Lottie Lucas lives in the countryside with her auctioneer husband, effervescent spaniel, and diva-ish rescue cat. Sometimes she wonders how she finds enough time for writing, let along anything else, but when she does get a free moment, she loves baking, walking, and getting the chance to read anything which isn't her own manuscript.

twitter.com/LottieAuthor
facebook.com/lottielucasauthor
instagram.com/LottieLucasAuthor

## Also by Lottie Lucas

*Ten Things My Cat Hates About You*

# HOW TO LOSE AN EX IN TEN DAYS

LOTTIE LUCAS



ONE MORE CHAPTER

One More Chapter
a division of HarperCollins*Publishers* Ltd
1 London Bridge Street
London SE1 9GF
www.harpercollins.co.uk

This paperback edition 2020

First published in Great Britain in ebook format
by HarperCollins*Publishers* 2020



A catalogue record of this book is available from the British Library

ISBN: 978-0-00-835365-0



Printed and bound in Great Britain by
CPI Group (UK) Ltd, Croydon CR0 4YY

*To my parents—for never once suggesting that I get myself a sensible job.*

# Prologue

"Are you ready?"

The gentle squeeze of my hand brings my attention away from the window. Outside, the scenery rushes past in a blur of azure sky, sparkling sea and golden sand, just visible over the edge of the cliffs.

I look into my sister's concerned grey eyes, and for the first time, I feel something inside me waver. With every inch the car advances up the winding hillside road, I'm aware that I'm getting further and further away from the life I used to have.

Everything's going to change. I'd thought I was so ready for that; I was too excited, too swept up in it all to stop and think. But now, as I sit between my two favourite people, my oldest friends and confidantes, I half wish I could turn the car around.

"Of course I am," my voice sounds overly bright even to my own ears. "This is an *adventure*! I can't wait."

Even so, I find my fingers clutching more tightly around the bouquet in my lap. A simple posy of almond blossom – all we could manage at such short notice. Even so, Rosie's done an amazing job; my hyper-organised sister wasn't about to let anything so inconsequential as mere time constraints get in the way of making this into a 'proper' wedding (her words, not mine). In fact, with more almond blossoms dotted in my hair, and the ivory maxi dress I found in a boutique back in Limassol, I *almost* feel like a bride.

Rosie opens her mouth to say something more but then closes it again, to my immense relief.

I *know* she wishes we'd waited a little longer. I know she has her doubts. But when he swept down onto one knee like that, in the middle of our graduation ceremony… I mean, yes, it was a shock for everyone, not least me. I can still remember it now, so vividly. The nerves as I stood on the steps, waiting my turn to go up and collect my degree certificate. The way the mortarboard wobbled on my head each time I moved – I had visions of it falling off, perhaps hitting the Dean in the eye as I reached forward to shake his hand. Didn't I hear about someone once who actually managed to knock themselves out with their mortarboard? They threw it up into the air and the sharp point of it hit them on the top of their head, and…

And then they were calling my name, the sound ricocheting around the cavernous hall.

"Belle Delphine."

Someone nudged me in the back and I lurched forward,

into the blazing spotlights which shone mercilessly onto the stage. I could see Ed walking away in front of me, certificate already clutched in his hand. I watched the back of his shoulders, using them as my anchor. And then he turned, and he was … walking *back*? I froze, my hand halfway extended towards the Dean, who was looking equally perturbed. For a moment I wondered if it was a trick of the light, but no, he was definitely coming back towards me, his gaze fixed on mine as the distance between us lessened with each purposeful stride.

A murmur rippled through the crowd. I could hear someone behind me in the wings hissing, "He's going the wrong way. Why is he going the wrong *way*?"

And I… I was still frozen. Watching him advance ever closer, unsure if the fluttering feeling in my chest was more horror or anticipation. Because the one thing I'd learned in the short time we'd been together was that with Ed, you never knew what to expect. When I was with him, I felt alive like I never had before. I also felt more *anxious* than I ever had before. He was dazzling, brilliant… and wholly unpredictable.

"What are you doing?" I demanded in an undertone once he was within earshot, uncomfortably aware that the sound was probably carrying in the echoing old hall. "Are you crazy? Get off the stage!"

"I've just had a thought," he said simply. "I thought you might like to hear it."

I could feel my face beginning to burn under the avid gaze of so many onlookers. Somewhere, out in the blurred sea of faces, Rosie was sitting. I could practically feel her outrage from here.

"What… right now?"

My voice held a distinctly strangled edge but he didn't appear to notice.

"Why not? This is the first day of the rest of our lives, isn't it?" He took my hand, which was still hovering in mid-air, and looked at me with eyes the colour of a twilit sky. "I think we should get married."

I stumbled over my own feet, even though I was standing perfectly still. My mortarboard lurched to one side.

"That's not funny, Ed," I gasped.

"I'm deadly serious. Look."

And the next thing I knew, he was down on one knee. There was a collective intake of breath from the crowd. The Dean coughed awkwardly.

"Marry me, Belle." Ed flung out his arms, a grin spreading across his boyish face. "Come on, what do you say?"

I just stared at him speechlessly. My mind seemed to have given up working all together.

They say that women always know when a proposal is on the way. But I couldn't have been more stunned if I'd tried. Ed and I… we were so *new*. A matter of months. Intense, magical, life-changing months, granted, but still…

I could feel the weight of expectation, like a physical force. The hall had gone utterly silent, everyone leaning forward to hear what I would say. I took a breath, looked into Ed's blue eyes, and teetered on the brink of my future.

"Yes." The word rushed from my lips of its own accord. I certainly didn't recall deciding to say it. But then I had, and it seemed like it was the right choice because the entire room exploded into a cacophony of cheers. And then Ed was kissing me and the sound became even more deafening.

"It's so romantic," one of the lecturers whispered to the Dean, dabbing at her eyes with a tissue.

"It's all *so* romantic," Tess chimes in supportively now, jolting me out of my memories as she smooths over the tense beat of silence which has settled within the car. She's good at that, Tess; she always knows how to say the right thing. She rearranges one of the blossoms in my hair with artistic precision. "There. You look absolutely stunning, Belle. He's going to be knocked off his feet when he sees you."

The car crunches to a halt at the top of the hill, sending up little clouds of dust from the packed dirt road. As I step out behind Rosie, trying to keep the hem of my dress off the ground, the intensity of the midday sun beats down upon my shoulders. The air is tinted with the heady scent of pine mingled with salt blowing off the ocean below, and as I straighten up to look around me, every single remaining doubt in my mind just melts away.

*This* is why I said yes. The whitewashed chapel with its blue domed roof sits perfectly on the crest of the hill, with panoramic views all around. Hot pink bougainvillea clambers across the front of the squat little building, hanging down across the doorway like a curtain.

It's perfect, every inch of it. It's paradise. It's the sort of thing only he could have come up with. If it had been left to me… well, I don't know what I'd have done. I didn't exactly have a lot of time to think about it. But it wouldn't have been this. I would certainly never have suggested that we didn't wait, that instead we just jump on a plane to Cyprus. A spontaneous wedding, as spontaneous as he is. The very reason why I love him.

And suddenly, I really can't wait to see him. I can already picture him standing at the altar. He'll be wearing his cornflower-blue suit, the one that brings out the colour of his eyes. It's pretty much the only suit he possesses, so that's a fairly safe bet. His dark blond hair will be falling over his forehead as usual. He'll turn and smile, because he's not the sort to wait with his back to me while I walk up the aisle. And when he does, that dimple will appear in his cheek, and I'll fall for him all over again, as I have every single time he's smiled at me for the past ten months.

Rosie and Tess link arms with me on either side as we navigate the last few metres of stony ground which lead up to the church. It's hard going, and not for the first time I begin to wish we'd gone for flat sandals like I'd suggested. But there's only so much informality my sister can take; I think it would have finished her off altogether if I'd insisted.

A figure moves out of the deep shadows which encircle the doorway.

"Leo," Rosie hisses, as we approach. "What are you *doing* out here? You're supposed to be inside with Ed."

"Well…" Now we're closer, I feel a small tremor in my glowing self-confidence of a moment ago. I've never seen Leo look worried before. He casts a quick glance in my direction. "There's been a small delay, that's all."

That's diplomatic speak for something's gone wrong, even I know that.

"You mean he's not *here* yet?" Rosie shrieks. Then she glances at the door of the church, which is wide open, and drops her voice. "He's only staying in the village. It's a two-minute walk away."

She arranged it that way on purpose. She knew he'd be late. He's *always* late.

"Why weren't you with him?" Rosie's demanding now. Leo tugs at the neck of his shirt. He must be roasting in that dark navy suit and the full power of Rosie's ire can't be helping. Nonetheless, he's used to it by now. God knows they've been together for long enough.

"He wanted to be by himself for a few moments," he replies calmly. "He must have just… lost track of time."

Tess is nodding vigorously as though she has some inside confirmation that this is exactly what has happened.

There's a tense, anxious silence during which they all dart worried looks between each other, apparently under the impression that I won't notice.

"Oh, for goodness' *sake*," I burst out, exasperated. "This is ridiculous. *I'll* go and look for him."

"Oh no you won't," Rosie yanks me back with such

force she nearly rips my arm out of its socket. "He can't see you before the wedding."

"You know we've never cared about any of that, Ro."

"I'll go," Leo volunteers quickly, after a look at Rosie's mutinous expression. "I'll be faster."

The wait seems to go on forever, although in reality it can only be about ten minutes or so. The three of us hover around outside under the shade of the pine trees. I wanted to go in to the church, not least because I'd be willing to bet anything that Mum is already subjecting the priest to her unwanted attentions, but Rosie won't hear of it. And for once, I haven't got the energy to argue with her.

Eventually, Leo comes striding back into view. For a heartbeat, I wait to see the familiar dark blond head behind him, the flash of cornflower-blue linen. But it's not there. Leo's on his own.

As he draws closer, I almost do a double take, wondering if the heat's beginning to affect my vision. I've never seen him so lacking in composure. His hair is standing on end, as though he's been running his hands through it.

"Belle, he's not there."

Almost of its own accord, my heart begins to thud in my chest, even as I tell myself that there's a perfectly innocent explanation. I force a laugh.

"He'll have gone for a walk or something and got lost. You know what he's like."

He'll turn up, I reassure myself firmly. Any moment now, he'll come around the corner with that gorgeous lopsided grin of his, full of apologies for being late. He's done it so many times before.

"No, you don't understand. I mean he's *gone*." Leo looks anguished. "His room's empty. And the rental car's gone too. He must have taken it."

Suddenly, I'm feeling dizzy. I lean back against the trunk of the pine tree, no longer caring about my dress.

"That can't be right," Rosie insists, although she's gone uncharacteristically pale. "There must be another—"

"There isn't." With a ragged sigh, Leo turns to me. "Belle, I'm sorry, but I don't think he's coming."

His words sound as though they're travelling from far away. It's so hot; I can feel the heat rushing through my body in waves, shooting up into my head. Black spots are dancing in front of my vision.

"No." My voice comes out thickly. "No, he wouldn't do that."

"Belle?" Tess clasps my arm. "Maybe you should sit down."

But I shake her off, already moving forwards. My shoes catch on the uneven ground, slowing me down, and I kick them off, gathering my skirt up in my hand so I can break into a run.

*He wouldn't do this. He wouldn't do this.*

The words pound in my skull as I pick up momentum going down the steep, twisting hill which leads into the village. Sharp stones stab into my bare soles, but I scarcely notice. My entire focus is on the blue door at the end of the street.

The village is deserted at this time of day, everyone having retreated inside to escape the searing sun. It radiates off the white painted facades of the buildings, creating a dazzling, disorientating effect which makes my head spin.

Finally, I reach my target. I grasp the handle; it's hot, and the metal burns my palm, but I ignore it, flinging open the door. It scrapes across the stone floor within, carving a groove through the rough surface.

The downstairs of the cottage is shadowed, silent. And empty. My heart leaps into my throat, and I will my nerves into steadiness, turning towards the wooden ladder which leads to the upper floor.

"Ed?" I poke my head through the gap, horrified at the way my voice shakes. "Are you here?"

A bare room stares back at me. Leo was right; he really has left nothing behind. No clothes slung across the bed, no toothbrush in the bathroom. The great irony is that he always manages to forget something; he loses things left, right, and centre. And yet, today, of all days… it's like he was never even here.

I traipse back through the village in a daze. I'm not even bothering to lift the hem of my dress off the ground anymore; instead, it drags in the dust. I don't know what to think; it's like there's a torrent of emotion, of pain, somewhere beneath the surface, just waiting to be unleashed, and yet…

*He wouldn't do this. Not to me.*

Everything feels unreal. The blazing sun on my head, the church on the top of the hill, the people gathered in a nervous cluster in front of it. The people I know so well, suddenly looking like strangers. Looking at me like *I'm* a stranger, like they don't know how to act, what to say… it's all too awful.

"Belle…" Rosie begins.

I hold up a hand to silence her. My mind is racing, turning over every possibility. I mean, the packing… It doesn't mean he's *gone*, does it? Maybe he's booked us a honeymoon suite somewhere, and he's driven off to prepare it for later. Lost track of time, like Leo said.

The thought sustains me; I cling to it like a life raft. I can't imagine the worst; I just… can't. Everyone else has already decided; I can tell it by their faces. And if I allow myself to doubt him, to condemn him… well, what'll be left?

"He'll be here." I'm amazed at how strong my voice sounds.

Tess's eyes widen, then dart across to Rosie for guidance. Ro sighs.

"Belle, I understand that you don't want to believe it…"

Her face is soft, pitying. So unlike my sister, who always says it like it is. I can't bear it. I look away, not wanting to see.

"He'll *be* here." Even I can hear the stubborn desperation which tinges my voice. "And I'm not moving until he comes."

Selecting a rock, I sit down. It's not exactly comfortable, but that's the least of my concerns right now.

"Belle…" This time it's Leo's turn to look uneasy.

"You can all go if you want." I prop my chin on my hand, squinting down the road for any signs of a car, the tell-tale puffs of dust rising from the loose surface. "I don't expect you to stay."

They all share a look. I can just about see it out of the corner of my eye. But more than anything, I can sense it. I hold my breath.

"Of course we'll stay." Rosie settles down next to me, not even pausing to survey the rock with distaste as she usually would. "We'll stay for as long as it takes."

I don't know how long we sit here for but gradually, the sun begins to sink in the sky, making the white walls of the church glow pink and amber. The vicar passes us on his way home with an apologetic look which I do my utmost to ignore. Mum takes Gran back to the hotel, promising to return as soon as they get a call from us. And still I sit there, trying not to think. Just hoping.

It's dark by the time Rosie finally touches me on the arm.

"Enough, Belle. Let's get you back. You're freezing."

It's only then that I realise she's right. I'm shivering violently in my thin dress. I try to speak, then find that I can't. It's like all the voice has gone out of me, along with all the light of the day. So I just nod. And in that moment, I release my grip on every dream I had for the future.

Leo drapes his jacket over my shoulders. Rosie takes one of my arms, Tess the other. And together, we begin the long walk back down the hill.

# Chapter One

"Delphine? Are you with us?"

Steve's booming voice, accompanied by the sound of meaty fingers clicking imperiously next to my ear, makes me sit bolt upright. The sight of dazzling sunshine on whitewashed walls dissolves from my mind's eye, to be replaced with the familiarly dingy outline of the *Illuminator* newspaper's office. It's even worse than usual on a day like this, with the rain lashing down from a mercilessly leaden sky – a typically British May day, the sort that could easily be mistaken for February if one didn't have the benefit of a calendar to prove otherwise.

Steve's still glaring down at me expectantly, hands on hips. His shirt is half untucked, as it permanently seems to be, and his tie – faded pink spots against a brown background, which I suspect came with the shirt – has that same spot of ketchup on it which has been there since the day I first met him six years ago.

"I was just… thinking about this article I'm writing," I lie hastily. Luckily, I've never been ashamed to bluster my way out of a situation. I've had a lot of practice. When I introduce you to my family, you'll begin to understand why. I frown at my screen in what I hope is an intelligent manner. "There's a lot of… nuance there. Lots to consider."

His gaze flickers disbelievingly to my screen, where the headline, "Streetlamp Timers to be Altered in Bid to Cut Energy Costs" is clearly visible in stark black font.

All right, so perhaps I misjudged that one. I resist the impulse to shrink down into my chair.

"It will impact a lot of people, you know," I add staunchly. "They might fall into potholes, or… or… get attacked by foxes!"

What am I *talking* about? Why don't I just stop before I make it any worse?

Steve's heavy eyebrows have been descending further and further down his forehead with every new word out of my mouth. By now, his eyes have almost completely disappeared.

"You're a terrible liar, Delphine," he says flatly. "Has anyone ever told you that?"

Not for the first time, I privately wonder if he even *knows* my first name. I've certainly never heard him use it.

"It has been mentioned on occasion," I admit dolefully.

For a moment, I think I see the edges of his lips twitch. But within the space of a blink, his face is as dour as ever once more. I must have imagined it, then.

"Daydream on your own time in future," he snaps. "If I catch you again there'll be hell to pay."

He says that every time so I'm not unduly worried. One day, maybe I'll actually find out what this hell is that I'm expected to pay. Then again, maybe he'll just keep throwing idle threats about the place.

"Tut tut," Darren snipes gleefully from the desk next to mine, as Steve shuffles away out of earshot, presumably to terrorise someone else. "Caught slacking again, Delphine. You don't do yourself any favours, do you?"

"Shut up, Darren," I snap. Usually, I wouldn't let him get to me, but today I'm feeling flustered. I'm annoyed with myself, not because I lost concentration – I mean, streetlamp timers, for goodness' sake; that would challenge anyone's attention – but because of where I found myself. Back in Cyprus, with my white dress fluttering around my ankles and almond blossom in my hair. I hardly ever think about that day anymore. I've long since trained myself not to; it belonged to another lifetime. Another person. I've become very good at pushing it to the back of my mind.

But the problem is that today isn't just any old day, no matter how much I might try to pretend otherwise. Today's *the* day. Six years ago, on this very date, my life changed forever. *I* changed forever.

And suddenly, it feels like no time has passed at all, like the distance I've put between myself and that fateful day is reduced to nothing. Like all of the work I've done to move on, to grow into a new person, to build a solid foundation for myself... it's nothing more than a castle built of sand, swept away by the breeze of past recollection. All of the pain, the old feelings… they're still there, pulsing vividly in my chest, in my soul.

It's nothing I'm not prepared for. It's the same way every year, even though each time May rolls around again, I pray that it won't be. That this day will fly by like any other. Sometimes I dream I might even forget about it all together, only realising after it's already passed. In my darker moments, though, I wonder if that'll ever really happen. Or if this date will haunt me forever, a ghost I can't shake.

The one bright spot of this whole experience is that I know it's only one day. It doesn't last. Tomorrow, I'll wake up and the pain won't be there anymore. Not in the same way, at least. It'll have retreated to whichever dark corner it hides in for most of the year, and I'll feel like myself again. Tired, wrung out, empty, but myself. And I'll realise that it was all an illusion, that what I've built for myself *is* real, that it means something. That I still mean something, even after everything.

Knowing that it's only temporary – even if it *feels* like the longest day of my life at the time – is what keeps me going. Still, it's hard. Particularly when I have such bothersome colleagues grating on my already stretched nerves.

Darren holds up his hands in mock surrender.

"*Touchy*. It's not my fault you got caught out."

I suppress a sigh. For reasons which utterly escape me, Darren has convinced himself that we're in competition somehow. The way he carries on, you'd think we were contestants in the final of some lurid reality TV show, not two lowly junior reporters working for a slightly archaic Edinburgh newspaper.

I don't even know why he bothers; it's not as if there's a lot of career progression in print journalism these days. And his toadying approach is woefully misguided when it comes to Steve; watching the expression on his face when Darren puts up his hand like he's in a classroom is the highlight of my day. It's like he's discovered an entirely new species of fungus.

The whole thing would *almost* be worth it… if the layout of the office didn't enforce close proximity to Darren, day in, day out. Our desks are so tightly packed together I could practically reach out and touch him, should I be gripped by a sudden desire to do so.

Needless to say, I never have been to date. I can't see that changing any time soon.

The *Illuminator* offices occupy a deceptively prestigious address just off the Royal Mile, in the heart of Edinburgh's famous Old Town; alas, once you get inside, the impression doesn't last for long. We're on the top floor, for one thing. The seventeenth-century building might boast a historically interesting service lift, but nothing which was designed to carry a fully grown human. Which isn't to say that it hasn't been attempted a couple of times during the latter, hazier hours of the office Christmas party, but that doesn't really count. But anyway, I'm digressing. The point is that every trip to and from my desk involves six flights of narrow, uneven servants' stairs. Which, admittedly, is excellent for my thighs, but that's about the only plus side I can think of.

It's not even like it improves much once you're up here. The tiny porthole windows hardly let in any light, casting the place in a perpetual layer of gloom. Which is probably just as well, as what you can see certainly doesn't invite closer inspection. The decor doesn't appear to have been changed since the 1950s; there are still cigarette burns on the dark stained mahogany desks, and a smoky atmosphere pervades the air, no matter what anyone does to try and dispel it. It's like a museum set; the office that time forgot.

I glance over at Steve, who's scowling with disproportionate ferocity at a proof copy on his desk. I bet *he* still wishes it was the 1950s, when the newspapers were experiencing a golden age, and editors could shout and swear and do anything to get the story without fear of such pesky inventions as employee rights and regulating bodies swooping in and spoiling all the fun.

I mean, don't get me wrong, he still shouts and swears with reckless impunity, but the rest… well, journalism's not what it was. The rise of online platforms has changed the face of news, and little publications like us struggle to keep up. As it is, it's only our age and reputation which keeps us afloat, although we've had to adapt over the years. Once a satirical Victorian start-up, we've now evolved into more of a niche local opinion piece, commenting on the goings-on in Edinburgh, both colourful and mundane.

Unfortunately, my role seems to lean heavily towards the more mundane side of things.

Look, it's not like I'm *bored* or anything. I mean, maybe it wasn't exactly what I'd planned when I left university with my shiny new degree in journalism, but then, to say that life hasn't always shown the utmost respect for my plans would be a laughable understatement. I've had to learn to make do with what's available to me.

And the *Illuminator is* a respectable publication. People are always impressed when I say I write for them; I expect they think it's all very glamorous, being a journalist. If only they knew.

Patting a yawn, I half-heartedly type a few more words onto the end of my article. Well, if you could really call it an article. That would be stretching it a tad.

Okay, so yes, I suppose maybe I am a *bit* bored. Under-challenged, as my grandmother might say.

Which, unfortunately, doesn't tend to bring out the best in me.

Especially not on a day like today, when I need distraction more than ever. Otherwise, I have to find it in other places.

Taking aim, I ping a rubber band at the back of Darren's ear. It misses by a mile.

Damn.

I'm just loading up another missile when a familiar voice floats down from above.

"Working hard as ever, I see."

---

I count out five long seconds before I allow myself to look up. My heart's already skipping in my chest; I can't help it, even if it is to my intense annoyance.

Nate D'Angelo is about the most handsome man I've ever laid eyes on in my life. And I don't say that lightly; believe me, I'm particular about these things. Hemlines started rising office-wide when he joined the paper three years ago as a senior journalist, and they've never gone back down since.

Combine sun-drenched Italian looks with the softest hint of a Scottish accent, not to mention an easy-going nature and a winning smile… well, even Margaret who does the accounts perked up considerably, and she'd looked pretty much fossilised before.

"Just… ah… taking a creative break." I pretend to stretch, wondering what the hell I'm doing. "Getting the juices flowing."

Great, now I'm *blushing*, I think crossly. What am I, a teenager?

"I see," he's nodding intelligently, though his eyes are sparkling with amusement. Why do I always get the feeling he can see right through me?

"Yes, well," I blurt out. "Got to… you know, carry on. Articles don't write themselves."

Ugh, now I sound like Steve. Perish the thought.

I turn back to my screen, trying to ignore the fact that I can feel his gaze on my face.

The truth is, Nate brings out mixed feelings in me. I mean, yes, he's gorgeous. Yes, he's charming. And yes, I've always had the sense that there's something between us, a fluttering attraction which makes every bantering exchange charged with extra meaning. But he's just a bit… well, maybe I'm jaded and cynical, but those things kind of leave me cold nowadays. He's just a bit *too* confident, a bit *too* smooth. It makes me wary. Because I had someone who was all of those things once before, and all I ended up with was a broken heart and a torn, dusty, white dress.

I'm not venturing there again. That much I'm adamant about. And I'm really not up for dealing with Nate right now; I'm feeling far too fragile. I just want him to go away.

Okay, so I'll just… look efficient. Pretend that I'm so wholeheartedly engrossed in my latest scintillating article on streetlamp timers that I simply have no time to idle away on mindless chitchat. Or flirting.

*Definitely* no flirting.

Briskly, I begin to type on my keyboard in what I hope looks to be a suitably efficient manner, glancing up at him cursorily.

Which turns out to be a mistake. The moment I look into his warm, brandy-coloured eyes, my fingers crash across the keys, spilling a load of gibberish across my screen. Because, at the end of the day, I'm only *human,* for God's sake.

"Are you all right, Belle?" he enquires mildly.

I jerk upright from my keyboard. "Yes! Yes! Why wouldn't I be?" I splutter. At the same time, I feel a flash of irritation. Seriously, is there nowhere else he needs to be right now? Why won't he go *away* and leave me in peace? Miserable peace, granted, but still.

"You just… look a little flustered, that's all."

"It's the streetlamps, you see," I hear myself saying, even as I curse myself for doing so. Why do I keep on with these streetlamps? Haven't I learned that it never ends well? "There's so much…"

"Nuance?" He supplies, with a wry smile, as he perches on the edge of my desk.

Ah, so he heard that, did he?

"There *is*," I say defensively. "Think of the chaos. The whole of Edinburgh plunged into darkness…"

"Of course," he says gravely. "People getting eaten by foxes, and such like."

"I never said that," I say hotly, although my lips are turning up at the corners. Oh God, here we go. This is what happens. This is what he does. It's impossible to stay annoyed with him.

Immediately, it sets all the alarm bells clanging in my head. Because if there's one thing I've learned from bitter experience, it's that no one should possess both pulchritudinous looks *and* an engaging disposition. It's a recipe for disaster. With a face like that, he ought to be withered inside, like Dorian Gray.

Maybe he is. I kind of hope he is. It would make it all so much easier.

"So this is how one generates creativity, is it?" He picks up one of the rubber bands between his forefinger and thumb, raising a brow at me.

I tilt my chin impishly. If he wants to play that game, then fair enough. I can play too.

"It's very effective. You should try it."

That'll get rid of him, I think smugly. He'll never do it. He's far too responsible, far too—

"All right." Before I can blink, he's stretched the band back and pinged it at Darren.

I clap a hand over my mouth to stifle a gasp. But the rubber band narrowly misses Darren's head, landing soundlessly on the floor instead.

One might even say that it was a perfect miss. *Too* perfect, I'd say.

"Spoilsport," I accuse him, in a hushed voice. "You missed on purpose. You could easily have got him from there."

"Of course I did. Can't have senior journalists injuring the staff, can we? What kind of example would that set?" He leans in across the desk. "But it was fun to watch your face when you thought I'd do it."

He's close. Too close for my liking. And the teasing expression has completely slid from his face. My breath hitches, and I steel myself.

"Belle," he begins haltingly, after a couple of seconds. "I was wondering…"

A heavy file of council minutes crashes onto the edge of the desk, making us both jump.

"*Thank* you," Steve thunders sarcastically. "I'm so glad I've finally got your attention." He allows for a dramatic pause before continuing. "Now, what the hell is going on here?"

I can't decide if I want to bow at Steve's feet or will the floor to open up beneath them. Emotions crash together, turgid and confused. I blink, trying to keep a handle on my thoughts.

Not that I need to. Nate steps in, ever ready with a smooth answer.

"Just a bit of research, sir."

My head swivels around. *Research?*

"Research?" Steve unwittingly echoes my thoughts. He still looks suspicious, but less so. Unlike me, Nate has a spotless reputation.

"Belle has agreed to help me with a story," Nate explains easily. I blink. Who knew the man was such a good liar? I'd always had him down as Mr Perfect, the ultimate goody-two-shoes. "I could really use her expertise…" he hesitates deferentially, then adds, "with your permission, of course."

I almost choke on air. *Expertise?* I'm not sure I have any. Not anymore. Maybe once, when I was fresh and young and full of confidence in myself. Now, I'm just pretending. Pretending that Ed didn't drive away with that all-important piece of me, along with everything else he threw into the boot of that ubiquitous hire car. I wanted to be a fashion journalist before it happened; these days, I can scarcely trust myself to choose the right shade of lipstick or throw an impromptu supper party for my friends. Things which I never would have thought twice about before now seem almost dizzyingly daunting.

Steve looks as surprised as I do by the suggestion I might actually be of some use to anyone.

"Well, if you really *need* her…"

"I do." Nate's eyes meet mine, and an involuntary shiver runs through me. My heart sinks with foreboding.

"Fair enough," Steve grumbles, already half turned away. "If you're willing to put up with her, then by all means. It's your funeral."

Charming. I grit my teeth together and try not to scowl.

"Brilliant." Nate pushes himself away from the desk, as though nothing out of the ordinary has occurred. He starts to head back across the room, but stops to throw back over his shoulder. "Oh, and Belle?"

I sit upright.

"Yes?"

He smiles.

"Try and get *some* work done today, won't you?"

I glower at his retreating back, then forcibly smooth out my features. At this rate, if I'm not careful, I might get stuck like that.

# Chapter Two

There's a parcel on the mat when I get home; one of the neighbours must have brought it upstairs. Bending down to retrieve it with one hand I somehow manage to juggle my keys in the other and wedge myself backwards through the front door.

"Belle! You're home," Tess's soft voice floats through from the living room. Rounding the corner, I find her reclining on the kingfisher-blue sofa, a magazine open on her lap. Her naturally blonde hair is gathered up in a loose topknot, with tendrils delicately framing her face. Even in a baggy, off-the-shoulder sweatshirt and fluffy pink socks, she looks amazing. If she wasn't my oldest friend, I could easily be inclined towards jealousy.

There's a generous glass of rosé on the coffee table next to her elbow. Following my gaze, she motions towards the kitchen with her head.

"The bottle's open on the counter. I thought you might... you know."

She tactfully turns back to her magazine article, and I have to blink against a sudden surge of emotion. Of *course* she's remembered what today is. Tess never forgets anything like that.

"Thanks," I say brightly, as I set about divesting myself of coat, handbag, and bulky parcel forthwith. Rain droplets are showering off me onto the carpet; I put a tentative hand up to my hair, which I can already feel is plastered to my head.

The rain didn't let up all afternoon. By the time I left the office, it was coming down in sheets, the waterlogged streets devoid of all their usual bustle and life as people retreated into hotels and restaurants. The whole place had a dank, oppressive feel to it; on a day like today, it's easy to remember why they call Edinburgh one of the most haunted cities in the world. It feels like the ghosts have the run of the place.

"How did you get on today?" I ask cautiously, casting an eye around the flat, which appears unusually tidy. It's been unusually tidy for so many weeks now that actually, it's starting to not be so unusual after all.

In most cases, a tidy home is nothing to complain about, but in this instance it's beginning to get me concerned. I'll explain. Tess is an illustrator; she creates these incredibly stylised, willowy fashion drawings in ink and watercolour. They've been featured all over the place, in fashion magazines, on book covers. I still get ridiculously excited every time I spot one, even if Tess just rolls her eyes and looks faintly embarrassed. She hates any kind of attention. Anyway, she's super talented, and when she's in a good place, perfectly productive. But sometimes, usually when something's bothering her, she just… dries up. She stops drawing, and that's when she starts cleaning. Which is fine; in fact, I've always thought it rather convenient. It means the flat gets a good once-over a couple of times a year.

Usually, though, these phases only last for a week or two.

Tess studiously avoids the question, instead looking at the parcel I've set down on the floor.

"Is that another one for Rosie? I didn't hear the intercom buzz."

"You were probably hoovering," I reply mildly, trying not to look pointedly around the spotlessly clean apartment.

My sister appears in the doorway to her bedroom, her arms loaded with bags of what appears to be confetti.

"Is that for me?"

"They're always for you," I say flatly. As usual, there's no preamble from her. No polite greeting, or enquiries about my day. Rosie prides herself on ruthless focus on the matter in hand.

She harrumphs.

"Well, it's about time. I've been waiting ages for that to arrive."

I already know I'm going to regret this next question.

"What exactly *is* it, anyway? Surely you can't need any more wedding stuff."

The look she gives me is part censure, part pity.

"Favours," she replies grandly, dropping the bags of confetti into a heap in the middle of the floor. Tess looks far from thrilled, but as usual she doesn't say anything. Tess always opts for the peaceful route in any given situation.

Rosie, on the other hand… well, you'll see. She's a veritable force of nature. Even I scarcely dare to contradict her.

Nevertheless, sometimes it must be done.

"Don't you already *have* favours?" I venture, hanging my trench coat on the last available hook. It's half coming off the wall, and you have to get the balance just right, or the coat simply slides right off again. It's a shame that Tess has no proficiency for DIY, come to think of it. There's loads of stuff which needs fixing. I could blame it on ours being an all-female household, but in this modern age that's not really an excuse. "What about all those boxes of sugared almonds you made us hand emboss about a month ago?"

I will *never* forget doing that. It took *hours*. Sometimes I still dream about it, and every time I look over at the pile still left to do, it keeps getting bigger, and…

I suppress a shudder. Rosie's wedding day cannot come soon enough. Let's just say it will be the happiest day of my life for more than one reason. I never want to see another scalloped edge, or pastel hue, or hand-lettered initial, as long as I live on this earth.

"These are other favours," Rosie says deliberately, as though I'm a complete simpleton and the whole thing should be transparently obvious. "You know, *secondary* favours. Give people a bit of variety. It's in all the magazines."

That is not a thing. She's just made that up. I know, because she's made me read all of those magazines. Part of my duty as maid of honour, apparently.

Tess catches my eye with a minute shake of the head. I know what she's saying. Sometimes, it's just easier to go along with it once Rosie's set her mind to something.

I watch my sister now as she rips into the box with alarmingly careless abandon for someone wielding an enormous pair of scissors, marvelling at how two people who share DNA can be so totally different. I mean, granted, we do *look* very similar. We're what's affectionately known as Irish twins, which means that we were born less than a year apart. We have the same tawny hair, although hers is cut to brush the tops of her shoulders while mine cascades down my back. And we have the same heart-shaped face, with large, wide-set eyes, except that hers are a pale dove grey whilst mine are striking violet blue.

But apart from that... well, what can I say? Rosie's just so single minded, so focused. She's always known exactly what she wants, and she won't give in until she makes it a reality. She met Leo whilst we were all still at school. Their eyes met across a crowded GCSE English lesson, and that was pretty much that. She decided that he was the one, and she's never wavered from that conviction since. Neither of them has.

I'm more emotional than that. I make decisions recklessly, assuring myself that in going with my heart, I must be making the right choice. It hasn't always worked out quite as I'd hoped. But let's not go into that right now.

Tess looks on in dismay as Rosie delves into the box, sending polystyrene nuggets spilling over the side and all over the carpet.

"Couldn't you store some of this stuff at Leo's?" I ask, wearily, picking my way across the sea of chaos towards the kitchen. "We're beginning to drown under wedding paraphernalia here. And he's got loads of space at his flat."

Oh, yes. That's another thing. Rosie and Leo have elected not to live together until after they're married. I suppose it's rather sweet, really. Rosie claims it will give them something to be excited about after the wedding's over, and the honeymoon, and everything starts to get back to normal. The novelty of living together for the first time, after almost twelve years as a couple. I suggested that the prospect might be more exciting for her than for Leo. I'm still not sure the poor man knows exactly what he's letting himself in for.

Alas, my little jest was not well received.

But in all seriousness, I'm not really looking forward to the day Rosie moves out, and I know that Tess feels likewise, even if her characteristic reserve means she's never said it in so many words. I know what she's thinking. After so many years, we *all* know what each other is thinking.

It's always been the three of us; because Rosie's birthday falls in September and mine the following July, we ended up in the same school year. After our parents' divorce, we moved up from Hampshire to Edinburgh to live with my grandmother. At first, we stuck out like sore thumbs at our new school, with our English accents and our mismatching uniforms, because we'd started in the middle of term. But Tess wasn't bothered by any of that. We became friends in the first week, and by the end of the term, we were practically living in each other's pockets. The only time we've ever really been apart was at university; we all went our separate ways then, me to London to study journalism, Rosie up to St Andrew's to be with Leo while she did her criminology degree, and Tess to art school in Oxford. I've never been so lonely. I missed that love, that closeness, so much that it hurt. Looking back, perhaps that's why I did what I did. Why I allowed myself to be swept up in something which promised all of those things and more.

And then, six years ago, when it all blew up in my face and I was desperate for a fresh start, it seemed that moving back to Edinburgh was the best option. Rosie was already here, she and Leo both having found jobs. Tess was so thrilled that she sorted the whole thing out so we could live together. She persuaded her parents to buy her the flat on the grounds that she needed somewhere to pursue her art. How she convinced them that a four-bedroom apartment was required to do so I've never been certain, but she managed it. She has a studio set up in the spare bedroom, so technically it wasn't a lie, I suppose. Not that I think they'd even have the chance to notice; they've never visited. They both have high-powered jobs in banking, and have always been chronically unavailable in both a literal and emotional sense. I think I've only met them a handful of times. When Tess was growing up, she all but lived with us and they never seemed to object.

Anyway, it was all worked out and Rosie and I found ourselves a home beyond our wildest expectations. With our salaries, we were staring down the grimy barrel of a studio flat in one of the less salubrious corners of town. Or – and I'm not sure which would have been worse – returning to the house we'd grown up in, where Mum and Gran still live. Well, Mum, Gran, and the latest in the constant stream of Mum's boyfriends, at any rate.

I'm shuddering just thinking about it.

Anyway, the rent we pay here can safely be described as a pittance, and we even had to fight Tess over that. Initially, she didn't want us to pay her anything; I've never seen her get so stubborn over an issue before. In the end, we reached a compromise, although she doesn't even take the money. It stacks up in an account, where it ends up paying for spa breaks and weekend getaways.

Which means that the good news is that at least we won't need to find anyone else to fill Rosie's room once she's gone. But that's small consolation. Rosie might be vexing, and dictatorial, and lacking a certain degree of tact, but it's going to be very strange without her. Strangely quiet, that's for sure.

Rosie, who's busy producing a set of tiny bottles from amongst the wrapping, doesn't give any sign that she heard my question.

"Look! Aren't they adorable?"

Adorable indeed. What is *happening* to my sister? The woman who handles gory evidence for a living and who organises her life with a ruthless efficiency. This wedding is turning her into someone I barely recognise. To be honest, I'm beginning to wonder how I'm going to get through it.

I can still hear her waxing lyrical about mini bottles of elderflower gin as I reach the relative safety of the kitchen and pour myself a glass of wine. It's a pale, peachy blush colour and I swirl it around in the glass, watching the way the light catches it as I lean back against the counter.

The truth is, I'd love to be excited about all of this. The person I once was would have gushed over miniature bottles of gin, would have thrown myself into the parade of pastel with unbridled enthusiasm.

But I'm too jaded to take joy in that sort of thing anymore; Ed's actions knocked all that romantic dreaminess out of me. They turned me into someone different, someone I'm not sure I even like that much. Someone I certainly never would have chosen to be.

I look at my left hand, wrapped around the stem of the wine glass. The bare finger where there ought to be a ring. I can still picture it: the three tanzanites embedded into the band—violet, like my eyes, Ed said, when we bought it together in Limassol, two days before our ill-fated wedding day. I was so happy then, so full of visions for the future. That ring… it symbolised everything I'd hoped for. Me and Ed, both blue-eyed like the stones. Maybe a blue-eyed baby one day to complete the trio.

I never saw it again after that day. It disappeared along with him.

They say we block out the worst moments of our lives, but I find I can still recall what happened afterwards with a vividness that almost seems clearer than the present. I wish I could go back and erase it all, just for the next ten days, just until after Rosie's wedding is over. I wish I could go back to how I was before, open-hearted and reckless, confident that life was always on my side.

I take a meditative sip of my wine, then another as I realise it's actually quite good. Rosie must have chosen it; Tess has unfailingly poor taste in wine. Her entire selection system comprises of choosing the one with the prettiest label.

"Belle!" As though telepathically responding to her name, Rosie hollers from the next room. "What are you *doing* in there? Come and help us fill confetti cones."

I briefly consider stalling, but the guilty thought that I'd be leaving Tess on her own is enough to change my mind. With a sigh, I resign myself to another evening of wedding preparations. At least the sheer monotony of it might keep my mind off the past, if nothing else.

## Chapter Three

"By the way…" Rosie says casually, after about ten minutes of concentrated work rolling up confetti cones and sticking them together. I know what you're thinking; it doesn't *sound* like a task which requires much concentration. But you'd be surprised at how fiddly it is.

Any hopes that we might finish the job within an hour are fast fading. But then, I shouldn't be surprised; I'm learning the hard way that most wedding-related things are far more complicated than they first appear. This is why, when I had the choice, *I* eloped.

I look up sharply. I know that tone. It too is far more sinister than it first appears. "What?"

"Mum's left a message on the answer machine. She wants to speak to us."

Somehow, I've managed to get my fingers all stuck together with tape. Alas, I've never been particularly artistic. I glance enviously over at Tess, who's assembling a confetti cone with an air of capable serenity, then back at Rosie.

"Really?"

I thought we'd agreed not to give Mum the house number, for the sake of our sanity. We'll have to play our usual game of rock, paper, scissors later to decide whose job it is to call her back. It can go on for a surprising number of rounds.

Rosie holds up a pristine confetti cone, inspecting it with a critical eye.

"She obviously has news."

My heart sinks a little. The words 'news' and 'my mother' rarely bode well when associated with one another.

"Maybe she's broken up with Carlos at last," I suggest, brightening at the prospect.

Rosie shoots me a reproving look, but as she turns her attention on to the next confetti cone, I definitely hear her mutter under her breath, "We can but hope."

As you might have gathered, neither of us is all that keen on Carlos. Oh, he's all *right,* I suppose. He possesses all of the usual requirements my mother asks for in a suitor: younger, muscular, and with a limited grasp of the English language. Where she finds them, I don't know, and I hope I'll never have to ask. Mum and I pursue a strict policy of live and let live. Anything I don't need to know, I have no desire to find out. And anything she doesn't need to know about *my* life… well, she does everything in her power to try and find out. It's a bit of a one-sided policy, I suppose.

Of course I *want* her to be happy. I do. And if Carlos,

with his dazzlingly white teeth and unintelligible Spanish accent is what makes her happy, then that's just… it's… I'm beyond…

I mean, for all the mercy in heaven, though, is it *really* too much to ask that just once she might fall for someone even *remotely* sensible? Someone who's not half her age would be a start. Someone who doesn't wear white skinny jeans would be even better.

Finally, I've finished one of these blasted confetti cones. Wrestling the fold into place, I survey my creation dubiously. Out of the corner of my eye, I can see Rosie's face. It's a picture of horror.

"Er, Belle, why don't you start on the confetti?" She asks, in an overly bright voice, tossing one of the cellophane packets onto my lap.

Tess and I exchange a knowing smile. Rosie's efforts to be subtle are so bad it's almost endearing at times.

"Oh, I don't know. I think I'm getting into a rhythm with these," I say airily, holding the cone up to the light as though to admire it. I know I shouldn't play with her, but sometimes it's just too hard to resist. She's such an insane perfectionist about things. Admittedly, my effort isn't *quite* as neat as theirs, but it's perfectly passable. Especially when you bear in mind that people hold them for all of thirty seconds before discarding them. Certainly, I can't see any of the guests performing a full-scale inspection of their craftsmanship. Only Rosie would do that, and as she's the bride, she won't even be given one.

She takes a steadying breath and I can tell she's dying to

say something else, but to my astonishment, she lapses into restrained silence instead.

It's so strange, Rosie being quiet, that eventually Tess clears her throat.

"So, Belle. Anything to report from today?"

"Not really," I say, keeping my eyes studiously focused on the task in hand. "Just the usual. Steve bellowed, Darren sneered, and the coffee machine broke down. Everything one would expect from a day at the *Illuminator* office." I shoot her a suspicious look. "Why?"

She doesn't look at me, but a faint smile tugs at the edges of her lips.

"You just looked rather… sparkly when you walked in, that's all."

*Sparkly?* I certainly didn't feel sparkly. No one could after a day spent in the crepuscular environment of the *Illuminator* office. You can almost feel yourself reanimating with every step you take away from the place.

"Did you speak to anyone this afternoon, by chance?" Tess presses, in a voice laced with honey. "Anyone gorgeously Italianate?"

Despite myself, I feel my cheeks begin to glow with warmth. Oh God, I don't like where this is going.

"I'm *always* sparkly," I murmur defensively, although even I know I don't sound very convincing. Especially not to the two people who know me best in the world. "It's my default setting."

I distinctly hear something that sounds like a tut from Rosie's direction which I stoically ignore.

Tess claps her hands together gleefully.

"I knew it! I'm never wrong about these things." She leaps up, showering confetti all over the floor. "I'm going to get the rest of the wine. I want to hear this."

"There's nothing to tell!" I protest, raising my voice so it follows her through to the kitchen. "Seriously. When are you guys going to let this drop?"

Rosie raises a disdainful brow. I notice she's abandoned all pretence of folding confetti cones, and have to suppress a smile. She pretends she's not interested but she clearly is. "Maybe when you finally admit that you like him?"

I frown. I can't believe they're pressing me on this, today of all days.

"I do not like him! Look, you guys are reading way too much into this. He seems like the sort of person who flirts his way through life. I'm just one in a line, I'm sure."

Rosie leans forward, resting her elbows on her crossed legs.

"You're doing him a disservice, Belle. He's really not like that. I know he can come across as a bit…"

"Arrogant?" I suggest pointedly, then immediately feel guilty. I'm on the defensive; I didn't mean to be so harsh. But I'm not feeling especially generous towards the male population today.

Rosie narrows her eyes.

"Not every good-looking man is a player, Belle."

Busted. I should have known I couldn't hide anything from her. Even with the preoccupation of an impending wedding, she still manages to keep a laser-like focus on what's going on.

"Anyway, Leo says he goes very quiet whenever you're mentioned," Rosie adds slyly.

The thought sends a ridiculous flutter through my chest, which I hasten to extinguish.

I always forget that they know each other. It's a weird, small world when your soon-to-be brother-in-law is an old university friend of your dashing work colleague. It also, as I quickly discovered, has the potential to be highly embarrassing. Rosie's evidently decided that Nate and I are perfect for one another, and she's determined to make it happen. Whether I like it or not.

Tess reappears, bottle of wine in hand, eyes luminous with excitement.

"You should ask him out! Wouldn't that be fun?"

The thought of walking up to Nate and asking him out strikes me as anything *other* than fun. It makes my blood chill in my veins.

"God, no. I couldn't do that." The words are out of my mouth before I can stop them.

"Why not?" Rosie's watching me like a hawk.

"It's not like there's anyone else, is it?" Tess gives a tinkling laugh. "You would have told us."

If only she knew. If only they both did.

"Look, why all of the attention on *my* love life?" I say abruptly, desperate to steer the conversation away from the unwelcome subject of my feelings. "Haven't you two got other things to be focusing on? There's the not insignificant matter of a wedding ten days from now. Shouldn't you be devoting your energies to that?"

"We just want to see you happy, Belle," Tess says softly, settling down on the floor next to me, tucking her long legs under her as she always does. "Is that so terrible? We're not the enemies here."

Suddenly, there's an uncomfortable sort of lump in my throat, and I take a gulp of wine to wash it away. Sometimes, I wish Tess wouldn't be quite so lovely all of the time. When she looks at you with those soft, understanding green eyes, it just makes you want to burst into tears and reveal the deepest torments of your soul. I've seen perfect strangers on the bus break down and tell her their entire life story.

As it stands, she already knows mine. They both do. I look at my two best friends, and I feel myself relent a little. I'm lucky to have people who care about my happiness. Even if their interference can be excruciating at times, it comes from a good place.

Of course, they don't know the whole truth, that there's still only one man on my mind, even now. I've worked hard to hide it from them. As far as they're concerned, I never think about Ed anymore. I never think about what might have been, save perhaps on this one day each year. I couldn't bring myself to disappoint them, not after they've been here for me for all these years, bolstering my confidence, being my cheerleaders.

"I will consider… I said *consider*," I reiterate sternly, as

Tess's eyes light up, "the possibility. That's all I can promise."

Tess beams and starts topping up the wine glasses. Even Rosie abandons the confetti cones to join us.

I'm smiling at their enthusiasm but inside I'm wondering what on earth I've just agreed to.

"To asking a man out," Rosie proclaims, as we clink glasses. "How hard can it possibly be?"

## Chapter Four

I absolutely *cannot* do this.

I'm hovering in the hallway by the entrance to the *Illuminator* office. If I lurk out here for much longer, I'm going to be late, but I just can't seem to make my feet move.

Last night I lay in bed running the scenario over in my mind until I managed to make it all seem just about okay. Because it's not like it's a big deal, is it? Asking a man out, I mean. Women all over the world are doing it every single day, and the place hasn't imploded yet.

Except, I woke up this morning with a sort of weird shivery feeling, and it's stayed with me ever since. It was there when I made myself a cup of tea. It was still there half an hour later, when the cup of tea had gone cold and I was trying to decide if my new skirt was inappropriately short for workwear. It was there as I stood on the tram, pretending to read the news on my phone. It got even worse when I emerged on to the pavement in front of our building, and now it seems to have stopped me in my tracks altogether.

I have no idea why I'm so nervous about this. I mean, I'm doing it for Rosie and Tess, really. And all right, so perhaps a bit for myself, too. To be honest, after yesterday's conversation, I couldn't shake the feeling of embarrassment, like I was hiding a dark, shameful secret. And I suppose I am; pining over a man who left me without a backwards glance isn't exactly something I want to emblazon across my life CV.

By the time I'd rolled out of bed this morning, I was resolute. I owe it to all of us to try and move on. Even if I just make a *show* of moving on, just take the first step by asking another guy out, then it's something. It's a statement of faith in myself, in my ability to heal.

Besides, it's a fairly safe experiment to begin with, because it's highly unlikely that Nate's going to say yes. He doesn't exactly strike me as the dating type. He'll probably just look at me in utter incomprehension, which'll morph into pity as he concludes that I've deludedly mistaken his friendliness for something more meaningful. I'm sure it happens to him a lot. He probably even has a stock response, a way to let them down gently, to assuage the embarrassment.

Luckily for me, I can deal with embarrassment. It's an old friend. And if it finally convinces Rosie that this vision she has of me and Nate isn't going to happen, then so be it.

"What the hell are you doing hovering around out

here?" Steve barges past me with a scowl. "Come on. We're about to have a meeting."

I blink at him in surprise. We *never* have meetings. Meetings are one of those things that glitzy, modern companies do. They have special meeting rooms with a projector screen and comfortable chairs, and croissants in the middle of the table. We just have… well, we have our dingy, time-worn newspaper office. We don't discuss things, as such. If Steve wants something doing, he yells it at you, and if there's something he wanted doing which he forgot to yell at you, then he yells at you for not doing it anyway. It's not exactly a democratic process, but it's how things are run. From what I can gather, it's how things have been run since time immemorial. Something monumental must have happened to change that.

Forcing myself to follow Steve through the doorway into the office, I make a point of not looking to the right as I make my way towards my desk. That's where Nate sits and I just can't look at him yet. In a minute, maybe, when I've gathered up my courage. It's one thing telling myself it's easy when I'm running through it in my head; in practice, my heart's still pattering with nerves.

I busy myself hanging up my jacket, taking files out of my bag – all the normal, routine things I do when I first arrive in the morning. Of course, normally by this point I would already have looked across the room towards Nate's desk. I would have smiled at him and he would have smiled back. And then I would carry on with what I was doing, and when I next looked up he would be there in front of me and we'd share a light, joking conversation and…

The thought makes me pause, discomfited. I had no idea that he'd become such an important part of my day. When did *that* happen?

"Right," Steve booms, leaning back against the edge of his desk, which is conveniently positioned at the front of the room. All the better to keep an eye on us serfs, I suspect. "Are we all here? Let's start."

Don't look over, I will myself. *Don't* look…

"As you're all no doubt aware, the paper has recently undergone a change of ownership," Steve says gruffly. He never exactly looks pleased but he looks even less pleased than usual at having to say the words. "And apparently our new American proprietors have their own ideas about how things should be run."

His voice is filled with disdain. "Not that I see much wrong with how things are now, of course. We've run along just fine for decades. But people will come in with their airy-fairy ideas…"

How exactly basic health and safety standards constitute "airy-fairy ideas" is beyond my comprehension, but I decide it's better not to voice that comment. The urge to look over at Nate is almost overwhelming. I know he'll be trying not to smile at the same thought. He's better at keeping a straight face than I am, mind.

Freya, who's been patting a small yawn and looking indescribably bored up until now, visibly perks up.

"Ooh, are we going to get a coffee bar?"

"No, we are not," Steve snaps. "You've got a vending machine, haven't you? What more could you want?"

Silently, thirty heads turn to look at the object in question. It's leaning to one side, propped up on a stack of old papers, the flickering light within illuminating a single cereal bar and a banana milkshake. Both pre-date my arrival here.

Freya sniffs disdainfully, but makes no further protest. Instead, she flips open her mirror and begins to reapply her lipstick. It's a bright bubble-gum pink, the sort of colour I could never even hope to pull off. But on her, it works.

To be honest, I've always been slightly suspicious of Freya; she's far too glossy-looking for my liking. Even when it's twenty-eight degrees outside – which, granted, doesn't happen often up here –she always looks picture-perfect.

*She* wouldn't have a problem asking Nate out, I think glumly. In fact, I'm amazed she hasn't already. She certainly doesn't hide her interest in him very well, although, come to think of it, I've never seen him flirt back at her. He only ever appears politely courteous.

I mean, not that I've been *watching* them or anything. It's just… hard not to notice things in an office of these proportions, that's all.

Steve coughs, evidently aware that the conversation is veering off on a tangent.

"Anyway, there are a few things we've got to do. Put a few posters up and the like. Should keep them happy. Doubt they'll check, but we'd better show willing. It's all nonsense, of course," he adds bitterly. "If it ain't broke…"

He slaps a hand down on his paper-strewn desk to illustrate, sending a cloud of dust billowing into the air.

I bite my lip to swallow a laugh.

To hell with it. I glance across at Nate's desk, prepared to catch his eye.

It's empty.

A part of me knows I should feel relieved but instead I just feel a sharp thud of disappointment. Even though I know I won't find him, I cast a surreptitious eye around the room just in case. But no, he's not here.

And suddenly, everything seems a little less bright. Admittedly, the sun does retreat behind a cloud at that moment, casting our already gloomy office even further into shadow, yet I can't help but feel that's only pathetic fallacy of a kind.

I can feel Freya watching me, her sharp, assessing gaze on the side of my face, and I quickly turn my head away, pretending to be interested in something on my desk.

"Do you think they'll send an inspector?" Darren's asking eagerly, clutching a pad of paper to his chest. He genuinely appears thrilled by the prospect.

I give him a disbelieving look.

Steve, meanwhile, looks revolted by the idea.

"I bloody hope not! That's the last thing we need. It's all very well this bloody nannying but we've got a job to be getting on with. The paper doesn't produce itself, you know."

I presume that's a rhetorical statement, and apparently

everyone else does too, as there's an awkward beat of silence.

"So, er, is there actually anything you need *us* to do?" I ask. I feel that someone ought to move this meeting on, lest it turn into one long diatribe on the evils of modern employment legislation.

"What?" Steve looks as though the thought hadn't occurred to him. "No, why would I? Don't talk nonsense, Delphine. I'm just giving you all a heads up, that's all. Now, get back to it, all of you. I'm not paying you to stand around wasting time."

As everyone disperses, I sidle up to Steve's desk.

"Do you, er… know where Nate is this morning? He missed the meeting."

I kind of hate myself for asking but suddenly I find I really want to know.

Steve's heavy brows draw together.

"Of course I know. Don't you think I run this place?" He shuffles papers around his desk clumsily, somehow only managing to put them in worse disarray than before. "He's at the courthouse, following up on a story. *Working*, like you should be now. I want the streetlight article on my desk by lunchtime."

"Oh. Okay." I make to leave, but he clears his throat, stopping me in my tracks.

I turn and blink in surprise at the transformation. For once, his angry bluster is conspicuously absent. Instead, he looks… well, if I didn't know better, I might even say *embarrassed*. But surely that's impossible. The man's like a brick wall.

"Er, Delphine, while you're here." His tone has dropped low, so low I can barely hear him. I've never heard him speak in anything quieter than a dull roar, so this is a revelation in itself. "There is *one* other thing..."

---

I push my way out of the glass doors and onto the street. The weather has perked up considerably, all trace of yesterday's apocalyptic atmosphere already seeming a distant memory. Pale sunlight filters down from a cloud-dotted sky, shimmering through the last of the late spring blossoms. It's the kind of day that can put anyone in a good mood. I'm convinced everyone looks a little bit happier than usual, even though it's lunchtime and the streets are absolutely heaving.

I make my way towards the café where I've arranged to meet Leo, weaving through the sea of people. I make a quick dash across the street, only just managing to avoid getting hit by a stealthy taxi which looms up on my left side. Raising a hand in tentative apology, I reach the relative safety of the opposite pavement unscathed, vowing to be more careful next time. Edinburgh might be much less chaotic than London, but it's still a big city.

It can be easy to forget though, I acknowledge, as I turn off into one of the steep, narrow-stepped side streets, and immediately the quietness envelops me. It's one of the things I love best about it here, how you can still find pockets of tranquillity without having to look too hard for them. They almost seem to find you, somehow.

Pulling open the door of the café, I'm hit by the familiar wave of heat and sound. The clatter of spoons on saucers, the deep whirr of the coffee grinder, the tinny sound of whisks beating against metal jugs. As coffee shops go it's not big or even particularly quirky. In fact, it's pretty nondescript, with squashy leather sofas and pictures of Italy on the walls which never seem to hang quite straight. But it's cosy and inviting, and they take an indulgent view of customers who linger for over an hour with a single coffee, so it's become something of a favourite haunt.

One of the baristas catches my eye with a half-nod of recognition, something which back in London would have been the equivalent of someone throwing their arms around you and declaring you an old friend. Here, it's not so uncommon. With an answering smile, I settle myself at a table tucked away in the far corner of the room and order a cappuccino and chocolate muffin while I wait for Leo to arrive.

When he does, it's with his usual punctuality, on the dot of half past one. He's clearly in business mode, wearing a smart grey suit and a stern expression, his dark blue eyes scanning the room. When he spots me, though, his face breaks into the wide, boyish grin I recognise.

"Belle," he gives me a warm hug before sprawling across from me, catching a passing waitress to order an Americano in brisk, impatient tones. She nods so vigorously

I'm worried she'll give herself a crick in the neck, before scurrying off to do his bidding. I look on in fascination. I've never understood how he manages to have two such different personalities. I'm always just me, no matter who I'm with, or what I'm doing. Perhaps that's why I'm not particularly high-powered, nor do I ever look likely to be.

"I'm afraid I haven't got as long as I'd hoped," he's saying now, drumming his fingers on the polished wood of the table top. "Things are a bit hectic at the office today."

I raise an eyebrow.

"Aren't they always?"

Leo has one of those convoluted, important-sounding jobs that involves lots of intense meetings around glass-topped tables (no doubt piled high with croissants) which go on for hours. He's paid exceptionally well, from what I can gather, and the whole thing seems to be taken very seriously. He certainly frowns a lot whenever he's talking about it.

So, I'm sure it's all very vital and all of that... but honestly, I have to admit, I have absolutely *no* idea what he actually does. It is a complete and utter mystery to me. He's explained it on more than one occasion – I can tell you it's something to do with advising on political policy, but that's it – and each time I've nodded intelligently, all whilst ending up none the wiser.

Secretly, I don't think even Rosie completely gets it. She pretends she does, but if you ever challenge her about it, she gets all defiant and blustery. That's a sure-fire sign she's lying.

He gives a self-deprecating smile.

"I know, I've worn out that excuse over the years, haven't I?"

I wave away his apology.

"Seriously, don't worry about it."

I half-expected it anyway, hence why I only ordered coffee and cake. Lunch was *never* going to happen.

"So, let's get the business out of the way first," Leo reaches inside his jacket pocket and produces an envelope. "Here's the special licence form. I've filled in everything in my section. She just needs to sign it, and…" his expression turns incredulous as a muffled bark sounds from somewhere under the table. "What on earth was *that*?"

As if on cue, the little Scotty dog pokes her head out from behind my handbag and trots over to inspect Leo's shiny black shoes. I give Leo a sheepish smile.

"This is Frou Frou. It's a long story, but don't worry, it's not a permanent arrangement. She belongs to my boss. Well, his ex-wife. Or at least, *one* of his ex-wives…" Aware that I'm making more amendments than the average council bill, I take the paper from his outstretched hand, stowing it away in my bag before I forget. It would be just like me to leave it behind on the table, and heaven only knows what the fallout from that would be. Rosie would probably have an aneurism. "Thanks for this, by the way. She's been tearing her hair out over it."

As it turns out, even my sister couldn't foresee absolutely everything. Apparently, when one gets married in a parish separate to one's own, two sets of banns have to be read before the marriage can take place. Somehow, this piece of information slipped the net and Rosie and Leo only found out about it a couple of days ago, and now it's only ten days until the wedding, and Rosie…

Well, you can imagine how that went down.

My suggestion that a little bit of tension only adds to the excitement was not well received, let me tell you.

"Can't think why," Leo shrugs, looking unconcerned. His coffee arrives at that moment, and he pauses to take a sip. It must be scalding hot but he doesn't seem to notice. "The special licence essentially does the same job. It's nothing to get worked up about."

You see, *this* is why they're so great together. This is why it kind of just seems to work between them, even though in many ways they seem totally unsuited. When he's not at work, Leo's the calmest, most laid-back person I've ever met, the complete opposite of my neurotic whirlwind of a sister. I like to think they neutralise each other, creating a perfect balance.

Although, maybe the reason they work is simply that Leo is just very forbearing.

"You know Rosie doesn't believe in Plan B," I remind him lightly.

She didn't even bother to accept a second choice of university. Madness, if you ask me, but there you have it. I went to my second choice and I had a great time. Sometimes, life takes you in a direction you don't expect. That doesn't mean it's wrong. I've learned to believe in that.

I've had to, really. In a way, you could say that my life so far has been one long Plan B.

I put my drink down in its saucer and as I look back up, I feel a prickle of awareness skimming across my skin. Like static. I look around, searching for something that might have sparked the sensation.

And then it happens. I see someone out of the corner of my eye. A familiar profile, a dark blond head, ruffled in a way which is so heart-wrenchingly familiar that for a moment it seems to stop my breath in my throat. But when I refocus my gaze, they're gone.

My heart is hammering against my ribs in an irregular pattern and I grip my coffee cup with shaking hands, feeling foolish for getting so worked up. This hasn't happened for a long time; I thought it had stopped.

Dimly, I become aware that Leo's talking again.

"Belle? What do you think?"

I jerk to attention to find him looking at me expectantly.

"Well, um…" I stir what's left of my cappuccino, playing for time. "Of course, you're right. It's very…" At his raised eyebrow, I give up. "I wasn't listening, sorry. What were you saying?"

I daren't tell him what I thought I saw. I don't want him to worry about me. He has enough on his plate as it is.

He shows barely a trace of impatience as he dutifully repeats himself.

"I said, do you think Rosie is handling all of this okay? She seems a trifle stressed to me."

It's one of my absolutely favourite things about Leo that

he can get away with using words like "trifle" in utter seriousness and still maintain an aura of credibility.

"She's *always* stressed," I point out. "It would be stranger if she weren't. She loves being stressed; it gives her a sense of accomplishment."

He smiles, but I notice that it doesn't quite meet his eyes. "I know. It just… she's so wound up. Nothing I say seems to make it better. I know she wants the day to be perfect, but…" He shakes his head, pushing his coffee cup away. "You're right, of course. I'm imagining things. We're just both so tired. It's felt like a very long engagement, you know?"

When Rosie and Leo first got engaged, he was all for taking off with a handful of family and friends to the coast for a tiny ceremony and a weekend with the people who matter most to them both. I thought it was a pretty sound idea, actually, and I expected that Rosie would too. Despite all her organisational tendencies, she normally can't stand a fuss. And she detests frills and flounces. I didn't think she'd have either the inclination or the patience for a big white wedding.

And I was right. To begin with, at least. She was totally on board with the idea; we were looking at little chapels in Dumfries and Galloway, and simple off-the-peg wedding dresses. She was still planning to organise the hell out of the whole thing, of course. She wouldn't be my sister otherwise. But it was all heading towards a small, intimate wedding. No fuss, no frills. Ideal.

And then, one day, without explanation, everything

changed. Suddenly, she wanted it all: a grand country house hotel for the venue, a bespoke designer gown, a four-course wedding breakfast. The whole circus. And we were *all* getting dragged along for the ride.

It has been, in a word, exhausting.

"I know I can be honest with you, Belle," Leo says, rubbing his forehead wearily. For the first time, I notice just how tired he looks. There are dark smudges beneath his eyes, tense lines around his mouth. "I'm getting to the point where I can't wait for this wedding to be over and done with. Is that terrible of me?"

I almost want to smile, despite how despairing he looks. Frou Frou has curled up on his feet and seems to be dozing peacefully. She's the same colour as his shoes, and if it weren't for the diamanté on her baby-pink collar sparkling under the lights, she would be rendered almost invisible.

"Of course not. Leo, this happens to *everybody* in the final weeks before a wedding. It's perfectly normal." I'm not sure who I'm trying to convince more, him or me. I pause, then add an afterthought. "I still wouldn't mention it to Rosie, though. She's probably a bit too fragile at the moment to be reasonable."

He holds up his hands.

"I don't have a death wish. I learned early on in our engagement not to voice even the slightest objection to anything wedding-related." He stops, looking shame-faced. "Listen to me. I'm sorry, Belle. I know all this must be difficult for you."

He's the only person who's ever really addressed the

lingering spectre of my wedding-that-wasn't. Everyone else just edges around it; I suppose they think it's easier to simply not talk about it. The classic Delphine way of coping with anything uncomfortable.

"It's fine. *I'm* fine. Honestly."

I'm not sure how true that really is, but it's the line I've been parroting for so long I can't even remember what lies behind it any more.

He sighs deeply, running a hand through his hair, making it stick up in the unruly way it used to when he was a teenager, and suddenly he looks exactly the same. Despite the suit and the world-worn lines at either side of his mouth.

"I just want everything to go back to normal, that's all."

Leo and I have known each other for a long time. We're practically siblings. So I have no compunction whatsoever about what I do next.

I burst out laughing. Frou Frou starts at the sound, emitting an affronted yap.

"What?" Leo pretends to look put out, but his lips are turning up at the corners, giving him away. "I fail to see why that should be so hilarious."

"Leo," I splutter. God, the man is *so* naïve. "You're going to be living with my sister. You're going to be married… *to my sister*. Clearly you haven't grasped the full implications of what that means." I shake my head, reaching across to place a hand on his arm. "Enjoy these last few days while you can. Because, believe me, things will *never* be normal again."

## Chapter Five

I give Leo an extra-long hug as we part ways outside the café. I feel he needs it at the moment. I watch him walk away, his broad shoulders disappearing into the crowd, and I try not to think too much about what he's said. It's really not my job to police his and Rosie's relationship, after all. They're both adults, even if one of them *is* as mad as a box of frogs. They'll sort it out. They always have before.

I turn and head back towards the office, Frou Frou bustling along by my side. She's not exactly fast, with those short little legs of hers, but I don't mind. I'm happy to take my time. It's not often I get to enjoy a sunny Edinburgh afternoon. As I said, the life of a junior reporter isn't quite as adventurous as one might expect. In reality, most of my time is spent typing up puff pieces to fill the sidebars at the edges of the pages; it's a rare thing for me to be released from the office.

I'm not certain Frou Frou will be able to manage the

steps going back up the street so I decide to take a different, more meandering route through one of the ancient alleyways – or closes, as they're known here – which cut between the buildings. I don't use them often and soon I remember why. It's breath-squeezingly tight down here and shrouded in a sort of perpetual twilight by the cramped overhanging buildings on either side. It's as though sun hasn't penetrated this space for years; it's deathly cold and I shiver. I can easily imagine myself falling back in time, to an Edinburgh which wasn't known as the beautiful tourist spot it is today, but a dark, brutal place, overcrowded and drowning in plague.

I shake my head, telling myself I'm being over-dramatic. Still, I don't fancy hanging around.

"Come on, Frou Frou," I mutter, with a gentle tug on her lead to encourage her to pick up the pace. "Let's get out of here."

But she doesn't move. In fact, she's rooted to the spot, staring at something in the shadows. Her teeth are bared, a faint, menacing growl rumbling from her throat. My pulse kicks into gear, muscles locking into place as fear sweeps over me. Heart hammering, I peer into the shadows, but everything's still.

"There's nothing there, girl," I'm trying to sound calm, but my voice is shaking. "Probably just a trick of the light."

She comes, albeit reluctantly, tail down, glancing around her as though expecting at any moment that something's going to pounce out of the darkness.

Finally, we emerge from the shadowy side street into the

hubbub of the Royal Mile, and I release a breath I hadn't even known I was holding.

Usually, I find the chaos of this part of town more of a nuisance than anything, something to be navigated on my way to and from work. It's at its worst in August, when the Fringe engulfs every square inch of space. Even now, at the city's supposedly 'quiet' time of year, the street throngs with people.

Well, I *say* street; if I'm being technical about it, it's actually a succession of streets, running between Holyrood Palace at one end and the imposing castle at the other. It's a total tourist trap – every other shop seems to sell exclusively tartan – and with its eclectic medley of churches, pubs, and museums all bunched up against one another, I can see why, even if it is a major inconvenience from my point of view.

Although, right now, I've never been so pleased to see it. Being surrounded by other people all getting on with their day, oblivious, is enough to bring my heart rate back to something approaching normality, although the sight of someone dressed up in a beak-like plague mask advertising ghost tours does make me flinch involuntarily.

People are pressed close around us, and, after a moment's consideration, I pick Frou Frou up, worried she might get trodden on. Not that I think Steve would mind much, judging by some of the colourful language he used about the ex-wife in question – I *think* it's the most recent one, but decided it was wiser not to ask – who seems to have gone off on a world cruise of indeterminate duration with her new boyfriend, leaving Frou Frou on Steve's doorstep.

I look down at the dog who's snuggling closer into my arms. Despite the ridiculous name and the hideously spangled collar, she's actually rather sweet. And she *did* try to protect me. I just hope she doesn't find Steve's living standards too much of a shock after the pampered existence she's been used to.

Letting myself into the office building, I begin the long trudge up the stairs. Already I'm starting to wish I'd brought something else for lunch. It's not like I wasn't prepared; I don't think I've ever managed to sit down with Leo for more than fifteen minutes since he got his latest promotion. Even if it's not during office hours, his phone will be buzzing away with some supposedly vital matter or another. It's going to drive Rosie absolutely crazy when they're living together.

I pop Frou Frou into Steve's office, fluffing up her pink crown-shaped bed and making sure her water bowl is topped up. I head back to my desk and am in the process of collapsing into my computer chair when a hand grasps me lightly beneath the elbow and pulls me back up.

"Ah, good, you're back. Come on, then. Let's go."

Go? Is he serious? I've just walked up six flights of stairs in high heels. And now he wants me to go all the way back *down* again?

"We've got some great leads," Nate announces, to no

one in particular. I stare at him, wondering if he's gone slightly mad.

Which would be a shame, as he's about the only sane person around here. He's about the only sane person in my *life*. It's kind of what I like about him.

That final thought sends me into a minor flap. When I say… I mean, not what I… oh God, what is *wrong* with me today?

"Just go with it," he murmurs out of the corner of his mouth, when he sees me about to protest.

Which I do, but only once the heavy door has closed behind us and we're in the echoing corridor outside the office. I dig my heels in, forcing us to a stop. Folding my arms, I glare at him. Handsome he may be, but I have *very* low blood sugar right now, and he's just got between me and the chocolate crunch bar I've remembered is hidden in the bottom drawer of my desk. I know my priorities.

"All right, what's going on?"

It had *better* be good.

"We," Nate says airily, taking my elbow and steering me along the corridor, "are going for lunch."

I really wasn't expecting him to say that.

"We… we are?" Cursing myself for stumbling over my words, I make a concerted effort not to stumble over my feet, too. I'm struggling to keep up with Nate's long strides. To be fair, my new lilac sandals aren't helping; they're probably a bit on the high side for work, if I'm being honest, but when my legs look this good in them, who cares? "Won't Steve have a fit when he finds out we've gone?"

I've seen Steve lose it before. Many times, as a matter of fact. It's nothing new. But still, it's not something you willingly want to incite.

"He's too busy to care at the moment," Nate replies with a shrug. "This whole load of documents came through an hour or so ago regarding the new health and safety targets. They're sending an inspector out next week."

"Darren's got his wish, then," I mutter darkly.

"When I left, Steve was staring into the first aid box with a vacant expression and scratching his head," Nate continues. His voice is perfectly neutral, but as I steal a glance at his face I can see the humour in his eyes.

"I wasn't even aware we *had* a first aid box," I say, trying not to smile.

I don't imagine it's that well stocked. It probably dates from the last war. Despite myself, I can't help but feel a twinge of pity for Steve. He's from another age himself. All of this must simply be incomprehensible to him.

Great, now I'm feeling sorry for *Steve,* of all people. I must be quickening for a fever.

My feelings must be apparent on my face because Nate says wryly, "I think he'll be just fine. Darren's beside himself with excitement. He's already appointed himself in charge of the new accident book."

I roll my eyes. God, he's going to be insufferable, isn't he?

Although, I suppose anything's got to be better than the previous accident policy, which comprised of Steve responding to every complaint with, "If you're not dying, then get back to work."

"Of course, there *is* a plus side to all this," Nate adds, opening the door and standing aside to let me go through. "Amidst all this chaos, no one will take much notice of what we're doing. When I told Steve we were going out together to gather eyewitness accounts for our story, he just told me to bugger off and leave him alone."

"Is that a direct quote?" I arch an eyebrow questioningly.

"What do you think?"

"Wait," I wheel to a stop, turning to face him in confusion as my brain finally catches up with what he's just said. "You told him that we're *still* collaborating?"

Why would he do that? I mean… it was just an excuse, surely? I never thought he actually *meant* it.

"Of course," Nate shrugs, as though it were the most natural choice in the world. "It's a pretty good cover, don't you think?"

"For *what*?" Now I'm hopelessly confused. I really don't know what he's talking about. Is there some covert journalistic operation I've missed? This is what comes from disappearing off on long lunch breaks. If I stayed at my desk, eating soggy homemade tuna sandwiches like Darren does, then maybe I'd be more up to date.

Nate raises a dark brow.

"To finally spend some proper time together, of course."

He says it so casually, but nonetheless it makes me freeze

to the spot. All of a sudden, I'm very aware of everything that's going on in this moment: the soft breeze tousling his hair, the kids splashing around in the puddle over his shoulder, the loose blossom petals dancing around our feet.

"Unless the idea strikes you as particularly repugnant," he continues lightly, "in which case, I shall naturally return you to the office without delay."

"No, it's not…" I'm struggling to take all of this in. Just a minute ago, we were walking along, and everything was fine. Normal. He was gorgeous and I was rambling, and… well, not much has changed in the last sixty seconds, except now I don't know what on earth is going on between us. It's like the ground has shifted.

Throughout this entire mental interlude, Nate's been waiting patiently, his eyes fixed on my face.

"I'm not doing a very good job of this, am I?" He shoves his hands in his pockets and rocks back on his heels. "I should just say what I mean. God knows, I've had enough chances, and I've… well, I seem to keep screwing it up." He laughs, but there's a nervous edge to it. "Much like I'm doing now."

"Oh," I stutter, momentarily unable to summon anything more. "I… I see."

Immediately, I curse myself. Because I really *don't* see. What is he talking about?

"Actually," I blurt out. "It *might* be quite useful if you would… you know, elucidate."

"Of course." He takes a formal breath. "I'm *trying* to ask

you out. On a date," he adds, deliberately. "Just so there can be no more ambiguity."

The sense of surprise hits me square in the chest, blooming outwards. I can feel my lips parting, my eyes widening. I've never been able to stop my inner workings from playing out across my face.

He's watching me silently. He's better than me; he doesn't give much away, but there's a flicker of trepidation in his eyes, and with a jolt, I realise that what I say next matters. It matters a lot.

The realisation that behind all of his confidence, his insouciance, lies someone fallible, forces me to look at him in a whole new way. This is a man who could have anyone he wanted. Someone like Freya, who's glamorous, accomplished… the kind of woman who has it all together. Who doesn't spill tea over herself every other day of the week, for starters.

And yet, it's me he's standing here in front of, looking earnest, and, dare I say it, even a little nervous? Not words I would ever have dreamed of matching to Nate before this moment. Can it really be me who's done this?

I can't deny it; it's an intoxicating thought. It makes me stall, the automatic rebuttal which was hovering on my lips dissolving. Because of course I was about to turn him down. I always turn them down. It's as natural now as breathing.

But then I remember what I promised myself last night. What I promised Rosie and Tess. If ever there was such a thing as a celestial shove in the shoulder blades, this would be it.

And there's something else, too. Something I never expected. A sort of sparkling interest in this new version of Nate. The truth is that if he'd asked me in another way – his usual way, all smiles and charm and effortless confidence – then I might feel very differently about the whole thing. But watching him bungle it so hopelessly… well, it's refreshing. It kind of makes me want to give him a chance.

"Look, can we just forget I ever said anything?" He scrubs a hand through his hair, his jaw tight. "This is why I was afraid to ask you. I never wanted to make things awkward between us."

"What? No!" I blurt out, slightly taken aback by my own vehemence. Suddenly, I find that forgetting it is the last thing I want. "You took me by surprise, that's all."

He looks at me, and his gaze is searching.

"You've never thought about it, then?"

"Er, well," I hedge, all the while wondering why I can't just tell him the truth. That I haven't allowed myself to think about anyone in that way for a long time. "It's not really been… I mean, we're friends – sort of – and you… well, you're so…" I trail off, suddenly not sure I want to go there.

"So what?"

Damn. He's actually expecting an answer. I was hoping to just leave it hanging. There's no polite way to tell someone that you've always thought of them as an arrogant, superficial inveigler.

"So… impossible!" I fling my hands up in exasperation. "You're so self-possessed, and charming…" I can feel myself starting to redden and his answering grin tells me he's seen it too.

"You think I'm charming, then?"

He *would* have picked up on that part, wouldn't he? I'm beginning to wish I hadn't been so tactful.

"Now we've sorted that out," he steps closer, until I'm looking deep into his brandy-coloured eyes. And he's back again, the shiny veneer in place. But it doesn't bother me so much now, I find. "Shall we go?"

I tilt my chin defiantly. I'm not going to fall that easily. Someone has to make it difficult for him every once in a while.

"I've already had lunch."

"There's lunch and there's lunch," he offers his arm and we begin to walk again. "We've been over this, remember? Chocolate cake doesn't count."

"I know, I know, it offends your Italian sensibilities," I roll my eyes, but already I'm smiling. He has a way of putting me at ease no matter the situation. I wish I knew how he does it.

"Food is a serious business in my family."

"Nothing is a serious business in mine. We're all equally ridiculous."

He laughs, and the sound seems to tingle through me, right to the tips of my toes. Immediately, I want to make him laugh again. The thought is so unexpected, so startling, that it almost makes me falter.

"Come on. I know somewhere that does great pasta. I

see it as my mission to convert you to proper sustenance. I won't rest until I've succeeded."

And as we set off into the sunshine together, it occurs to me that, against all the odds, I actually can't think of a nicer proposition.

## Chapter Six

"Well, it might have been a somewhat unorthodox beginning to a first date," Nate remarks, as we stroll back through the streets of Edinburgh. "But it didn't turn out *so* badly, did it?"

"Not at all," I say softly. In fact, if anything, it's only left me feeling more confused than ever.

I didn't expect any trouble when we walked into the restaurant. Actually, I was congratulating myself on my mature, worldly approach to the whole thing. All right, so maybe I was panicking a little bit. After all, it was my first date in six years. My first date as a proper, fully fledged adult. Ed and I just *happened*; we never had any formal dates. In fact, the last time I did this, it was all sharing a tub of popcorn in the back row of the cinema before getting the last bus home.

So I could admit it was probably past time I had a practice date. Just so I didn't forget how to do the whole thing. Follow the formula… order food, trying to avoid anything which had the potential to fly off the plate like a missile, or anything with rivers of bright red sauce; chat about uncontentious, superficial subjects… I mean, if anyone's a perfect candidate for that sort of thing, it's Nate. He's practically at professional competition level when it comes to light banter.

Except, somehow, it didn't go quite how I'd planned. Somehow, I found that we were talking about all sorts of things… or at least, he was. He told me about his father's cancer diagnosis, the reason he came back to Edinburgh and took the job at the *Illuminator*. He told me about the editor at the broadsheet he'd been working for in London who threatened that if he left, he'd never get back into serious journalism. He told me about the girlfriend he'd been living with, who wasn't prepared to do long distance. He told me all of it with such simple openness, and I…

Well, I talked too. I told him about my crazy family, about my salt-of-the-earth Scottish grandmother, who practically had to drag Rosie and me – and Tess, when she was there – up into some sort of respectable adulthood while my mother swanned in and out like a diva at the opera. I told him about how Rosie and I spent the first summer trying to learn the accent so we'd fit in better at school, except we ended up sounding more Russian than anything and our teacher put us both in detention for being 'disruptive'.

But I glossed over it all, playing it for laughs. I didn't talk about how I really felt. I didn't stray towards anything too meaningful. Even after everything, I still can't bring myself to do that, not with anyone. The impenetrable wall of my armour is rusted into place. Because I told someone else all of these things once before. I handed my heart to him, and he ran away with it.

Deflection is nothing new for me; I've spent most of my life doing it. But today it bothers me. I feel… guilty. Like I've cheated Nate, somehow, by not returning his honesty. And it's not just that; I'm painfully aware the whole time of the person hovering just beyond the edge of my vision. It's like I can feel Ed watching us, like he's a physical presence, taunting me with the knowledge that I'm not free. That, fundamentally, I still belong to him.

I'm so lost in my introspection that I follow Nate without thinking and it takes me a moment to realise we're standing outside the gates to Greyfriars Kirkyard, Edinburgh's most famous cemetery. I falter in my step and he looks askance at me.

"Are you okay?"

"Fine." My voice sounds strained; I swallow and try again. "Just… I haven't been through here in a while, that's all."

"Does it bother you? We can go around it if you like."

"What? No. That'll take ages. It's fine, honestly. It's just… been a weird day, that's all." First the inexplicable sighting outside the café, then Frou Frou growling at nothing in the alleyway, and now this. I'm beginning to feel pretty shaken. "I had a… um, strange experience here once, when I was in my teens," I explain. "Rosie and I were walking through late one night, and we..." I hesitate at this part. I've never told anyone about this before. "Well, we saw something."

Or at least, I did. Rosie's never spoken about it; I don't know if she even remembers. We'd been to a party; no doubt there had been several cans of lurid mixed drinks involved.

"A ghost?" He raises an eyebrow, but not unkindly. Even so, I feel myself flushing.

"I don't know what it was. It was so quick. More like a shape than anything."

I look over towards the spot where I saw it all those years ago. In the bright sunshine, on a glorious spring day like this, it suddenly seems very foolish. It's hard to reconcile this peaceful place with the infamous tales of ghost attacks and body snatching which have become so synonymous with its name.

"I'm sure we imagined it, anyway," I say briskly. "We were young, impressionable." A bit drunk, too, although I don't say that part aloud. "It was dark. There are a lot of stories associated with this place. You can see how it happened."

He's watching me carefully. I can't tell what he's thinking.

"And yet you've avoided coming back for all this time? It must have had quite an impact."

I look away, pretending to admire a sarcophagus.

"I think that's more out of habit than anything."

*More lies*, I think, with a flash of guilt. How many am I going to stack up?

Because he's right; it did shake me. To the core. And I've never been able to convince myself that it was a flight of imagination. I know what I saw. I pushed it to the back of my mind but the truth is, the way I look at the world changed that day. Irrevocably. My faith in a steady, explicable universe was shattered forever.

He doesn't question me any further, and we walk the rest of the way back in companionable silence. Or at least, he seems comfortable with it. My thoughts are churning.

"I have a small confession," I blurt out, as we reach the front of the *Illuminator* building. I really don't want to tell him this, but I feel I owe him one small truth, at the very least. "*I* was supposed to be asking *you* out today. You kind of… beat me to it."

"*Supposed* to be asking me out?" He looks quizzical. "That sounds ominous. Did Rosie have anything to do with it, by chance?"

He knows my sister far too well. You know, come to think of it, it's amazing that Nate and I never crossed paths before serendipity brought us together at the *Illuminator*. There must have been countless parties where we were orbiting the same room and yet somehow never managed to meet. I knew that he existed, of course. I'd heard about him from Rosie and Leo, but even after we finally met I never dared to ask them too much about him. The last thing I wanted was for Rosie's antenna to start twitching.

"She might have been the… er… catalyst," I admit reluctantly. Since when isn't she?

He pauses at the top of the stairs, turning inwards to face me. For an instant, I wonder if he's going to kiss me, and I freeze. I can feel my heart rate kicking upwards, the blood pounding in my ears.

"We should probably go in separately," Nate murmurs, and I start, the spell popping around me like a burst balloon.

With an effort, I try to focus on the practicalities. It's almost four o'clock; we've been gone for hours.

"You're right." I find myself nodding a bit too fervently, trying to cover my confusion and embarrassment. What the hell was *that*? Of *course* he wasn't about to kiss me, not right here. Not after one sort-of-date. "Even Steve will probably have begun to wonder where we've got to by now."

It's not even like I wanted him to kiss me, I remind myself feverishly. It was just… a moment of madness. It didn't mean anything. Immediately, Ed's face swims into my mind, and I force it away as I'm overwhelmed by a sudden, sharp kick of guilt, followed immediately by self-directed shame and anger. Why, after all this time, after everything he's done, do I still feel like I owe him fidelity?

"I'll go first, I think." Nate smiles down at me. "Your face will give us away in a second. You certainly don't look like you've just spent a tedious afternoon gathering witness statements. You look far too perky."

*Do I?* My hand automatically flies to my face, as though I'll be able to feel the evidence there. That can't be good.

I would give anything in this moment to rewind a couple of hours, to change the course of events. I wish I'd never seen the moment of vulnerability in his eyes when he asked me out. I wish I didn't know anything about his life. That he's a good son, that he's capable of a long-term relationship, that he values family over career. I wish I could still look at him and see a one-dimensional player, intent only on flirting his way around the office.

"I'm glad we finally did this." He runs his hand through his hair, tousling his espresso-coloured curls. "I should never have waited so long."

"Why did you?" The words are out of my mouth before I can stop them and I curse myself, but at the same time I wouldn't take them back even if I could. I want to know.

He smiles ruefully.

"Belle, I don't think you realise… you're kind of intimidating, you know."

I'm stunned into speechlessness. Of all the words I might have associated with myself, intimidating is not one of them. *Rosie* is intimidating. My grandmother is *definitely* intimidating, especially when she starts waving her walking stick around after a few glasses of sherry. Even my mother is at a stretch, in an alarming, what-will-she-do-next sort of way. But I… well, I fall over my own *feet*, for Christ's sake. I'm about as intimidating as a new-born kitten.

And yet he said it so earnestly. He wasn't joking. Nate D'Angelo genuinely finds me intimidating.

I'll have to tell Rosie about this. She'll be *thrilled*.

Before I can summon up a reply, a door bangs further down the corridor. It seems to refocus Nate's attention.

"I'll see you in a minute. Try to look a little less cheery when you walk in, if you can manage it."

"I'll think of Darren," I choke out, forcing myself to joke, to act normally. "That ought to do it."

He grins and squeezes my hand briefly before releasing it and walking away.

I lean back against the wall, waiting until he's out of earshot before letting the breath whistle out from between my lips.

I can't afford to like him. Not even a little bit. I'm not ready; I can see that now. When Ed walked away like that, he left so many unanswered questions, so many trailing threads. If we'd just broken up, it might have been different. There would have been an ending, a sense of closure. But this way… Perhaps I'm cursed never to have that.

I've pushed myself away from the wall and am sloping along the corridor, disconsolately pondering the notion, when suddenly, from nowhere, there's the most almighty crash from somewhere behind me.

I all but screech to a halt. What was *that*? It sounded like the whole building's in the process of falling down.

Although, that may not be so surprising. It's hardly state of the art. There's a ceiling tile above my desk that's been looking decidedly precarious ever since I started here. Every day, I'm half waiting for it to fall on my head. A part of me almost wishes it would, just to end to suspense.

There's another crash, of slightly lesser magnitude than

the first, although this time it's accompanied by the addition of a rather choice expletive.

Avidly curious now, I find myself turning despite myself, retracing my steps back along the corridor.

It seems to be coming from the stationery cupboard, although of course, it can't possibly be. Who would be flailing around in *there*?

It's all gone quiet. Suddenly, I'm very aware of my heartbeat, of how alone I feel out here in this dark, empty corner of the building. If I were to scream, would anyone in the office even hear me? The sound would have to travel along rambling corridors, through stone walls probably metres thick in places. The thought gives me a shiver.

The temptation to back away is overwhelming. Every sense in my body is firing, my muscles aching to move. But I don't. Telling myself I'm being ridiculous, I edge towards the door warily. At least if I open it, I can prove to myself there's nothing…

The door bursts open. I leap backwards with a piercing scream.

"Surprise!" A very familiar figure looms in the doorway.

For a long moment, I just stare. The world has begun to blur around the edges. It takes everything I have to gasp out the single syllable on which my world once turned.

*"Ed?"*

# Chapter Seven

"Of course it's *me*," he says, pouting a little as he picks a pencil out from where it has lodged behind his ear. "Who else would it be?"

He utters this last sentence as though there aren't literally billions of possible answers, but that's the least of my concerns right now. I feel like a struck gong, shock waves reverberating through my body, wave after wave, each more paralysing than the next. I just stare at him speechlessly. I don't think my lips could form words, even if I wanted them to. Every muscle seems to be locked into place, crystallising into stone.

I've played this moment over in my mind a hundred times. I've envisaged meeting him again in dozens of different ways, under countless circumstances. But nothing could have prepared me for the reality of seeing him standing there. I almost can't believe he's real. I wonder if the frequency with which he's been on my mind lately has summoned a hallucination, a manifestation of my guilty conscience.

The thought is like a pinprick of light lancing through the debilitating shock, giving me something to hold on to. I take a deep shuddering breath, trying to bring my heart rate back to something less precarious.

"Are you all right?" He's watching me warily. "You look as though you're about to faint."

"I never faint," I murmur thickly, but I lean back against the wall nonetheless. Stars are blooming and bursting in front of my eyes and there's a ringing sound vibrating through my ear canal. The outline of the corridor seems fuzzy and I shake my head, trying to clear it.

"Are you sure? Should I get you a…" he looks wildly around the cupboard, then, seeing no chair, finishes lamely, "*something* to sit on?"

I ignore him, closing my eyes against the still-dancing stars. He's not real, I tell myself. It's just a vision. I'm imagining him.

But it's not enough to stop the memories from closing in. Standing outside the church, the baking sun upon my shoulders. Waiting, praying that he'd appear. I had so much faith in him. Then the look on Leo's face when he came back. I'll never forget that look. It was the moment my faith crumbled, even if I couldn't admit it at the time. It was the moment I knew.

The world isn't spinning quite so vigorously anymore, and I risk opening my eyes. He's still there. I blink, willing him away, the first stirrings of doubt beginning to play a faint tune. Why is he still here? He looks so real up close. I can even see the hint of green in his blue eyes. Like the Cyprian sea. The thought brings a fresh twist of painful recollection.

And then I realise something else. His hand is on my shoulder. I can feel the weight of it through the thin fabric of my dress. And in that moment, the bottom falls out of my whole existence. My whole life here in Edinburgh. Everything I've built since it happened. Blown away like dust.

"Belle?" He repeats. "Can you hear me?"

"You're…" My voice is papery, like it's about to crumple in upon itself. "You're really here, aren't you?"

"I haven't handled this very well, have I? Maybe the whole 'surprise' thing was a bit inappropriate, with hindsight." He chews on his lip. "I just thought… well, I don't know what I was thinking, to be honest. I suppose I thought it might make it all a bit less… intense." His face falls, blue eyes widening in remorse. "You know I'm no good with this sort of thing."

"What are you doing here?" I've found my voice, and it's steadily rising with each word. Is this what hysteria feels like?

He blinks, as though this is a strange question.

"In the cupboard?"

Well, yes, actually, now that he mentions it. And at any other time, that might be the most pressing question. But right now…

I breathe deeply, placing the flats of my hands against

my temples and squeezing, as though I can block all of this out somehow. Suddenly, I feel like I'm suffocating under the full force of it all. This can't really be happening, can it?

Suddenly, footsteps sound further down the corridor. Swift footsteps. Heading in our direction.

"Belle!"

Nate's voice. And then it hits me, like a bucket of iced water, sweeping the numbness aside temporarily as my focus narrows onto a single thought.

I can't explain this. Not now, not to anyone. I have to get Ed out of here.

Quick, Belle, think. Something ingenious.

In a panic, I grab Ed by the arm.

"You've got to get back into the cupboard."

He looks appalled.

"No way! It's a deathtrap in there. I almost got lacerated by an open box of staples last time."

His words barely register through my panic. I shove him inside and yank the door shut, just as Nate comes skidding around the corner, Darren and Steve – who's carrying Frou Frou in his arms like a baby – at his heels.

"Are you okay?" Nate looks adorably concerned, I can't help but notice. "We heard you scream, and… well…" he trails off, evidently conscious of Steve and Darren lurking behind him. Neither of them look half as concerned to find me alive and well, I can't help but notice.

"What the bloody hell's going on, Delphine?" Steve grumbles, although the effect is ruined somewhat by Frou Frou, who chooses that moment to lick his chin. "Can't have all of this. Screaming and such the like. Most unprofessional. People will think we're not…"

"A safe and caring environment?" I suggest innocently. I wonder if they'll notice that my voice is higher than normal, taut with strain.

Steve colours, then coughs.

"Quite. Of course."

"You'll be pleased to hear that I'm fine, then," I grip the door handle tighter as Ed begins to push against it from the other side. Belatedly, it hits me what I've done. This is a disaster. A *disaster*. I can't just stand here chatting like everything's normal. How on earth am I going to pull this off? "I was just alarmed, that's all. I, er…" They're all looking at me expectantly, and I realise with a sinking feeling that I have no idea where I'm going with this. I'd kind of hoped they'd have lost interest by now.

"A rat!" I exclaim, triumphantly, before realising that I shouldn't be sounding so pleased about it. "I saw a rat," I reiterate in a smaller voice, hoping I look suitably pathetic enough to add credence to my story.

"A rat?" Darren looks about ready to climb onto Steve's back. "Where?"

Frou Frou's ears prick up hopefully. Steve looks decidedly bilious.

"Oh, God. Not right before the inspection. This is a total nightmare."

Nate doesn't say anything. He just watches me, with a steady look that makes me feel slightly uncomfortable. He's not buying any of this, I can tell.

Ed gives the door a sharp shove, and I brace my shoulder against it.

"Are you struggling with that door, by any chance?" Nate asks mildly.

"What? No, not at all." I execute what I hope looks like a nonchalant lean, all whilst still barring the door. It's not easy. I pray that Ed doesn't try and break out again, or I'll probably find myself sprawled on the other side of the corridor. "I was just… you know… brainstorming headlines. For our new project. It needs something striking, you know? Something…" What on earth am I banging on about? Why do I do this whenever I lie? I'm *such* an over-embellisher. It always trips me up. "…Thought-provoking."

Steve and Darren look none the wiser, which makes three of us. Frou Frou seems to have fallen asleep, so she's out. However, Nate is nodding.

"Right," he says, with great gravity. "I see."

I'm momentarily taken aback. *I* don't.

Steve grunts.

"Well, so long as you're alive, Delphine…"

"And not about to sue," Darren adds helpfully. Steve glares at him and he quails.

"Back to the office, everyone," Steve barks, making the dog in his arms start. "D'Angelo, I need to talk to you about the Newell case. Do you have the notes?"

"Yes, sir." Nate sounds reluctant. His eyes flicker back to me and I hold my breath. But then he turns away. "I'll get them for you now."

I exhale heavily as they round the corner, their voices

fading out of earshot.

"Belle!" Ed hammers on the door and I start, letting go of the handle.

The door swings open. He's standing there as though poised for battle, a mop clutched in his hands. The sight is so farcical that it should dampen my reaction somewhat but instead it hits me all over again – if anything more powerfully than ever. To think I could ever have convinced myself that I was imagining him, I brood, with a misery-laced stab at humour. Even the wildest corners of my imagination couldn't have conjured up something like this.

"You trapped me in here!" He gasps. "I thought I was going to have to employ this as a battering ram."

Through the mental fog, one thought glows brightly. I can't deal with this here. Edinburgh was supposed to be my new life; no one here at work knows anything about what happened. I have to remind myself to take my next breath. Something which should be automatic suddenly seems more and more challenging.

"Look, we can't talk here." I'm amazed at how level I manage to make my voice. As if it isn't taking every ounce of focus to keep my mind on the practicalities, to hold everything else at bay just for a while longer. "I'll see if I can get away early. Go downstairs and wait for me outside."

He doesn't look convinced.

"How long will you be?"

It's like having a ten-year-old. Suddenly he looks appealingly unsure of himself, and my heart turns over. I will myself to ignore it.

"I don't know, five minutes? I just need to wrap up a couple of things but I won't have any trouble getting away."

All I have to do is make the most veiled hint about my period and Steve will practically shove me out of the door. It works every time. Actually, I only used it last week when I had an emergency manicure appointment, but thankfully he doesn't seem to have much of a grasp of the feminine reproductive cycle.

"All right, then." Ed slinks out of the cupboard. "I'll wait."

"Great," I say brightly, struggling to keep the tremor out of my voice. I *cannot* fall apart here. I have to keep it together. "And then we'll go…"

Actually, that's a good point, I realise, with a new wave of panic. Where *can* we go? Nowhere I'm likely to bump into anyone from work, which rules out anywhere around here. Nowhere I'm likely to bump into any acquaintances, come to think of it. Knowing Ed, he'll cheerfully blurt out our history to anyone we meet. And definitely nowhere public. I really don't want to have this conversation in the open.

Which doesn't leave many options. In fact, I acknowledge, with a sinking heart, it only really leaves one.

---

With hindsight, I'm not convinced this was such a good idea.

I turn my key in the lock tentatively, pushing open the door a crack so I can poke my head through into the flat. Everything seems quiet. Although, Tess is stealthy by nature; quiet of voice, quiet of tread. She's made me jump countless times by appearing behind me when I thought I was alone.

It's definitely curtailed my spontaneous dancing habit, that's for sure.

I edge my way inside, Ed close on my heels.

"Tess?" I call softly. "Are you here?"

No one answers and I breathe a sigh of relief, dropping my bag down on the sofa.

The whole way home, I was terrified that someone would recognise me. I kept my gaze ahead, not looking at Ed, not speaking to him. Well, every now and again I sneaked a glance, just to remind myself that he was really there. A part of me still half expected to turn around one moment to find that he'd gone again, disappeared, as is his wont.

"This is a nice place," Ed says, gazing around the flat in wonder. I'm not sure if I should be flattered or insulted. "Very… grand."

"It's Tess's, really," I perch on the edge of the sofa, watching as he wanders over towards the window. He never could stay still. "Rosie and I are just squatters."

He spins around, the colour draining from his face.

"Rosie lives here too?" he stutters. "She won't… she isn't here *now*, is she?"

"She doesn't finish work until five. She'll be at least an hour yet."

I can't believe we're having this conversation so normally, as if we're just old friends catching up. It feels wrong, false, when there's so much pressing at the edges, far more important things to be said. And yet, I know we're just circling the issue, neither of us wanting to go there first.

"Oh," he sinks down onto the sofa next to me, although he still looks edgy. I'd forgotten how afraid he always was of Rosie. I think he always sensed that she didn't approve of him, wasn't bowled over by his charm and wit the way everyone else was. She knew he'd break my heart. I wouldn't believe her at the time; I thought I knew better, as younger siblings always do. I wanted to prove myself; look how that turned out.

Knowing I can't put it off forever, I take a deep breath and allow myself to properly survey him for the first time. The reaction is instantaneous, a rush of love and longing so potent it's like being punched in the chest. He looks the same as he ever did; I could swear he hasn't aged a day. Trust him to still look twenty-one. His dark blonde hair falls over his forehead the way it always did. It's ever so slightly sun bleached at the ends, which, combined with the light tan which colours his skin, only makes him look more vital, more glowingly youthful than ever. By comparison, I'm sure I look pale, haggard, dull.

He raises an eyebrow, as though reading my thoughts.

"I have to say, you look good, Belle. I'm glad you kept your hair long. It suits you like that."

"Don't," I choke, horrified at the catch in my voice, the raw emotion. "Don't do that. Don't try and charm me, Ed. I'm not—"

*I'm not strong enough.* The thought slams into me, making me turn away. What was I thinking, bringing him here, into my home? Into my new life? Now all I can see is how he would have looked here if he'd stayed. Now I'll never be able to look at this place in the same way again.

"I'm not trying to charm you, Belle." He rubs a hand across his face. "I… Jesus, I don't know what I'm trying to do. I don't know what to say to you. Nothing seems right."

At least he can acknowledge that.

"You should never have come." I'm shaking my head fervently, even as the words twang at my heartstrings. Because I don't mean that, not really. "Why did you come?"

"I wanted to see how you were." His blue eyes are earnest. "I… I never forgot you, Belle. Or today."

I stare at him. I can feel my face hardening.

"If you mean our anniversary, that was yesterday."

"Oh." His face drops, and he has the grace to look ashamed. "Well, you know what I'm like with dates."

I look away. I don't want to dignify that with an answer.

"It took me ages to track you down, you know." He's shrugging off his denim jacket, making himself at home. He still dresses like he's twenty-one, too. Although, frustratingly, he manages to pull it off. "As soon as I landed in London, I went to the offices of that fashion magazine you were supposed to be working for and asked after you. I fully expected for you to have made assistant editor. I couldn't believe it when they said you'd never worked there." He raises his eyebrows. "What happened, Belle? You had the job all lined up. It was everything you wanted."

He *landed* in London. The information lodges itself in my brain. So he's been abroad. Something akin to relief nudges through me. I couldn't face the thought that he'd been nearby all this time, living a life in parallel to mine and yet not with me.

I realise I'm absently rubbing the joint of my ring finger, as though twisting around a ring which isn't there. Mental association, I suppose. I half want to ask him what he did with the ring, if he still has it, but I hold myself back. Most likely he sold it; if that's the case, I'd rather not know.

"Yes, it was," I agree, forcing my voice to a neutral level. Some small skein of pride which still runs through me insists upon it. "But I couldn't face being in London anymore. That was meant to be *our* life, Ed. I didn't want to do it on my own."

He frowns, a line creasing his smooth forehead.

"I did want to get in touch before, honestly. But I was… well, it wasn't possible."

Oh, how badly I want to believe that. But I'm not the naïve girl I once was.

"Not very hard, obviously." I fold my arms, partly to stop the trembling which is running stealthily through my body. "You could have found me if you'd wanted to. It's not like I've been hiding. *I* wasn't the one who disappeared off the face of the earth," I can't help adding bitterly.

He sighs.

"Okay, you're still really upset with me. I can see that now. Maybe this wasn't such a great idea, me coming back."

I stare at him, wishing I could scream out loud in frustration. He still has that childlike simplicity which borders on the pathological. For the first time, something new lances through the sense of longing and regret. A bolt of anger.

"Yes, I'm *upset* with you! You—"

I stop myself almost as soon as I've started, dropping my head into my hands. Because instinctively, I don't want to go any further with that. Because the truth is, I already *did* all of this. I did it years ago. I ranted and raved and cried and threw things. I hated him and felt sorry for myself. I went through the whole process. And now he's here and I can say it all to his face, all the things I once dreamed I'd be able to tell him.

But I don't want to. Not because he doesn't deserve to hear them, but because I can't face going back over it all again. One day, we'll have to have that discussion, but not right now. Not when I'm still trying to get my head around his sudden reappearance. Not when these feelings are still so fresh, so intermingled that I can't even begin to separate them and work out what's real. Shock, love, anger… right now, they're all the same, all shaken up together like a snow globe. I have no idea how I really feel.

I raise my head and look at him, trying to anchor myself with a more practical angle.

"Where have you *been*, anyway?"

It's an innocent enough question, I think, but he starts,

leaping to his feet as though he's been scalded.

"Look, you're still in shock. Upset. Let's take this one step at a time, shall we? I'll make you a cup of tea. I can see the kitchen through there."

He scuttles away and I let him go. I know better than to try and get a straight answer out of him when he's in this mood. Besides, I appreciate the distance to let my thoughts settle for a moment. I feel like I've been picked up by a tornado and dropped from a great height.

"Hey," Tess appears in the doorway, rubbing at the side of her face. "What's going on?"

The mere sight of her is enough to bring long-suppressed tears to my eyes. After the day I've had, a bit of normalcy feels like paradise. Then I take in her tousled hair, her sleep-flushed cheeks, and despite everything I find myself frowning.

"Were you *asleep*?"

"I was taking a nap," she says defensively. "I was up late last night dusting."

Dusting? In the middle of the night? Someone really needs to have a sit down with her at some point.

There's a clatter from within the kitchen and Tess's head swivels.

"Surely Rosie isn't back yet?"

Before I can even begin to flail my way through an answer, Ed pops his head around the kitchen door.

"Cup of tea, Tess?"

For a moment, nothing happens. Then, as if in slow motion, Tess's eyes widen, her mouth dropping open in a frozen gasp. She takes a step backwards, almost stumbling over the wooden doorstop which keeps the fire door open. It's only by my grabbing her wrist that she manages not to fall over. Tess is ballet-school trained; seeing her innate grace desert her like that makes me feel slightly better about my own reaction earlier. A scream doesn't seem so overblown now. In fact, it seems perfectly fitting.

Of *course* it was perfectly fitting, I remind myself in exasperation. It's only Ed who seems to think there's nothing untoward about any of this. Only Ed would be so naïve to think that he could just walk back in here and no one would so much as bat an eyelid.

As if to prove my point, he raises his eyebrows sardonically.

"Is that a no, then?"

"Belle," Tess manages, in a strangled voice. "Can I talk to you for a moment?"

She tugs me with uncharacteristic force to the other end of the living room. Out of the Georgian sash window, I can see people wandering past on the pavement below. This street is unusual in the sense that there aren't any houses opposite, only a line of trees before the landscape falls away down the side of the hill. In the middle distance, just visible through the branches, Arthur's Seat looms over everything like an ever-watchful sentinel. Usually, I love that, the sense of smallness, that the city, nestled as it is amongst the immense landscape, is only here by the tolerance of nature. But today, it feels oddly oppressive.

"What is going *on*?" Tess hisses frantically. "Where did

*he* come from?"

She jabs a finger towards the doorway, where Ed still lurks, watching us. He waves. She frowns and turns back to me.

"I know, I'm sorry," I say miserably. Now I feel guilty on Tess's account, too. I'm sure he's the last person she wants in her home. "He just turned up, and… well, there wasn't anywhere else… I didn't want to be seen with him."

"It's all right," she takes my hand, squeezes it, and I feel my heart rate decelerate a little. Thank God for Tess; her calmness is infectious. "I understand. But seriously. Belle. Do you want him here?" Her celestial blue eyes rake over me with concern. "After everything he's done. You don't owe him anything, you know. Don't feel you have to… I mean, we can get rid of him."

She could, too. Her willowy frame is deceptive. She looks as though a strong breeze might blow her over, but years of yoga have given her a core of iron. I envisage her manhandling Ed out of the flat, and for the briefest of moments, I'm tempted. It would be tantalisingly easy to just pretend this never happened. That he never came back and detonated a bomb beneath the fragile façade of my new life. But just as soon as the thought passes through my mind, I know it's not an option. If I'm being totally honest, I've only ever really been on hold, waiting for this moment. Now he's here, I have to see it through.

"No, I can't hide from this. I need to talk to him… alone," I add firmly, as she makes to sit down. "Preferably before Rosie—"

As if on cue, the lock rattles.

"I'm back," Rosie trills, from somewhere in the hall.

Tess and I look at one another in mute horror. It flashes between us, a single thought; Rosie *cannot* know he's here. The ensuing eruption would put Krakatoa's more spectacular efforts in the shade. I doubt the Earth could survive it.

"You distract her," I command, thinking on my feet. "I'll get him out of here…" I flounder. There aren't exactly many options. Short of pitching him out of the kitchen window there's only one way out of this flat, and Rosie's currently blocking it. "Somehow," I finish lamely.

"They let me out early," Rosie continues to shout through, oblivious to all of this. "I thought we could use the extra time to do some place settings."

"Great!" I call desperately. I'll do all the place settings in the world if I can just pull this off.

"That met with less resistance than I was expecting," Rosie remarks, appearing in the doorway. She looks in better humour than I've seen her for ages.

Oh, the irony.

Sidling towards the kitchen, I motion with my head to Tess to keep Rosie talking. Then I back through the doorway.

"Okay, so there's been a slight—" The words die on my lips for the second time that day as I turn around to see…

Nothing. Absolutely nothing. The kitchen's completely empty. I stand there, dumfounded.

Where on earth did he go?

## Chapter Eight

"I'm so glad we're all here together," Mum gushes, raising her glass of prosecco in the air. Her scarlet talons glint under the twinkling fairy lights which trace a web across the low vaulted ceiling of the restaurant. It's like being under a starry sky. In reality, we're underground in one of Edinburgh's many stone cellars, which has been transformed into a rather retro little Italian restaurant. The kind where they still serve bread in gingham-lined baskets and the menus are laminated and presented in a faux leather folder. The food's amazing though, and it's always packed. I'm surprised Mum managed to get us a table for tonight. She must have done some serious flirting.

Then again, when doesn't she?

"It's *so* nice to do things as a family, isn't it?" She says, placing a hand on her heart. "It feels like we never see each other anymore."

Rosie fidgets in the chair next to me and I sidle her a

look. The fidgeting has been steadily intensifying since the moment we sat down twenty minutes ago. I can tell she's dying to tell Mum to get on with it.

Because we're here for a reason; we all know that. It's nothing to do with family gatherings. Mum has something to boast about, and she wants us all to know. The only thing is, she takes *such* a long time to get around to it.

"What are you wittering on about, Valerie?" Gran barks. "We see the girls all the time. And you *live* with me. We're hardly starved of each other's company."

Mum purses her perfectly glossed lips in annoyance, and despite my churning emotions, I have to suppress a smile. Trust Gran to tell it like it is; she's about the only person in the world blunter than Rosie.

To be honest, this dinner was the last thing I felt like tonight. I feel like I've been slugged with a sack of bricks, both physically and emotionally. And trying to act normally is only making it worse. But I have to; I can't risk letting on to any of them that something's going on. Ed's disappearance rocked them almost as much as it did me, after all. I don't want them dragged into this.

Unfortunately, Rosie's chosen tonight to be unusually quiet and preoccupied. Under normal circumstances, I could rely on her to be the loud one, allowing me to sink into the background. As it stands though, now I have nowhere to hide. Which means I have to pretend to be extra sparkling to make up for it.

"Yes, but it's so nice to do something *special* for once,"

Mum perseveres, apparently undented by Gran's lack of enthusiasm.

"Does Rosie's wedding not count?" I ask innocently, spearing an olive with a cocktail stick. "It doesn't get much more special than that."

"Well of course," Mum gives a tinkly laugh. "But you know, there are *other* things going on. It's not *all* about Rosie, you know! No offence, darling," she adds mildly. "But you have been monopolising the attention just a *teensy* bit of late. Not that *I* mind, of course…"

Rosie appears to be making a detailed study of her bread plate. With a surge of sisterly protectiveness, I snap my menu shut.

"Shall we order?"

Preferably before Mum manages to make the atmosphere any tenser.

I don't know why she has to do this. All that's required of her is to get through ten more days of smiling and being supportive and then she can gladly have the limelight back again.

Believe it or not, she *is* trying. But she just can't help herself.

You see, Mum's always believed that she could have had a career on the stage, if only she hadn't fallen pregnant with Rosie when she did (and me barely ten months later, it might be added, so I think the blame can safely be landed on her. Obviously, she didn't learn from the first time; had the woman never *heard* of birth control?).

I mean, she loves us, I know she does. But she's never

quite been able to get past the dream of all that might have been. The glamorous lifestyle, the stream of lovers, the exotic travel… although, I've long suspected that most of that was merely a fantasy of her own creation. She's always been vague about what this great job she'd been offered was, but Gran let slip a few Christmases ago after one too many sherries that it was actually an understudy role for Nell Gwyn at a theatre in Bolton.

So, hardly the staircase to stardom that Mum has always made out. Nonetheless, she's convinced herself that it could have been the start of something amazing. Perhaps she's needed to believe that all these years. I wouldn't mind, really, if only the repressed theatrical ambition didn't spill over into every area of her life.

And, by extension, ours.

"Excellent idea!" Gran booms, slamming her menu down and making the couple at the table behind us jump. "I'm utterly starving."

I don't see how she possibly can be, given that she's hoovered up most of the bread and over a third of the olives. And that she'll be eighty in a few months. Aren't people's appetites supposed to abate as they get older?

Then again, it might just be her way of deflecting the conversation. You wouldn't think it to look at my Gran – she's brusque and earthy and suffers no fools – but she's strangely perceptive. She brought Rosie and me up with a fierce no-nonsense sort of love. Her advice during our teenage years might not have been particularly gentle, but it was always spot on (in most cases, it was "dump him"), and our diet might have been reminiscent of wartime (lots of stew with unidentified bits of animal floating in it; it haunts me to this day) but it was always on the table, and I never once heard her complain about the job that had been foisted upon her. I'm sure she must have despaired of Mum's capricious approach to parenthood, but she never let it show in front of us. She still holds her counsel even now; I think she has an iron-clad view that children should never hear criticism of their parents, no matter how old they might be. That's the children, not the parents, although goodness only knows what Mum's psychological age is. Probably younger than Rosie and I are now.

When we've ordered our food, which is a painful experience involving Mum dissecting everything on the menu before eventually requesting a dish of entirely her own invention, a febrile sort of silence settles upon the table.

It never used to be like this. It's the wedding; natural topic of conversation it might be, considering it's taking over all of our lives, but the mere mention of it makes Rosie stiffen and Mum sulk. Which somewhat limits the options.

"So, Gran," I blurt out desperately. "How's bridge club?"

"It's such a *shame* that Carlos can't be here," Mum says, as though I hadn't spoken. She fiddles with the gold bangle on her wrist, which he gave her obscenely early on in their relationship. "But he knew that I wanted to spend some time with just my girls. And you, Mother," she adds, somewhat unnecessarily. "Although you can't really be classed as a girl anymore."

Gran just harrumphs.

"Neither can you, dear."

Mum ignores that pointedly.

"Did I tell you about the spa Carlos and I went to over the weekend? He booked us the most *divine* suite: roll-top bath, views over the parkland..." She pauses for effect. "And the bed... well, let's say it was very *generously* sized."

Gran takes a fortifying slug of wine. I wonder if it would be impolite to stuff napkins into my ears.

Only Rosie looks unaffected. She's toying with an olive, looking far away.

"That's great, Mum," she says flatly.

She won't be this quiet when she finds out about Ed, that's for sure, I think, with a flip of guilt. I wonder how long I can keep it from her; she really doesn't need the stress at the moment.

All right, so maybe that's not the *whole* reason why I'm so panicked at the thought of her finding out. There's a bit more to it than that. I'm protecting myself as much as her. Protecting myself from her crushing disappointment. Because Rosie was always right, from the start. She knew it would end badly. And afterwards, when she stopped me from staying on and scouring the island for him, when she booked me onto the next flight home, practically marching me through the airport and onto the plane... well, I didn't resist. How could I? What grounds did I have? She was so resplendent, so dynamic; she took care of everything. She created this new life for me, up here in Edinburgh. She handed me a future. And when we got home, and she told me to forget about him, to pretend that he'd never existed, of course, I agreed. I let her believe that I hated him as much as she did, because I was too ashamed to admit otherwise. That the truth couldn't be more opposite. How could I ever tell my strong, proud sister that I was still in love with the man who'd betrayed me? Betrayed us all?

If she finds out I brought him back to the flat today… well, she won't understand. She'd have sent him packing the moment he burst out of the cupboard. She wouldn't have given him a single chance to explain.

Where did he *go* earlier? I wonder for about the sixtieth time this evening, as Mum continues to regale her unwilling audience with all the lurid details of her and Carlos's spa weekend. I've been twisting my brain around in knots trying to work out how he got out of the flat without any of us noticing. Maybe he really did jump out of the window. But it's three storeys up; there's no way he could have done it.

But I know, really, that question is just a front for the real one which is gnawing at me. The issue isn't where he went, it's whether or not he'll be back. When it comes to Ed, there are no guarantees.

"…So we went to our couple's spa treatment. They mashed up strawberries and put them all over our bodies," Mum's enthusing now. "Heavenly for the skin, they told us. Takes *years* off." She squints at her arm, then thrusts it in front of Gran's nose. "I can already see it, can't you?"

Gran just stares at it, bemused. I don't think she's ever been within forty feet of a spa. Her idea of beautifying is a cold sponge bath with a bar of carbolic soap.

"Then they put you in the sauna," Mum carries on, not waiting for an answer. Which is probably just as well. "*So* detoxifying. I could book one for you and Leo, darling," she turns to Rosie. "It would get all that stiffness out of you both. Do you a world of good."

Rosie looks less than thrilled by the idea.

"Unfortunately, the heat was too much for my poor, darling Carlos," Mum sighs woefully. "He fainted, right into my arms."

Rosie looks at me then, and I know what she's thinking. The image of Carlos, semi-naked and covered in strawberries, swooning into my mother's arms, is almost too much. I can't decide whether it's grotesque or the first real laugh I've had all day.

"Isn't he Spanish?" I choke out, mainly to distract myself.

"What?" Mum looks put out to have been interrupted. "Oh, well, yes. But he's always… stayed in the shade. Anyway, it was a *terrible* moment. I thought I'd lost him *forever*. But then he awoke, and looked up at me with those beautiful brown eyes of his, and he said…"

My phone buzzes in my pocket. Surreptitiously, I check it beneath the tablecloth; it's not a number I recognise. As soon as I scan the first line, though, the mystery clears, and I suck in a breath.

*Sorry I ran out earlier…*

I can't read any more here. I need some space. Hiding my phone in my palm, I get to my feet, hoping my jangled emotions aren't showing on my face.

"I've just got to nip to the ladies'."

Mum pouts.

"But darling, I was just getting to the important part!"

"Sorry. I'll be back in a minute."

I push my way into the bathroom, checking that there's no one else in any of the stalls before I lean back against the sink, unfurling my fingers so I can read the message on the screen.

*Sorry I ran out earlier. I've really missed you, Belle. I didn't realise just how much until we saw each other today. Can I see you again? Promise I'll stick around this time. Ed x*

My heart feels like it's about to burst out of my ribcage. Of course, I knew he still had my number. I never bothered to change it after the wedding; there didn't exactly seem a lot of point. After all, he ran out on *me*; I wasn't worried about him bombarding me with communications. Or at least, that's the story I told Rosie.

I chew on my lip, staring at my pallid reflection. He's missed me. He wants to see me again. Those things should make my heart soar; instead, I just feel sick with nerves. Although, in a way, it still feels like none of this is actually happening; I feel removed from it all, as if I'm having a very confusing and convoluted dream.

Very glad that no one's around to witness what I'm about to do next, I tentatively raise my hand and, screwing up my eyes in anticipation, give myself an experimental pinch on the arm.

"Ouch!" Jesus Christ, that hurt. Tears spring to my eyes and I rub my arm furiously, trying to assuage the pain. There's going to be one hell of a bruise there tomorrow.

"What are you *doing* in here?" The door swings violently open. "You left me on my own with them!" Rosie grinds to a halt, staring at the red mark on my arm. "Did you just hit yourself?"

"No, I just..." Where to begin? Rosie knows most of the nonsense which goes through my head, but this is one ridiculous thing too far. Preferably, *no one* should ever know about this. "Look, never mind. I'll come back through. Before Mum throws a full-on sulk."

To my surprise, though, she blocks the door.

"Not until you tell me what's going on. You've been weird all evening."

I feel like firing back, *you've been weird for months. What of it?* but I feel that now's not the time to open up that particular issue, so I hold my tongue.

Something which, incidentally, I appear to be getting pretty good at these days.

"And don't bother lying," Rosie folds her arms and fixes me with a menacing look. "You're no good at it and you know we're not leaving this bathroom until you tell me the truth."

I sigh internally, feeling my shoulders sag. That's no idle threat; she once barricaded herself in her bedroom for eighteen hours. I can't even remember why anymore; it was probably fairly inconsequential. The point is, her strength of will is indomitable.

"Okay." I turn, perching back against the edge of the sink. "But you *cannot* lose it. Promise me?"

Her lips twist, but eventually she nods tersely.

I take a breath. Best just to come out with it, then.

"Ed turned up this afternoon."

For a couple of seconds, she just carries on looking at me. Then…

"He *what*?!" she explodes.

"Whatever happened to not over-reacting?" I hiss, grabbing a small vase of flowers which is wobbling precariously on the shelf and righting it.

She throws her hands up in the air.

"Screw *that*. That's when I thought you were going to admit to spilling coffee on the bunting I left out."

Ah, so she's noticed that, has she? I'd been hoping I could throw it in the washing machine when she wasn't around.

"Just wait till I lay my hands on him," she fumes, prowling around the bathroom like a caged tiger. "I'll kill him." She pauses, looking thoughtful. "And I know how to get away with it too. That's one of the upsides of my job."

"Ro, you need to calm down," I soothe. You see, I *knew* this would be a disaster. This is why I kept it from her.

Rosie doesn't seem to have heard me.

"You sent him on his way, of course. Told him what a prat he is. I'd have liked to have seen that." When I don't speak, she stops and turns to me with narrowing eyes. "You did... didn't you?"

Here we go. I put on my metaphorical tin hat, take a breath.

"Not... in so many words, no."

She purses her lips, and in that moment, she looks just like Gran.

"What does that mean exactly? You might as well tell me. You didn't give him an opening, did you? Because you know what that man's like; he'll worm his way in..." Then her face clears, mouth falling open in horror. It seems to happen in slow motion. "Oh my God. When I got home this evening. You and Tess were acting strangely." She points a finger at me, as though accusing me of witchcraft. "He'd been there, hadn't he? I can't *believe* you! You invited him into our home!"

"I had to *talk* to him, Ro," I say desperately, defensively. "I couldn't just... slam the door on him. Not when there's so much left unanswered."

"Why does it matter?" she shoots back, clearly exasperated. To her it must seem so simple. "Why do you *need* answers? He's gone, out of your life. You've moved on."

I swallow guiltily at that last sentence.

"We're not all the same, Ro. For me… it's just not as black and white as it is for you."

That's as far as I'll go towards admitting my true feelings. Even that feels more than far enough.

"It has to be, Belle." Rosie moves forward, grips my shoulders urgently. "Because I'm damn well not going to sit back and watch him trample all over your life again. I just can't."

I look into her grey eyes, filled with love and stubborn concern, and I feel myself relenting a little. Maybe she *is* right. Yet again. Maybe this is the only way. Before I end up getting hurt again. Before I end up right back where I started, six years ago. Like nothing I've done in the meantime even matters.

"Don't talk to him again," she urges, her nails digging into my shoulders. "Promise me?"

I can practically feel my phone burning into my palm. She doesn't know about the message, and in that moment I decide it's better that way.

With a sigh, I wrap an arm around her shoulder and nudge her towards the door. "Come on, let's get back. Before Gran eats our starters."

## Chapter Nine

If I was hoping for some time and space to work out my conflicted feelings, then clearly I'm not about to get it. Over the next couple of days, Ed texts me three more times, with increasing plaintiveness. He calls, too. More than once I just sit there, watching the phone ring out, frozen with indecision.

A part of me still feels I deserve answers, and I'm not going to get them unless I agree to see him. Plus, I can't deny that I *want* to see him. But then, maybe Rosie's right; maybe that's exactly why I shouldn't. I can't afford to soften towards him, and I know that the longer I spend with him the more the botched-together cracks in my heart will begin to reopen, letting him back in. I won't be able to help it.

With a force of will, I steel myself. I should listen to her. She knows me better than I know myself, after all. She knows what's good for me, and Ed certainly isn't it.

And yet… my emotions swing dizzyingly back as if on a

pendulum. I can't deny that this is totally unlike him, being so persistent. He's never had to work for anything; if something doesn't come easily then he simply shrugs it off and moves on to the next. Or at least, he always did.

He must really have meant it when he said he's missed me.

The very notion sends a shiver through me, and I immediately retract it. Thoughts like that are *not* helpful. I need to be logical, impassive. I need…

Oh God, I don't know what I need. Except a cup of tea. A biscuit or two, maybe. That always puts everything into perspective.

I elbow my way through the heavy fire door into the office, balancing the latest stack of council minutes in my aching arms. Although even the *Illuminator* has embraced the twenty-first century and moved much of its editorial system onto computers by now, there are still certain things which have remained stubbornly in paper form. Invariably the most boring things, I might add. If it were something exciting, I might not mind as much lugging it halfway across the building.

I've still got my back to the room, catching the door with my foot so it doesn't bang shut, when I hear a familiar shout of laughter. Immediately, my whole body stiffens.

Please, God, tell me I'm imagining things.

With a sense of doom, I very slowly turn on the spot. And my highest hopes and darkest fears are realised simultaneously.

Ed's lounging against the window at the far end of the

room, one leg crossed casually over the other. He's chatting away to Freya, who's gazing up at him rapturously, her lips formed into a pretty, practised-looking moue.

She tosses her shiny dark mane back over one shoulder, leaning closer towards him. I blow a strand of my own – decidedly less lustrous – hair away from my sticky forehead. My insides wring out with a sharp twist, making me gasp.

Why is he *here*? Panic and anger clash together, striking sparks. Doesn't he know how I hate to be cornered?

If we're going to talk, then it should be in my own time, when *I'm* ready. Just the thought of being forced into a confrontation in the middle of my workplace… it feels like I'm suffocating. I feel like I'm losing any grip I might have had on my own life. Like all my agency is being stripped from me.

"You all right?" The sound of Nate's voice over my shoulder, though low, is enough to jolt me back to reality. I don't stop to think; something primal in me takes over, urging me into action.

Unfortunately, its idea of 'action' is flinging the stack of files randomly at the nearest desk, which happens to be Darren's. They sprawl across the surface, sending a potted cactus flying and causing disarray to the line of stationery he arranges each morning with military precision.

He's going to *kill* me when he sees this. But there's no time to worry about that now.

Nate looks at the carnage with raised eyebrows and I

take advantage of the distraction to grab his arm and shove him unceremoniously through the doorway.

"Let's go out here." My voice is garbled, strangely pitched. "There's something I need to talk to you about."

He looks at me quizzically but to his credit he doesn't resist.

I drag him along the corridor, hoping I'm not coming across as irretrievably unhinged. Luckily, he doesn't appear to alarm easily.

"Okay," he says at last, when I deem we're a safe enough distance from the office and finally let go of him. He leans back against the wall, folding his arms across his chest. "What's up?"

"Er…" I'm saved from having to answer by the sound of the fire door banging further down the corridor, accompanied by the murmur of voices. Immediately, I can feel the panic rearing its head again. It might be Ed, it might not. But I can't take the chance.

"Not here." I shake my head emphatically.

Nate looks equal parts exasperated and amused.

"What's wrong with here?"

"There's a… draught." Snatching his arm again, I drag him blindly through the nearest doorway. A wave of relief swallows me; okay, crisis averted for the time being. I yank the door closed behind us.

We're plunged into total and utter darkness.

Ah, okay. Not *quite* what I was going for.

"Er… much better," I manage weakly.

Nate's voice registers a tone which I can't quite identify. Or perhaps I just dread doing so. "Belle..."

He breaks off momentarily and a second later, the lights flicker on. It's only one dim bulb, so it doesn't provide a lot of illumination, but it's enough for me to see the frown on his face.

"Would you care to tell me exactly what we're doing in the stationery cupboard?"

I'm hoping it's dingy enough in here that he can't see the flush that's stealing up my neck. Rather belatedly, it hits me what I've done. What was I thinking? Why on earth did I even drag Nate into this? Just because he happened to be the nearest thing to hand isn't much of an excuse. Now I have to try and salvage this.

"Because..." I stutter, "because... of these folders!" I exclaim triumphantly, waving an arm wildly in the direction of the shelves. Which isn't easy, given that there's barely enough space to extend an arm in the first place. "The way they're stacked is... um, atrocious. A real health and safety risk. I think we should inform Steve, don't you?"

He nods gravely.

"I wasn't aware that health and safety was a particular passion of yours."

He's laughing at me. Even in the gloom, I can see the subtle spark of humour in his eyes. It piques me. All very well for him to find it amusing; *he* hasn't got a persistent ex chasing him about the place.

"*I've* been reading the flashcards," I retort, with as much dignity as I can manage. "Clearly, you haven't."

Don't even get me started on the flashcards. They're Darren's latest thing. We've only had them for a day and already I want to set fire to the lot of them.

"I've had other things on my mind," he says, softly. And something in his tone tells me that we're not talking about health and safety any more.

I blink up at him, reminding myself to breathe. I can't help but notice that he looks extra amazing today, in a mint-green shirt which he's rolled up to the elbows, revealing his tanned forearms. How has he managed to get a tan in Edinburgh? Then again, come to think of it, he looks that golden all year round. Maybe it's not a tan at all, just his Italian genes, and… hang on, why am I *thinking* about this now? Why must my brain go galloping off on these rambling tangents? No wonder everyone thinks I'm mad. Perhaps I *am* mad.

I'm a little surprised at my own reaction. He hasn't been in the office for the past couple of days, and to be honest, with everything that's happened, he's slid somewhat to the back of my mind. Our date seems like a lifetime ago. But of course, to him it's still very current.

Which is probably why, with hindsight, he's the *last* person I should be sequestering with in a dark stationery cupboard.

*Way to go, Belle. Really great work there.*

"Perhaps I really wanted a debate on alphanumeric versus terminal digit filing systems," I manage, wondering why my voice sounds an entire octave higher than usual.

He raises an eyebrow.

"You *have* been reading the flashcards. I underestimated you."

Actually, I wandered into the wrong lecture room one day in my first week of university and thought it would be impolite to leave, so I ended up having to sit through an entire PowerPoint on filing systems. Perversely, the astonishing dullness of the information has somehow meant it's been retained in my brain all these years. But I'm not about to tell Nate any of that.

"Many people have," I say, trying not to sound too pointed. "But they learn in the end."

He laughs.

"Touché. I apologise." He reaches across and tucks my hair behind my ear, his voice lowering with intensity. "I've missed you. It's felt like a long couple of days."

I gaze up at him and something in me responds, a sensation in my chest quite unlike any of the others I've experienced lately. It's warm, tingling… and quite alarming. Trying to shake it off, I say brightly, "You only saw me this morning."

"I saw you across the office. And I had Darren in my eyeline the entire time." He pulls a face. "All I've been able to think about is getting you to myself."

Despite myself, his words make a thrill run through me. I bite my lip, wondering what on earth is going on with me. My hormones must be all over the place. That's the only explanation.

At least I've managed to pick the most unromantic setting I could find, I console myself. That ought to cool any ardour. I don't think I even knew this cupboard was *here* until three days ago, and now it appears to be the scene of every—

And then suddenly he's kissing me, and this dusty, poky cupboard morphs into the most romantic place in the entire universe.

Okay, so that's perhaps rather fanciful. But I couldn't care less about our surroundings; the moment his lips touch mine, my conscious mind takes flight and something else takes over. Something beyond my control. It's as though years of pent-up desire are finally being unleashed. A fevered urgency surges through me and I wind my arms around his neck, pushing him backwards until he bumps against a filing cabinet. A box of rubbers topples off the shelf above us and bursts open, its contents raining down upon our heads. Nate pulls away, laughing.

"We seem to be wrecking the cupboard."

"I don't care." My words come mechanically, my gaze not leaving his lips. I'm already reaching for him again but he hangs back, looking at me wryly.

"Such wanton destructiveness today. Is it something to do with me?"

For some reason, his words are like a bucket of cold water over my head. I freeze, horror stealing across my skin in goose bumps as my mind begins to clear.

What the hell was *that*? I want to bury my head in my hands. This is a *disaster*. An absolute, unmitigated, wonderful—

Wait, what? What am I *saying*? This is *terrible*. Appalling.

Not the kiss, which was, I have to say, rather electric, but everything else. This whole situation.

"No, you bring out the best in me," I croak, smoothing down my jumper, which had rucked up in our entanglement. "Which is why I'm going to suggest that we head back to the office now, before we're missed."

I just need to get out of here. Away from those molten eyes, from the memory of what we just did. Preferably, before we do it again. Clearly, my willpower is not to be relied upon.

Confusion crowds my mind, making my head hurt. *Again?* Surely, it was just a moment of madness. I mean, I still love Ed. That's well established. I couldn't possibly think about anyone else romantically. There wouldn't be room, for one thing.

It must be a mistake, I decide. I must be confusing my long pent-up feelings for Ed with something else. This was just… an outlet. A way to let off steam.

The hallway seems almost dizzyingly bright after the gloomy interior of the cupboard. I blink, then blink again when I see the unwelcome outline of Darren looking at us in astonishment, still in mid stride. He grinds to an uncertain halt, his eyes widening as Nate appears behind me.

My heart sinks. Great, that's just what I need. Now it'll be all over the office.

"Good afternoon, Darren," Nate says mildly, as though there's nothing untoward whatsoever about two colleagues enjoying proximity in a dark stationery cupboard. How does he *do* that? I feel like I'm about to expire with nerves and embarrassment, but I try to keep my face impassive.

Darren's eyes are swivelling between us suspiciously. I can practically hear his brain whirring, and apparently Nate does too, because he casually moves away from me.

"Nate, Steve's looking for you," Darren says at last, although he still looks uncertain. "Not you," he adds, levelling a disapproving look in my direction. "He doesn't care where *you* are."

Charming. I glower at him.

"Well then," Nate says affably, "I'd better see what he wants, hadn't I?"

And then he saunters off, although not before shooting me a smile over the top of Darren's head. The kind of smile which, despite everything I've just told myself, makes me feel so bewilderingly warm and glowing inside that I'm only vaguely irritated to come to my senses several moments later to find Darren still standing in front of me with his annoying, suspicious face.

"Can I *help* you?" I ask, in a strained voice.

He scowls.

"Something's going on here, I just know it."

I feel like telling him he couldn't imagine the half of it if he tried, then think better of it.

"Just two colleagues bonding over the filing system," I say blandly. "That's all."

And then I brush past him, head held high.

## Chapter Ten

By the time I make it back to my desk, Ed has completely disappeared, for which I'm eternally relieved. Especially after what's just happened. If I thought I couldn't face him before, then this has just added another layer to an already tangled situation. I'm braced for Freya to come over and announce that he's been here looking for me, but it never happens. Instead, she avoids turning in my direction. It must be deliberate; I can see her screen from where I'm sitting and I find it impossible to believe that she could possibly be that engrossed in formatting an advert about erectile disfunction.

I reflect back to the way she was fluttering away at Ed earlier and decide that the omission is definitely a calculated one. Which makes me feel a little peeved, I suppose, but not all that surprised. She's not really one for the sisterhood, Freya.

It's quiet in the office all afternoon. Under any other

circumstances, I might even manage to get some work done. But my emotions are careering wildly back and forth like a pinball. Jealousy over Ed and Freya flirting, annoyance that Ed was here at all and yet half longing for him to come back, guilt over kissing Nate…

*Nate.* That's a whole other issue. I look across at him now, sitting at his desk on the other side of the room. The light slanting through the window illuminates his bone structure so nicely as he frowns over the latest copy. It's fascinating to watch his face as he concentrates, the way the muscles tense beneath his skin, the coffee-coloured curls which fall over his forehead again and again, even as he shoves them back impatiently.

No matter how much I try not to look at him, that's somehow where my gaze ends up, over and over again. I can't stare at him too hard, though, because every now and again he glances up and smiles at me. I never quite know when he's going to do it, and more than once there's an awkward fumble as I hastily pretend to look at my own screen, or in one particularly inspired moment to clasp a hand to my chin as if I'm deep in thought, knocking my coffee cup over in the process. His eyebrows raise infinitesimally and I feel myself flushing as I right it. At least it was empty.

Clearly, this isn't just about me projecting my feelings for Ed. I chew on the end of a pencil thoughtfully, something I haven't done since school. Immediately, I realise why; it tastes awful. I dash it down in frustration. How could I have been so *careless*? I should never have let myself get anywhere near Nate. I should never have agreed to that date. And I certainly shouldn't have dragged him into a dark, out-of-the-way stationery cupboard. How could I have been naïve enough to tell myself it would be harmless, that nothing would change between us?

How am I supposed to make it through the days now, knowing he's just on the other side of the room?

There's only one feasible solution, I decide wildly. I'll have to build a wall of folders. Then I won't physically be able to see him. I'll tell Steve I have a light sensitivity or something.

I'm diverted at that moment by a small brouhaha (I'm a journalist; I like to exercise my vocabulary from time to time) when Darren discovers the carnage I made of his desk, but I deftly manage to offload the blame onto Steve, who's shut up in his office poring over his health and safety guidelines so can't leap to his own defence. In a way, it's a bonus that he spends so much time throwing things around in that heavy-handed way of his; granted, it's not so great when a file clips your ear, but it does mean he can be blamed for all sorts of things which one might not wish to own up to. To date, I've saddled him with a broken chair, three lost USB sticks, and more tea spillages than I can count.

By the time I turn off my computer and head home that evening, it's like the world is doing its best to cheer me up. The low early evening sun casts a rich pink glow across the New Town's leafy boulevards, painting the elegant

Georgian frontages a pastel shade which matches the abundance of frothing cherry blossom to perfection.

Even I can't fail to feel my spirits lift a little in the face of such lavish beauty. The world is pink, the wine which I'm going to pour myself as soon as I get in will be pink, and maybe – the wine might help with this, I'll admit – I can just forget about everything that's going pear-shaped in my life for a short while and enjoy an evening with my two favourite people. Rosie and Tess should be home by now; maybe we can have a girls' night, like we used to. There'll be an embargo on all wedding-related talk. Instead we'll order pizza and watch old romantic comedies back to back. It's sounding perfect already.

I unlock the door to the flat, closing it softly behind me. Not because I'm trying to be particularly stealthy or anything, just because I suppose a part of me subconsciously feels like I need to compensate for the way Rosie will come crashing through it in about half an hour's time, almost taking it off its hinges.

Or maybe not, I reassess, as I almost trip over her handbag, which is sprawled right in the middle of the floor. For someone who's so precise in just about every other way, her slovenliness is truly astounding. Not that I make any great claims to tidiness myself, but at least I don't turn our home into an obstacle course.

I nudge the bag aside with my foot crossly, moving towards the kitchen. That glass of wine can't come soon enough.

I haven't taken more than three steps, however, before I'm stopped in my tracks.

There are voices coming from the living room. Several, by the sounds of things. Apparently, we have guests.

"It's a Ceylon sapphire," Mum's voice rings out. "Look how it catches the light…"

My heart sinks. I know it shouldn't; she is my mother, after all. I should be pleased to see her. But I just can't help it; it's a primal reaction.

Besides, I saw her only two days ago. For the sake of my sanity, once a week is enough.

She'll be here to tell us her news, I realise, with sudden, bleak clarity. By the time Rosie and I got back to the table the other night at the restaurant, she was in a high dudgeon, refusing to say a word more about it. Apparently the *moment had been lost*.

To be honest, I'd rather forgotten about it. Mum always has 'news'; rarely is it anything which could sensibly described as such. She'll have found a new manicurist, or booked another holiday with Carlos. Sometimes I consider suggesting that she ought to just put everything into a weekly newsletter and send it to us; it'd be far more efficient.

"Lying in my arms," Mum sighs. "*So* romantic."

I suppose I'd better intervene, I concede reluctantly. I don't know who she's tormenting in there, or what on earth she's blathering on about, but someone had better save the poor soul. Where are Rosie and Tess, anyway?

"...He'd been keeping it in his swimming trunks. I can't believe I didn't see the bulge..."

Dear God. Okay, *definitely* time to step in. Before this person is permanently scarred.

"Mum," I launch myself into the doorway. "They really don't need to hear—"

Whatever I was about to say next dies a comprehensive and sudden death upon my lips.

Because sitting calmly on the sofa, with Mum leaning far closer towards him than is appropriate, is Ed.

Shock sweeps over me, turning me first cold, then red hot. I don't by nature have much of a temper – again, making up for Rosie's infamously short fuse – but I think even I can make an exception for this.

I can't believe he's here. Surely he's worked out that I'm not ready to see him by now? Or maybe he just doesn't care. For the first time since he reappeared, the relief at seeing him again, the overwhelming feelings I still have for him, fade into the background as anger blooms to the surface. Real, blazing anger, so powerful I know it's about more than just this moment. It's a delayed reaction, buried deeply for so many years, finally sparked into life by this one small act of thoughtlessness.

"Ah, darling, you're here," Mum fiddles with the folds of her skirt, dropping something into the pocket. "I was just telling Ed about my spa trip. He so wanted to hear about it." She shoots me a veiled look which seems to say, *unlike some people*.

"I'm so pleased for you, Valerie," Ed says, patting her knee. "I just hope he knows what a catch he has."

Mum twitters delightedly. I shoot Ed a glare over her head. He raises his eyebrows at me in faux innocence. Damn him and his charm; he's always known just what to say to Mum to get her fawning all over him.

And now, somehow, I'm the one feeling like an interloper in my own home. Which only makes me feel all the more infuriated.

"What are you *doing* here, Ed?" I grind out.

Mum looks shocked.

"Darling, that's not very polite."

I want to throw my hands up in the air and scream. Where *are* Rosie and Tess? I've never needed them more, if only to stop me putting my hands around my mother's neck. And Ed's too, while I'm at it.

"I don't need to be polite to him," I snap. "He rather gave up all claim to courtesy when he left me at my own wedding."

"Yes, but you've sorted out that little misunderstanding now, haven't you?" Mum waves away my explanation. "Ed told me you'd spoken about it."

The cheek of the man! We never sorted anything out, and he knows it.

"Oh really?" I say frostily. "He said that, did he?"

"Perhaps I'll go and help Tess with the tea," he says quickly, shaking himself free of Mum so he can leap to his feet.

Tea? What tea? Surely they haven't invited him to—

At that moment, the clink of china meets my ears as Tess walks in, balancing a tray of mugs. My mouth all but drops open.

You have *got* to be kidding me. This *cannot* be happening.

Her eyes widen in horror as she sees me, and she deposits the tray swiftly on the table.

"I can explain," she whispers out of the corner of her mouth.

Let's hope so.

"Milk!" She blurts out brightly. "We need more milk."

Grabbing my arm, she tugs me through the doorway into the hall.

"So," I begin, trying to keep my voice controlled. "Explain to me *why*, exactly, you're playing host to my reprobate ex-fiancé?"

"I didn't know what else to do!" She pleads, wringing her hands together. "He just turned up and your mum was here and Rosie went and barricaded herself in her room and he said that he needed to see you and that you wouldn't mind because you wanted to talk about it more – which you had sort of said – and I didn't know what was true and what wasn't because… well, you know what he's like, but I didn't want to do the wrong thing, and the tea… the tea looks bad, I know, but I couldn't leave them just *sitting* there, could I? I could hear my mother's voice in my head…"

I grasp her shoulders before she can ramble on anymore.

Somewhere, within that miasma of information, one thing stands out at me.

"Wait… why has Rosie barricaded herself in her room?"

Tess hangs her head.

"She said she couldn't trust herself not to murder him. At least, not until you'd given her the all clear to do so."

That's actually the most solid piece of reasoning I've heard all day. I wonder if that ought to worry me slightly. I clasp a hand to my forehead, blowing out a sigh, trying to get my emotions under control.

"Okay. I'll talk to her. And then we really need to get rid of Ed. Before one of us does something we'll regret."

Tess looks me up and down, a sorrowful look in her eyes.

"You're not built for prison. Rosie might be all right."

"Rosie would be running the place within a month," I mutter, turning the handle on her bedroom door. No point in knocking; she'll be expecting me. Knowing her, she's probably had her ear pressed to the wood the entire time, anyway.

Still, I jump about a foot when I open the door a crack to find her staring belligerently at me.

"I'd be running it within a week, thank you very much."

"Let's see if we can manage not to resort to anything illegal," I slip through the gap, closing it behind me.

Her eyes search my face.

"What's going on, Belle? I thought we agreed you weren't going to have anything to do with him?"

*Actually, we didn't agree anything,* I think silently. *You did.*

But as I'm inclined towards her opinion in this case, I don't say it.

I scan around the room for somewhere to sit, not an easy task given that every surface is littered with stuff. Does she never hang *anything* up? I can see why coming in here gives Tess palpitations. Pushing a lone shoe aside, I manage to clear a small square of bed, just big enough to perch on. "I've tried. But he just keeps turning up; he was at work earlier."

Rosie plonks herself down next to me on top of a straw hat, crushing it in the process.

"It's unlike him to be so persistent."

"He obviously really wants to talk to me, Ro." I sigh, pushing my hair away from my face. Suddenly all the fight seems to have gone out of me and I just feel tired. Bone tired. "Maybe I ought to give him the chance."

She stares at me in horrified admonishment.

"Belle, no! You can't be serious. This guy ruined your life, remember? He left you at the altar and disappeared without a word... for six *years*. You didn't know if he was alive or dead. What kind of person does that? There's nothing he can say that will make it acceptable."

"You don't know that, Ro." There's an edge to my voice, a defensive one. I know she has a point, but she needn't make it sound so irretrievably damning. Isn't there room for hope sometimes... just a tiny bit? "Maybe there's more to it than meets the eye. He *did* say he'd wanted to come back sooner but couldn't."

My imagination conjures up all sorts of scenarios.

Perhaps he was in prison – framed, of course, by the unscrupulous sorts he fell in with. He always was so innocent, so trusting of people. He thought everyone was on his side. Or perhaps he was left behind on a remote island with no way back. Or perhaps…

I draw myself up short. All right, these are getting a little ridiculous, even I'll admit.

Rosie's shaking her head ferociously.

"I knew this would happen. I knew he'd get under your skin. It's like you can't say no to him."

She makes me sound so weak and feeble; it stings horribly. It's always been like this with Rosie and me: I try to see the best in people, she the worst. What I regard as one of my greatest strengths, she sees as my Achilles' heel.

"That's not fair. I'm just trying to keep an open mind, that's all."

"You're deluding yourself!" She throws up her hands in frustration. "Belle, you know nothing about him. Nothing. For all you know, he could be here sidling his way back into your affections whilst somewhere in a nice semi-detached house in Chislehurst there's a wife and three children waiting for him."

Her words hit me like a blow, but it's not as bad as it ought to be. And when I try to imagine it, I see why. The vision of Ed mowing the lawn on a Sunday or picking children up from the school gates feels hopelessly false. From what I've seen, he's still the same old Ed. Just as debonair and pulse-skippingly irresponsible as ever.

"He told me he *landed* in London," I say quietly. It's not

the point, and I know it, but I have to say something to defend my point of view.

"A wife and three bambinos, then. What's the difference?"

"And he is not *sidling* his way into my affections, as you put it," I say crossly. "I'm not that gullible, Ro. I'm talking about hearing him out, not running off into the sunset with him."

She fixes me with a piercing look.

"So you wouldn't take him back, then? If he could explain it all away, if he wanted to try again? You're telling me you wouldn't even consider it?"

Before I can respond to that, Tess's head appears around the edge of the door, her blonde hair shining like a halo around her face in the reflected light from the lamp.

"I could use some backup out here. Your mum looks like she's about to climb onto Ed's lap!"

Rosie gives me a look which suggests that our conversation is only paused, not concluded, before pulling me to my feet.

"He doesn't really deserve saving, mind."

As we file out into the hallway, I'm expecting to hear Mum's high-pitched laughter, but instead, everything's quiet. We find her sitting on her own in the living room, sipping demurely at her cup of tea.

"Mum? Where's Ed?" Alarmed, I crane my neck around, as though expecting to find him crouched behind the sofa. "What did you do to him?"

"Nothing!" She shoots us an affronted look over the rim

of her teacup. "Why do you girls always assume the worst? It's your father's influence, that is. He's told you no end of lies about me."

We haven't seen Dad in over fifteen years, but I decide to let that one pass.

"He left, in answer to your question," Mum sniffs, putting her cup down on the table. "Suddenly got very edgy and said he couldn't wait any longer. He was *so* looking forward to seeing you," she adds reprovingly, as though somehow I've done him a great disservice. "In fact, he was saying how much he's missed all of us while he's been away." She sighs rapturously. "He is *such* a sweetheart."

I can't even be bothered to feel indignation. Instead, my whole body seems to sag with relief. Thank God for *that*; I really didn't want to have that conversation here, in front of everyone. It's something that needs to be one-on-one; there's no room for onlookers.

Rosie sits down and picks up the milk jug, raising her eyebrows at me.

"What a shame we missed him."

Sarcasm drips from her voice and I wince internally. Flopping down on the sofa next to her, I reach for a biscuit. Oh well, I reason. It's better this way. At least now I can decide for myself when—

"Oh, you don't need to worry about *that*," Mum says mildly, as she flips open her compact to reapply her signature red lipstick. "You'll be seeing him tomorrow night. You can talk then."

I freeze, the biscuit halfway to my mouth. Rosie almost spits her tea back into her cup. Tess, who's sitting quietly in the other chair, looks as though she'd like to hide behind a cushion.

"Mum…" I struggle to form the word. "What have you done?"

She rubs her lips together, coating them evenly in flaming scarlet.

"I asked him to the party tomorrow night. You know, Rosie and Leo's… whatever it's called."

"Sten Do," Tess supplies feebly. "It's a cross between—"

"Not the time for an etymology lesson, Tess," I say, in a strangled voice.

"Mum!" Rosie yells, ignoring us both. "What were you *thinking*?"

She blinks.

"What? What did I do wrong?"

I close my eyes and drop my head into my hands.

Suddenly, tomorrow night is looking very ominous indeed.

## Chapter Eleven

Maybe he won't turn up.

I cradle a glass of champagne in my hand, scanning the room surreptitiously, looking for a familiar tousled blond head. Not that I'm even certain I'd be able to spot him in this crush; I never realised Rosie and Leo had quite so many friends.

I'll admit to being a bit nonplussed when Rosie announced they were eschewing the traditional stag and hen parties in favour of a much more modern and civilised-sounding 'sten do'. But I suppose it makes sense when you've been together for as long as Rosie and Leo have and you're not even sure whose friend was originally whose anymore. Everyone's mingling happily, no one appearing to object in the least to the lack of inflatable penises or L-plates which are the mainstay of the more traditional segregated form the festivities usually take.

It helps that Rosie certainly knows how to throw a party.

The vaulted space of the Italian restaurant looks almost unrecognisable tonight, with all of the tables taken out. She's even managed to convince them to take down the gaudy decorations somehow, and has replaced them with tasteful, pastel-coloured bunting and banners. The only thing she's left in place is the net of fairy lights which adorns the ceiling, twinkling merrily above the assorted company.

I never thought she'd take up my tentative suggestion of using this place when she couldn't get the ornate hotel function room she'd wanted for the occasion. But I'm glad she did; the whole atmosphere is relaxed and informal – much more, in fact, what I'd once expected this whole wedding to be like. I glance across at her now; she's chattering animatedly over by the buffet table, looking more at ease than I've seen her in months.

*I* should be enjoying myself too, I think bitterly, knocking back my champagne in one gulp. This is meant to be a celebration. Instead, I'm on a razor's edge, jumping every time someone taps me on the shoulder…

…Or whacks me in the shin with their cane.

"What's wrong with you, lass?" Gran demands, appearing at my side. "You've been skulking about all evening with a face like a wet kipper. It's not like you at all."

Well that's a relief to know, at least. If not terribly flattering in the present moment.

"I know. Sorry." I didn't realise it was that obvious. I need to make more of an effort; the last thing I want is to spoil the party for Rosie and Leo. It took me half of yesterday evening to convince her not to tell him about Ed's last-minute invite; she was all for having him bundled out the minute he dared set foot upon the threshold. "It's just…" I hesitate, unsure how much to tell Gran about Ed. One the one hand, I don't want to alarm her, but then, if he's going to turn up… well, she'll find out anyway, won't she? And in much more spectacular fashion. God knows what that'll do to her blood pressure.

I'm momentarily diverted from that train of thought as she lifts the glass in her hand to take a long draught. "Gran, is that whisky?"

She gives me a gimlet eye.

"And why not? This is a party, not a funeral. Lord knows, I go to enough of those as it is. Now listen to me," she leans in close. "I know what's going on. You're worried that fly-by-night you were foolish enough to get engaged to once is going to walk through that door any minute and meet your newest model." She gestures to Nate, who's standing several feet away, laughing at something Leo's said.

I choke theatrically on my champagne.

"Your mother is hardly discreet," Gran says dismissively, thumping me on the back. "Sometimes I wonder what rattles around in that woman's skull. The notion of inviting him here! But I suppose he said a few sweet words and it all went to her head, as usual. And as for the other," she raises an eyebrow. "Well, I might be old, dear, but I'm not dead yet. I know when sparks are flying between two people. I take it by your skittishness that he doesn't know about the… *unfortunate incident*?"

She needn't make it sound quite so sordid. I know she never really liked Ed all that much, but it was a perfectly respectable wedding… or it would have been, if he'd ever bothered to turn up.

"He is not my 'newest model'," I protest levelly. "We're just…"

I trail off as I realise I don't really know *what* we are. Workmates who kissed in a cupboard? Friends who went on an almost date? Either way, we can never be any more than that, so what does it matter?

Gran lets out a hoot of laughter.

"I expect you've been far too busy, and I can't say I blame you. He's got a pretty face and no mistake."

"Gran!" I hiss, feeling my face flaming. Thank God it's loud in here. I eye the empty glass in her hand. "How many of those have you had?"

She looks as if I've just deeply insulted her.

"A Scotswoman can hold her whisky, Belle. Now, that boy hasn't been able to keep his eyes off you all evening. Why don't you put him out of his misery and just go and speak to him?"

I look over to where Nate's standing. Our eyes catch and he gives me a warm, if slightly more reserved than usual, smile. I feel a now-familiar thud of guilt. I don't blame him for being confused; I've been avoiding him all evening. I've been carefully engineering it so we're circulating around the room at the same speed and therefore never actually end up in the same conversational group. Ever perceptive, he's taken my lead and hasn't approached me. God only knows what he must be thinking.

I'm being a coward, of course, and I know it. I ought to be over there right now, telling him that the kiss was a mistake, that I'm not in a position to get into anything at the moment, however casual it might be. But somehow, I keep finding excuses.

"I promised Rosie I'd watch out for Ed arriving…"

I also told her I'd get rid of him. It was my way of trying to show her that I don't relish the situation as I think she secretly suspects I do. This is *my* worst nightmare too. Just because I'm prepared to see Ed again doesn't mean I want it to happen here, in front of all these people I know.

In front of Nate. The thought draws me up short. Why do I care so much about this? I ask myself irritably. After all, I barely know the man. I didn't even *like* him until a few days ago.

"Don't you worry about Edward," Gran ripostes. "I'll deal with him if he turns up. What do you think I brought my stick for?"

That's the kind of comment which by rights should generate a lot of questions, but I don't even know where I'd start. I scrub a hand across my face, feeling exhausted all of a sudden.

"All right, I'll talk to him."

I look towards Nate again, and this time I feel my resolve harden. I owe him the truth, or part of it, at least. I can't bear the idea that I might be stringing him along, even unintentionally. I've tried so hard to be a good person these past few years, almost as if I could counter-balance what happened to me. As if I was terrified of letting myself off the hook, lest I become someone like Ed. Lest I hurt someone else like he hurt me.

It's time to do the right thing.

I put my empty glass on the edge of the bar and collect two freshly poured ones. Then, pushing back my shoulders, I make a beeline for him, cutting through the crowd.

He sees me, of course he does. I'm hard to miss, in a shocking pink shift dress, standing out against the dark suits and pale, floaty summer frocks. I bought it yesterday in my lunch break, in an act of rebellion against all the pastels I'm going to have to wear during the next week. Fitting closely against the contours of my body, with a deep v neckline, it's more daring than I'd normally go for. But then, I think I needed to feel daring again, to feel strong. This sense of helplessness… it's not me. It never has been.

I walk right up to Nate and hold out one of the glasses of champagne.

"Hey."

Just be breezy, Belle. Pretend that everything's okay. Like it's no big deal. You're good at that; God knows, you've had plenty of practice.

He hesitates for the briefest of moments, and I feel my pulse thud nervously. But then his face relaxes, and he takes the glass from my outstretched hand.

"Thanks."

We're both just looking at each other, my face tilted

upwards. I'm trying to read the expression in his eyes. I open my mouth to speak, but another voice cuts in.

"What, don't I get one?"

My head whips around. Leo's looking at us, patently amused.

"Here." I thrust my glass at him with a *go away* look.

He just stands there, showing no signs of moving.

"So, what shall we all talk about?" Then, at our astounded faces, he grins. "All right, *all right*, I won't torment you anymore. I know when I'm not wanted."

God, I hate him sometimes. He's better when he's in serious business mode.

"I heard Rosie say she has some jobs for you," I say sweetly. Time to get my own back. Stretching my neck, I make a show of scanning the room. "Shall I point you out to her?"

Alarm flickers across Leo's face.

"Okay, I surrender. I'll go." He turns to Nate. "Be careful with this one. She's mean, I'm warning you. Always has been. Don't let the big blue eyes fool you."

"I won't," Nate says softly. Or at least, I think that's what I hear him say. But Leo's brushing past me, leaning down to murmur in my ear, "Rosie seems better tonight, don't you think?"

All the teasing has left his voice.

"It's been a big build-up, that's all," I reply reassuringly. "See? Nothing to worry about."

He squeezes my shoulder briefly before moving away, disappearing into the throng. I watch him, reflecting that as men go, he really is one of the good ones. I need to remind myself of that every time I catch myself thinking that such a thing doesn't exist.

"He's very protective of you, you know," Nate says quietly from behind me. "He sees you as a little sister."

I shrug.

"We've known each other for a long time, I suppose. Almost half our lives." That draws me up short. "Actually, I've never thought of it like that before. It makes me feel rather old."

Nate's lips curve in a smile.

"I think he was sounding me out, trying to work out if I'm good enough for you. It was a bit nerve-wracking, to be honest."

I feel heat surge to my face. Oh God, how mortifying. How did he even *know*, anyway? I was careful not to tell Rosie about the kiss; I thought it might be one revelation too many for her to deal with. Why does Leo have this strangely omniscient way of working things out?

"And…?" I manage. I'm wishing I hadn't given my champagne away now. It would provide a displacement tool for my fidgeting, give me an excuse to look away. Every alarm bell in my head is screaming that I shouldn't have asked that question. I should be shutting this down right now.

"Actually, he seemed almost… relieved." Nate raises an eyebrow. "Clapped me on the back and said I was better than the last contender. Is there anything you want to tell me? You haven't got some serial killer lurking in your dating history, have you?"

He's joking, of course. And yet, I feel myself stiffen. Because this is it, isn't it? I'm not going to get a better opening than this. It's like the universe has handed it to me on a platter, with neon letters blaring, "Tell him!"

Except, I don't. I can't. I look up into his unfathomable eyes and the words freeze in my throat. At once, I'm aware of how close we are. I can practically feel the warmth of his body through his shirt, and the crisp, clean scent of him… It's slightly citrussy; it reminds me of the Mediterranean somehow. If I closed my eyes, I could easily trick myself into believing we were standing on a beach somewhere, beneath a glaring, glittering sun. With an effort, I will myself to focus on the present.

His face turns from teasing to serious in an instant.

"Look, Belle. Clearly this isn't a social visit. Why don't you just say what you came over to say?" He watches me levelly. "It's all right; I'm an adult. I won't take it personally."

The directness of his assertion makes my next words come out in a gasp.

"Why… what makes you think…?"

"I was an investigative reporter for over two years back in London. I know when someone's avoiding me." Suddenly, he looks weary. "Even when they're not so spectacularly obvious about it as you are."

"Look, it's nothing like that…" I don't know what I'm

saying. After all, he couldn't make it easier for me. But for some reason, that consideration, that kindness, is the very thing which prevents me from saying what I know I ought to. That and the fluttering in my chest, like a thousand captive butterflies. Instead, I grasp at the best excuse I can come up with. "It's my family, really. They're… well, they're a bit mad, to be honest. You've seen what they're like whenever they think I'm the slightest bit interested—" I break off, reddening. "I mean… I was trying to shield you, that's all."

It's not a total fabrication, to be fair to me. After all, even if Ed wasn't enough to put him off me for life, half an hour with my mother ought to do it.

He surprises me by catching my chin in his fingers, tilting my face up to look at him.

"And that's all it is? You're sure?"

"Of course." My voice trembles slightly on the lie, but I manage to hold his gaze. "What else would there be?"

Oh, God. Suddenly, a wave of nausea hits me, and my head reels. I am the worst person in the world. I feel like any moment demons will reach out of the floor and drag me down into hell.

"Well, that's good news for us, then." The warmth is back in his eyes, his lips tilting up at the corners. "Because they all seem to be otherwise occupied at the moment; in fact, isn't that one of yours over there?"

I twist my head around and try not to let out a groan. My grandmother, never one to resign herself to a life of twinsets and embroidery, appears to be sinking Jägerbombs over by the bar, surrounded by a cheering group of Leo's friends.

"I would ask if we should intervene, but it looks like she's drinking them all under the table," Nate observes mildly.

"Tomorrow morning when they're all nursing hangovers, she'll be right as rain. She'll be up at six grilling kippers," I joke weakly. "Then again, I shouldn't mock. That could be me in fifty years' time."

"In which case, I sincerely hope I'll still know you. You certainly won't be dull."

Even though his words are said lightly, they make me go still. Because I'm not used to thinking about the future, even in a jesting, theoretical way. I stopped doing that even before my ill-fated wedding. Ed never liked to think too far ahead; in the end, I stopped trying to make him, and soon enough I became the same way. Especially after it all fell apart; I think I became afraid of forming expectations. It's why I've always envied Rosie; she's never doubted that she and Leo would be together forever, that they would get married someday, have children. She's courageous enough to put her faith in something she can't completely control. I'm not sure I could ever do that, not anymore. I'd always be braced, waiting for the other shoe to drop. For something to come out of left field and smash my dreams to pieces, to punish me for daring to try and predict the future.

Of course, Nate doesn't realise any of this. To him it was nothing but an easy, throwaway comment. The privilege of someone who's never had it all taken away from them in a moment, I suppose. So I force myself to smile and reply in kind.

"To be honest, turning into my grandmother would be the easy option. It could be so much worse. I could become my mother instead. You can't imagine what *she's* like."

"Er... actually, I can." He's looking over the top of my head. "She's standing up on the bar as we speak."

"She's *what*?" I wheel around so fast I almost go over on my ankle. Mercifully, though, I'm still holding on to Nate, so I manage to keep my balance.

Sure enough, he's right. I'd half hoped he might be joking. Really, I ought to have known better.

Mum's balanced on top of the bar, teetering in her stilettos on the polished surface, holding a glass of champagne in one hand and a spoon in the other. For a second, I'm confused, then it hits me. She's going to make a speech.

Then it hits me all over again, wave after wave. Oh no. *She's going to make a speech.*

Mum rarely misses an opportunity to make a speech. I think she sees it as a replacement for the Oscar acceptance address which she's convinced herself was in her stars. Until Rosie and I ruined it, of course. Hers tend to be long, self-congratulatory monologues which bear little or no relevance to the people they're supposed to be toasting.

"Mum," I hiss, lurching forwards. "Get down from there!"

She looks down at me petulantly.

"Why?"

"Because you're causing a scene, that's why." I blink, taking a step backwards. "And because I can see up your skirt!"

I notice that Nate has politely averted his eyes. Not all of the men present are doing the same, mind.

"It's all right, I've waxed," she says idly. "Now, if you don't mind..." she stretches out her arms, tapping the spoon against the side of the glass. "Everyone! I have something to say!"

I'm beginning to wish those demons would hurry up. Being swallowed into a hole in the ground is sounding pretty appealing at the moment.

Then again, why should *I* have to be the one to go? No, I decide savagely, I wish it would swallow *her*, black lacy pants and all.

At least she is actually *wearing* pants on this occasion. It's not always a given.

I crane my neck, looking around for my sister. I should be by her side for this. But I can't see her anywhere.

"Tonight is a wonderful celebration," Mum begins, her voice ringing out across the now hushed room. "My darling Rosie is marrying the man of her dreams, and we couldn't be happier."

I release a breath I hadn't even known I was holding. This doesn't sound so bad; in fact, I might even venture to say that it sounds like a nice speech. Perhaps I was wrong after all. Maybe she really is going to let it be Rosie's—

"But there is more than one reason for celebration tonight," Mum continues, looking smug.

This sounds ominous. I can feel myself tensing.

With great fanfare, Mum moves her hand around the glass so that her fingers are facing the crowd. Something glints beneath the lights. My stomach contracts; even before she's said it, everyone knows.

"Carlos and I… are engaged!"

## Chapter Twelve

There's a beat of confused silence. Then someone cheers, and the room erupts into a cacophony of applause. I'm not sure any of them even know what's going on, let alone who Mum is – these are Rosie and Leo's friends, after all – but the effects of an open bar are beginning to hit. They'd cheer for anything right about now, I'm willing to wager.

Not that Mum seems to care. Flushed with delight at the vociferousness of the response, she's taking a bow as if she's on stage in a West End production. I can only watch helplessly as she yanks a bemused but beaming Carlos – I'm not entirely convinced he knows what's just happened, either – up onto the bar top with her, and proceeds to kiss him passionately. That earns them a fresh round of cheers, with the odd wolf-whistle thrown in for good measure.

It's the single most hideous moment of my entire life. And bear in mind that there's quite a bit of competition.

This sails straight over being jilted and comfortably takes the top spot. I'd volunteer to be jilted again if only it would erase this moment. I'd gladly go back over and over, like Groundhog Day. That's how bad it is.

I can't even look at Nate. I'm hot with shame; it prickles all over my skin like a rash.

Why couldn't she manage to be a normal mother for *one* evening? Why couldn't she just smile, and say how proud she is, and wear sensible underwear? Is that really too much to ask, just this once?

The saddest truth of all is that I already know the answer to that question. I've asked it of myself many times before: when she hijacked my school play and muscled her way into playing the lead, when she got tipsy at my graduation and fell into the Dean's lap, when she wore a cream-coloured dress to my wedding…

She simply can't do it. She can't let anyone else have their moment; it's like an addiction. No wonder Rosie and I have our issues.

Rosie. The thought jolts me into action. If this is bad for me, it must be ten times worse for her. At her own hen party, surrounded by all of her friends…

"I have to find my sister," I yell over my shoulder. I still can't bring myself to look at Nate, can't bear to see the pity I know must be in his eyes. But he clasps my arm before I can get away.

"I'll help you look."

I dive off into the crowd before he can say any more, squinting through the bodies for a glimpse of Rosie's emerald-green dress. The task just became a lot harder; Mum's antics seem to have reminded everyone how drunk they are. The volume has increased markedly and people are bumping against each other. Some are even dancing to the music, their arms up in the air. If it was difficult to locate someone before, it's all but impossible now.

A hand catches my wrist, and I spin around to find Leo looking down at me. Gone is the relaxed persona of mere minutes ago; the tense lines are back around his mouth, his face drawn.

"I can't find her," he says hopelessly.

"She must be here somewhere. I'll carry on looking, while you—" I glance back across the room, where Mum and Carlos are still cavorting on the bar.

He understands what I'm saying. With a curt nod he carries onwards and I breathe a sigh of relief. That's one less thing to worry about; Leo's good at damage control. The least we can do for Rosie is to make sure it doesn't escalate any further.

I've just about managed to fight my way to the far wall when someone else lays a hand on my shoulder.

"She's not anywhere in here," Tess says in my ear. "I've already circled the whole room once." At my look of astonishment, she simply shrugs and explains, "sharp elbows. They were clearing a path for me by the end."

Having been on the receiving end of one of her bony elbows to the ribs more than once, I can easily see why. But I'm getting distracted. I shake my head, trying to focus.

"She must have stepped outside for a minute." Hope flares in my chest. "Maybe she missed it altogether."

God, I hope so. I'll still have to tell her, of course. But perhaps I'll be able to carefully omit some of the more… graphic elements.

Tess looks across the room, biting her lip, the way she always does when she's worried.

"Leo seems to be getting it back under control, at any rate."

"You mean my mother isn't gyrating on top of the bar anymore," I say drily. But the words come out with a bit of a wobble, nonetheless.

Tess takes my hand and gives it a reassuring squeeze.

"Belle, no one's going to remember this tomorrow. Look how far gone everyone is in here. It'll just be a blurry recollection they'll assume they half-imagined."

*But I'll remember*, I think desolately. *Just like I remember all the other times.*

Over at the other end of the room, I can hear the deep rumble of Leo's voice. I can't make out what he's saying, but judging by the answering ripple of laughter from the audience, he's doing what he does best. Skilfully smoothing it over, making it all seem like nothing.

Thank heavens at least one of us can. If it were me standing up there, I'd probably just burst into angry tears.

Tess nudges my arm.

"Heads up. Your mum's coming over."

My heart sinks. She's the last person I want to see right

now. How did she even spot me from all the way over there?

Then I remember: the dress. I scowl down at it, hoping that blaming an insentient object might somehow make me feel better. I'd give anything to blend in to the wallpaper right now.

"Belle, *darling,*" Mum can make her voice surprisingly loud when she wants to – all those years of drama lessons with teachers booming at her to "project her voice!" seem to have paid off, even if none of the rest of it did. I automatically want to shrink backwards, the way I used to as a kid in the playground at school pick-up time, when Mum would come sashaying through the gates in a leather skirt that redefined the term 'mini'. Even though everyone knew she was my mother, my childish logic told me that if I avoided her, perhaps no one would realise we were related.

Unfortunately, I'm an adult now, even if sometimes I wish I weren't. And I can't pretend not to see her. Especially when she thrusts her engagement ring right under my nose.

"Aren't you going to congratulate us?" She preens.

I feel a spike of temper. Honestly, she's just so *pleased* with herself, isn't she? She has no idea what chaos and embarrassment she's just caused. She's got what she wanted, and in her mind that's all that matters.

I'm about to say as much when a deep voice sounds next to my ear.

"Of course she is." Nate places a hand on my shoulder and gives it a subtle squeeze. "She's just getting over her surprise, aren't you, Belle?"

For a split second, I'm confused, then I hear the inflection in his voice, feel the light pressure on my skin, and realise what he's doing. He's cautioning me, giving me a moment to think before I speak.

I spot Carlos hovering a little behind Mum, his muscles straining at the fabric of his too-tight white suit. He looks as if he might be about to burst out of it altogether. Although, in a less literal sense, I can't help but notice that he seems to be bursting with pride, too. I've never seen him look so thrilled, and the realisation deflates my anger slightly.

And now I find myself in a tight corner. Because really, what can I say? Of course, I want nothing more than to yell at Mum for being so selfish and idiotic, but one look at Carlos's face reminds me that after all, they *did* just get engaged. Even if they did do it in the most horrendous manner imaginable, there's no getting away from the fact that this is a precious moment in their lives. Can I really bring myself to ruin it for them forever?

Besides, now I've drawn back from the situation a bit, I notice that quite a few heads are beginning to turn in our direction, unable to resist following the unfolding drama. And I have to ask myself: do I want to make an even worse scene than we've already had tonight? Would Rosie and Leo truly thank me for that?

Oh, bugger it. This is going to hurt.

Swallowing down my pride, I try to nudge my lips into something approaching a smile. I fear it comes out as more of a grimace, if the horrified look Tess darts me is anything to go by.

"Congratulations, Mum." I have to force each word out. "Carlos. I'm really pleased for you both."

Nate releases my shoulder, and I feel a rush of gratitude for his quick thinking. But there's no time to thank him, even with a silent look. I can feel him moving away tactfully, blending back into the crowd. Presumably, he didn't want to intrude on a family moment, but I find myself desperately wishing he was still here, beside me, steady and reassuring. Something to hold on to as everything else whirls around me.

"*Graçias, bomboncita.*" Without warning, Carlos crushes me against his rock-hard chest. "Your blessing, it mean everything to us."

He sounds worryingly like he might be about to cry. But then, it doesn't take much. He cried once when he found a café selling churros near Holyrood Park. Said he thought he'd never taste one again.

"Er, no problem," I gasp, reaching behind myself to remove his left hand, which is straying rather lower down my person than is appropriate. Not knowing what to do with the hand I'm now awkwardly holding, I pat it a few times before returning it to him. "Don't you think you could have chosen a better time to announce it, though? Like, say, *any* other time?"

My voice rises a little on that last sentence. Well, I had to say *something*, didn't I? I couldn't completely let it go.

Mum doesn't miss my sarcasm. She frowns reprovingly, little lines appearing between her perfectly waxed brows.

"I did *try* to tell you, darling. Here at the restaurant the other night. But then you and Rosie disappeared for half the evening."

We disappeared for all of ten minutes, but I bite my tongue on that point.

"And then I came over last night to try again," Mum sighs dramatically, as though it had all been such a trial. "It wasn't *quite* as I'd planned, but I wanted you two to be the first to know. Yet again, though, you never gave me a chance. At least Ed was pleased for me, even if no one else cares."

"Wait… what?" My brain is struggling to compute this. "You told *Ed*?"

"Yes, of course." She inspects her ring, turning it this way and that so the light catches it. "He was *very* interested. He always was such a sweet boy. I was *so* looking forward to having him as a son-in-law, you know. Why you couldn't make it work with him, I can't imagine."

I stare at her.

"Mum, he *jilted* me."

She blinks.

"Did he? Oh yes, so he did. But apart from that, he was simply *lovely*. *Such* a catch. It was a *teensy* bit foolish of you to let him go, really, darling, if I might say so."

A strangled scream rises up in my throat. If I don't leave right now, I think I might kill her.

"I can't talk to you," I throw my hands up in the air. "You're just… impossible. Completely and utterly impossible."

"I don't see what all the fuss is about," Mum says, her

face darkening with annoyance. Clearly, this isn't the rapturous reception she was expecting.

"You!" I can't contain myself any more, and the word bursts from my lips. You see, *this* is why I needed Nate to stay. "It's always you. You have no consideration for anyone else, do you? You don't even *think*." I break off with a frustrated sigh. "Oh, what's the point? You'll never understand."

And in that moment, I realise I'm right. Her mind just isn't capable of compassion, of thinking about anyone else. In a way, it's not her fault.

There's a charged silence. Even Carlos looks awkward.

"Er, let me see the ring!" Tess blurts out, grabbing Mum's hand. "Oh, how lovely. Did Carlos choose it all by himself?"

Mum melts like butter on a hot scone.

"It a Ceylon sapphire," she purrs. "Don't you see how it matches my eyes? That's why he chose it."

So *that's* what I overheard her going on about in the flat; I recall how she studiously hid her hands when I walked in. Waiting for a grander moment to announce it, I suppose. Perhaps she'd already planned this, even then.

Tess gives me a meaningful look out of the corner of her eye and my heart swells with love for her. Sometimes it's easy to take her gentle presence for granted, but at moments like this I'm reminded how lucky I am to have her. God only knows how many times she's saved my sanity over the years.

I slip away quietly, leaving Tess waxing lyrical about my

mother's resplendent irises, and make my way to the ladies'. Wincing at the washed-out reflection which greets me in the mirror, I search around in my clutch bag for my new lip gloss. Twisting off the cap, the synthetic strawberry scent catapults me right back to my teenage years. It's oddly soothing – Lord knows why, because from what I remember of that time it was decidedly tempestuous.

And my mother was still *exactly* the same. How can we have come so far and yet nothing's changed?

When I press the applicator to my lips, I find that my hand is shaking with pent-up emotion. Clearly I haven't calmed down as much as I'd thought. I reach for a tissue to correct my smudged lip line, willing myself to breathe deeply.

I have to say, the bathrooms here are very plush – surprisingly so, in fact. I didn't get much chance to notice the last time I was in here; I was far too preoccupied with the text from Ed. The mirrors are edged with lights, like a theatrical dressing room, and there are little wicker baskets with rolled up hand towels next to each of the basins. There's even a burgundy velvet love seat pushed up against the far wall, presumably so you can sit and chat while waiting for one another to wash their hands or put the finishing touches to their makeup.

It's the sort of room that makes you realise why men complain so much about women disappearing to the bathroom for hours on end. To be honest I'm pretty tempted to hide in here for the rest of the evening, but then a gaggle of girls burst through the door, breaking my introspection.

Reluctantly, I refasten my bag, knowing I have to go back out there. After all, I still haven't managed to trace Rosie, for starters.

As soon as I re-enter the party, I'm hit by a wall of sound. I'm not looking forward to the prospect of pushing my way through the crowd, but as it happens, I don't need to. A gap seems to open up between the bodies, like a glade in a thick forest, and I can see Nate. Well, part of him at least. He looks like he's deep in conversation with someone but I can't see who.

I bite my lip, wondering what to do. Rosie ought to be my priority, really, but seeing as he's right *there*... I should take a moment to thank him. God knows if I'll be able to find him again in this crush.

I weave my way towards him, determined not to lose him again. He moves in and out of sight as people get in my way, but I keep my sights fixed on the top of his head, the mop of tousled curls that is so distinctive. His face comes into view again, ever so briefly, and I blink at the expression on it. He looks almost... grim, which is unlike him. I crane my neck, trying to see around a pair of broad shoulders, trying to convince myself I must have imagined it. Or else it was a trick of the light. A beam falling across his face in just the wrong way, distorting his features. Like an optical illusion, I tell myself, but nonetheless, my heart is beginning to patter. Because let's face it, in my life, with my family, it's never just nothing.

Please, *please* don't say that my mother's got her claws into him. That would be more than—

I duck under an outstretched arm, and suddenly I can see everything. And immediately, I wish I couldn't. Because it's *so* much worse than that. It's worse than I could possibly have imagined.

Ed's standing with his back to me. I can't hear what he's saying, but I don't need to. Because the look on Nate's face says it all.

And I know in that moment it's all over.

# Chapter Thirteen

"Nate—" with increased desperation, I surge forward, elbowing aside the last few people who are unlucky enough to be in my way. I *have* to get to him; that's the only thing on my mind.

But he's already looking away, shaking his head. And then he's gone, disappearing into the crowd and out of view, beyond my reach.

Ed's already turning around, searching for the source of the commotion. He looks as fresh and unruffled as ever in a crisp linen suit, his hands shoved carelessly in his pockets. The sight of him should be enough to make my heart skip, but tonight it doesn't happen. For once, he's not the only man on my mind.

"Ah, there you are," he says, as I finally reach his side. "I was beginning to think I might never find you. Pretty rammed in here, isn't it?"

"What did you say to him, Ed?" I demand, grabbing his sleeve urgently. "What have you done?"

"Who? Him?" Ed asks, looking shifty all of a sudden. He moves his weight from foot to foot. "Oh, we just had a chat, that's all. Why does it matter?"

"What did you *say* to him, Ed?" I repeat, in a low voice. I'm trying very hard not to let my agitation show.

"I just wanted to check up on him, all right?" Ed looks up at me then. His eyes, still vivid even in the dark, flash with defiance. "I wanted to see who this guy was, that you're—" his face seems to crease in pain"—that you're… *replacing* me with. I was *trying* to look out for your interests." He folds his arms. "I don't want you to make a mistake, Belle."

I stare at him in utter disbelief, but he doesn't appear to notice the irony. He seems perfectly earnest.

"I…" My voice has dried up. It sounds papery, afraid. I realise I was about to say, "I could never replace you." The very thought that I almost voiced that aloud, that I could lay myself bare like that, vulnerable to his mercy, terrifies me. "You didn't tell him who you are, did you?"

It's a pointless question. I already know the answer.

Oh God, what must Nate be thinking right now?

Ed's shoulders hunch defensively.

"It's not *my* fault. How was I supposed to know that he was in the dark about it all?" He has the audacity to look faintly disapproving. "I assumed you would have said something to him. It's not exactly the best start to a relationship, is it?"

I don't trust myself to speak. This from the man who's almost pathologically playful with the truth. It took me ages to untangle all the creative fiction he fed me at the beginning of our relationship. Some of it was minor, but some of it… not so much. I forgave him back then; in my mind, so long as he was faithful, nothing else mattered much. But then, I was much more pliable in those days.

There's the beginning of a headache pulsing faintly in my right temple and I press a hand to my head.

"There is no relationship. It's nothing."

It's the complete truth, and yet it feels very much like a lie. The realisation disquiets me.

Ed doesn't look convinced either. He raises a blond eyebrow.

"Then why are you about to go after him?"

My natural inclination is to deny it but I know what it's like with Ed. One stupid argument can spiral on endlessly, and I don't have the luxury of time right now. I open my mouth, then close it with a bitten-off curse of frustration, pushing my way past him. I *have* to find Nate before he leaves.

I don't know where it's come from, this reaction, this panic. After all, if I were being logical, I know I ought to be feeling something more akin to relief. At least it's out in the open now. Everyone knows where they stand. I just wish I'd been brave enough to do the job myself. I don't want to leave it like this.

I race up the stairs and burst out into the street, the cool night air fluttering against my face. It's delightful after the heat of the party, but I scarcely notice it. My eyes are too busy scanning the dimly lit pavement, looking for a tall figure striding away. But there's nothing. It's completely empty.

"Are you looking for me?"

The voice emerges out of the shadows to my right, making me start. My head whips around and there he is, leaning back against the side of the building, his dark eyes fixed upon me.

"Oh," my hand has automatically fled to my throat in surprise, and now my fingers find the silver pendant which rests in the hollow there. I fiddle with it nervously, wondering what to say next. Sensing that whatever it is, I need to tread carefully. I can't identify his mood, not with him half in shadow like that. "I thought you'd left," I finish lamely.

"I needed some air."

My ears strain to pick up the inflection in his voice, but there isn't any. What a time for him to pick to become utterly inscrutable, I think despairingly. Just when I really need to know what he's thinking.

"It was pretty hot in there, wasn't it?" I'm painfully aware that I'm rambling, that this conversation isn't real, not in any sense that matters. It's nothing more than a veil, a smokescreen. Inanity, a pretence at normality. And all the while, the real conversation simmers and boils away under the surface, waiting while we circle ever closer. The question is, am I brave enough to go there? I get the sense that he's not about to. He's waiting me out, and maybe he should. After all, this is my fault, my failure.

"Do we… need to talk?" I venture, hating how tentative I sound. But I'm no good at this sort of thing; in my family, if something goes horribly wrong, we don't *talk* about it. We just brush it cheerfully under the carpet and pretend it's all fine, and, soon enough, it is. It's perhaps not the most mature approach on the planet, but it's always worked for us.

Well, after a fashion. Maybe tonight wasn't the best example; Mum's announcement seems to have brought up a barrage of old feelings which I'd thought long dissipated.

"I don't know," he sighs, scrubbing a hand through his hair, disarraying his curls in a way that makes my stomach flutter. I bite my lip. What is wrong with me? *Definitely* not the time for such thoughts. "I suppose so, but to be honest, I'm beginning to wonder if there's any point."

The defeat in his tone takes me aback. I'd expected… well, I'm not sure what. For him to be angry? Maybe. But this… it's something else. Something that makes my heart beat a warning patter.

He's giving me the out I wanted, I realise. *Again*. He's giving me the chance to walk away unscathed. I should take him up on it. It's for the best. But something within me can't let it go. I feel inexplicably desperate to explain, to make him *understand*.

"Nate, I never—"

"You never lied to me?" Even through the shadows, I see

his eyes flash. "No, I suppose that's true, if we're being technical about it."

The bitter sarcasm in his voice makes me flinch.

His quietness is deceptive; he *is* angry. That response was revealing. It gave away more than I think he intended it to. Yet despite everything, I find myself breathing a small sigh of relief. At least I know what I'm dealing with now.

"So it's true, then." Nate's dark eyes are scanning my face.

I wish I could look away, but I know that's not an option. He deserves to know the truth. I take a fortifying breath.

"We were engaged once, yes. But it was all such a long time ago," I add quickly, as his gaze begins to turn shuttered. "I was young, Nate. Barely out of university. I was just so… caught up in the romance of it all."

The dizzying, reckless romance. I can still just about summon up the memory of it, if I allow myself to. The absolute conviction that we could run off into the sunset, hand in hand, and nothing could ever possibly go wrong, could ever touch us, so long as we were together.

Now, of course, I know better. But hindsight is a fine thing, isn't it?

"But I promise you, I hadn't seen him for *years*. Until he turned up the other day, he honestly could have been dead for all I knew. After he walked out on our wedding, I never—"

"Wait, after he did *what*?" I can hear the shock reverberating through Nate's voice.

Of course. He doesn't know this part. I strive to find the right words, even as I wonder what on earth I'm doing this for. I told him the first part out of a sense of obligation, but I don't owe him the whole story. Whatever I say next, it's because I want to, even if I don't know exactly *why* I want to.

"Ah, yes." I clear my throat. "I was… um, somewhat… jilted." I frown, more to myself than anything. "I wish there was a better word for it. It sounds so…"

"Christ, Belle." He doesn't sound angry any more, at least. But he's looking at me… my heart sinks. The way I never wanted him to look at me. Like I'm someone to be pitied. "I'm really sorry. I had no idea." He holds my gaze as he says it, at least. Most people have to look away. "Leo never told me."

"He's never told anyone. I asked him not to." I've twisted the pendant around and around until it meets my throat. Now I release it and it spins back into shape. "Besides, it's the sort of thing you don't tend to bring up in polite conversation."

"No, I can imagine." He sounds a little dazed. I suppose I did rather land it on him.

"I mean, we all have a past, right?" I edge closer, feeling my way. I can sense that he's softening, that maybe he's beginning to understand. That he might even forgive me. The thought assuages my guilt a little. "Didn't you do anything reckless when you were twenty-one?"

"Wait," he steps forward into the light, but the

expression on his face seems to darken before my eyes. "You think *that's* what this is all about?"

There's a heavy beat of silence during which I just stare at him in confusion.

"I don't believe this." He looks away, shaking his head in apparent disbelief. "You think I'm angry because you were *engaged*? Belle, I couldn't care less about your past. What matters to me is now, and the fact that you chose not to tell me what's been going on. I thought we were friends. I thought..." He lapses into silence for a moment. When he speaks again, his voice is low. "I thought a few things. But perhaps I was mistaken."

I scrub a hand across my face, suddenly feeling exhausted. This whole thing's beginning to catch up with me. I'm out of fight, out of excuses. Perhaps it's time to just be honest, even if it is a little belated.

"I'm sorry, okay? Really, I am. I don't know what else I can say to you. I was just confused about everything, and I guess I was afraid that..."

"I wouldn't understand?" He interjects. "That I'd want nothing to do with you? Is that the kind of person you think I am? If you'd just told me, I would have handled it all differently. Trodden more carefully. I would have—" He breaks off, looking pained. "Wait... is that why you agreed to go out with me? Because he was back on the scene?"

"No!" I feel a jolt of horror as I realise where his train of thought is heading. "No, it was never about that. I didn't even know he was here then."

He doesn't seem to hear me. He's looking past me.

"And the kiss... Was any of it even real?"

I just stare at him in desolation, not knowing what to say or how to make him believe me. I don't even know how we got here. I never, ever wanted to hurt Nate. To be honest, I never thought I could. He's so breezy, so self-assured. I never thought anything could affect him.

It was just supposed to be a bit of fun, I think with a kind of frantic despair. It *was* a bit of fun. It was never meant to go like this.

He opens his mouth to say something, then stops himself with a single shake of the head.

"You know what? Don't answer that. I'd rather not know."

"Belle!" The door next to us crashes open and Rosie bursts breathlessly onto the pavement. "You *have* to come. Something's happened."

# Chapter Fourteen

Honestly, talk about timing. My family has some of the worst in the Western Hemisphere.

"I'll be down in a minute," I say, not taking my eyes off Nate.

But Rosie doesn't move. Instead, she hops from foot to foot, wringing her hands.

"We really need you *now*."

I bite back a sigh of frustration, turning towards her. Can she not see that I'm—

I do a double take when I see her face. She looks awful: her colour is high, her eyes bright with agitation. My heart plummets, and I feel a stab of guilt. I'm not the only one having problems this evening. She's probably just found out about Mum, it occurs to me. She must be devastated. It sounds inconceivable, but with everything that's happened since, I'd temporarily managed to forget about it.

What an evening this is turning out to be.

"It's important." She presses, still looking off into the half distance in that odd way which is so unlike her. "It's about Ed."

I feel Nate go still next to me.

"Of course," he says quietly. I get the sense that he's looking at me, but I can't bring myself to meet his gaze.

For the first time, Rosie seems to notice his presence. She darts a quick, curious glance at him; I can practically see her trying to work out what she's missed.

Nate's shrugging on his jacket, turning the collar up against the chill evening air.

"I think that's my cue to leave. It sounds like you have more vital things to deal with."

I see Rosie's eyes widen at the pointed note in his voice. She opens her mouth as if to say something, but then closes it again with a snap. For once, even my sister seems lost for words.

And I… I just stand there. Watching him go. Wishing he wouldn't. Wondering why it feels so final, like he's taking something with him I never even realised was important.

Rosie's watching me beadily, obviously bursting to unleash a barrage of questions. I hold up a hand wearily.

"Not now, Ro, okay?"

Her eyebrows shoot up in an overblown protest of innocence.

"I wasn't!"

"You were," I push myself away from the wall with an effort. My whole body feels like lead. I force myself to focus on something else. Anything but that retreating back, disappearing into the night. "What was it that you wanted me for, anyway? Something about Ed?"

She starts, anxiety sweeping back across her features, transforming her before my eyes. She grabs my arm, pulling me back towards the door.

"Yes, but not out here. I don't want to risk being overheard."

I glance around the empty street, perplexed by this sudden descent into covert operations.

"I think it's unlikely."

Even as I say it, a group of four ascend the stairs in a burst of laughter, coats over their arms, the girls teetering slightly in their heels, men offering a steadying arm. I don't recognise them especially – they're probably work friends – so I hang back politely, waiting while they engage Rosie in a protracted goodbye. I swipe the screen on my phone, checking the time, feeling a jolt of surprise to see that it's already five to midnight. The time when people will be starting to drift towards the door. Soon enough, there'll be a steady stream traipsing past us, all stopping to give Rosie their congratulations, to twitter excited nothings about the wedding, even though they'll all be seeing her in a week's time anyway.

Eventually she extricates herself with a supercilious look that clearly says, 'I told you so.'

"All right, fine," I say testily. She's such a pain when she's right. She's a pain when she's wrong, too, come to think of it. "Let's go. And this had better be as critical as you say, or I swear, I'm going to be—"

"Oh, it is." She gives a jittery laugh and I dart her an apprehensive look from out of the corner of my eye. She's beginning to unnerve me. "You might say it's a matter of life and death."

I want to roll my eyes. She's such a drama queen. I wouldn't be that surprised to find out this is all some wild goose chase dreamed up in her fertile imagination. You'd think that a three-year criminology degree and seven more working for the police would have tempered her more fanciful notions, but apparently not.

My uncharitable thoughts are vindicated as I watch her peer around a corner, craning her neck in an exaggerated fashion.

"In here will have to do," she mutters eventually, pushing open a door and shoving me unceremoniously inside.

I blink to find myself in the bathroom. Yet again. This is getting like the stationery cupboard at work; I just can't seem to get away from the place.

Rosie props a spindly little chair under the handle, looking pleased with herself.

"There. That should give us some privacy, at least."

"For *what*?" I'm getting exasperated now. This is no longer feeling so amusing. I'm exhausted. I'm having what has to be the worst evening of my life. I just want to go home and fall into a deep, uneventful sleep, then wake up tomorrow and hope it all feels just a little bit better. "I'm in no mood for amateur dramatics, Ro. Not tonight. In fact, I think it's time I went home." I move towards the door, but she makes a sideways leap in front of me.

"Wait, Belle. Just hear me out. Believe me, you're going to want to once I've started. If I can even work out *where* to start." She sighs, twisting her engagement ring round her finger. "I had a phone call about half an hour ago. One I'd been waiting for. I went outside to take it."

At least something has started to make sense. So that's where she'd disappeared to when Mum was making a spectacle of us all.

She's already shaking her head at herself, biting her lip.

"No, that's not the right place to start. I need to begin with a confession." She looks up then, her dove-grey eyes meeting mine squarely. "I called in a favour with one of the detectives at work and asked them to look into Ed's disappearance."

"You did what?" That definitely wasn't what I was expecting. I stare at her, hopelessly confused. "Why? He disappeared entirely of his own accord. There was nothing suspicious about it."

"I wanted to know where he's been." There are two high spots of colour on Rosie's cheeks, her chin tilted in a defiant look I know well. It's the same look she got when we were seven and she raided the fridge and ate my last piece of birthday cake. She knew she was in the wrong, but she was utterly unrepentant nonetheless. "What he's been doing all this time. What was so bloody important that he had to… to *leave* you like that, on what was meant to be the best day of your life."

She looks so fiercely protective that I have glance away, heat building behind my eyes.

"I couldn't stand to hear you making excuses for him, Belle. I wanted to… no, I *needed* to prove to you that he's no good. That he doesn't deserve a second of your compassion." She looks down at her hands, curled into fists at her sides. "I didn't think we'd turn up much, the odd parking ticket, but at least it might show where he's been. Just getting on with his life, while yours fell apart." Her eyes flick up to meet mine. "But what we found…"

The door handle rattles, startling us both.

"Out of order!" Rosie bellows. "Use the gents'."

The rattling stops. Rosie looks at me, uncertainty clouding her features. As if suddenly she's not sure she's doing the right thing. I can read her like a book; I know exactly what she's thinking.

"Just tell me, Ro," I say gently, surprising myself with how calm I sound. In reality, I feel sick with trepidation. But I need to know. "It's not going to get any better for waiting."

If it's something really bad, I tell myself, trying to breathe through the churning in my stomach, I'll do my best to take it gracefully. For Rosie's sake. I won't let her see how much it still has the power to hurt me. If there was another woman whose arms he ran away into on that fateful day, or he was involved in something shady, or…

"No, it isn't." Rosie tucks a strand of chestnut coloured hair behind her ear, then takes a breath. "It's—"

The door handle rattles again and I feel a hot flash of irritation.

"Out of order!" This time it's me who yells, before Rosie can even open her mouth.

"It's me," Tess's voice floats through the panelling. "Let me in."

Rosie pulls the chair away from the door and yanks it open, bundling Tess inside.

"I saw you coming through here," Tess says, with an uncharacteristically reproachful look between us. "What's going on? Something's happened, hasn't it? Tell me."

Rosie and I share a look, and a silent communication. It's right that Tess should be here; after all, it's always been the three of us. Most of the time, I think of myself as having two sisters, not one. I move towards Tess, linking my arm through hers.

"Tell *us*."

Rosie scrubs a hand across her forehead, and I notice how tired she looks, how lacking in her usual vibrancy. But then, maybe she's been looking like that for a while now. I don't know. I haven't exactly been paying that much attention lately, I'm ashamed to admit.

"There was a car crash," she says at last, her voice neutral. "Three miles away from the church, on the mountain road. It broke the barrier, went right over the edge. The whole thing went up in flames. There was almost nothing left." She looks away, as if it's difficult for her to recount. "The worst part was that it landed in a wooded valley; no one even knew it was there for years. When they finally found it, there were the remains of a body in the car. A complete John Doe. Everything that could have identified him was long gone. It was a young man, that was about all they could deduce, with what they had left to work with."

Tess shivers beside me.

"That's horrible."

"It is." I can't even begin to process that. What a way to go. My heart goes out to whoever it might have been, but at the same time my exasperation is beginning to get the better of me. "But Rosie, we're supposed to be talking about *Ed*. You said that's what all this was about."

She stands her ground.

"We are talking about Ed."

"No, *you're* talking about some random body in a car," my voice is rising in frustration, the long, stressful evening having shortened my temper considerably. I jab a finger in the direction of the door. "*Ed* is out there, probably sinking Jägerbombs with Gran by now."

"You're right, he is." Rosie nods. "But also… he isn't."

I throw my hands up in the air.

"This is like talking to Mum! You're making no sense at all. I don't have the patience for this, Ro. I'm going home."

My hand is on the door handle before her shout stops me.

"Look!"

I turn slowly on the spot. Rosie's holding out her phone, an image filling the screen. Something in an evidence bag.

"Thrilling," I say dryly. "One of your work photos. Should you even be showing me that?"

"Just look at it," she snaps, pushing the phone closer to my face. "Don't you recognise it?"

I squint at it, wondering why the hell I'm even bothering to humour her. The habit borne from being a younger sister, I suppose.

"It's a watch," I conclude sullenly. "What of it?"

She stifles what sounds like a rather rude retort and instead swipes across the screen, flicking to the next photo. A close-up this time of the back of the watch. There's an inscription there, engraved in swirling script.

*To T from A*
*May luck be with you*
*18.5.43*

All of a sudden, I feel very cold. Freezing, in fact, as if all the blood has drained from my body. All I can do is stare at the photo in front of me, heart hammering against my ribs, breath stopped in my throat.

I'd know that inscription anywhere.

"It's Ed's watch," I whisper. The one he told me was a family heirloom, given to his grandfather during the war; in fact, it turned out he'd bought it from a pawn shop. Just another seemingly innocuous untruth which should have set alarm bells ringing. As it was, it just made me want to protect him, the boy without a family who made up stories about relatives he'd never known.

"It was thrown from the car in the blast," Rosie says, watching me carefully. The way I've seen her do with victims at work. Looking for signs that they're about to break down. "That's why it survived."

"But it can't be..." My mind is spinning. Now I really do feel sick. I close my eyes, willing my stomach to stop tossing and turning. "It must be a coincidence. Ed must have dropped it there, or someone stole it..."

Rosie shakes her head.

"I thought of that. So I turned to the skeleton. The collarbone had been broken in two places. Recently, too. Within the previous year."

Tess has been watching us both silently, mouth frozen open in shock. Now, though, she lets out a gasp of recognition.

Ed broke his collarbone six months before the wedding. He'd gone skiing with some uni friends, and, reckless idiot that he was, decided to go down a black run on his first attempt. He'd had to be airlifted off the side of the mountain. I was absolutely furious with him when I found out. It was one of the few times his careless attitude to life really frightened me.

A host of other facts come rushing towards me, things I'd long forgotten. Leo saying that Ed had taken everything, including his passport. Everything that could have identified him. The questionable hire car company Ed had booked with because he'd left his one job until the very last minute, as usual. I'm not even sure if they *were* a company, with hindsight. He just screeched around to the airport in this rusted old banger and told us he'd sorted it.

"I can't believe I'm really about to say this out loud," Rosie says at last, in a strange, faraway voice. "It's beyond crazy, but…"

"You think the body in that car was Ed," I finish, astonished by how bland the words sound, out there in the open. As if I'm relaying a particularly boring fact.

Rosie looks levelly back at me.

"Yes. Yes, I do."

"And so that man out there…" I gesture towards the door. "He's… what? A doppelganger?"

But I know he's not. We all know he's not. That's Ed, without a doubt. No one could imitate his particular idiosyncrasies.

Rosie shrugs helplessly.

"I didn't say it makes the first bit of sense."

Silence settles on the room. None of us really seem to know where to go from here. We've had so many conversations, the three of us, ranging from the sublime to the ridiculous. But nothing like this. Nothing even close.

And then a voice speaks from the far corner of the ladies' bathroom. A distinctly male voice.

"It appears I've got some explaining to do."

# Chapter Fifteen

We all whip around in unison. Ed's leaning against the closed door, watching us steadily.

"You… you can't be in here. It's the ladies'," I stammer, before cursing myself for making such a trite assertion. Of all the things I could have chosen to say first… but it was just instinctive, torn from my lips by rote. The sort of thing you say mindlessly when you've had a shock.

He raises an eyebrow in surprise.

"Does it really matter, I mean if he's…" Tess blurts out, then blushes as she turns to Ed. "I mean, er, if *you're*…"

Apparently, she can't quite bring herself to utter the word.

Rosie's uncharacteristically silent. I can practically see her engaging that forensic brain of hers, trying to piece it all together, working out how best to gather the facts.

At least someone's managing to keep a coherent head, I

think dazedly. I feel like I'm floating, far up above all of this. As though it couldn't possibly be real.

I mean, it *can't* possibly be real, can it? Surely, this has all got to be some kind of sick joke. That would be just like Ed. He always thought everything was one big jest. It never occurred to him that it might sometimes be wildly inappropriate, even poor taste. I used to find it mortifying when we were together, and…

The thought hits me in a rush, lighting up the room.

Of *course* it's all just a prank! That's the only explanation. How could I have been so ridiculous as to think otherwise? Too relieved to feel truly irritated, I look around the room, expecting a camera man to leap out of a cupboard and capture our shocked faces. I can see it all now; Ed will burst out laughing, his face creasing into dimples the way it always does when he finds anything utterly hilarious. And I… well, I'll laugh along, won't I? Pretending I never believed any of it for a moment. That I was just playing the game.

And pray I can pull it off. It'd be too embarrassing otherwise.

I look at Rosie. She's folded her arms, staring at Ed with a furious expression. She's doing a great job, I think approvingly. Who knew she was such a good actress? I would never have guessed that she was just stringing him along. But of course, she probably worked it all out long before I did. If she's willing to play to the conclusion, then I'll follow her lead.

I mean, it *might* have been nice if she'd given me a

heads-up, I have to say. But I can see why she didn't, I guess; she knows I'm a terrible liar. She probably thought I'd give the game away.

I turn back to Ed, trying to keep my face serious. But, feeling ebullient and a little bit emboldened, I can't resist a subtle dig.

"Should you really be revealing yourself to those of us on the mortal plane?" I quirk an eyebrow at him. "Isn't there some sort of celestial rulebook prohibiting that sort of thing?"

To my surprise, his face falls dramatically.

"Yes, as it happens, there is. I'm going to get into huge amounts of trouble for this."

I try not to roll my eyes. Does he really expect me to buy this rubbish?

"You," he jabs a finger at Rosie, a scowl darkening over his eyes. That surprises me. I know he's acting but I could swear he looks genuinely upset. "Why couldn't you have just left it alone? You always were frustratingly meddlesome."

"And *you,*" Rosie snaps back, colour high on her cheeks, "always were stupidly careless."

I look between them, starting to feel anxious. They really do look angry with one another; I haven't heard them bicker like this in years. It's probably time I broke it up.

"Okay guys, you can give it up now." I hold up my hands in a mollifying gesture. "It was a good joke. I'll even admit you almost had me for a minute. But let's not take it too far, shall we?"

They both stare at me as if I'm completely and utterly mad. Suddenly, I feel cold, the first stirrings of doubt beginning to rear up in my mind.

"Belle?" Tess lays a soft hand on my arm, peering at me with concerned green eyes. "I... I don't think they're joking."

"Of course they are." My voice sounds as though it's coming down a long tunnel, several seconds' delay between the words leaving my lips and resounding in my ears. "They have to be. Because if they're not, then it means..."

I try to drag in a breath but it's not working. I can't seem to get enough air.

Rosie's head whips around. She looks blurry at the edges. I narrow my eyes, trying to bring her into focus.

"She's about to go," she says shortly. "You'd better stand behind her, Tess."

"I'm not—" I try to protest, but it's already too late. The black spots are obscuring my vision, dancing ever faster.

I sway towards the floor and everything goes dark.

---

When I come to, I'm lying on the chaise longue at an awkward angle, my arm twisted underneath me, legs akimbo over the side.

"She's awake," Tess trills from where she's perched on the velvet upholstery next to my hip.

I struggle into a semi sitting position, wincing as pain throbs through my shoulder socket.

"You didn't catch me, then?"

"I did *try*," Tess says, a touch defensively. "But you sort of… fell on me."

"Like a tranquilised rhinoceros," Rosie adds descriptively. "Practically flattened her."

I swallow a groan. What an image. Evidently I'm not a graceful, Austen-esque sort of swooner. More like a bulldozer taking down everything in my path.

As if I'm not already humiliated enough.

"Next you'll tell me that it took both of you to get me onto here." I pat the seat next to me with my good arm. That's not something I particularly want to envisage, either. Being hoisted like a sack of potatoes. Perhaps I should start going to the gym with Rosie in the mornings like she's always badgering me to.

"Oh no, Ed did that."

Following Tess's gaze, I whip around to find Ed seated at my other side. Instinctively, I recoil; for a few seconds, I'd forgotten he was here. Or maybe I'd half hoped I'd imagined it all.

Except, I know I didn't. Just like I didn't imagine what I saw that night at Greyfriars Kirkyard, all those years ago. Over a decade now, without a single further supernatural experience, and yet the one was enough to make me sure, without a doubt. Haven't I been secretly carrying around the knowledge for years, resigning myself to the fact I would never find out for certain? Not even *wanting* to know, really.

If I believed in fate like Tess, I might even say that

sighting in my teens was put there deliberately in order to prepare me for this moment.

"There's no need to look quite so horrified," Ed murmurs, sounding hurt. "I thought you'd prefer not to wake up on the floor, that's all."

"No, it's not that, it's just…" The thought of Ed scooping me up into his arms, of being pressed against his chest… the intimacy of it sends an involuntary tingle across my skin. "Thank you," I manage stiffly. "You didn't have to do that."

"No worries," he says quietly, sidling me a meaningful glance. "I kind of owed you one of those anyway."

My chest squeezes as I catch his meaning. The motion of picking me up and carrying me over the threshold was one we'd joked about practising but never did. He'd said it should only be done once.

Now, finally, it's happened, but six years too late. Too late in so many other ways, as well. In the most fundamental way there is. The thought sends a fresh wave of shock reverberating through me, locking every muscle in my body.

"I think we should leave you two alone," Tess says suddenly, already beginning to rise to her feet. "You need to talk." She inclines her head towards the door, blonde hair gleaming under the spotlights. "Come on, Ro."

My head jerks up and I stare at her in horror. Wait… they're going to *leave* me?

"What?" Rosie splutters, apparently equally dismayed. "No way. I have so many questions—"

"And you can ask them," Tess says calmly. For once, she's the only one *not* losing her head; in fact, she hardly seems fazed at all. But then, I suppose this is her field; she has all sorts of strange belief systems. "Later. I'm sure Ed understands that he has a lot of explaining to do – to all of us." She gives him an unexpectedly stern look. "Don't you?"

Ed, looking utterly wrongfooted, just nods mutely.

"And he knows that if he says anything to upset Belle then he'll have both of us to deal with," Tess continues, in a honeyed voice. "Isn't that right, Ed?"

"Er..." Ed tugs his collar away from his neck before offering a wavering, "Yes?"

"Good." Tess shoves Rosie towards the door with less than her usual gentleness. "We'll be just outside, Belle. Shout if you need us."

Rosie looks like she's about to protest rather hotly, but Tess gives her another sharp push in the small of the back and they're out of sight.

I watch them go with no small sense of trepidation. The desire to leap up and rush out after them, to go back to the party with its colour and sound and people and the sense of safety a crowd brings, is almost overwhelming. But my head is still swimming; I doubt I could get up right now if I tried, and even if I could, I know that would be a mistake. Because Tess was right, as she almost always is. We *do* have to talk about this. And for once I can't hide behind other people, behind the safety net of our trio. They've always been there to protect me; Rosie rather more loudly than

Tess, granted, but the effect has been the same. But this… this, I really do have to do on my own.

An awkward silence has settled upon the small room. I clear my throat.

"So…" Where do I begin with this? What precedent is there for this kind of conversation? "You really *are* dead?" I hedge, as though hoping he might suddenly slap a hand to his forehead and pronounce that it's all been a misunderstanding. "You're really… you know, *sure*?"

He fiddles with a tassel on the edge of the seat.

"I'm afraid so. It's not a state which is easily confused with other things."

"But… you *can't* be." I insist. I'm still really struggling to accept this. Even though my heart whispers that it's true, my logical mind is in overdrive, telling me there must be some other explanation. "You're *here*," I conclude, lamely.

He looks up at me then, as though surprised.

"The two aren't mutually exclusive, you know."

"But I can *see* you," I persist. I know there are a lot of emotions I should be feeling right now; I can feel them, boiling beneath the surface. But I can't even begin to open the lid on them now. Instead, I force myself to focus on the more immediate practicalities. Fortuitously, I find I have a *lot* of questions I want answering; they crowd the front of my mind, blocking out everything else. "And so can everyone else. How is that possible, if you're…?" I frown, a new thought striking me. "What exactly are you, anyway? A phantom? A poltergeist? A *ghoul*?"

He visibly shudders at my final suggestion.

"I prefer apparition, if we really must employ terminology," he says primly.

I have to fight the urge to roll my eyes.

"Fine. Whatever. But how does it work?" I stand, feeling bolder, and prod his arm with a finger. It feels completely solid. Not exactly warm, now I'm making a study of it, but not cold either. Sort of weirdly ambient. Either way, not like I'd expect a ghost to feel.

He sits there patiently, letting me poke him. It's only when he winces slightly that I draw away, feeling instantly embarrassed. Here I am, manhandling him like he's a waxwork exhibit. Although, in truth, it's hard to see him as anything other than human. He's nothing like the apparition I saw that night in the cemetery. He still looks so… alive, for want of a better term.

*Too* alive. I fold my arms, narrowing my eyes at him.

"If you really *are* a ghost—"

"Apparition," he interrupts doggedly.

"Then how come you felt that?" I demand, ignoring his protest entirely. "I know you did; I saw you wince."

Apparently he's been expecting this question, because he hardly misses a beat.

"Because I'm supposed to be undercover. The powers that be up there don't want anyone working out what I really am; when that's happened in the past, it's caused pandemonium." He raises an eyebrow. "All of those ghost sightings are testament to that, the stories don't ever seem to go away. This city is about the worst reminder of it they can get – a whole trade built around past mistakes, tours raking over every slip-up." He shakes his head. "They try to be more careful these days. If I seem very human, it's because I'm supposed to blend in with the rest of you. So I can send texts – as you've discovered," he adds, with a self-deprecating smile. "And I can drink tea, and yes, even feel pain."

It's quite a neat explanation; I have to admit that it does make sense.

And yet… something nags at me.

"That can't be it, though, can it?" I blurt out. "I mean, how did you get in here, for one thing? How did you disappear into thin air that day in the flat? There must be more."

He's not telling me all of it, I realise. It's like it always was, him picking and choosing which pieces of himself to share. Well, it's not like that, not anymore.

He looks shifty.

"I can't… it's against the rules."

"What about this isn't?" I shoot back. "I think I deserve the whole truth. It's the least you can give me now."

He still looks defiant, but as I continue to stare at him challengingly, he deflates with a sigh.

"Oh, fine. I'm already in trouble anyway; you might as well see the rest."

Before my very eyes, he appears to be fading, becoming more and more translucent until he's just a watery form. I can only watch, struck dumb, as he begins to return, his colours growing brighter until I can't see the wall through him anymore.

I blink several times, making sure my eyesight really is working. But no, he looks completely normal again. And not a little bit smug.

"How…?" I manage faintly. I think I need to sit down. Luckily, the chaise longue is still right behind me and I sink onto it, my legs having lost all desire to function. It's one thing listening to someone tell you that they're a ghost; it's another thing believing them, but it's something entirely and indescribably different to see the evidence of it with your own eyes.

"It's kind of like a dimmer switch," he says, fading in and out as he speaks as though to demonstrate. I can hear the excitement in his voice; clearly, he's been desperate to show someone this. He always was fascinated by how things work. "I can become as solid or as invisible as I like. It's really rather ingenious. When I'm in 'human' form, as I suppose we ought to term it, you'd never know I wasn't one of you. But when I'm like this…" he fades into a smudge of colour. "I can move about as I please." He swipes an arm though my head with an impish grin.

I shudder. Even though I couldn't feel it, I still feel pretty violated.

"Do you *mind*?" I say testily. "Keep your arm to yourself."

His mouth drops open. It would almost be comical in any other situation.

"Wait… you saw me do that?"

"Of course I did."

"You can *hear* me too?" He frowns thoughtfully. "That's

interesting." He says the word 'interesting' in such a tone that I'm in no doubt that he what he really means is 'inconvenient'. I get the sense that I've ruined his fun, somehow. "Although I suppose it *does* make sense that you'll always be able to see me even when others can't. I am haunting you and all of that."

I elect to say nothing. I'm not sure how I feel about being haunted. And I daren't ask what 'all of that' might be.

"That's not even the best thing." Suddenly, he's animated again, his boyish enthusiasm overtaking his sense of pique. "I can pop up—" he disappears, materialising over by the door, then disappears again, "—anywhere I want. It's great fun."

"Will you stop that?" I groan, as he materialises to my right. "It's making me feel nauseous. Can't you just… sit down for a second?"

"Oh, right." He suddenly looks a bit sheepish. "Yes, of course. Sorry. This must be a lot for you to absorb. I kind of take it for granted by now."

He flings himself down next to me on the sofa with such barely suppressed energy that the seat cushion bounces up and down. It doesn't exactly help with the nausea. I dig my fingers into the upholstery, trying to breathe deeply. There are still about a million questions which need asking, but right now I only have the strength left for one. And it's a big one.

"Ed, I need you to answer me honestly. Have you been watching me all these years?"

The thought makes my skin crawl with embarrassment.

In a way, I'd rather not know. But at the same time, I have to ask.

He looks at me steadily. I get the impression he's trying very hard to sit still and, as usual, failing dismally. His feet are tapping against the floor in a miniature jig.

"No. Not because I didn't want to," he adds hastily, as though worried I might take offence. "But what I told you the other day, about not being able to come back… well, it was true. Just not for the reasons you probably thought. Until I they sent me down here a week ago, I honestly had no idea how you were doing."

I'm so busy basking in the relief that he hasn't been witness to some of my more mortifying moments that it takes a moment for the ramifications of what he's just said to come home to me.

"Hang on… a week?" A memory races to the front of my mind: sitting in a café, the conversation dissolving into white noise as I was gripped by the overwhelming feeling of being observed. But when I looked up… "That *was* you! You *were* watching me!" I yelp accusingly. "When I was having lunch with Leo."

He has the grace to look faintly chagrined.

"Ah yes, well, I might have done a little light observation. To find out how the land lay before I made my entrance. But that was it," he adds quickly, as my expression darkens. "I promise. Nothing more."

I'm not sure whether to believe him or not. I suppose I'll have to take his word for it; I don't exactly have much choice anyway. "You said that *they* sent you," I begin haltingly. "Who exactly…"

But he's already shaking his head.

"I can't tell you everything, Belle. I've already said too much as it is. But never mind," he continues in a rallying voice as my face falls in disappointment. He puts an arm around my shoulders and gives me a reassuring squeeze. "You'll find out for yourself someday. We all do. No escaping it. It may even be sooner than you think."

How consoling. I choke back something which could either be a sob or a hysterical bubble of laughter; alarmingly, I'm not even sure which.

He gives me a strange, wary look.

"Are you… all right?"

Am I all *right*? Is he *serious* right now?

"No, I am not all right!" I snap shrilly. Suddenly, the sheer scale of it all overwhelms me; my brain feels in very great danger of bursting right out of my skull. I'm beginning to see why people have mental breakdowns after supernatural encounters. I feel like I've been shaken upside down and dropped into a parallel universe, where nothing's quite the same. And the worst of it is that it never will be again. "What are you even *doing* here?" I ask hopelessly, my eyes prickling with angry, despairing tears. "Why *now*?"

"I don't know," he says simply.

My head shoots up. Suddenly, I don't feel like crying any more. Instead, I stare at him in consternation.

"What do you mean, you don't know?"

He shifts awkwardly.

"Bureaucracy doesn't only exist in the last of the living, Belle. I have no idea where the order came from. No briefing or anything. All I know is that for years I've been requesting to come and visit you and they wouldn't allow it. They kept finding other things for me to do. But then suddenly..." He shrugs. "To be honest, I'm as much in the dark as you are about all of this."

I surge to my feet, too wired and jittery to possibly stay still while I process this latest development. I take three paces forward then stop and whirl back to face him.

"So let me get this straight." I utter each word slowly, not wanting there to be any room for misinterpretation. "You're telling me that neither of us has any idea what you're doing here?"

He shrugs helplessly.

"Sorry, no."

"And presumably you're stuck here until you've accomplished whatever you need to do," I persevere.

He scratches his head, looking up at a painting on the wall.

"I presume that's the sort of thing. I don't know. Like I said, I've never done this before."

It crosses my mind to enquire what exactly he *has* been doing for the past six years, but now isn't the time. It's hard enough to keep him on topic as it is. He has all the concentration span of an eight-week-old cocker-spaniel puppy.

"Okay." I massage my temples the way Tess taught me

to when things are getting to me. "So that means…" I take a deep breath, then release it. "I don't know what that means," I conclude hopelessly.

"I think it means…" he gives me a sideways look. "You're not going to like this. I'm warning you now."

My heart sinks like a stone.

"Go on."

"We're stuck together." He regards me levelly. I can't tell how he feels about the idea. "For as long as it takes."

"So, what? A week, a month, a year, or even…" I fall silent, unable to voice the rest, but we both know how the sentence ends.

Forever.

## Chapter Sixteen

It's on Sunday morning that it really hits me. I wake up, staring at the familiar hairline crack in the ceiling, the sunlight streaming through the sash window. For a few minutes I lie there nestled in my duvet, blissfully unaware of anything except the fact that I'm warm, and that my alarm isn't blaring at me, and I'm so comfortable that I could easily turn over and go back to sleep.

Although, now I mention it… I flex my toes experimentally and wince as pain lances through them. The kind of ache that only comes after an evening spent in killer heels. Where *was* I last night? It takes a good few seconds for the answer to reach me.

Oh yes, Rosie's party. Lots of champagne. Pink dress. Ed—

I sit bolt upright, the edge of the duvet still clutched in my hands.

Oh my God.

Oh. My. *God*.

There's a knock on the door and Rosie enters, mug in hand.

"I brought you some tea."

I just stare at her.

"Last night… Ed… he's a…"

"Ghost, yes." She sets the tea down on the nightstand, outwardly calm, although I notice that the colour has gone from her face. "Obviously, we weren't imagining things that night when we were teenagers. They really do exist."

"You remember that?" I thought she'd forgotten it, dismissed it as nonsense. I thought it was only me who still secretly wondered.

"Even I couldn't erase something like that from my memory." Rosie sits on the edge of the mattress. "It really scared me at the time."

"I didn't know that." She never mentioned it again; I suppose I thought… but now I see that maybe she was just trying to protect me, to be strong for both of us, like she always does. I pick up my tea as a displacement activity and stare into its amber depths. "But I mean… *Ed*. He died. In that awful, lonely way." I realise that my hands are trembling so much that the tea is in danger of sloshing over the rim. "And I wasn't there. None of us… we weren't *there*, Ro." My voice is rising in anguish.

Last night I was so consumed by the practicalities, and he seemed so cavalier about it all, so healthy and full of life, not a mark on him. It was easy, I suppose, to forget what lay behind it. But now, in the light of morning, it all comes sweeping in. Guilt, anger, sorrow… like a tsunami, crashing over me, threatening to drown me completely.

"I know." Rosie prises the cup gently from my fingers and puts it safely out of the way, pulling me into a tight hug. "I know, believe me."

I know what she's thinking, even if she won't say it. She's wondering if we were wrong not to look for him. If we should have tried harder. If she should have let *me* try, like I wanted to. If what she's told herself was for the best all of these years was actually a terrible mistake.

Of course, she thinks I don't know any of this. She doesn't realise how well I can read her thought processes. She still thinks she can protect me. She'll carry it around inside her, a silent burden, something else to feel responsible for.

---

I spend the rest of the day under the duvet, sobbing my heart out. Grieving both for what happened and for what can never be. For what, in truth, perhaps I always knew could never be. Whatever impression I might have given Rosie, there was never any need for her to be alarmed. I could never have gone back to Ed, not after everything. Missed him, yes. Dreamed about him, certainly. Loved him, absolutely. But been *with* him? Picked up where we left off, as though none of it had happened? No. I couldn't have done it to myself. Something irrevocable was shattered that day outside the church in Cyprus, a trust which could never be repaired. And without trust, love is nothing. It's empty, lost.

And eventually, through the haze, I begin to see that the problem is the same as it ever was. That Ed was always lost to me. That the ghost of past love has been haunting me for six years, a broken component in my heart, unable to be either realised or extinguished. Trapping me in an endless cycle.

By the time Monday morning rolls around, I'm wracked dry, hollow with fatigue and spent emotion, but the worst of it is out of my system. I get up mechanically, get dressed for work, put on far too much makeup in an attempt to disguise my pale face and sunken eyes. I get on the tram into the Old Town, walk down the Royal Mile towards the office, telling myself that I can do this. That I've been doing this for years. I'm a Delphine. My childhood was lived on constantly shifting sands; nothing ever stayed the same for long. I learned very young how to adapt to sudden change. You get good at accepting things, at not looking back.

People coming, people going, homes changing, schools changing, engaged then not engaged, phantom ex-fiancés popping up left, right, and centre… What's the difference, I think, with an attempt at dark humour. It's just something else I have to try and take in my stride.

Because that's my thing, apparently. The phrase has bounced around me like an echo throughout my life, from teachers to relatives to well-meaning acquaintances. "Oh, Belle will be all right. She takes things in her stride." After I came back from Cyprus, it seemed to pop up in every conversation. I suppose people didn't really know what else to say. I'm not sure what I'd say to someone who was jilted, even now, even having been there myself. Nothing seems right in that situation. I definitely didn't *feel* like I was taking it in my stride. But everyone else wanted me to, so very badly. They were desperate for me to be okay. So I obliged; or at least, I pretended to. I didn't want to let anyone down.

And I can't let anyone down now, either. Whatever my feelings about the whole thing, I have to try and push them to the back of my mind, because the alternative is hiding under my duvet for the rest of the year. I saw Rosie and Tess's worried faces when I sloped out of the flat this morning – I owe it to them not to fall apart. I owe it to Steve to be here, getting on with my job, in my own fashion at least.

And there's something else, someone else, who I know I need to speak to. I need to clear up this misunderstanding between us. I can't bear to let it continue.

Nate's not at his desk when I walk in and I breathe a small involuntary sigh of relief. Despite all my claims of readiness, I wouldn't mind a moment to prepare. Rosie always says that one can never be too prepared. Usually I wouldn't entirely agree – see wedding planning that would have any self-respecting fascist regime weeping at their own inadequacies – but in this case, I'm more inclined to concur.

I sidle into my seat, keeping my head down. The last thing I want is for Steve to notice me and start bellowing instructions, not just yet, anyway. Flipping open my compact mirror, I check my makeup, feeling a lurch when I see the apprehensive violet eyes which are reflected back at me.

With everything else I've had to deal with over the past few days, a minor misunderstanding with Nate should barely even register in my mind, let alone be gnawing away at me like this. I'm telling myself it must be my conscience working overtime. There's no other way to explain it.

With a shaking finger, I smudge along my cheekbone, where I've been somewhat over-zealous with the highlighter.

All right, so maybe not *quite* so minor when you throw in the whole ghostly angle. But Nate doesn't know about that anyway, so we can ignore that for now.

Other than that… well, it was just one *little* omission. Now that he's had time to cool down, he'll be feeling more forgiving, surely? I'm sure if I just explain to him that whatever happened between us, however confused my feelings might have been at the time – however confused they still *are* – I certainly never meant to use him. He'll be able to understand that, won't he? And then maybe we can begin to return to something approaching normal.

I begin to dust powder over my face, feeling distinctly more robust as I continue my new train of thought.

Nate's not the type to hold a grudge, I reason to myself. He's one of the most level-headed people I know. He'll probably walk over here, with his most engaging smile, and…

"You're late, you know," Darren says sourly, from the desk to my right, breaking into my introspection.

I glower at him. I was having important thoughts, can the man not tell? Does he have no sensitivity at *all*?

I watch as he scratches behind his ear with a pencil, then inspects the resulting bounty with interest. I give an inward shudder.

No, he definitely doesn't. He really is beyond hope.

"Hardly," I roll my eyes towards the clock above the door. "It's two minutes past."

"Still late," he chirps, making a note with the offending pencil. "It's going in the log book."

He looks utterly thrilled. It's quite revolting.

"What log book?" I ask, cursing myself even as I do so. What is *wrong* with me? Why am I prolonging this conversation? "I thought you were in charge of health and safety, not—"

"It's a new initiative," he says crisply, stroking a finger lovingly down the page. "To keep better tabs on everyone. Some people," he gives me a sharp look, "have had a tendency to abuse the system. Don't think it wasn't observed that you had two lunch breaks last Tuesday."

He really is insufferable. I reply with forced sweetness.

"That was a work project. Nate and I are writing a story together."

"Are you?" He leans forwards, his eyes glinting behind his wire-rimmed glasses. "Because we haven't seen much evidence of it."

I shift backwards as subtly as I can. I'm more alarmed by

his use of 'we' than anything. Why is he referring to himself in the plural? I'm pretty sure no one else is party to this madness. Who else would bother to lurk around spying on people, for one thing?

"It's still in production," I say coolly. "We're trying to keep it quiet for the time being."

"Oh, yes?" He smirks, lounging back in his chair. "I'm sure you are. Steve wouldn't be too thrilled if he knew the truth, would he?" He clicks his tongue. "Junior and senior reporter… might be considered a conflict of interest, wouldn't you say?"

Something cold trickles through me. Even though I suspect he's fishing more than anything, it doesn't stop my heart from beating faster. Because he has a point, even if it is a loathsome one. In a way, Nate is sort of my boss. Not directly, but still. I can practically hear the whispers of favouritism even now, every time he okays one of my articles with minimal editing, or gives me a byline. It won't matter that we only went on one date, that nothing even really happened between us. It won't matter that Nate has a reputation for honesty which has never been questioned before. In a competitive world like journalism, it'll suit a lot of people to believe it.

I lunge out of my chair.

"Give me that book."

I want to see what insidious things he's been writing, if nothing else. But he's too quick for me. He scrabbles for it, clutching it to his chest just as my fingers find purchase. I cling on to the corner which is in my possession and tug. He tugs back.

"Get off. It's private."

"How can a company log be private?" I snap. "I have a right to see what's in there, especially if it's libellous nonsense."

He looks deeply offended.

"It's painstakingly researched, I'll have you know."

"Sneaking around the office eavesdropping on other people's conversations is *not* research!" I retort, still refusing to let go. "It's just a pathetic attempt to create trouble, and —agh!"

The page has torn off in my grasp, sending me toppling backwards into my chair in an inelegant heap.

"You ruined it!" Darren inspects the mangled book with dismay. "Must you cause chaos wherever you go? Is *nothing* sacred?"

That seems a bit melodramatic, even by my standards. Anyone would think I'd just smashed a priceless Ming vase. Then again, I wouldn't put it past myself, the way things are going at the moment.

"You started it," I groan, rubbing my elbow, which is smarting from its encounter with the edge of my desk.

Darren doesn't come back with a snarky reply, which I think is a bit odd. Then I notice that a shadow has fallen over my desk.

Reluctantly, I look up, and Nate's standing there, wearing a decidedly unfriendly expression.

## Chapter Seventeen

My heart plummets all the way down to my lilac soles. First impressions are not looking promising.

"Nate," I fix a smile upon my face, hoping it doesn't look too stretched. "I—" I hesitate, glancing across at Darren, who's making a good pretence of frowning at his screen as though engrossed in work. Not that I believe it for a moment; he's listening intently, I can tell. I really don't want to have this conversation in front of him. But I have to say *something*. I hover, wracked with indecision, wondering how many seconds can trail by before the end of a sentence has to be given up for lost.

As it turns out, I needn't concern myself. Nate seems to be in no such quandary. He slams a file down on my desk with what I deem to be unnecessary force.

"This needs proof-reading by tomorrow," he says crisply. "I want it back first thing."

His tone makes me wince. Okay, so he hasn't defrosted

quite as much as I'd hoped. But no matter, I was prepared for something like this. I gear myself up to deliver a patented Belle Delphine charm offensive.

"Nate?" I say, in my most sing-song voice.

He's already half turned away, but he stops, then, very slowly, turns back around.

"Yes?" he says, in a tone that could make the Sahara desert freeze over.

I offer him my most engaging smile. The one which has got me out of more detentions and speeding tickets than I can count. It never fails me.

"Can we talk?"

He gives me a hard look.

"I don't think so."

Then, without another word, he marches off. I stare after him, my mouth dropping open in shock.

Wait… he can't do *that*, can he? He can't just go around delivering cutting remarks and then stalking off like a villain in a gothic novel. Not when I'm trying to make things better, trying to *explain*. I mean, surely there's some sort of etiquette in these situations?

Next to my elbow, my phone starts to ring. Biting back a curse of frustration, I snatch up the offending device without even looking at the screen.

"Yes?" I fume, then immediately hope it's not a professional call.

"Aren't you going to go after him?" Ed's voice barrels down the line, making me jump.

"Where…" I begin to whirl around, but he speaks again.

"Don't do that. You'll look completely bonkers. I'm over here."

Turning my head slowly, I spy him in the corner, a translucent, shimmering shape behind the water cooler. At least he's had the presence of mind not to turn up in human form, I think, with a small rush of consolation. That really *would* have put the cat amongst the pigeons. Then I do a double take at my own calmness, how practical my thoughts are. How come I'm not freaking out over this?

The answer comes to me almost immediately. *Because you're relieved, that's why. Because it proves you weren't imagining things at all. You haven't been going insane these past ten years, believing in something that doesn't exist.*

"What are you doing here?" I hiss. I don't know what I expected to feel when I saw him again, but it wasn't this surge of hostility. I might have spent all of yesterday crying over his death, but somehow, in his presence, I can only remember why I'm angry with him. Dimly, I'm aware that it's probably irrational, even a bit unfair. But it's easier to be angry with him – for leaving me, for dying, for all of it – than the alternative, which is to drown in grief and regret. "This is none of your business."

"Technically, everything you do is my business, seeing as you're the reason I'm here in the first place."

Have I been spending too much time with him, or did that just make some vague sort of sense? I shake my head at myself. Never mind looking mad, I must be *going* mad. And no wonder, with everything that's been happening.

Besides, I thought ghosts were meant to just float about the place? I never realised they could be so… intrusive.

"Will you just go *away*?" I mutter furiously, turning away to cradle my hand across the phone, away from Darren's flapping ears. The last thing I need is to give him even more ammunition against me. "I'm handling this."

He just raises a sceptical brow.

"Oh, just…!" Truly irate now, and lost for a smart rejoinder, I stab the red button on my screen, cutting the call. I'll show him.

Tossing my phone aside, I stalk across the cracked linoleum floor towards Nate's desk.

"What, so you're not even going to hear me out?" I demand, drawing to a stop in front of him. I half consider smacking a palm down on the wooden surface, the way Steve does sometimes, but decide that's a step too far, so instead I just fold my arms mutinously. "That's just… *it*, is it?"

He rolls his chair forward, tapping his keyboard to bring his computer screen back to life.

"Yes."

He begins typing briskly, his gaze fixed on the screen.

I stare at him, torn between dismay and irritation. This is *not* how it was supposed to go. I knew he was upset with me, of course I did, but I thought…

I draw up short at that. What *did* I think? That he'd just forget about it? That he'd pretend none of it had happened? Maybe. Probably. That he'd give me a chance to talk him around, at the very least. But it seems that he's just going to shut me down.

"But—but that's not fair!" I stutter. I probably sound childish, but I'm beyond caring. I don't understand him; it's like he's not even interested, like none of it matters. I don't know how to get through to him when he's like this. He's not someone I recognise, and suddenly I'm hit by a wave of discombobulation.

Because Nate… well, he's a rock. Easy going, honest, ready for a laugh. When I turn up at work, no matter what else is happening, I can count on him always being the same. Always being there when I need him. I never realised how much I'd come to lean on that dependability until it's missing.

He just carries on typing as if he hasn't heard me.

"I think he's ignoring you," Ed's voice flutters the air next to my ear, sounding indignant on my behalf. He scowls at the top of Nate's head. "That's not on. I can pull his chair out from underneath him if you like. That'll get his attention." He's already edging towards it, one hand outstretched.

I shoot him a warning look. He retreats reluctantly, leaning back against the desk, absently flicking a pen out of his way. It skitters across the scarred wooden surface, and I hurriedly clamp my hand down upon it as Nate looks at it with a questioning frown.

Somehow he manages to avoid looking anywhere near me in the process, even though it requires him to turn his neck at a rather awkward angle. And suddenly I feel absolutely, furiously, exhaustedly fed up with the entire male gender. Suddenly, I'm done with trying to be the mature one. I've spent the past six years trying to rise above it all, to do the right thing, to keep my head down and get along. And look where it's got me. Why should I bother anymore, if this is the way they behave?

I perch pointedly on the edge of his desk.

"All right, well I'll just stay here then until you decide you're ready to speak to me again." Leaning across him, I pull open the top drawer and peer inside. "Do you have any biscuits?"

A muscle twitches in his lower jaw, but he doesn't respond. I feel a flash of vindictive triumph; I'm getting to him, then. Good.

"No, you don't seem like the sort of person who would," I say regretfully, nudging the drawer closed again. "Far too healthy. Have you ever wondered what everyone in this office would be if they were all turned into biscuits? Kind of their spirit biscuit, if you will. Like a spirit animal."

Ed looks highly entertained by this notion. Unsurprisingly, Nate doesn't.

"Darren would be a fig roll," I decide swiftly, before turning to look through the glass into Steve's office, tapping a finger thoughtfully to my lips. "And Steve, he's a garibaldi. Old-fashioned and an acquired taste. Freya, now she'd be a pink wafer, I'm sure. And you…" I survey him for a moment, admiring his classical profile, the dark sweep of his lashes. "Actually, that's obvious. Amaretti, of course."

"Dry and bland and only palatable when dunked in liqueur?" Ed quips, his eyes hard chips of ice.

I move to kick his ankle under the desk, before realising there's no point as I'll just go straight through him. Instead, I turn back to Nate, eyebrows raised in question.

"What would I be, do you think? In my more fanciful moments, I'd like to say Viennese whirl, but perhaps that's ambitious."

"Jammy Dodger's more like it," Ed mutters.

I'm not sure how to take that, but at least I've got Nate's attention at last. He stops writing and glares at me.

"Belle," he says through gritted teeth, clearly trying to hold on to his temper. "Haven't you got something more pressing you could be doing? That work I just gave you would be a start."

I open my mouth to make a suitable retort then realise that for once, I don't have one. Damn. My eyes rove the room, landing on Darren, who's tending to the spider plant on the edge of his desk with such rapt devotion that it could almost be endearing. In anyone else, that is. In any event, it provides the inspiration I need.

"*This* is work," I point out, unable to keep the smugness out of my voice. "We have a story to write together, in case you'd forgotten. We can't very well do that if you're refusing to speak to me, can we?"

Now he's in a corner. Good hand, Belle. One point to me.

"The story's been canned," he says flatly. "I told Steve it had hit a dead end."

Or… not. I blink, confused.

"But… why?"

Finally, he looks at me.

"*This* is why, Belle." He gestures between us, the frustration palpable in his voice. "Clearly the two of us can't be professional… under any circumstances," he adds, lowering his tone. "We've got too close and it's not doing either of us any favours. I think it's better if we just stay out of one another's way."

It's like putting a sparkler in a bucket of water. All the fight in me fizzles out as he says those words, the adrenaline ebbing away to leave nothing but a kind of stunned, heavy resignation as it hits me that he really means it. I realise that for all my outward nerves, I really had thought I could smooth this over. That he might put on a show of being annoyed for a bit, but that would soon fade. I thought it was all a game. Now, looking at his resolute face, that seems so excruciatingly naïve and complacent.

"Oh," I stutter, dully. "Well, I mean… if that's really what you want, then…"

Something passes across his face, but suddenly, it feels too awkward to look at him, and I turn away before I get a proper glimpse of it.

I intend to go back to my desk but when I find my legs veering towards the door of their own accord I don't fight it. The cool, dingy quiet of the corridor greets me like a haven. I sag back against the wall, head tipped back, drinking in the air. Wondering what this dull ache in my chest might mean.

"Are you all right?" Ed materialises next to me, hands in pockets.

I shrug, aiming for a dispassionate air.

"I'll live."

"The guy's an idiot. You should have let me deal with him."

I can tell he's furious, despite the flat tone of voice and the casual posture. It surprises me; Ed rarely gets in a temper about anything. I turn my head to look at him, his watery outline flickering slightly like an old transmission on an analogue television. It's quite unsettling on the eye.

"He's not," I say wearily. "He's just… hurt that I didn't tell him the truth. He feels humiliated. Used. And maybe he's right to."

His eyes widen.

"What?"

A swell of frustrated emotion rises within me and I whirl on him, the nearest target.

"This is *your* fault," I poke him in the chest with a finger. It goes right through him and stubs against the wall. I draw back with a shudder; I'll never get used to that. "If it weren't for you, I wouldn't even *be* in this situation! What are you even here for anyway? I can't believe that you were sent down to actively ruin my life. I'm not that bad a person."

His expression sharpens at the unprovoked attack.

"If you must know, you're just about tipping the scales. I'd be a bit nicer to Darren if I were you. And stop cheating during the pub quiz. That might just help to land you in the right place at the end of it all."

There isn't much that can stun me into silence, but that does it. My throat works soundlessly for several moments. He claps a hand to his mouth, looking horrified.

"The… *right* place?" I manage at last. "You mean there really *is* a…"

"Yes, well, anyway," he interrupts hastily, with what I could swear to be a nervous glance up towards the ceiling. "Let's not get off topic. There's no need to turn on one another."

I'm almost tempted to push it, but the look on his face gives me pause. Perhaps it's best not to toy with powers beyond my understanding. With my luck, we'll probably both end up banished to some sort of celestial wilderness together for eternity.

There's a short, tense silence. He draws circles on the floor with his foot.

"I never wanted to ruin your life, you know," he says at last, in a small, hurt voice, and I immediately feel terrible.

"I know." I sigh, rubbing a hand across my forehead. "I'm sorry I said that." I shouldn't have taken it out on him. We're in this together, after all. He doesn't have any more say in his being here than I do. "And I'm sorry about… well, everything. I'm sorry that you're here, like this. I know you never chose to die." It's the closest I can get to expressing everything which has been crashing through me in the past thirty-six hours. "It's just… I feel like everything's been turned upside down. Even Nate's not the same, and I…" I trail off miserably, at a loss to express feelings I'm not even sure of myself yet.

Ed hangs his head like a schoolboy caught flicking ink at the teacher's back.

"I'll fix it," he mumbles into his collar. "I can make it better."

My head snaps up and I try not to look as horrified as I feel. Ed getting involved is absolutely the last thing that's going to help. Especially since his idea of tackling a problem tends to be heavy on enthusiasm and light on thought process.

"Ed, no. You don't need to—"

But he's not listening to me. Instead, his eyes are shining with new purpose.

"I'll make it up to you, I promise. Just leave it with me; I'm sure I can come up with something."

And then he vanishes into thin air, leaving me alone with the disquieting sensation that I might just have made yet another monumental mistake.

# Chapter Eighteen

"And?" Tess demands, swinging her endless legs over the edge of the lounger so she can stare straight at me. "You can't just stop *there*. What happened next?"

"Who says anything happened next?" I say evasively, flipping unseeingly through the magazine which I've been pretending to read since we got here.

Rosie lets out an unladylike scoff from the lounger to my left.

"Oh, all right," I throw the magazine aside irritably. "But you're not allowed to say *I told you so,*" I add, with a pointed glance.

She stretches out her toes to admire the shimmery lilac nail polish. Quite a bold shade for her, I have to admit. I was impressed. Usually when we go for a pedicure, I have to crowbar her away from the neutrals. But then, it does match her bikini perfectly, which I suspect might have swayed her choice.

It was Tess's idea to come to the spa this evening. She booked it a week ago, when we were still elbow deep in confetti cones and last-minute scrambles for the special licence. With her customary presentiment, she seemed to know that we would all need it. Somehow, she even managed to keep Mum out of it, by recruiting Gran into fabricating a WI meeting that she insisted she needed a lift to. To be honest, I think that's been the greatest gift of all; Mum has a way of sucking the relaxation right out of a gathering. Besides, I think we're all still a little raw after Saturday. Rosie hasn't said much on the subject. Leo broke the news to her in the end and I think he's managed to persuade her not to rock the boat so close to the wedding, but that doesn't mean she isn't stewing over it. Rosie can forgive, with time, but she doesn't tend to forget. She can bring up something I did in 1997 like it's a fresh wound.

Tess props her elbows on her knees and leans forward, blue eyes sparkling with expectancy, as though she's a child waiting to see a magic show. At least someone is getting some entertainment value out of my life, I think dully.

"Okay," I sigh, rearranging my towel so I can lean back comfortably. "It started when I got back to my desk after lunch…"

*I didn't even notice anything was wrong at first. I unlooped my bag from my shoulder, hung up my jacket on the lopsided coat stand as usual. But there was something… odd. A prickling of awareness across the back of my neck. I turned slowly, eyes scanning the room. Everyone was at their desks as usual, but there was a change in the atmosphere. Like a low buzz of expectation. And was I imagining it, or were people watching me out of the corners of their eyes?*

*I caught Freya staring at me then quickly pretending to examine her nails. Okay, so definitely not imagining things, then. I wasn't sure whether that was reassuring or not.*

*And then I saw them.*

*A colossal bouquet of red roses sat proudly on my desk. And when I say colossal, I mean it; when I sat in my chair, I couldn't even see around them. I reached for the card, which was pushed into the blooms at such a jaunty angle that it confirmed my suspicions that it had already been plucked out and—*

"Wait," Rosie interrupts, looking incensed. "They *read* the card? That's outrageous!"

"Aloud, too, I expect," Tess chirps. "They probably have an office-wide pool going by now."

"I should enter," I say drily. "Seeing as I have as little idea of what's going on in my life than anyone else."

"What did it say, then?" Rosie demands, sitting bolt upright, all pretence of relaxation forgotten. "On the card?"

"I'm getting to that," I say airily. "I'm just setting the scene."

"Never mind Ed, we'll all be dead ourselves by the time you get to the point," she mutters darkly, but settles back to listen.

*I flipped the card over between my fingers, my heart skipping in anticipation and nerves as I wondered who—*

"Nate?" Rosie's brow crinkles in consternation. As

predicted, it didn't take her long to prise the information out of Leo. She doesn't seem all that pleased by the news, but then, I imagine she doesn't entirely approve of the timing. And to be fair, she probably has a point; look at what a disaster it's turned out to be. "But that doesn't seem like his style at all. He's not the showy type. So who else—?"

"If you stop interrupting me, maybe I'll get the chance to tell you," I manage, through gritted teeth. The tinkling spa music isn't having a noticeable effect on her levels of patience, that's for sure.

*"Impressive, aren't they?" Ed's voice made me start. "You can't miss them."*

*"You certainly can't." An errant bud was tickling my cheek and I batted it out of the way in a daze. "What did you do, raid a florist's?" Another thought occurred to me. "Wait… how did you even* get *these? You didn't…"*

*"Of course not," he looked affronted at even the implication. "I bought them, Belle, like any normal person."*

*"But you're not a normal person," I persisted, albeit in an undertone. The roses were providing a sight barrier to the rest of the room, but the last thing I needed was for everyone to think I was talking to myself back here. "You're a ghost. Ghosts don't use money."*

"Of course they do." Tess interjects reasonably, winding her hair into a topknot on her head. "He explained this to you before, remember? If you're posing as a person, you have to be able to act like one. Otherwise it would just be suspicious. Shall we go in the hot tub, by the way? It's just become free."

Damn, but she's got a point, I brood silently as I trail after her. She seems to be much more au fait with this whole ghostly thing than I am. Why couldn't *she* be the one being haunted? Knowing her, she'd probably even enjoy it.

"While you were pondering the financial arrangements of the afterlife, did it not occur to you that a more pertinent question might have been *why* he was buying you flowers in the first place?" Rosie asks archly, once we're ensconced in the hot tub amidst the broiling bubbles. "And red roses, on top of everything. You don't even like them."

I make a show of fiddling with the lemon-yellow straps on my bikini.

"I did point that out," I yell at last, over the thundering of the jets, which seem to be increasing in ferocity with every passing minute. The truth is, that was the first thing I'd noticed, and I couldn't get past it in my mind. It seemed to blot out everything. Red roses; what was he *thinking*? Had he really paid such scant attention when we were together? The thought was unexpectedly painful, even after all of this time.

"And?" Rosie presses. "What did he say?"

*"I know that." He raised an eyebrow, looking faintly affronted. "Give me some credit, Belle. I'm aware I wasn't great at lots of things, but I never forgot stuff like that. Have you forgotten our first Valentine's Day?"*

I'd frozen as a memory came back to me out of the mist.

He'd had my room at university filled with pink roses while I was out at a lecture. Dozens and dozens of them, scattered across every surface, filling the beige, boxy space with colour and scent. It was the most romantic thing anyone had ever done for me. It still is.

How could I have forgotten that? I suppose that, after a while, I'd had to carefully pack away all of the wonderful things he did. It was just too difficult to remember them.

Aware that I'm lost in thought and Rosie and Tess are waiting expectantly, I pull my mind back into focus guiltily. There's a reason I didn't share that part with them; God only knows what Rosie would say if she knew that I'd been entertaining such soft thoughts.

*"Anyway," Ed shrugged. "Red roses make a better statement." He inclined his head towards the door, through which Nate had just entered, frowning down at his phone.*

*A shiver of horror went down my spine as it dawned on me what—*

"Oh, no!" Tess claps a hand to her mouth. At least *she's* getting into my story. "I've just seen where this is going."

Rosie shoots her a disbelieving look as if to say, *really?*

*I leapt to my feet, grabbing at the bouquet—*

"What were you planning to do with it?" Rosie asks incredulously.

"I don't know!" I retort. Honestly, no Booker Prize winning novelist had to put up with this sort of thing. "Hide it, I suppose."

"Brilliant." Rosie deadpans.

"It was too heavy anyway," I admit glumly. "My spindly arms couldn't lift it."

"I told you you ought to have come to Pilates with me," Tess admonishes gently.

*"Help me!" I hissed at Ed, who just looked confused by all the fuss.*

*"I am* helping. *Trust me, I know how the male mind works." He patted me on the shoulder. "Don't worry, I've got this. Just play along."*

*"Wait—" I lurched forward. I didn't even know what he was about to do, only that knowing him, it was probably about to make everything ten times worse than it already was.*

"Now you're just getting melodramatic," Rosie tuts. "It's like having Mum here."

Stoically, I ignore her.

*And then somehow, inexplicably, the card was sailing through the air, caught on an invisible breeze. I followed its progress in mute horror, watching as it whisked over Darren's desk and swirled around the ceiling fan before making its descent, eventually fluttering to the floor and landing right at Nate's feet.*

I'm rewarded with a gasp from Tess. Rosie just looks stony.

*I stopped breathing then and there. I was frozen, helpless to do anything as Nate bent down to pick it up, turning it over to read the script.*

*I closed my eyes with a sense of impending doom. The message unscrolled helpfully across my brain, reminding me just how damning the whole thing appeared.*

***I had a great time last night. Ed x***

Rosie throws up her hands, spraying water everywhere. "Finally!" Then, belatedly, it seems to hit her, and her face falls. "Oh, wait. That's *bad*. That's really bad."

That about sums it up, I fume silently. Bloody Ed. Usually you can't stem his tide of flowery waffle, and he chose that particular moment to employ brevity and get straight to the point. The very suggestive point.

I don't want to recall the way Nate's dark eyes scanned the words, then flicked up towards the monstrous bouquet before settling on me. A look flashed across his face, just for a second, but it was enough. I knew exactly what he was thinking, and in that moment, I felt like the worst person in the universe. I don't want to relay it to Rosie and Tess, either. It's too difficult to share, even with them.

"You don't have to tell us anymore," Tess whispers, scooting over to put an arm around my shoulders.

"There isn't much more to tell," I sniff morosely. "He just said…"

*"I believe this is yours." He stepped forwards to hand the card back to me, his face completely neutral.*

Rosie winces. Tess gives her a reproving look.

"Sorry," she murmurs, shuffling around to my other side. "It's just…"

"I know." It's oddly comforting being sandwiched here between them. "I tried to tell him it wasn't what it sounded like, but he just walked away. He didn't want to know."

"You can't really blame him, I suppose," Tess ventures.

The jets cut out, and she stretches across to push the button once more. "Think how it looks to him; he probably thinks this is some twisted romantic game between you and Ed, with him as a pawn in the middle."

I blink back sudden tears, hoping the steam obscures them. Usually it's Rosie who lays it out with such brutal honesty.

"Just my luck to get a guardian angel who manages to wreck my life rather than improve it," I moan, sinking deeper into the bubbles. "I know he means well, but…"

"Hmm." Rosie purses her lips and looks away. My heart sinks; that's never a good sign. Rosie gets her lip pursing directly from my grandmother and it inevitably precedes a very unwelcome revelation.

"What is it?" I sigh. She's going to tell me anyway; why prolong the suspense?

"I'm just not so sure that his intentions really are that beneficent, that's all."

Tess gives her a wide-eyed look.

"Why wouldn't they be? It's not like he can exactly have her for himself anymore, is it?"

My mouth drops open and chlorinated water floods in, making me splutter.

"I don't pretend to know his motives," Rosie replies primly. "But I *do* know that he likes nothing better than to make trouble. I can't imagine death has altered him that much. He doesn't exactly seem to have transformed into a paragon of virtue, does he? In fact, he seems exactly the same as he ever was, except with the unfortunate development of being able to disappear at will."

"What are you saying?" Tess's brow crinkles. "That he's on some secret, malevolent mission to ruin her life?"

"I'm just saying I don't trust him, that's all. And if I were Belle, I'd be on my guard."

"Ro, sometimes you do have to give people the benefit of the doubt."

There's a sharpness to Tess's tone which is unfamiliar.

"Not if they don't deserve it," Rosie shoots back, eyes flashing. "He left my sister at the altar. I'll never forgive him for that, dead or alive."

"I'm well aware of that. I was there too, in case you'd forgotten!"

I manage to regain my voice at last, having swallowed an unpleasant amount of frothy water.

"Will you both stop it?" I look between them in dismay. This is the closest thing to tension there's been between them for as long as I can remember, and I don't like it. The three of us have always got along, even when we don't agree. It's the one thing I've always been able to count on. "Look, I don't know what to think at the moment, okay? But I do think I have to trust him, to some extent at least." I sigh, brushing a damp curl away from my face. The steamy atmosphere always plays havoc with my hair. "I mean, what else can I do? I'm stuck with him, and him with me, until we work this thing out. I have to believe that he's on my side, even if sometimes he does have a funny way of showing it. But whatever I decide to do, I need you both to support me. I can't do this without you. Both of you together." I leave a weighty pause to let that sink in before concluding, "Okay?"

They just continue to glare at each other. Then Tess stands abruptly, water running down her turquoise swimsuit in rivulets.

"I think I'll go for a swim."

I watch as she dives seamlessly into the pool, barely rippling the glassy surface. She becomes little more than a blur, moving away beneath the water.

"What's got into *her*?" Rosie asks incredulously. "She isn't usually so touchy."

That's the understatement of the year, but at least she's noticed that something's amiss.

"I don't know," I say thoughtfully. "I haven't seen her drawing for ages, though. I think she's blocked."

"Creative types," Rosie says disparagingly, reaching for her towel. "They're all the same. No common sense. All over the place. It'll blow over before long. Everything in life does eventually."

"What about in death?" I joke weakly. She gives me a sharp, assessing look.

"Just be sensible, okay? I know it's not your forte, but—"

"Thanks very much! What kind of pep talk is this?"

"The kind you need." She wraps the towel around herself and stuffs her feet into a pair of white spa slippers, turning to look at me sharply. "Belle, this can't carry on. I think you know what you have to do."

I look back at her, alarmed.

"What do you mean?"

"I've got a few ideas." She tosses my towel to me. "Now get out of there. Turning into a prune's not going to improve anything."

At least there's one thing we can agree on.

## Chapter Nineteen

I soon find out what Rosie was so cryptically alluding to last night. I'm picking my way to the kitchen first thing in the morning to make some tea when she pounces at me from behind the door frame wielding a handful of garlic.

"Ro!" I squawk, as she starts attacking me with it. "What the hell are you *doing*?"

"Protecting you!" She retorts, rubbing it all over my bare arms as I try valiantly to fight her off. "You want to get rid of him, don't you?"

I slap her hand away as it advances.

"Who?"

"Ed, of course!"

I'm so astonished that I stop flailing and just stare at her. "Rosie, he's a ghost, not a vampire!"

That seems to give her pause. She draws back thoughtfully, garlic in hand.

"Oh, no. I suppose he's not. Good point."

"It might have been nice if you'd double checked that *before* you started covering me in garlic juice," I mutter, rubbing my sticky arms. Let's hope that a long hot shower and half a bottle of strawberry shower gel will be enough to negate any ill effects. "And what's all this about getting rid of him?"

"Surely you can see that you don't have any choice?" Rosie stares me down, hands on hips. "Well-meaning or not, Belle, I know what he's like. He'll ruin everything for you if you don't find some way to stop him."

I hesitate, feeling torn. In a way, I know that what she's saying is true. In fact, it's nothing I haven't entertained myself. I even caught myself starting to search 'how to get rid of a ghost' on my phone yesterday, before pangs of guilt made me hastily delete it.

You'd think the notion of having the love of your life by your side forever would be a dream come true. But, as I'm beginning to discover, it's not nearly as simple as that. Watching the havoc Ed's managed to wreak on my life in just a few short days has been a jarring shock to the system, but it's made me see things differently. Because it is *my* life, and although I've always dismissed it as a pale imitation of what I could have had, now I find myself feeling rather protective of what I've built. For the first time, I can see what has been there all along, things I took for granted which now, on the verge of collapse, seem incomparably precious.

And yet, just the thought of betraying Ed makes me go cold. How could I live with myself if I sent him away?

But then, as a sensible voice interjects, he never chose to get stuck here either, did he? He never chose this situation, any more than I did. And wouldn't it be doing him a favour, in a way, if I could release him from an eternity spent on earth trailing around after me?

Oh God, I don't know.

"It's not just Nate," Rosie presses. "If he carries on causing trouble like this, you could lose your job. I won't watch him take everything away from you." Her lips set in a thin line. "Not again. If I have to get rid of him, then I will."

My eyes widen.

"Ro…"

"Take this." She pushes a small vial into my hand, curling my fingers over it. "It's holy water. Sprinkle it over him when he's close enough. It ought to do the trick."

I almost say, "Like the garlic?" but manage to refrain. I look down at the bottle in my hand.

"Where did you even *get* this from?"

"Work. Don't ask," she adds, automatically, before I've even had a chance to open my mouth. "I took it a while ago. I had a feeling we might need it."

"Isn't that illegal?"

She shrugs.

"There was plenty of it," she says ominously.

And suddenly, I'm really glad I didn't ask.

"Morning, Belle!" Freya chirps, a resplendent vision in a denim mini-dress towering over my desk. "How are you today?"

I regard her with utmost suspicion. Never, in the entire time we've worked here together, has she ever so much as ventured a greeting. She's certainly never lowered herself so far as to enquire after my health.

"Fine," I say slowly. "What's up?"

Freya gives her hair a practised little toss, then wrinkles her neat nose distastefully.

"Has someone got garlic in here?"

"Don't think so." I move my chair subtly away from her, hoping she won't notice. "Maybe Darren?"

He's not here so I can safely blame him. Besides, he's just the sort of oddity who might keep a bulb of garlic in his desk.

"Anyway, I was wondering if you could just check this ad for me," she proffers a proof copy of the middle page of the paper. "How exactly do you spell 'susceptible'? Is it with an s *and* a c, or just an s?"

"Isn't that what the spell-checker's for?" I say drily. How stupid does she think I am? I ponder that for a second, then decide not to pursue it. I don't think I'll come out of it very well.

"Of course!" She gives a tinkly laugh which sets my teeth on edge. Frou Frou, who's curled up neatly in her new favourite position next to my keyboard, raises her head with a small, agitated growl. "But I don't always trust it. It's forever changing words to their American spelling without asking me."

"I don't think there is an American spelling for susceptible, so…" More in hope than determination, I turn back to my screen.

"Thanks so much. You're a star!" She beams, revealing a flash of white teeth. There's a pause, and I could swear that she's counting to five before she speaks again. "So, that guy who was here last week… he's your ex, is he?"

Here we go. Steeling myself, I smile at her politely.

"Yes, he is."

Evidently, news has spread. Perhaps not surprisingly, considering that this is a news room, I think, with a fatal sort of humour.

"He's cute." The next time I look up, Freya's lounging, cat-like, across the edge of my desk. My heart sinks. It doesn't look like I'm getting rid of her anytime soon.

"Yes, I could tell you thought so," I say blandly.

Irritation flickers across her face like a ripple across a pond, here and gone in the blink of an eye.

"Yes, well, if you weren't so *secretive…*" The tinkly laugh has a strained edge to it now. She edges away from Frou Frou, who's staring at her with hostility. "But anyway, I can forgive you for that, because as stands, it works out quite well from my point of view."

God, but she has good legs. I can't stop staring at them. How does she get them so *smooth*? Mine invariably have little missed hairy patches on the knees.

"Oh yes?" I murmur vaguely. I have no idea what she's talking about.

She must wax, I decide. She seems like the sort of woman who would wax. Alas, my pain threshold couldn't stand it. I can only just about bear to pluck my eyebrows, and even then Rosie has to hold me down.

"Because it means that Nate's free after all."

It takes me a second for the meaning of her words to sink in. Then I'm sitting bolt upright, staring at her. Legs couldn't be further from my thoughts.

"What?"

Manicured fingers flutter across her plumped lips, formed in an 'o' of shock.

"Oh dear, did I say too much? I mean, I just *assumed*… with the roses and everything…"

She did read the card. I knew it; I just *knew* it would be her. No one else would have the gall.

"So you won't mind if I, you know…" she raises an eyebrow meaningfully.

It's not a question. It's a notification.

"I…" I stutter.

*Yes, I bloody well do mind.*

The words spring onto my tongue, surprising me with their intensity, and it takes an effort to hold them back.

Frou Frou is on her feet between us, fur bristling protectively. I put a hand on her back, trying to soothe her.

"I've always known he had a bit of a thing for you." Freya's watching me with a gimlet eye. It's like being in the sights of a bird of prey, paralysing in its intensity. She's not half as air-headed as she makes out, I realise now. It's all an act, a means to lull you into a false sense of security while she weaves her web subtly around you.

"But I never got the impression that you felt the same, and now I see why. You and this ex of yours clearly have unfinished business," Freya continues in a honeyed voice. "So it's not like you could possibly *mind*, is it? I mean, that would just be horribly selfish and, well, unreasonable, wouldn't it?"

I'm engulfed by a sense of hopelessness as I realise she's well and truly backed me into a corner. Immediately, it becomes clear why she came over here, why she bothered to stage this rigmarole in the first place.

She's setting me up for a fall, I realise. Whatever I say will get back to Nate; she'll make sure of that. And what *can* I say? I have no claim over him, no right to stop Freya asking him out should she so desire. But if I give her the go ahead, it'll sound like I don't care. Like he was, as he already believes, only ever expedient.

Of course, there is another option, and that's revealing the whole truth. But that's not my truth to tell. I'm not even sure I'd get the chance to tell it; I'd probably be struck down before the words were out of my mouth. I don't think the powers that be would consider the salvation of my fragile fledgling relationship with Nate a valid reason for blowing open the secret of the afterlife.

And so I do the only thing I can do. I say nothing.

Which is hard. I mean, really, really hard. Because I *never* say nothing. I always have some sort of riposte. And she's looking at me with the most infuriatingly smug tilt to her lips, and it takes everything in my power not to reach out a hand and shove her right off the edge of my—

"Package for you, Delphine," Darren lobs a beribboned black box onto my desk, knocking my now cold cup of tea everywhere. Frou Frou jumps behind my monitor, barking madly. Freya springs away from the splash with a shriek. Unfortunately, given that I'm sitting down, I'm not nearly so mobile. Nor so lucky.

"Let's hope it's not breakable, shall we?" I say crossly, grabbing a fistful of tissues and scrubbing at the wet patch spreading across the front of my dress. At least I wore the royal purple today; it's dark enough to hide the stain.

"Another present!" Freya plucks the box out of a puddle of tea and holds it up for inspection. It's still dripping everywhere, but she's apparently too excited to notice. "How thrilling. I wonder what's inside?"

A flicker of disquiet runs through me. I haven't seen Ed since yesterday; he did one of his famous disappearing acts right after the wars of the roses – as I'm terming it in my mind – and despite my best efforts to summon him, he's remained stubbornly elusive. He's up to something, I just know it. I've been braced all day for the first signs of trouble. I'm not taking any chances with this.

"I'll open it later." I reach for it hastily, but she holds it aloft with a disappointed pout.

"Oh, *don't* put it away. I'm dying to see."

Honestly, does she have no shame whatsoever?

"It's private," I say, through gritted teeth. "I'd rather not—"

"Oh, we're just girls here," she smiles winsomely. "We don't need to be shy, do we?"

She tilts her head to the side as she says it, a disarmingly childlike gesture for a fully grown woman. She's like one of those girls at school who were sharpening their claws on you one moment, then the next all sweetness and light. And you were so bowled over by their charisma, so grateful to be noticed, that you could forgive them anything. But I'm not a teenager anymore, and I'm not so easily swayed.

"Even so, I'd rather have it back, thanks." I hold out my hand expectantly.

A small dent appears between her dark eyebrows.

"Oh. All right, then." She shoves it back towards me ungraciously, but as she does so, her finger gets hooked in the ribbon, which begins to unravel. I snatch at the box, but it's too late. Something slithers out and drops onto the desk.

"Is that…?" Freya's eyes are round, dancing with sheer delight. "*Underwear*?"

I stare at the crumpled heap on my desk. Red satin, black lace. And not a lot of either. On autopilot, I pick it up, between my thumb and forefinger, as if it's a piece of evidence. It's as bad as I feared. They're see-through. They're so skimpy there's barely any point to them. The only saving grace I can find is that they're not crotchless. Thank *God* they're not crotchless. I almost want to do a little dance of joy.

Hysterical laughter presses behind my lips. What a thing to celebrate. It just shows how dire my life has become.

Great, now I want to cry. Blood rushes to my head, singing in my ears, pulsing behind my eyes. My cheeks are burning; they're probably the same colour as the pants by now.

I am going to *kill* him, I vow silently. I don't care that he's already dead. I'll bloody *resurrect* him if I have to, just so I can have the pleasure of killing him all over again. And this time, it's going to be slow. Very, very—

"What the hell's going on over here?"

Steve's voice booms across the expanse of desks, making both Freya and me freeze.

"Er, nothing really," Freya twitters, moving not so surreptitiously away. Disassociating herself from the scene. I glower at her. Traitor. Whatever happened to *girls together*?

"My point exactly," Steve thunders, stalking over. "Don't you think I have enough trouble keeping this paper afloat without my female staff idling away time in frivolous chitchat?"

It's little wonder that he's been divorced three times.

"It's not only women who socialise, you know," I say hotly, throwing my hands up in exasperation. Sometimes, one needs to defend one's sex, even if it will make absolutely no difference whatsoever. I've been trying to educate Steve for years. As far as he's concerned, Emmeline Pankhurst was just a pesky woman who liked to wear green and purple. "Men are equally capable of…"

I trail off. Steve's gone puce, his eyes bugging out of his

fleshy face. I fervently hope he's not about to keel over on my desk. He doesn't look healthy at the best of times.

"Delphine." He chokes. "Are those…?"

Slowly, I turn my head to the side, following his gaze. From my fingers, a scrap of lurid lace dangles. In my indignant support of women's liberation, I'd forgotten that I was still holding them.

"They're hers," Freya backs away, jabbing a slender finger in my direction. "Nothing to do with me."

I just stare at the offending article in mute horror. Wishing I could deny it. Wishing a lot of things, actually, most of them involving me being sucked into the floor never to be seen again.

Because really, where else is there to go after this? Every time I think I've had enough embarrassment for one lifetime, along comes something else. And each time, it's just a little bit worse…

Quick as a flash, a blur of black fur darts out from behind the monitor and snatches them from my fingers before jumping off the desk and running full pelt towards the door.

And then a little bit worse again.

"Should I… er…?" I stutter, making to stand.

"Get them *back*!" Steve says, in a strangled voice. "Now! And then remove them from my office!"

"All right." Face flaming, head down, I scuttle towards the door.

Behind me, I can hear Freya saying, "Of course, I *told* her it was inappropriate…"

Eyes blurring with angry tears, I slam the door behind me, ensconcing myself in the echoing silence of the corridor. The bloody dog's nowhere to be seen, and right now, I couldn't care less. I just want to be alone, completely alone, to wallow in my shame and mortification.

I stand there for a moment, hovering uncertainly. Because at once, I realise that I don't know where to go. I can't face the outside world, but I can't stay here either. People are always in and out of this door; it's only a matter of time before someone sees me.

Really, there's only one place I can think of that fits the bill.

The stationery cupboard is freezing cold. Fumbling around for the light pull, I'm rewarded by a dim, spluttering beam from above, barely enough to illuminate the shadowy corners in which numerous long-forgotten supplies still lurk. And God knows what else; something scuttles on one of the shelves up above and I cringe. As long as it doesn't drop on me, though, it's a small price to pay for solitude.

"What did I *do* in a previous life?" I manage, through chattering teeth. Wrapping my arms around myself, I rub my chilled skin in an attempt to warm it. How can humans go from being too hot to too cold almost in an instant? Just minutes ago, I was so broiling with humiliation I thought I might explode. Now, I'm in danger of frostbite. "Was I really so bad? Was I Jack the Ripper or something? I must have been to deserve this."

Silence reigns in response to my question. Not even the scuttling thing dares to move a muscle.

I collapse onto a precarious-looking stack of A4 pads, not even bothering to brush the dust off them first, and drop my head into my hands.

"This doesn't look good," Ed's voice pierces the musty air. "What have I missed?"

My body undergoes an instantaneous transformation, stiffening as ire floods through my every cell. I sit bolt upright like a possessed doll, fixing him with a furious glare.

"What have you *missed*?" My voice is unnaturally high, more than slightly tinged with hysteria, and rising with every word. "Well, let me think. You missed… oh yes, the moment my entire life was ruined. When I probably signed the death warrant on my career. That's not to mention the fact that everyone in the office thinks I'm completely incompetent. And to top it off, I've got a bloody *ghost* following me around causing havoc wherever I go!"

He edges away, wariness in his eyes.

"You seem a little… er, stressed. Should I come back later?"

"You're not going anywhere!" I surge to my feet, almost shaking with emotion. "You are not running out on me again. You're not running out on the wreckage you've caused. This time, you have to face up to what you've done."

He flushes but stands his ground.

"This is about the present, isn't it? I know it was a bit strong, but…"

"Strong?" I almost choke on the word. "It was insanity! What were you thinking? You can't just send lingerie to someone at work. Did it never even occur to you that I might be embarrassed?"

To my incredulity, he has the gall to look aggrieved.

"Why are you being so hard on me? I *am* trying to help, you know."

"So you keep saying," I snap. "But are you? Really? Because it doesn't feel like it. It feels like you're deliberately sabotaging me." Hot, angry tears are pulsing behind my eyes. "Why would you do that, Ed? Haven't I been through enough?"

Immediately, he loses his defensive demeanour. He kneels down in front of me, taking my hands in his.

"You're right, I'm sorry. Maybe I took it too far. I just… got jealous, I suppose. This is hard for me, you know. Watching you moving on."

"Hard for *you*? Are you kidding me?" I snatch my hands from his clasp, rising to my feet. I'm so incensed that I can hardly get the words out – they're staccato, breathless. "You left *me*, Ed. Not the other way around. I was the one who had to pick up the pieces, who was left with all the unanswered questions. I've barely even *begun* to move on; this is the first time I've even considered it. It's taken me six years to get to this point, but you… you don't care about any of that, do you?" My voice trembles. "You only care about yourself, your feelings. I can't believe I thought you might have changed. I wanted to believe it so much I've even been defending you to Rosie!" I clasp a hand to my forehead with a self-recriminating laugh. "But she was right; you're just the same selfish bastard you always were. You still destroy everything you touch. It's like you can't help yourself." My hand closes around the vial in my pocket. I wasn't going to use it; it hadn't even crossed my mind until this moment. "Ro's right; it's time you went."

And before I can think any more, I unstop the bottle and sprinkle the water over him.

Or at least, that's the plan. But it doesn't quite go like that. In my agitation, I use a little too much force, and the water shoots out, hitting him right in the face.

I don't know what I was expecting, maybe for him to start hissing like the Wicked Witch of the West, or to disappear with a pop. Instead, he just stands there, dripping and glaring, wiping the moisture from his forehead.

"You just drenched me," he says flatly.

"Er…" I look down at the bottle, as though expecting to see some previously unobserved instructions. Is there meant to be a time delay on this? "Yes," I admit at last, in rather a small voice.

He folds his arms.

"With what, exactly?"

"Holy water," I mumble. Hang on, since when did the tables turn? Why is he now making *me* feel bad? How does this always seem to happen with us? I steel myself and look at him defiantly.

He looks deeply offended by the notion.

"I'm not an evil spirit, Belle."

"So you say," I retort. "Based on past evidence, I'm yet to be convinced."

And with that, I slam my way out of the cupboard.

I stalk along the corridor, faintly aware that I'm shaking with repressed fury, at myself mostly. How could I have been so foolish to think he might have changed? How could I have been so naïve to believe he might have actually wanted to help me? That any of this mattered to him? My life is just an amusing toy to be played with then dropped, as it always has been.

Why did I let myself waste all of these years loving him?

That last thought hits me with such devastating ferocity that I almost crumble to my knees right there and then. But a faint shimmering in the air to my right makes me stand up taller instead. I will *not* let him watch me fall. Not again. I shoot a quelling glare in its direction.

"Don't even *think* about it," I warn raggedly. "I mean it, Ed. Leave me alone. I'm not in the mood for—oh!"

I've rounded the corner to find myself at eye-level with a blue-shirted chest. With an impending sense of doom, I drag my gaze slowly upwards.

# Chapter Twenty

There are times in life when I'm in no doubt whatsoever that the world enjoys a good joke at my expense. I mean, come on now. Of everyone in this building I could possibly have bumped into at this moment, there couldn't have been a worse choice. Send me Darren. Send me *Steve*, for heaven's sake. Even after Pantsgate, I'd take it. Anyone but Nate.

It's the sort of cruel practical joke that has Ed's handwriting all over it. At least, it would do, but I'm pretty certain he doesn't have that kind of power. Thank mercy for that, at least. He's already doing a sterling job of making my life difficult with what limited powers he does possess.

Nate doesn't look enchanted to see me, but at least he has the manners not to blank me completely.

"Not in the mood for what?" He enquires blandly, as though this is a conversation we've been having quite normally for the past few minutes, not something he's caught me ranting to myself in a supposedly empty corridor.

I sigh internally, surrendering to the fact that he just seems fated to think I'm mad.

He raises his eyebrows slightly in question.

"Are you okay?"

All right, so perhaps that sigh wasn't quite as internal as I'd intended. Quick, Belle, say something. Anything.

"I… ah… pickles!" I blurt out, before immediately wanting to die.

When I said *anything*… Perhaps I need to be more specific with the parameters next time.

"And you accuse *me* of ruining your relationship chances," Ed appears in a shimmering haze over Nate's shoulder, his face a picture of appal. "You seem to be achieving that all on your own."

"I mean… um, pastrami." I flail helplessly. Now I'm just shouting out random foodstuffs. It's not an improvement. "I was thinking about lunch," I finish lamely.

"Right." Nate's looking decidedly wary now. He jabs a thumb backwards over his shoulder. "Steve was looking for you."

My head snaps up.

"It's not about the pants, is it?"

The question tumbles out of my mouth before I can censor it.

Ed claps a hand to his forehead and groans.

"Er, no," Nate says slowly. "Actually, he wants us to go out on a story."

I blink in surprise.

"What? Together?"

"Apparently so." Nate doesn't appear particularly thrilled by the prospect. "He didn't give a reason."

I frown, considering the options.

"Do you think he knows about…" I can't quite bring myself to say, *us*. After all, I'm not even sure there was ever really such a thing. Even so, Nate seems to catch my meaning.

"That would be a bit subtle for Steve, don't you think?" he says dismissively.

I don't argue but deep down I'm not so sure. It seems a little too convenient. But then, maybe I'm just getting paranoid. All of this insight into the supernatural has made me think twice about everything, however innocuous.

"It's out in Leith, so we'll take my car." Nate jangles the keys in his hand. I get the impression he's keen to get on with it. Get it over with, more likely. I suppose it must be fairly galling to be forced into spending the whole afternoon with someone you've been trying so diligently to avoid.

I'm not exactly relishing the prospect either, I realise, with a swoop of dismay. Once I might have done, when we were friends, when our easy relationship was still the best thing about my working day. But now, things are very different between us. Nate's retreated to a place beyond my reach, and, after Ed's meddling during the past twenty-four hours, I've given up hope of ever being able to talk him round.

Suddenly, I become aware that we're being followed. I

throw a ferocious look over my shoulder, mouthing, "Don't you dare."

Ed pouts, but doesn't advance any further. Finally, he seems to have taken the hint. If he has any sense in his head, he'll stay well out of my path for the foreseeable future, at least until I've had a chance to simmer down.

There's a light rain falling as we stalk out into the car park. Well, Nate stalks, I sort of scuttle along in his wake, wishing I'd worn flats.

"Where are we going?" I pant, as I struggle to match his pace.

"The river." Nate obviously doesn't feel the need to elucidate any more than that.

My heart sinks as I envisage my new espadrilles doing the same into inches of river mud. Never mind flats, I ought to have worn wellington boots.

Nate presses the key in his hand, unlocking a gleaming silver car nearby. Don't ask me what it is – I'm useless with anything automobile related. I can tell you the colour, and that's about it.

I mean, to be fair, I've never technically owned a car. Not of my own, at any rate. I never needed one in London, and by the time I came up here there just never seemed a lot of point.

"It's very… er, shiny," I venture. I don't know what on earth I'm going on about, but I feel I ought to say something. Men seem to like being complimented on their cars.

My efforts are rewarded with a faintly pitying look. The

sort of look that makes my feminist hackles immediately begin to rise.

"What?" I demand. "What's that look for?"

He shakes his head, pulling open the car door.

"Never mind."

Right, that's it. I thrust out a hand, palm upwards.

"Give me the keys."

He eyes me warily.

"Belle…"

"Give me the *keys*!" I snap. "Now."

There's a pause and then, with a sigh, he hands them over.

"Am I even allowed to enquire as to when you last drove?" He asks, as we settle into the seats. I frown at all of the dials; I'm sure there weren't this many when I was last in a car. Ah, well, some things must be the same. The gearstick, for example. I remember that. Just about.

I feel a small lurch of alarm. Oh God, when *did* I last drive? It must have been during the university holidays, in Gran's purple tin can. It had wind-down windows and a sunroof which was taped into place, and you could barely hear yourself think over the din as it rattled along the road.

"Never mind that," I say briskly, scouting around for the lever which should move the seat forwards with increasing levels of frustration. Where the hell is it? Why do they make these things so hard to find? I press a button on the side desperately, but nothing seems to happen. I jab at it again, more forcefully. "It's like riding a… argh!"

Belatedly, the back pitches forwards, knocking my head into the steering wheel.

Wordlessly, Nate reaches down and flicks a lever, righting the seat once more and somehow moving it forwards to exactly the right position.

"Thank you," I mumble, turning the key in the ignition. The engine purrs to life immediately, which is pleasing. The tin can always used to take at least three attempts.

We drive for a couple of minutes in silence, only punctuated by Nate issuing directions and the occasional grinding of the gears, which I studiously pretend I can't hear. Nate winces every now and again, but doesn't comment.

"So," I venture at last, nervously, when I simply can't stand the silence any more. "This isn't… *so* terrible, is it?"

He slides me a cold glance.

"What isn't?"

"You and I, together in the same space." I half wish I hadn't said anything; I get the feeling I'm straying into dangerous territory. I indicate to the right, pulling out onto the main road. "And so far, nothing cataclysmic has happened."

"I'm not sure my car would entirely agree," he says dryly, as we narrowly miss a cyclist pedalling furiously along the edge of the road. "But I can't deny that there are worse choices of company. I'd still rather it was you than Darren. At least you're amusing."

That sounds like a backhanded compliment if ever there was one.

"Intentionally amusing," he rectifies, catching my suspicious glance.

Is that his way of saying he enjoys my company? My heart begins to patter at the thought, even as I wonder if I'm being ridiculous, reading too much into a throwaway comment.

Maybe he's wondering the same because he awkwardly looks away, out of the rain-streaked window, beyond which the world is little more than a watery blur.

"Stop here."

The command comes suddenly and I swerve in to a layby, which is already populated by several other cars and a couple of news vans.

"What exactly are we here for anyway?" I peer through the windscreen, trying to see what's going on. "It's not a body, is it?"

I've only had to watch them do that once before. It's not fun, standing on the bank watching them dredge some poor soul out of the watery depths. Immediately, my thoughts turn to Ed. I wonder if local reporters went to the crash site, stood around with their cameras and their Dictaphones, trying to surmise what happened, to condense it into a few curt sentences to fill the sidebar. A whole life, dealt with in a flash. It seems cold when you think about it like that.

I immediately quash that train of thought. I can't start feeling sorry for him already, not after what he's done. I deserve a bit of guilt-free stewing time.

"It's a dolphin, apparently." Nate's voice disrupts my thoughts, which I'm grateful for. "It swam up the estuary sometime during the night and was spotted this morning. They're going to try and coax it back out to sea." He glances dubiously at the rain, which is now lashing down. "I doubt they'll manage it in this, though. It's going to be impossible to see even if they do. We'd better wait for it to ease."

I sink down in the seat, wrapping my arms around myself. It's going to be a cold wait, and I'm only wearing a thin dress.

"Here." He starts to shrug off his leather jacket.

"Thanks." I nestle into it gratefully, savouring its warmth, the familiar scent of him which it carries. Like a lemon grove beneath an Italian sky.

"Well, I didn't exactly give you a chance to grab your coat," he acknowledges, with a rueful twist of the lips. "So I suppose it serves me right."

"Is that your roundabout way of saying that you were in the wrong?" I tease tentatively, and then immediately wish I could recall the words.

"Yes, it is." At my astonished expression, he raises an eyebrow. "What, is that really so surprising?"

"No, it's just…" I blink. "I'm not used to hearing people admit it, that's all."

You've met my family; we're an infamously stubborn line. Rosie, Mum, even Gran… hopelessly intractable one and all, convinced of their own correctness about every subject under the sun. Arguments could fester on for weeks in our house and I never won a single one. No one did, really. They just sort of petered out eventually, with each side privately assured of their own moral victory.

And then there's Ed. He'd swear that the sky was orange if it suited him to think so. I never won an argument with him, either. He'd always retreat, wounded, somehow making me feel that it was all my fault. Just like he did this afternoon.

It occurs to me that he still hasn't apologised for running out on our wedding. Not in so many words. Oh, he's talked around it. He's expressed contrition in one form or another. But he's never actually *said* it. The realisation stings, especially in the face of Nate's simple, unexpected candour. If he can admit that he was wrong over something as minor as dragging me out of the office without a coat, it just throws Ed's omission into even starker relief.

I look at Nate now, sitting so solemnly beside me, and I feel a wave of longing for the way things could have been. If the situation were different, if *I* were different. Nate… he's good, kind, honest. He's more complicated than I gave him credit for, admittedly, but then, who isn't? At least I don't have to second guess his motives. I don't worry about what's left unsaid. He's someone I can instinctively trust.

He's the sort of man I ought to have fallen in love with, I think, as my chest twists. With a man like this, I might have had a chance at happiness. For the first time, I feel something dangerously close to hatred towards Ed. Just a flash, just for a moment, but it draws me up with a silent intake of breath.

"While we're on the subject," Nate unclips his seatbelt, looking straight ahead. "The way I've been at work… it's unprofessional. I should be above all that."

There's a strange stiltedness to his voice. I frown, shifting around in my seat to look at him directly.

He takes a breath. "However I might feel about… events, I understand that we still have to work together. We need to put our personal issues aside."

I stare at him, dismayed. This has taken a bizarre turn. We were talking at last, and although it wasn't exactly comfortable, not by a long way, we *were* beginning to get somewhere. Or, I thought we were. But now he's started spouting some nonsense which wouldn't sound out of place on the back of a corporate leaflet.

"I don't understand…"

"Because sometimes people have to!" He cuts me off in a burst, his fingers tightening around the edge of his seat, knuckles turning white. "Because we can't always have what we want, Belle. It's a painful lesson which we all have to learn."

There's a silence during which I stare out at the rain, not sure what to say. That explosion of feeling knocked me totally off guard. I'm desperate to ask what he meant but something holds me back. A kind of fear, or self-preservation perhaps.

"Nate," I try for my most reasonable voice. "Look, I know things have been difficult, but can't we get past this? Can't we go back to how we were? You're talking like that isn't even an option."

"Because it *isn't* an option."

"Why not?" I smack my hand against the dashboard in frustration. Now he's just being deliberately obtuse.

"Because you're still in love with your ex-fiancé, that's why!"

The words seem to be wrenched from him. They echo around the interior of the car, fading into a new, charged sort of silence. For the next few seconds, I'm acutely aware of the blood roaring in my ears, the skip of my pulse.

"I know how it must look to you." I say at last, quietly. "With the roses, and... but honestly, it's not what it seems."

"Belle, you can sleep with who you want," he cuts me off, a faint flush tinting his olive skin. "It's none of my business. But I won't be used like this. Whatever's going on between you, I have no intention of getting in the middle."

"I would never do that." I shake my head fervently. "Ed and I... yes, it's complicated, but nothing can happen between us now."

His answer comes back almost immediately.

"He doesn't seem to think so."

I gape at him, disbelief and anger slamming together and showering into sparks.

"Never mind what *I* might think, then? Of course, that's not important."

His face darkens.

"Don't be sarcastic, Belle."

"Why not, when you're patronising me?"

He looks baffled.

"I'm not—"

"Telling me I don't know my own mind?" I blaze. "I think you are. I'm perfectly capable of deciding for myself. Women *can* do that these days, you know."

"Of course you can." He's trying to sound calm but I can tell his teeth are gritted together. "But please, Belle, don't insult my intelligence. It's very clear how things stand." He looks pained. "I don't understand why you're doing this. I never thought you'd be the sort to toy with someone."

I draw back, stunned. I feel like I've been slapped.

"You don't believe me, do you?" Knowing that he could think that of me, after all these years, hurts more than I can express. "It doesn't matter what I say."

His eyes flash, then just as immediately cloud over.

"Can you blame me? You haven't exactly been honest with me in the past."

The resignation in his voice twinges at my heart.

The worst of it all is that he won't quite meet my eye. Because our friendship has always been an equal one, despite the fact that he outranks me at work, we've spoken openly, without artifice. He's never once not looked me in the eye, not ever. I can see all of that crumbling away around us now, like a rock fall from a chalk cliff, while I can only stand and watch helplessly. It's an awful moment in a catalogue of awful moments, and yet somehow, even though this is perhaps the least dramatic, it's perhaps the most heart-wrenching of them all.

Because at last I can see it. He's never going to forgive me, is he? No matter how much we talk about it, or how much time passes. He won't wake up one day and forget about it all. This whole argument is pointless; his mind is made up. As far as he's concerned, I'm a different person to the one he thought I was. The betrayal and disillusionment are clear on his face.

And the worst of it is, it's completely my fault. I built this situation single-handedly, brick by brick, every time I chose not to tell him the truth. I can't blame him for not believing a word I say. Why should he?

"Things had to change between us at some point, one way or another." His voice is soft, regretful. "You and me, we were never really friends, were we? But I have to say, this wasn't the way I thought it would go." He looks out of the window with a sigh. "It's stopped raining. We should get out there, or we'll miss it. Bring the camera, won't you?"

And then he flings open the car door and gets out, leaving me alone in the cold empty space. And all I can think is how wrong I was when I predicted that Ed would make things ten times worse than before. Completely, utterly, woefully wrong.

Because right now, it feels more like a hundred.

## Chapter Twenty-One

It ought to have been a magical afternoon. By the time we got down to the river bank, the sun had burst from behind the clouds, scattering sparkles across the surface of the water. And through it all, a tell-tale shape looping above the ripples, light dancing across its back. Believe it or not, despite the fact that I've lived in Scotland for pretty much the past fifteen years, I'd never actually seen a dolphin in the flesh before.

And yet, all I was aware of was Nate's quiet presence standing next to me, outwardly as cordial as ever, but at the same time hopelessly remote. Something had altered between us in the car, this time irrevocably.

By the time I crash into bed in the night, I'm desperate to tumble into oblivion. My limbs ache from the blisteringly cold wind that whipped off the surface of the river and I feel almost like I'm coming down with a head cold.

But sleep evades me. I toss and turn, fling the covers off then pull them back on again. I plump the pillow then flatten it, lie on every side I possess, and do a mini meditation in my head which I dimly recall from a gong bath Mum made us go to. It involves lots of wafting around a garden, finding doors in walls and secluded benches. Soon enough, I get lost in my imaginary garden and end up by the compost bins. It feels like a metaphor for my life at the moment.

I have to hand it to myself; I stick it out. My phone reads almost 2am before I finally give up and swing my legs over the edge of the mattress, reaching for the fleece-lined hoodie I've left thrown over the end of the bed. Summertime it might be, but in the flat, eternal December reigns. Those Georgians might have known a thing or two about architecture, but they didn't set much store by the cosiness factor.

Tea, I think decisively, as I pick my way gingerly across the floor towards the kitchen, trying to avoid the wedding paraphernalia that's strewn about the hall. For the next two days, at least. I can't even see my way in the dark, but I've slalomed between it so many times over the weeks that my feet automatically know where to put themselves. Let's just hope no one's moved—

"Agh!" My foot catches on something and I pitch forwards, landing in a sprawl of limbs on the floor. It's only after a second that I realise all the limbs aren't mine; there are too many of them. My heart thuds painfully in fear as I realise there's an intruder in the house. I *told* Tess we should get that loose lock changed.

I open my mouth to scream again, when Rosie's irate voice cuts through the darkness.

"For God's sake, Belle! Keep it down. It's only me."

"Ro?" I flick the torch app on my phone, shining it in her face. "You scared me half to death!"

"And you're about to blind me." She screws up her eyes, putting up a hand to shade them. "Do you mind? Put the lamp on."

I reach up for the flex, clicking on the light.

"What are you doing sitting on the floor in the dark?" I ask incredulously.

"Just thinking." She opens out the blanket that's draped around her shoulders, inviting me to share. "What are you doing up, anyway? You normally sleep like the dead. No pun intended," she adds, with a rueful smile.

I groan, cocooning myself in the blanket.

"Don't talk to me about the dead right now. I've had about enough of them as I can take. I can see why they usually keep to themselves."

"Do I want to know?"

"Probably not." I sigh. It's like being children again, huddled up together under a blanket, talking in the dark. Except, these days our problems are way more complicated than who left the Valentine's card in our desk or how to do our hair for school photograph day. Sometimes I wish we could go back there. It all seemed so vital then, like the world would end if we got it wrong. If only we knew how blissfully banal our existence was. "The holy water didn't work, and it was too late anyway. Ed's ruined everything. I'm a pariah in the office and Nate doesn't want anything to do with me."

"Well, it was a long shot. Perhaps it's for the best." Rosie arranges her feet beneath the blanket, tucking it neatly beneath her toes to keep the cold out. "The situation was getting a bit untenable. Someone had to make a mature decision and clearly you weren't about to do it."

My head whips around in disbelief. That was the last thing I expected her to say. She's my sister; she's supposed to sympathise, to rail against the injustice of my life! Not sit there calmly and tell me I deserve it.

"Don't look at me like I'm a monster," she chides. "I'm only telling you the truth. You and Nate could never work. I see that now."

I feel my face falling. That's particularly heartless, even for Rosie.

"It's not like it was serious," she continues reasonably. "You spent three years insisting you didn't even like the guy. That can hardly have changed in a week. That's barely enough time to learn how he takes his tea, let alone anything else."

"I know how he takes his tea," I retort defensively. In a way she's right, and yet, the spasm of hurt that lances through me says otherwise. Because I didn't *know* him a week ago, not really. Not as a person. He was just a cardboard cut-out, a two-dimensional – if notably pleasing to look at – piece of scenery. Or at least, that was all I ever allowed him to be. Perhaps I was afraid even then, somewhere in my subconscious, of what would happen if I began to see him as more. If I let him in. Then again, perhaps that's just wishful hindsight, a way to justify the burgeoning feelings I can't pinpoint and don't really understand. "Why are we even talking about tea anyway?" I snap, with growing exasperation. "Why is it that every conversation in this family always ends up with us talking about tea?"

All right, so it's not really about the tea. In reality, I'm beginning to feel rather piqued at having to explain myself. Can she not simply be on my side, just this once?

She pats a small yawn, apparently unconcerned by my outburst.

"You know I'm a practical person. What do you want me to say? Do you want me to *lie* to you?"

"Yes!" I smack a hand to my forehead. "I mean, no. I just want…" I break off, frustrated. "I don't understand you at the moment. It's like you're going out of your way to be provocative. Do you not care about my feelings at all?"

"Frankly, in this case, no." Her eyes flash silver in the dark, her features hardening. "Amazing as it may seem, Belle, not everything in life revolves around you and your petty little problems."

"Petty?" I choke on a gasp. "Ro, there is a *ghost* following me around the place. An actual, undead person.

That's hardly a trifling everyday occurrence! It's not like I've lost my eyeliner, or we've run out of teabags."

"Yes, and it bloody *would* have to happen to you, wouldn't it, of all people," she snaps, throwing up her hands and sending the blanket flapping. "Because woe betide that anyone else ever got to be the centre of attention for once!" Her eyes shimmer with unspent tears. "God, between you and Mum… it's like a never-ending soap opera! You're both so bloody self-absorbed, so busy jostling for the limelight…"

"I am *nothing* like Mum!" I splutter, appalled. The thought alone sends a shiver down my spine.

"Oh, yes you are. Maybe it's not as conscious with you, granted, but it's there. You just don't want to see it." Her voice drips with bitterness. "You know, I reckon you even loved it when Ed left you like that. It just added to the drama, didn't it?"

My mouth drops open as shock reverberates through me.

"I can't believe you'd even think—"

She continues as if I haven't even spoken.

"Everyone fawning all over you, talking about you… and me, quietly in the background, having to pick up the pieces like always. Looking after my little sister, like always. Has it never even occurred to you that sometimes *I* might need to be looked after? That *I* might need to be supported? That I—" She draws in a shaky breath, scrubbing a hand across her eyes.

"Ro," horrified, I put a hand on her shoulder. Although

I'm still smarting over what she said, that pales into the background compared to the protective feeling that rears up within me. I can dissect my own feelings later. "What is it? Look, I'm here now. You can talk to me."

"It's just…" She draws a sharp breath, and for the first time I notice how angular she looks, sitting hunched over like that. "The wedding, it's so close now. So close. And I just want… no, I *need*… it all to go perfectly. Just for once. Just that one day." A fevered gleam lights her eyes and she balls the blanket between her fists. "Everything has to be absolutely flawless."

"No, it doesn't," I say soothingly. "Ro, no one cares…"

"I care!" She shrugs her shoulder away from my clasp with one rough movement. "God, you just don't get it, do you? I haven't worked this hard for it all to fall apart now. I have to show everyone that I can do this."

I daren't touch her again. She looks so fragile, as if she might shatter into a thousand pieces if I do. Just for a moment, I don't recognise my sister at all and guilt wraps itself around me like a vice. When did this happen? More importantly, how did I not notice? Maybe she's right after all. Maybe I really am so self-absorbed that I can't even see what's going on around me.

"I don't know what you're talking about." I lean closer, urging her to look at me. "Show who?" Then a thought strikes me. "Wait, this isn't about Leo's parents again, is it? Because we've talked about this."

Leo's parents are… let's say, precise. That's the nicest way to put it. They're the sort of people who turn up ten minutes early for every engagement and sit in the car. The sort of people who look horrified if an excited puppy comes bounding up to them in the street. I've only been to their house once and it terrified me. Everything was so pristine, so matching; I felt like my very presence was disarraying the place.

Their life is an endless carousel of bridge parties, and cruises, and lunches at the golf club. If Ed thinks Rosie and Leo are stiflingly conventional… Leo's parents practically invented the term. Emphasis on the stifling. They basically epitomise respectability, and, well, you can perhaps begin to see the issue. I'm not sure the word respectability is even in my mother's vocabulary.

I've told Rosie a million times that it doesn't matter. That Leo loves her, loves all of us, for exactly what and who we are. All right, so perhaps it's more the case that he tolerates Mum, but even in her worst moments, I know he harbours a sort of exasperated fondness for her. How could he not? He's been an honorary member of our family for a long time, just like Tess. No one could say he didn't know what he was letting himself in for, could they? In a secret sort of way, I suspect he enjoys the chaos and I like to think we've saved him from a stuffy existence. There's no time to be bored with us around.

Even so, there's no point in saying any of this to Rosie; I'll only sound like a broken record. For some reason, she's always had a major complex about it. I think Leo's mother is the only person who can make Rosie feel insecure about herself, about all of us, about everything she is. I've never been able to understand it. Since when has my sister ever cared what anyone thinks of her?

"No, it's not about that... not *just* about that," she amends sheepishly, as my expression turns disbelieving. "I just feel like..." She gives a frustrated sigh. "Like someone in this family ought to get it right. Make a success of something for once."

I stare at her in consternation.

"What is *that* supposed to mean?"

"Never mind." She begins to disentangle herself from the blanket, her tone dismissive. "Look, it's the middle of the night. We're both tired, and we've got work in the morning. Let's just go back to bed, shall we?"

I watch as she rises to her feet, indignation settling in my chest. She's brushing me off; even I can tell that.

"Ro..." I begin determinedly.

"You wouldn't understand." The words snap back at me before I've even finished uttering her name. They're stark, underscored with frustration. "Just forget what I said, okay? I'll take care of my own problems, and you focus on yours. For as long as they last, anyway."

I blink at her, confused. Sometimes, I wish she'd just say what she means.

"Haven't you worked it out yet?" She puts her hands on her hips and looks down at me impatiently. "Because it seems pretty obvious to me, even if it isn't to anyone else. Ed's here to help you move on. Why else would they have let him come? So if you really do feel anything for Nate, then you won't have to worry for much longer, will you? Ed will disappear from whence he came, and you…" Her features harden. "Well, everything will be rosy in the garden again, won't it? Just like it always is for my little sister."

Then she turns out the lamp and flounces away, leaving me on the floor in the dark.

## Chapter Twenty-Two

"Delphine." Steve appears out of nowhere, looming over my desk like a particularly portly Banquo's ghost. He startles me to such an extent that my fingers crash over my keyboard, spilling a load of gibberish across the screen. Probably not a lot worse than what I'd been writing anyway – the street lamp timers are back in force, and I've been tasked with doing a follow up. It's not easy writing an entire article which is essentially described in the headline, *Street Lamp Timers Revert to Prior Schedule*. I'm almost relieved to see Steve's scowling face; at least it gives me a break from wondering how many times I can repeat the same sentence by switching around the various words.

"Steve," I say cordially, surreptitiously swivelling my screen to the right so he can't see the nonsense I've been writing. "How nice of you to visit. Is this a social call?"

"My office." He's already half turned away. "Now."

An ominous request if ever I heard one. I sigh, getting

up to follow his retreating form as he marches across the floor back to his lair. I fluff out my skirt, wondering why I'm even bothering to try and look presentable; it's not like he puts a lot of effort into the endeavour himself. But it's a force of habit.

"This is it!" Darren wrings his hands gleefully. "He's going to *fire* you! I knew this would happen eventually. It was just a matter of—"

Suddenly, his chair screeches backwards. He flails, trying to hold on, but it's too late. He lands on the floor with a dull thud, glasses knocked askew, mouth a frozen 'O' of stupefaction.

"Someone walk over your grave?" I say serenely, stepping over him. And trying very hard not to smile.

Because I saw it. Just for a second, out of the corner of my eye. The air rippling, like a deluge of rainwater across a windscreen. Then gone.

Perhaps there *are* occasional benefits to having a pet ghost after all. He's been keeping a low profile since our argument; I think he's still a bit miffed that I tried to… well, to exorcise him. Which, to be fair, *was* a tad mean, but I still maintain that he deserved it. In any event, at least now he's reappeared, he's making himself useful. It's about time; he certainly owes me that, before he moves on again.

The final part of that thought inspires a twinge of sadness so strong and unexpected that it makes me falter a step, my hand automatically moving to my heart. What is *that* all about? I can't be going to *miss* him, surely?

I mean, by rights I should be thrilled at the prospect of

getting rid of him, I tell myself stridently. *Thrilled*. After all, he's been nothing but trouble since the moment he arrived… how long ago was it, now? Odd, but I seem to have lost all track of time. I do a swift mental calculation, then frown. That can't be right, surely. I run through it again, this time more slowly. And come up with the same answer. The same, inconceivable answer.

Eight days. Is that really it? I feel like he's been plaguing me for months. Years. Christ, scarcely over a week, and he's systematically managed to turn my entire life upside down and inside out. Is that really all it took? It doesn't say much for the foundations of my existence, does it? The solid ground I thought I'd built for myself, dashed away like it was never anything more than sand. It's a depressing thought.

Steve's already wedged in behind his desk when I reach the doorway to his office.

"Shut the door, won't you?"

I comply, wondering what this is all about. Steve never bothers to close his door; he's so loud that everyone on the entire floor can hear anyway, so it's little more than a formality. I turn back to him, hovering uncertainly.

He looks up then scowls, as though irritated to find me there.

"Well, aren't you going to sit down?"

I cast around. The only thing that could reasonably described as a seat is a rickety-looking stool covered in old copy and crisp packets. I'm unsure if it would be impolite to start moving it all, so instead I just perch on the very edge, hoping that nothing sticks to me.

Not that Steve is paying much attention anyway; he picks up a chipped mug which is balanced on a teetering pile of paperwork next to his elbow, peers distastefully at its contents, then reaches for another one several inches away. I begin to wonder how long they've been there – didn't I make him coffee in that mug three days ago? – then rapidly conclude that it's best not to pursue that particular train of thought.

It probably wouldn't even matter if he *were* about to fire me, I think, watching squeamishly as Steve downs whatever was left in the cup. This whole place is almost certain to get shut down when the health inspector arrives; they'll probably never have seen such a biohazard in their entire career.

Steve clears his throat at length. I fervently hope he's not choking on a piece of mould, but then he visibly makes an effort to sit up straighter, smoothing down his tie, and I realise he's just gearing up to his official mode. A bolt of alarm slices through me, knocking all irreverent thoughts to the side. Steve doesn't do 'official' very often. When he does, it's almost exclusively bad. If he's pleased with you, he just doesn't shout as much or throw as many things at your head. It's as simple as that.

Oh, God. I shrink down in my chair. What have I done *now*?

"I won't beat about the bush." Steve steeples his fingers, apparently unaware that Frou Frou has stuck her head in to the discarded coffee cup and is slurping from it loudly. "You're not the most dedicated reporter I've ever employed."

I open my mouth then promptly close it again. I can't really refute that; it's better not to try.

"You frequently miss deadlines." Steve begins to tick my transgressions off on his fingers. "You wind up the other employees, you conduct illicit office romances…"

"Just the one," I blurt out, before I can stop myself.

He glares at me, evidently not pleased that I would dare to interrupt him.

I curl my palms around the edge of the seat beneath me, wondering why I have to say these things. Why can't I just sit and take the lecture like anyone else would; why do I have to go and make it all worse?

Because it's *true*, a stubborn voice in my head reminds me. And God knows I'm in no position to preach on honesty at the moment, but that's all the more reason to stand up for the truth when it can be expressed.

"It was just the *one* illicit romance, if you could even go so far as to call it that," I mumble. "And I didn't think you knew."

Frou Frou jumps up onto my lap; instinctively, I put my hand on her head, stroking her wiry fur. She seems to be chewing intently on something. Something red. With a jolt of horror, I tug at the mangled scrap of lace, trying to get it off her.

"I'm a newsman, Delphine." Steve's voice is heavy with disdain. "I'd like to think I possess some degree of observation. 'Collaborating on a story', my arse. I know when something's going on between my reporters. Do you really think you two are the first?"

I can feel myself flushing beneath my embellished Peter Pan collar. Dear lord, was it really so *very* obvious?

"So you did send us out together on purpose yesterday?"

"Of course I did." Evidently, Steve's either forgotten completely about being official, or he's simply given up, because he leans back in his chair, propping his feet up on the desk. One shoelace is undone; for some reason, I can't stop looking at it. "I thought it'd give you two a chance to get your act together. And what happened instead? I lost my best reporter!" He slams a fist down on the desk, but there's no real heart in it. He looks thoroughly fed up. "Now I'll have to promote you, which God knows is better than Darren, but that's about the only good—"

"Wait… what did you just say?" I pitch forwards, mindless of the fact that I'm already on the very edge of the seat, and nearly topple off altogether. Frou Frou yaps indignantly, digging her claws into my knee, but she lets go of the underwear at least. Hastily, I stuff them into my pocket.

Steve looks loathe to repeat himself, but he does so.

"I said that you're better than Darren."

"Yes, but…" At any other time, that would be a welcome assessment, if an obvious one. Of *course* I'm better than Darren. Who isn't? But right now, my entire focus is on other matters. Namely the cold, foreboding feeling that everything's about to tip on its head. Yet again. I venture onwards, praying my guess will prove wrong. "I meant the bit before that. About Nate…"

"Leaving?" Steve flicks a salted peanut off the desk. At least, I hope that's what it is. In any event, it immediately disappears into the general detritus which litters the floor, probably never to be seen again. Frou Frou follows its progress with interest. "Right pain in the behind, it is. I tried to persuade him to stay, even offered him a sub-editor title. Nothing worked. He was adamant."

"Did he—" My throat feels constricted; I fight for air. "Did he say why?"

Steve grunts.

"Gave me a load of nonsense about it being time to go back to London. Didn't mention you, of course. No, he carefully left you out of it." Steve's accusatory tone suggests that the blame is well and truly laid at my door nonetheless. "Now you'll have to step up, fill his shoes." He doesn't look hopeful about the prospect. "It won't be easy, but I daresay we can make something of you yet. I've always thought there was a decent reporter lurking in there somewhere, beneath all the fluff. You just need to keep your focus on the job, not on your own life."

I'm not entirely certain what he means by 'all the fluff'. At least it's not my hair; I had that straightened at the spa. It's almost as mirror-like as Freya's now. But that feels like small consolation at the moment.

"You want me to *replace* Nate?" I manage, disbelievingly. I hear the words coming out of my mouth, but I can't connect them to myself. Everything seems sort of misty, far away.

"There'll be a small pay rise, of course," Steve replies gruffly. "I don't doubt you'd rather be writing about handbags and the like, but it's not a bad racket. You'll have more of a chance to chase down your own stories, get out of the office. You won't be writing about street lamp timers anymore, that's for certain."

I can only stare at him, speechless, overwhelmed by myriad conflicting emotions.

I can't believe Nate would *do* this. More importantly, I can't believe he'd do this without telling me. That's what really stings; that clearly, he didn't think I deserved to know first. That he thought it was okay for me to find out like this… I can't decide if I'm more upset or angry. I take a breath, trying to order my thoughts.

"Does he know you're offering me his job?"

I'm surprised at how cool my voice sounds, almost like I'm not really interested.

"Not his job anymore." Steve shrugs. "But as it happens, yes. In fact, he was the first to suggest it. He thought you should have the opportunity."

Oh, he did, did he? For some reason, that makes my temper flare. Because really, why does he get to do this? Why does he *always* get to be the bigger person, the soul of righteousness, while I'm left feeling like the lowest sort of worm? What am I supposed to feel? Grateful? While he waltzes off into the sunset, taking the moral high ground with him?

"Problem, Delphine?" Steve raises an untamed eyebrow. "Do I need to remind you what a great opportunity this is? I thought you'd be pleased."

Which just goes to show how much he knows. Even so, I feel a little guilty at my obvious lack of enthusiasm. After all, he *is* giving me a chance, which he didn't need to do. He could have skipped straight over me and hired someone more experienced. I know what I should do; I should smile, and thank him, and forget about Nate. I should look out for myself. And yet… it feels wrong. My head is spinning. I need a moment to think, to compute all of this.

"I…" I begin waveringly. I've no idea where I'm going with this. But then I see a flash of pale green shirt through the glass wall to my right and suddenly, I know exactly what I need to do.

"I have to go," I burst out, already halfway out of my seat. Frou Frou slides off my lap with a stubborn growl.

Steve's gaze flicks over my shoulder, then turns sardonic.

"Of course you do." He shakes his head, waving me away. "We'll continue this discussion later."

"Thanks," I mutter breathlessly, yanking open the door and racing out. "Nate! Wait!"

Bad enough that it rhymes; it's not exactly the dignified image I'd have chosen, had I the time or the opportunity to arrange it more to my liking. I can see Freya giving me a scornful look over the rim of her compact mirror, which once would have been enough to make me squirm, but these days, I'm not so easily embarrassed. I need to talk to

Nate. Now. If making a scene is what's required, then so be it.

His back is to me. I see his shoulders tense beneath the fine linen of his shirt but he doesn't turn around. Instead he scoops up his phone from the desk and carries on walking, making a beeline for the door.

I'd half expected it. God forbid that he might actually have to face me after pulling a stunt like that. Not to be thwarted, I follow him out into the corridor. Ed's hovering in the doorway as a transparent shape and I shoo him back inside. I don't want an audience for this. To my amazement, he complies. Is he actually gaining some degree of sensitivity? That would be a turn up.

"Nate!" I call, more forcefully.

"I don't want to talk about it," he says wearily, without even turning around. "I mean it, Belle. Just take the job. It's for the best."

We're almost at the stairs. I'm about to lose my moment. Before I can stop to think about what I'm doing, I tug open the door to my left and shove him inside.

"What the hell—" He blinks as I click on the light, looking around in bemusement. "What *is* it with you and this cupboard?"

I fold my arms defiantly.

"I want to talk."

"And I just told you that I don't." He makes to move past me but I sidestep, blocking his way to the door. He narrows his eyes. "Belle, let me past. You're being ridiculous."

"What does it matter if I am?" I shoot back. "Who am I trying to impress? You?" I give a light little laugh, which sounds hollow even to my own ears. "You're leaving anyway, so I'm told. Not *by* you, though, incidentally. No, *you* didn't have the decency for that. Instead, you took the coward's way out and made me find out second-hand. Very big of you, might I say."

He at least has the grace to look faintly discomfited by the ire in my voice.

"I thought it was easier this way. I thought you—"

"Oh, stop pretending that this is about me!" I burst out. My composure didn't last long, then. But somehow, he's making me feel so unlike myself, so angry. Even angrier than Ed has ever been able to make me. I jab him in the chest. "This is about you running away."

"I am *not* running away." He looks mortally offended that I'd even suggest such a thing, as though it's an insult to his chivalric honour. "How could you even think—" He sighs then, rubbing a hand across the back of his neck, his tone softening. "Look, this was only ever supposed to be a short interlude, Belle. I'd had a bad breakup, I needed to get away from London… that was all. I never meant to stay as long as this, never meant…" He breaks off, looking away. His face is cast in shadow. I can't see his expression but I can hear it in his voice. "None of this was meant to happen."

"Sorry to be such an inconvenience," I say sarcastically, but my voice trembles on the words, belying the emotion underneath. It always throws me when he speaks like this, with that raw, passionate Mediterranean brand of honesty. I'm British, for God's sake; I just can't handle that kind of thing.

"It was," he agrees, the barest hint of a wry smile curving his lips. "You are, on the whole, a very inconvenient person. At least you can acknowledge it."

I shrug.

"It's nothing new. I've been inconveniencing people since I was embryonic. My mother's never let me forget how unplanned I was."

He throws back his head and laughs. It's wonderful, unexpected, bittersweet. I haven't heard him laugh in… well, it's probably only days in reality but it feels like forever.

"You know Belle, I really am going to miss you."

Him looking at me like that… with warmth, affection, the way he used to look at me before all of this happened… it makes my heart ache with longing. Why couldn't I have noticed sooner what was there all along? I take a breath, knowing that what I'm about to say next might change everything. Then again, it might change nothing at all.

"Then stay." The words fall from my lips with a quiet resonance, seeming to shiver between us in the frigid air. Words I'd promised myself I'd never, ever say. After Ed left, I swore I'd never hold anyone down again. But I can't seem to stop myself. "Keep your job. I don't want it. I'll write about street lamp timers till the end of my days. I'll never complain about it again. I'll do it gladly, if you'll just…" I take a breath. "Stay."

It's as close to a declaration of my feelings as I've ever come. His eyes snap to mine and for a long moment we just look at each other. I realise I'm holding my breath. Then his gaze flicks away.

"I have to. And don't ask me why again," he adds warningly, as my lips begin to part. "Because you already know the answer."

This time, I don't even try to respond. Not with words, at any rate. Instead I just throw my hands up in the air, overwhelmed by sheer frustration. I give up, I really do. I mean, this is an intelligent man I'm talking to here. Someone with a university degree and a competent grasp of the tax system. And yet I might as well be talking to Frou Frou for all the good it's doing.

What *is* it with men? I think despairingly. They can be so astonishingly dense when they set their minds on something.

Sometimes I feel we'd be better off if the world were populated solely by women. There'd be some procreation issues, granted, but once we'd got that side of things worked out, then we'd be laughing. I mean, I grew up in an all-female family, and look at—

Actually, on second thoughts, don't look at that. It didn't turn out all that well.

"Christ, Belle, why do you always have to be so stubborn?" he blazes, clearly interpreting my silence as a revolt. "I'm trying to make things easier for you here, and you just won't have it, will you?" he runs a hand through his hair, dishevelling it even more than usual. "He's the one you always wanted. It was never me. I can accept that. But please, let me go. Before this whole thing sends me mad. Before I fall any deeper in—" He breaks off, a flush tinging his olive skin.

I've frozen to the spot. My mind is stuck on the last part of that fractured sentence. It revolves around and around my head.

"What did you just say?" I manage, in a dazed voice.

"It was a turn of phrase," he mutters, not meeting my eye. In his palm, his phone lights up, and his shoulders visibly drop with relief. "Look, I have to take this. It's a source."

He brushes past me to the door and this time I don't try to stop him. I just stand there, thinking that there's no secret in the universe I'd rather know than how that sentence would have ended.

## Chapter Twenty-Three

The sound of the doorbell clanging through the quiet flat is almost enough to make me jump out of my skin. I huddle closer into the sofa, staring sightlessly at the magazine in my lap as though pretending to be busy might somehow will whoever it is away. I'm not expecting anyone. In fact, I actively want to *avoid* people right now.

For once, I have the entire place to myself, an almost unheard-of occurrence. Rosie has gone off for a final dress fitting – with Mum, of all people. No, I wasn't quite sure why, either – and Tess is… I frown, splaying the magazine across my lap. Good question, actually. Where *is* Tess? As far as I'm aware, she hasn't left the house for weeks. I suppose, then, that her absence can only be a good thing; maybe she's sketching in Holyrood Park, like she used to do, or browsing the paintings at the National Gallery of Scotland for inspiration. There's a John Singer Sargent on display there that she's always adored. She can sit in front of it for hours, studying its gossamer-like paint strokes, or "absorbing it's energy", as she's explained it to me.

Recalling that makes me smile. I've missed her madness of late, the way she used to stop in the middle of the street and admire the play of sunshine over the craggy outline of the castle. Always when we were in a hurry to get somewhere, as well. It used to make Rosie apoplectic. Or how we'd have to make strange, spontaneous detours because she'd just seen someone with the most interesting face and she wanted to take a closer look. I always half thought we were going to get arrested, following some random person around. I was certain that one day they'd notice, but they never did.

The doorbell rings again, more insistently this time. I'm not even sure if that's possible; after all, it only has one chime, but it certainly sounds that way to my ears. I frown, pulling the blanket up over my head, like I'm making a fort. It's probably just a salesperson or a courier with a parcel for one of the flats below. I can't face interacting with anyone today; for one of the first times I can remember in my entire life, I actually *want* to be on my own. The only other was after I'd been jilted; I can still remember everyone jostling around me, trying to be comforting, trying to be kind. And I just wanted to scream at them all to get out, to leave me alone with my thoughts. With my misery.

I couldn't, of course, and I didn't. I felt guilty even for thinking it. These were the people who loved me, cared for me, and they were trying so hard. I couldn't hurt them like that. But I felt it all the same.

And now I feel it again. Except, this time, I really am alone. I have my wish. And it feels… well, certainly not any worse, but not any better, either. My heart aches. It's as simple as that. And it would be as simple as that wherever I was, and whomever I was with. Nothing can change it. Even if I don't understand it, I know that's how it feels.

The doorbell rings once more. Evidently, they're not going anywhere, whoever they are. With a sigh of annoyance, I unfurl myself from the warmth of the sofa and pad across the carpet to answer it.

For a good half a second, I'm convinced that there's nobody there. Then I adjust my gaze downwards by a foot and do a double take.

"Gran?"

"For the time being," she answers crisply. "Although in the time it took you to get here, I might well have shuffled off this mortal coil."

"I didn't know it was you," I mutter helplessly. She certainly knows how to make you feel awful, doesn't she? I can see where Mum gets her flair for the dramatic. "What are you doing here?"

"I wasn't aware I required a specialist permit to visit my own granddaughter," she ripostes, navigating the doorstep to sweep past me into the living room. I trail in her wake, still feeling a little dazed.

"Of course not. But… how did you *get* here?"

Gran abhors public transport. She claims it's the devil's creation, not to mention a breeding ground for any quantity of previously undiscovered superbugs. I'm not sure why that should be a particular concern for the woman who used to pick mushrooms out of the park for breakfast and boasts that she has the constitution of an ox, but still.

"I drove," Gran says airily, as though this isn't a bombshell of the most alarming variety. "Gave old Martha a good spin. Still runs like a dream."

"You… what?" I scuttle over to the window. Sure enough, there's the ancient purple car, parked at a haphazard angle across a double yellow line. Let's just hope the police aren't cruising around in the vicinity. "Gran, you're not supposed to drive! You promised, after your hip…"

"Och, it was fine." Gran waves away my concern dismissively. "I just said that to keep those doctors quiet; never had any intention of sticking to it. Why should I?" She puffs herself up proudly. "Been driving my whole life and no harm's come to me yet."

Down in the street, a van hoots its horn as it swerves up onto the pavement to avoid Gran's car. I wince.

Gran, as usual, seems oblivious to the cacophony she's causing. She's glancing around the room hopefully.

"See here, I don't suppose you've got any gin?"

I blink, taken aback by the random request.

"Er… no. I don't think so. I can offer you tea."

"That'll have to do, then." She follows me through, an incongruous sight in our poky little kitchen, robed in swathes of black velvet like a Victorian doll. She fixes me with a reproving stare, and my heart immediately sinks.

"Now, let's get straight to the matter in hand. You're not moping, are you?"

I start guiltily, then turn my back to the counter to hide it. I was not expecting that. The family grapevine must be working overtime.

"Of course not," I lie, striving to appear sufficiently buoyant as I busy myself with the kettle. How exactly one can make tea in a buoyant fashion I'm not certain, but I'm damned well going to try.

Obviously it's working, because Gran looks palpably relieved.

"Good! I wasn't looking forward to that conversation." She leans on her stick with a satisfied air. "You've had a hard time lately, your past catching up with you and all that. But it's a sensible attitude you're taking, I have to say. I'm impressed. I would have expected you to lose your head. You're like your mother, you see. No fortitude."

I magnanimously decide to overlook that very backhanded compliment.

"Er… thanks?"

But Gran hasn't finished yet.

"And as for that nice boy, Nathaniel. Well, it's a shame, but you've just got to accept that it's finished."

I fling teabags blindly into the pot. Okay, this really isn't making me feel any better.

'…Kaput."

I fill the teapot more vigorously than perhaps is wise, sloshing boiling water all over the side.

"…No hope for it whatsoever."

"Would you like a biscuit?" I blurt out desperately, brandishing the packet in front of her face. Anything to stop her from talking.

"Don't mind if I do," she selects one, then uses it to point in my direction. "But look here, I haven't just come to see the curtains."

I freeze, a biscuit halfway to my mouth. What is she *talking* about? I swear, she gets more and more erratic with each passing day.

Before I can ask what exactly about the curtains – especially considering that we have blinds – she's installed herself regally on the sofa, fixing me with an assessing eye.

"So you're just going to let him go, then, are you?"

I'm not about to get out of it that easily, then.

"Yes, Gran." I say dully, sitting down next to her, cradling my cup between my palms. "I really am. Believe me, you don't have to worry. I'm going to do the right thing; I won't make it any more difficult for him."

Finally, I've had to accept that Rosie's right, as usual. I'm no good for Nate. And I don't want to hurt him anymore. If that means slinking away quietly, then that's what I'll do.

"No!" Gran explodes suddenly, banging her stick against the floor, making me start. "I can't listen to any more of this wishy-washy nonsense. What's *wrong* with you, girl? Have you lost your mind?"

My heart is still thudding against my ribcage at the shock; I'm not sure how I've managed not to spill hot tea everywhere. I put the cup down carefully with shaking hands, not wanting to tempt fate.

"But you just said—"

"Never mind what I said! I was trying to get the spirit up in you, that's all." She shakes her head disgustedly. "I was waiting for you to tell me that I was wrong, that you weren't going to be beaten so easily. Don't you have feelings for the boy?"

Blood rushes to my head, heating my face. Gran has never been shy when it comes to a direct question.

"I-I don't know," I stutter. I didn't think I did. But to be honest, even I don't trust myself anymore.

"Of course you do!" Gran snaps. "You forget that I basically raised you two girls while your mother was off galivanting. I know everything about you. You think I don't," she adds, in an admonishing tone. "But I do. And you, Belle, have always known your own mind. At least, until you let someone put doubts into your head. Who have you been listening to this time? Your sister?"

I open my mouth, then close it again. I probably look like a fish.

"Hmm, I thought so." Gran breaks a biscuit in half. "Well, you don't want to pay any attention to what *she* says. She's got the bluster, but that doesn't mean she's got all the answers. This is a woman who's making herself and everyone else miserable over a few fripperies, when she's got a man who loves her and couldn't care less if they got married in a cowshed! Is that really who you want to be taking advice from at the moment?"

I cringe internally on Rosie's behalf. She doesn't mince

words, does she? God only knows what she says about *me* when I'm not around.

Gran leans forward, narrowing her eyes at me.

"Unless… this isn't about Rosie at all, is it? It's about Edward."

Gran is the only person I've ever known to use his full name. It's the first time I've heard it since… well, since our wedding day, now that I think about it. Gran never mentioned him again after that morning. It was like he ceased to exist.

Which, in an ironic way, he rather did.

"I'm right, aren't I?" Gran thumps her stick triumphantly. "It *is* the reprobate!" Then her expression turns serious. "Why does he still have a hold on you, after all this time? You can't think yourself still in love with him, surely?"

I take a subtle glance around, just in case he's lurking somewhere. But the tell-tale shimmer is conspicuously absent.

And suddenly the urge to talk about it is overwhelming. To open my lips and finally voice the awful truth.

"I don't think I can ever stop loving him."

If I'd imagined that saying the words out loud would make me feel better, then I was wrong. Hanging in the air between us, they sound worse than ever. Hopeless. Pathetic. Filled with bitterness in a way they never were before. Once, I just meekly accepted that it was the case, part of my identity, but now… things have changed. I've seen what freedom might have looked like. Freedom to love someone else. To be happy.

Gran regards me with uncharacteristic tenderness. "Why not, dear?"

"Because it'll never be finished." The words are tumbling from me now, beyond my control. Truths I didn't even know existed, finally being freed. "Because I should have looked for him. Should have gone after him. I should have known…"

The fleeting tenderness has vanished, to be replaced by puckered disapproval at such a dismal lack of rationality.

"He left of his own accord, Belle. Clearly, he had no wish to be found. Why should it have been your job to search for him?"

Because he had no one else. No family, no close friends. He was a drifter, making connections wherever he was, then moving on. He was charismatic, magnetic, always the life and soul, always surrounded by people. And yet, at the same time, always alone. I think I was probably the first person he ever really tried to stick with, to carry with him from one place to the next.

And of course, Gran doesn't know the whole of it. She doesn't know what happened after he left. Really, she can't possibly understand what I'm getting at, how I'm feeling; I ought to be having this conversation with Rosie or Tess. But somehow, it's Gran I want to talk to. I need some of her wisdom, even if we will be talking at cross purposes to an extent.

I know what she would say even if she knew the truth;

that I couldn't possibly have known what would happen, that it wasn't my fault. But I can't forget that while I was here, building a new life in Edinburgh, he was lying at the bottom of a ravine, then in a cold, sterile morgue somewhere. A part of me feels I ought to feel as dreadful as possible about it all.

And perhaps losing Nate… that's the price I have to pay. My penance.

"Is that why you've been making excuses for the boy?" Gran presses, disbelief evident upon her face. "Because you feel… culpable?"

"I just…" I bury my face in my hands, not knowing how to express myself better. "I can't explain, but… it *is* my fault. When he left…"

"It sounds to me like you're confusing guilt with love." Gran shakes her head solemnly. "They're not the same thing. Not the same thing at all." She sighs. "Whatever burdens you're carrying, I don't presume to understand, but they don't shackle you to the boy forever. It's all right to move on, you know. You're not sentenced to love him now just because you once did. That's not how it works." She eyes me sharply. "Don't get to my age, dear, and wish you'd done it all differently. Give yourself a chance to find out what could be."

I sit there, pondering the notion. Gran is generally a woman of few words, but the ones she saves up, she uses to great effect. You might emerge on the other side feeling like you've been beaten with a thousand birch twigs, but you can't deny that she's right.

Is it possible, even the tiniest bit possible…? Just the notion is like cracking open a door, letting a chink of light spill into a dark room. I can practically feel my chest expanding as I ponder it, the crushing pressure of it beginning to lift slightly off my back.

"Think about it," Gran says briskly. "That's all I ask. Can't knock the sense into you; you'll have to do that yourself." She takes a slurp of her tea, her lips turning down at the corners. "This tea needs whisky. Don't suppose you've got any of *that*, have you?"

## Chapter Twenty-Four

"There." I lean back to admire my handiwork, before belatedly recalling that I'm balanced rather precariously at the top of a ladder and hastily gripping the rung more tightly to steady myself. "How does that look?"

Tess peers up at the ceiling, chewing her lip doubtfully.

"I don't know. Maybe to the left a bit?"

I try not to scowl. It looks fine to me. But she's the one with the artistic flair, and in any event, I'm trying to enter into the wedding spirit, so I scrunch up every inch of my remaining patience and nudge the ribbon a couple of inches further along the wooden beam.

Tess cocks her head to one side, blue eyes assessing. "More."

I stretch out, the heel of my foot raising off the step as I try to reach. The ladder wobbles beneath me, and my heart takes a swooping dive. I squeeze my eyes shut, wondering what on earth possessed me to volunteer for this. Then again, someone had to take one for the team and I think Tess would have burst into tears before she'd reached the second rung. She's even worse with heights than I am.

The ladder mercifully comes to a stop and somehow, I'm still upright. I breathe an internal sigh of relief, prising open my eyes. These bloody decorations had better be worth almost plunging to my death for, I think darkly.

"Er..." Tess raises a tentative hand, as if we're in the classroom. "Actually, I think it needs to go a little to the right."

She has got to be kidding me. Very slowly, I turn my head to look down at her.

"It just *came* from the right," I say frostily.

She pinkens delightfully, then coughs.

"Are you trying to tell me," I say evenly. "That it was better off where it was in the first place? *Before* I almost broke my neck moving it?"

"Well, um..." She scratches her jawbone, her voice dropping to almost a whisper. "Yes."

I take a very deep breath, trying to maintain my equilibrium. *Remember the wedding spirit, Belle. Sweetness and light and... oh, to hell with it.*

"Tess!" I yell admonishingly, the sound ringing around the high-vaulted space of the barn.

"Sorry!" She wails, twisting her hands together, the way she does when she's really stressed. Which, in truth, isn't all that uncommon. Especially not at the moment. "It's just...

with Rosie so tense, I don't want to get anything wrong, that's all. It's making me nervous."

The genuine worry in her voice makes me swallow my instinctively sarcastic retort. Instead, I climb down the ladder, legs shaking with relief as they meet terra firma once more.

"I doubt even Rosie will have time to notice one paper pompom tomorrow, whatever she might say today."

Despite my outward confidence, I find myself casting a critical glance over the floating sea of white and peppermint green ruffles suspended over our heads, checking for any glaring inconsistencies. If it were my own wedding, I'd simply throw up my hands and wander off to crack open the champagne, but it's not. It's Rosie's day and I'm trying to be supportive. So that means resisting my naturally lackadaisical attitude and doing things the way she would want them. It's not been an easy ask, particularly when every effort is met with curt disdain by the bride in question. A little appreciation might not go amiss here and there, but I've given up hoping for it.

If I'd anticipated that getting to the venue this afternoon might dispel some of the tension, then I'd have been sorely disappointed. If anything, she's worse than ever, snapping at anyone who dares to cross her path. Leo's stalking around with the sort of pinched expression usually reserved for a particularly fraught upcoming acquisitions meeting, not what's supposed to be the happiest day of his life. Gran's lips are permanently pursed. Even Mum's picked up the mood and is noticeably muted. It's certainly not the celebratory atmosphere one might except from the day before a wedding. I wouldn't exactly know, considering that my own was hardly conventional, or indeed planned, but I'd imagined that there'd be a sort of merry camaraderie, endless rounds of fortifying tea, even a picnic lunch on the lawn outside. Nothing like this. It's like we're setting up for a funeral. A very pastel funeral.

I stretch, my shoulder blades responding with an audible crack. It's been a long day. Eschewing the venue's standard decorative scheme might have seemed fine when the wedding date was still a comfortable ten months away, but now it's upon us, I'm past beginning to wish that my sister had just taken the easy route for once in her life. I'd give anything to be relaxing in a bubble bath in my plush ensuite right now, running over my speech in my mind and wondering which earrings to wear tomorrow. Instead, there's a half-decorated barn staring back at me, stacks of chairs waiting to be set out, and plates still languishing in their plastic catering bags.

"I hope you're right," Tess says glumly. "Because we're running out of time. The rehearsal's in an hour."

I slap a hand to my forehead and groan. I'd forgotten about the rehearsal. That just ramps up the pressure even more.

"All right, well let's set the tables at least. Then I wouldn't mind a chance to freshen up. I've been awake since five this morning."

I didn't even get a chance to wash my hair. It was a case of throwing on the nearest top, throwing some coffee down my throat, throwing some coffee down my top too, throwing some water onto my top to wash the stain, throwing an entire cargo load of wedding gear into the boot of the little purple car, then squeezing everyone into the gaps between. I was in the back with Mum and Tess, having drawn the shortest straw of all by sitting in the middle. My head was bent at an awkward angle for the entire hour and a half journey up to St Andrews.

Having said that, at least I didn't have to sit in the front with Carlos, who had, by a mysterious sort of vote which none of us recalled taking, apparently been elected to drive. That dubious honour fell to Gran, which was probably just as well because out of all of us, she's the one with the nerves of steel.

I thought we were going to die on that journey, I really did. Carlos seemed to be labouring under the misapprehension that he was still in Spain and accordingly spent most of the time on the right-hand side of the twisting country roads. And if Nate thinks *my* clutch control is bad…

By the time I practically fell out of the car onto the sweeping gravel drive in front of the hotel, I'd already sweated away about half my body's moisture in sheer terror, and that's before I'd even started on an entire afternoon of lifting and carrying. I've probably never needed a shower so badly in my life.

Tess, needless to say, looks as fresh as a daisy. I must prise her secret out of her one of these days, I vow silently, pushing a sticky strand of hair away from my even stickier forehead. I really hope it's not just down to genes; that would be too depressing.

I did catch her sneaking a quick meditation in the formal garden earlier when she was supposed to be fetching the orders of service from the car. Maybe it's all this stretching and yoga and reiki and colour healing that she's always doing that gives her such a beatific glow. Although to be honest, that doesn't make it much more attainable from my point of view. I just haven't got the mind for meditation; I always end up wondering about my next meal, or if those shoes I saw on sale in the window earlier are still there.

Why can't the holy grail of fresh-faced serenity be as simple and attainable as a new lipstick, I think despairingly. Come to think of it, why can't the solution to *every* problem lie in the purchase of a new lipstick? Maybe then I might stand a fighting chance of sorting out my life.

"Do you think…" Tess hesitates, a stack of plates cradled in her arms. "I mean, nothing's going to be the same after tomorrow, is it?"

Something in her tone of voice, a kind of childlike wistfulness, makes my hands pause in the process of sorting napkins. I stare at the pattern on them, a kind of swirling, stylised foliage, pale green on brightest white. Perfectly matched, like everything else.

It's the sort of question that can't simply be dismissed with a thoughtless platitude; it demands a proper answer. I'm not sure I have one, but I can say what I feel, I suppose, which is better than nothing.

"Not completely, no." As I speak, movement is restored

to my body and I begin arranging napkins on the plates she's laid out, following her progress around the snowy white table cloth. "How can it? It's the end of an era, in a way. Rosie's moving out, and I…" I break off, not ready to finish that sentence just yet. What *will* I do? It's something I've promised myself I'll think about, after the wedding's out of the way. Until then, it's ostensibly put to one side, but the questions still lurk over my shoulder like shadowy vultures, provokingly pervading my consciousness every now and again, taunting me with everything I don't yet know and can't yet answer.

Can I bear to stay in Edinburgh after everything that's happened? But then, if I leave, what will I become? Someone who just flits from place to place, from disaster to disaster? Someone who runs away?

Although, aren't I already just that? A small part of me whispers that I'm the worst kind of hypocrite for accusing Nate of doing something of which I'm as guilty as anyone. I ran away from London, from a job I'd worked so hard to attain, because I couldn't face the memories that seemed to be everywhere. They were like a mist, in every breath I took. Or at least, I thought they were. I blamed the place. I thought I could run from the past, and yet look what happened; it found me anyway. Even if Ed hadn't turned up, it would have found me, because in truth, it never left me in the first instance. The fear of falling for someone again, of getting it wrong again, has coloured every moment since I saw that look on Leo's face when he came around the side of the church.

"You what?" Tess is watching me anxiously, her vivid eyes wide.

"Nothing," I say hastily, turning away to reach for a bundle of cake forks. The last thing I want is to alert Tess to what I'm thinking. It'll only stress her out even more. If she knew I was so much as considering leaving… well, it'd be too much. She's not great with sudden change. She never has been.

"I hate it when things change," she says miserably, as though reading my thoughts. She often does that. Sometimes, in my more fanciful moments, I wonder if she really might have some sort of extra sensory perception. She traces the rim around the plate she's holding, looking pensive. "I know they have to, and I'm pleased for Ro, but… they've been so much fun, these past few years."

"They have," I agree softly. "I'm going to miss it too. I don't know how I would have managed without you both."

"You'd have been fine, Belle." She smiles sadly. "You and Rosie, you just… keep going, no matter what. You make things work. I've always been so envious of that." She sighs. "You two… your lives will move on. I've always known it would happen one day. I'm just so afraid that I'll be the one left behind."

Instinctively, I feel myself frowning. I hate it when she talks like this about herself.

"Tess, things can change for you too, if you want them to. Life isn't fixed; opportunities are everywhere. You'll find a way forward. Something will turn up, I promise."

"Oh, it already has." He eyes shine with emotion.

"That's half the problem. I just don't know if I have the courage to take it."

"Okay." I exhale slowly. I sense that we're approaching a pivotal moment here. Dropping the forks onto the table, I lift a couple of chairs off the nearest stack and set them down next to one another. "Come on. Tell me about it."

# Chapter Twenty-Five

I pat the seat next to me encouragingly, feeling like a therapist. Even more so when she looks at the chair with a kind of horrified suspicion, as though expecting a trap. I stare her out, though, and eventually she perches reluctantly on the edge.

"I had a call from my agent a couple of weeks ago," she begins haltingly. "A production company had got in touch with her about a new programme they want to pitch. They're looking for an illustrator, and they'd seen my Instagram…" she trails off, reddening beneath her over-long fringe.

"Oh my God!" I squeal, practically leaping out of my seat in sheer excitement. "Are you *serious*? You're going to be on TV! Tess, this is *amazing*!"

My mind is already racing away. Maybe I'll get to visit her in the studio, and then, when she's a massive star, I can say—

"No, I'm not!" She blurts out violently, then claps a hand to her mouth, shrinking back into her seat. "I mean, I'm not sure," she mumbles. "I haven't decided yet."

I blink in stupefaction.

"What? You mean you haven't said yes yet? Are you crazy?"

Her face falls and immediately I regret my reaction. I always forget how sensitive she is.

"No, I'm not," she says stiffly, and I can tell she's hurt. "But I'm trying to protect myself. You don't understand, Belle. How could you? You might think it sounds like a dream, but to me, it's my absolute worst nightmare. To be up there in front of everyone…" She visibly shudders. "I feel like I'm about to hyperventilate just thinking about it. I'll probably have a panic attack before every single show. These past two months, just trying to psych myself up to agreeing to it… it's been awful, Belle. I haven't been able to do anything, I haven't even been able to work, I'm behind on about a million deadlines…" She drops her head into her hands. "It's paralysed me. I'm miserable. I've never been so miserable in my life, and I haven't even started yet. I don't know how I'm going to cope."

"Why didn't you tell me any of this?" I ask gently. I'm trying to sound calm, but there's a tremor beneath the words.

She sounds so broken, so defeated, that it's like a stab wound straight to my heart. How did I not know that she was going through this? I knew she wasn't working as usual, I knew she was off her game, but I just assumed…

well, I assumed what I *wanted* to assume, didn't I? What was easier to assume, which was that it was just a phase, a regular case of creative block. Because I simply didn't have the energy or attention span to allow for the possibility that it might be more complicated than that. Because I had enough going on elsewhere, and I didn't want to open up another door of responsibility. That's the harsh truth of it. It's not pretty, and it's not something I like to admit, but there it is. And Tess being Tess, she would never say anything voluntarily; she wouldn't want to burden anyone with her problems.

But the truth is that it was never her responsibility to tell me that something was wrong. It was mine, as her friend, to notice, to be there. At once, I feel a rush of emotion; a mixture of guilt and gratitude. Because, despite that, she's not blaming me. She'll never blame me, even when it's my fault. I don't deserve her.

"I just couldn't face disappointing you both." Her answer, when it comes, is unexpected, enough so to make my head snap up. She looks on the verge of tears. "My agent is furious with me for making them wait; she's probably about to drop me, but I don't care. And I don't care what my parents think either; they hardly notice what I'm doing anyway. I've never cared what the world thinks, so that's not it. But you and Ro have been there for me since the start. You encouraged me to apply for art school when I was too scared to show my designs to anyone. You helped me with my first submissions when I was looking for an agent. You've cheered on every single commission I've got.

And to know that after all of that, I might be about to let both of you down..."

"Tess." On impulse, I grab her hand, forcing her to look up at me. "Don't do it."

Her mouth drops open, and for a couple of moments, her lips form soundless words. When she regains her voice, it's slightly strangled.

"What did you just say?"

"I said don't do it." The words come out in a rush, gaining momentum as I go on. I don't know where all this is coming from, only that it's exactly the right thing. Because for once, it's not about what I think, or what I would want. I've made a lot of mistakes lately, but finally, I have a chance to get it right. For someone else, at least, even if not for myself. "Tess, we did all those things because we wanted you to be *happy*. We wanted you to be successful because it was something you wanted for yourself, not so we could say our friend was a famous artist." I take a breath before carrying on. "Look, nothing is worth feeling the way you've been feeling over this. Nothing is worth having panic attacks over. If you really feel that doing this TV show will make you unhappy, then *don't do it*. There's no shame in saying that something isn't right for you, in saying no, even if you feel like everyone around you would say yes. You have to make the best decision for yourself, not let yourself be pressured into something that later you know you'll regret."

As I say these words, a memory flashes before my eyes: a hall filled with people in black gowns and mortarboards, everyone I knew, all staring at me, willing me to say yes. I can still feel the faint sense of panic fluttering in my throat, the unspoken sense of expectation pressing against me, forcing words from my lips without giving me the chance to consider if they're the ones I really want to use. I push it away firmly, bringing my attention back to the present.

"You will always be my best friend, Tess. I don't care where you live, or what you do. I don't care how outwardly successful you are; I only care that you feel successful *inside*. Do you understand what I'm saying?"

"Yes." As I watch, her face breaks out into the most radiant smile. I haven't seen her look like that – like Tess – for so long now, that emotion swells in my throat, and I pull her into a fierce hug.

"I'm sorry that I haven't been here," I mumble tearfully into her shoulder. "I'm sorry about everything. I've been blaming Ed, telling myself that everything's gone wrong since he turned up, but the truth is, it was all going wrong before, wasn't it?" I draw a ragged breath. "All he's done is bring it to the surface, force me to confront the things about my life that I didn't want to see."

After I'd bundled Gran into a taxi yesterday, I did exactly what she'd asked. I sat there in the flat for hours, the room darkening around me as the sun set, and I let myself think about what she'd said. I opened up my soul and questioned the truths I'd accepted so long ago that they seemed almost rusted into place. And somewhere, within that suspended period of time, I set myself free.

*You don't have to love someone forever just because you did once.* The idea is both euphoric and terrifying all at the same time. Because loving Ed… it's the only thing I feel like I know. It's become such a part of me that if I take it away, what'll be left? *Who* will be left?

"I think…" I pull away, scrubbing a hand across my eyes. How freeing it is to be bare faced; no need to worry about smudging mascara. I hesitate, reluctant to voice this next part. "That maybe I haven't been coping quite as well as I was pretending to."

And then Tess does something which surprises me. She throws back her head with a laugh.

"Thank God you're finally admitting it! I've been waiting six years for you to come out with that."

I just stare at her, open-mouthed, not knowing how to respond.

"Six years." She shakes her head. "Watching you pretending to be perfect, to be invincible, to have it all together. You put on a good show; I almost bought it for a while. But I knew it could never be that easy, even for you." Her face turns serious. "Maybe it's partly my fault. I've always looked up to you, admired how lightly you take things. Everyone has. No one's ever allowed you to be vulnerable, have they?"

Oh, God. Talk about turning my soul inside out. My eyes are pricking with tears all over again, hot and insistent. This time, though, I'm afraid if I let them fall, I won't be able to stop. So I grit my teeth and hold them back.

"Maybe if Ed coming back has done one good thing, it's

letting you admit that it's okay not to be okay sometimes." Tess squeezes my shoulder. "In fact—"

Whatever she was about to say next is drowned out by the clanging of church bells in the near distance. We both leap to our feet like we've been scalded, all introspection forgotten.

"Crap," I mutter, rummaging in my bag for a compact mirror. That's a shower out of the question – Rosie will have us hanged, drawn, and quartered if we're late for the rehearsal – but maybe some setting powder will make me look halfway more human.

I flip open the mirror and wince, immediately retracting that thought. My face is pallid, and my eyes are a horrific combination of tears and tiredness, red-rimmed and purple smudged. I'm certainly not going to be a radiant bridesmaid tomorrow. If I manage not to make any of the children scream, I'll consider it a success.

"We'll have to continue this later. Come on," Tess stretches her arms above her head, her jumper riding up to reveal her washboard flat stomach. "Let's get this over with, shall we?" Then she pulls a face. "God, that sounds awful, doesn't it? We ought to be enjoying this."

"And we will," I say decidedly, linking my arm with hers as we head out into the summer's evening. "Tomorrow."

We begin to walk up the slope towards the chapel, the late sunlight washing over us, and I wish more than anything that I'll turn out to be right for once.

"Well, *that* was stressful," Tess mutters half an hour later, as we all file out of the church.

"You're telling me," I exhale. "I thought Rosie was going to strangle Mum."

"She *did* whoop when the vicar said the part about 'with my body I honour you'," Tess points out tentatively. "It was perhaps not wholly incomprehensible."

"It was a small whoop," I protest feebly, before wondering why I'm even bothering to defend the woman. After all, she brings it on herself. It's not like she even cares what anyone thinks; it's the rest of us who feel the embarrassment on her behalf.

Just thinking about the expression on Leo's parents' faces is enough to make heat rise in my cheeks. Poor Rosie. No wonder she looks like she's about to implode. At least I won't have to see them every Christmas and Easter for the rest of my life. It's easier for me to laugh it off.

To be fair, it wasn't just Mum. It seemed like everyone was on their worst behaviour this afternoon. It started at the introductions, when Carlos ignored Leo's mother's outstretched hand and instead yanked her against him for an uncomfortably long kiss. On the plus side, it's the most animated I've ever seen her husband; I was half hoping he might challenge Carlos to a duel then and there. Alas, he just shrank back into his collar instead, muttering something about foreigners as Leo diplomatically funnelled everyone inside.

Not that things got any better in there. What with Mum's whooping – at one point, I think there was even a wolf whistle – and falling out of her top, and Gran sitting there like the spectre at the feast, all wreathed in black and in a particularly militant mood, thumping her cane every time she disagreed with something…

"Let's just hope they've got it all out of their systems tonight," Tess ventures, although she doesn't appear to harbour much hope.

"All it needed was Ed to round things off," I say, with an attempt at dark humour. "He's as bad as the rest of them."

"No sign of him yet, I take it?"

"No, thank God. He seems to have taken the hint, for once."

I'm under no illusions that it's sensitivity which is keeping him away, although I daren't admit that to Tess. In truth, I'm half terrified he's lurking in the shadows somewhere, gearing up to a big, showy entrance. It's just the sort of idiotic thing he would do.

"It's for the best," Tess says softly. "It's easier on you, at any rate. At least you won't have to contend with having him and Nate in the same room tomorrow."

The sound of Nate's name is so unexpected that it knocks the air out of my lungs, stopping me in my tracks. Literally, as it turns out; Carlos almost walks straight into the back of me. Tess eyes me in alarm.

"You *did* know that Nate is coming, right?"

"Yes, I mean… no… it's just, I thought he'd already gone

to London," I finish helplessly. "I thought his new job needed him straight away. I…"

"They do. But he wanted to be here for the wedding. I think he's going down afterwards." Tess looks apologetic. "Sorry, Belle. I thought you knew."

"No, it's fine." I breathe in and out, trying to still my fluttering heartbeat. Trying to convince myself that it really is fine, when patently it isn't. It couldn't be any further from fine if it tried.

I mean, of course I want to see him. There's a part of me which doesn't care if he's angry with me, so long as I can be near him one more time. And yet, the other part of me – the more cowardly part, I suppose – is afraid. Knows that it's safer just to let it go, pretend it never happened. That I never began to feel anything more; that it doesn't hurt, it ending this way.

And yet… I can't forget what Tess said to me, back there in the barn. How long can I keep doing this, trying to shrug life off like it doesn't mean anything? Like I don't feel, when nothing could be further from the truth?

I can feel Tess's eyes on me. She knows it isn't fine; she knows it matters. Just the knowledge that for once I don't have to pretend… it's more reassuring than I ever could have imagined.

"I think I might take a walk," I say, in a shaky undertone. "Could you cover for me? With everyone else, I mean? I don't want them asking—"

"Don't worry. I'll tell them you have a headache or

something. They're all too exhausted and preoccupied tonight; they won't question it."

I put my arm around her in a quick approximation of a hug.

"You're wonderful."

"I do my best." She gives me a gentle shove. "Now go. Get away from this madness for a bit. It'll all still be here when you get back."

Despite my churning emotions, that dredges up a small smile onto my lips.

"That's one thing I can rely on."

## Chapter Twenty-Six

I walk straight up the hill towards the woods. On the edge, I pause, turning to look back at the hall, which is nestled so neatly in the natural dent in the landscape. It's an elegant Georgian structure, a perfect cube, without any of the jarring Victorian additions that usually feature on British country houses over a certain age. I can see why Rosie loves it; it's only been a hotel for the past twenty years or so, and they've done it well. You can't even see the barn where they hold weddings from here; it's tucked around the back, so the place still has the feel of a private house. I can imagine centuries' worth of inhabitants walking up into the woods, following the same path that I am now.

When Leo brought Rosie here for a weekend break two years ago, no one had any idea that he was about to propose. Least of all my sister. They'd always spoken about it so openly, with their customary efficiency. I think she expected them to simply agree on it one day, mid conversation. She certainly wasn't expecting the ultimate traditional, romantic gesture. Down on one knee in the rose garden, surrounded by her namesake in full bloom. An antique emerald engagement ring in a plush velvet box. A bottle of champagne hidden behind the arbour, two chilled glasses at the ready. The only thing missing was an orchestra in the bushes.

In essence, the very last thing my ultra-modern, practical sister would have wanted.

I don't know what he was thinking. I have a sneaking suspicion that he wanted to surprise her for once, to do the unexpected. Or then again, maybe it was just love. Maybe Leo is as susceptible as the rest of us to the head-turning, heart-flipping tumble of finding the one person who makes everything else make sense.

I pause, Leo's stern face floating into my mind's eye. Okay, so maybe that's stretching it a bit far. It's more likely the former.

In any event, it almost didn't pay off. She *almost* said no. Or at least, so she claimed afterwards. Personally, I'm not so sure. I think she was just trying to maintain her reputation.

Of course, that was back when my sister made sense. When I knew her inside out. When she knew what mattered and what didn't. If that person were here today, she'd be walking up this hill with me, drinking in the views and laughing about all the stuff that hadn't got done.

And in that moment, I miss her so much that it almost sucks the air out of my chest. I miss the way things were. Tess is right, it feels like everyone's changing: Rosie, Nate…

the people I leaned upon. It's only recently that I've realised just how much. They were my stability. Without Rosie's strength growing up, I don't know how I would have managed. It was never really me; she led the way, and I simply followed in her wake.

I'm not sure I've ever really stood on my own. Oh, I've fooled everyone well. But the truth is that I'm a fraud. First it was Ro, then Ed, then Nate… I've just passed myself from person to person, praying that they'll be my anchor. But at the same time, praying that they'll never realise just how much I need them to be. Praying that no one will ever know.

And now they're moving away from me. For the first time, I really am on my own. And I haven't the first clue what to do about it.

I step into the trees, the shadowy quiet enveloping me like a blanket.

Except, as my eyes adjust, I realise that it's not really dark at all. Sunlight pierces the canopy above in golden lances, creating a misty, ethereal luminance in the cathedral-like space. Above my head, the new leaves are vivid, rustling gently in the evening breeze, and around my feet, like a constellation of violet-coloured stars, there are bluebells. Thousands upon thousands of them, stretching in every direction, as far as the eye can see. They mould to the shape of the ground, rising and falling like waves, dazzlingly intense in the encroaching twilight. The effect is breathtaking – in the literal sense. For a moment, I can only stand there, looking around me in wonder.

Suddenly, everything else seems very far away. Whatever thoughts I'd been wrangling with are just hazy concepts dissolving into a sea of purple. For the first time in ages, I feel a sense of peace, the tightness in my chest beginning to ease. I breathe in the scented air; a proper breath, deep into my lungs. Why don't I do this more often? When was the last time I got out of Edinburgh? Really out, into the countryside? Holyrood Park is all very well, but it's not quite the same. There are always so many other people around for one thing, whereas here, I'm completely and utterly alone. And that's fine. In fact, it's… well, it's almost *nice*.

That last thought brings me up short. And then, slowly, a smile breaks out across my face; a giddy smile, unbidden. Because it's true; it *is* nice. For once, I'm alone, but I'm not lonely. Not in the slightest. Not here. And all right, so it's just one walk, but it's a *start*, surely? If I can be happy by myself in one moment, then it follows that I can be happy by myself in another. And then maybe another after that.

Maybe I might just be okay after all.

A spark of hope ignites within me and I carry on walking up the hill, the bluebells brushing against my jeans, releasing more of their heady scent into the air with every step.

The incline levels off a little the further I climb, but it's still an effort, and my heart is beating hard. I pause for a moment, leaning back against a tree to catch my breath.

"Thank God you've stopped," Ed's plaintive voice materialises from the other side of the tree trunk. "I'm not as fit as I was, you know. There's no time for the gym in the afterlife."

I jump, but not as much as I would once have done. I'm not sure if that's worrying or not; am I actually getting *used* to having a ghostly stalker?

"Have you been following me all the way?"

"Well, not exactly *all* of it," he shimmers into view, his expression sheepish. "I sort of materialised at certain points along the path to see where you'd got to. I wasn't about to walk the whole thing."

I fight the urge to roll my eyes.

"What do you want from me now?" I'm aware I sound hostile, but damn it, I was enjoying the time to myself. And now, just as quickly as the feeling began, it's been stamped all over by the realisation that I'd forgotten one small, undead, omnipresent factor. Frankly, if we can't find a way to move him on, I might never truly be alone again. There's a sort of bitter irony to that. "Come to destroy some other aspect of my existence? Because you're out of luck. I don't think there's anything left."

He looks wounded. Not in that theatrical way which he does to get attention, but really, genuinely hurt. The guilt almost swallows me whole. All right, so perhaps that was unnecessarily harsh. I know it's not all his fault, not really, but it's just so easy to blame him. It's habit. I've been blaming him for years. And now I'm having to face the fact that some of it wasn't him, it was me, and… well, it's just uncomfortable. It's hard. And that doesn't make it right, but…

Oh, *fine*, I think crossly, silencing my conscience before it can run on any further. I'll just apologise, shall I?

"Sorry," I mumble. "That was uncalled for."

"That's all right," he shuffles his feet, still hanging his head. "I haven't exactly been an exemplary spirit guide, I know." A faint smile crosses his lips. "It's a good thing you can't leave a review."

My mouth practically falls open in astonishment.

"Hang on, I need a second to process this." I clap a hand to my forehead. "Am I dreaming, or are you actually admitting that you did something wrong?" I pause for emphasis. "Out loud?"

A frown disrupts his smooth forehead.

"I don't recall saying those words," he hedges, but his lips are turning up at the corners a little. "Not technically, anyway."

I nod gravely, smothering the grin that threatens to spill across my cheeks with a cough. We both know what he meant; there's no need to torment him. I'll let him save face.

"No, of course not. Nothing of the kind."

He slants me a knowing look out of the corner of his eye.

"Come on," he says suddenly, reaching for my hand. "You should see this."

"What?" I ask, bewildered, as he drags me along. "Where are we going?"

"Have you never heard that patience is a virtue?" He tuts. "Yours certainly hasn't got any better. It's like our wedding all over again; you *would* have it straight away."

That's such an outrageous lie that I gasp.

"That was your idea!"

"Was it?" He stops, blinking in confusion. "To be honest, I don't remember. Life… it all seems so long ago now."

The way he says it seems so wistful, so sad, that I can't help but be moved.

"Not… all of it, I hope," I say hesitantly. "I mean, we did have some good times, didn't we?"

He smiles.

"Yes, I remember those. We were pretty great together, weren't we?"

"For a while. It was certainly exciting. And passionate," I confess, cursing myself for the blush that tints my cheeks. What am I, fourteen? "I thought that was enough, once."

"It was never about you, you know." The words come out of his mouth in a rush. My head snaps up and our eyes meet. Blue on blue. He swallows; I watch his Adam's apple move up and down his throat. "It wasn't… I mean, I *did* love you, Belle. In my way. It was just… the whole thing. Marriage. Forever." He looks pained even now at the thought of it. "I tried, I did. I wanted to be capable of it. And if it could have been anyone… if I could have done it for anyone, it would have been you."

As I stand there, listening to words I never thought I would hear, I half wonder if I ought to feel surprised. Comforted, maybe? That it never was about me, after all? That there was nothing lacking, that it wasn't about me not being enough.

You might wonder, might have been wondering for some time, why I've never asked Ed what might appear to be the most pertinent question of all. The question most people would probably have asked first. Why? Why did he leave that day? Why did he leave *me*?

Except, he didn't leave me, not really. I think I've always known that, deep down. What he was running from was far bigger than any one person. It was an institution, an expectation, that he should be something he wasn't. That he should be the kind of person who loves, who commits, who stays where they're placed, or else he wasn't much of a person at all.

And so I simply shrug and say, "I know."

He eyes me strangely.

"You do?"

"Yes," I say firmly. I don't want to talk about this anymore. I'm done with talking about it, done with thinking about it, done with trying to work out who to blame. If I'm going to move forwards, I have to put it behind me. "It's the past now, Ed."

"Obviously it isn't." He raises an eyebrow. "Because I'm here. Someone, somewhere must think that there's unfinished business between us."

I rub my arms with my hands; it's starting to get cold. I'm exhausted after a long day, and my patience is not what it was.

"What were you going to show me?"

"This." He spins me around, and suddenly, I find myself gazing out across the most fantastic view, visible through a break in the trees. It's like a doorway into another world. On impulse, I step through, onto a natural outcrop. It's obviously a favoured spot with someone, because there's a bench positioned at the perfect angle for the sunset which is just beginning to settle upon the horizon.

"Wow." I breathe, positioning myself on the seat. I'm pretty sure I can see for miles, the sun skimming over the landscape, sparkling off the surface of a distant sea. "What a stunning view."

"You're not wrong there." Ed's voice is close to my ear.

*Very* close, now that I mention it. I turn my head to find that he's sidled right up next to me on the bench, gazing at me with appealing blue eyes. I recognise that look all too well; it sets off about a hundred alarm bells in my head.

"Er… what are you doing?" I ask warily.

"Looking at you," he says simply. "Thinking about what could have been. Us, together. Maybe we'd have kids by now, be living in London. You'd be at the fashion magazine, I'd be…" He pulls a face. "Well, I don't know about that, but I'd have some kind of steady, sensible job to keep us all in organic Earl Grey and expensive granola."

Those words… they should make my heart soar. To know that he's wished for the same things I once did; to know that he regrets walking away. It's the closest thing to an apology I've ever had from him.

The life we could have had… I've played it over and over in my head so many times. And yet, hearing it now, from his lips, it doesn't ring true at all. It sounds faintly ridiculous, like a hopeless fantasy.

I can't look at him, so I turn my head away. The view is just as lovely in this direction, with the sides of the valley folding inwards on each other in graceful, grassy slopes. Unfortunately, my eyes rake over it almost unseeingly.

"Ed, you don't really believe that, do you?"

He materialises in front of my face, looking confused.

"What? Expensive muesli instead? Organic Darjeeling?"

I massage my temples, trying to work out if I have the courage to say what needs to be said. It's time to end this charade, for both of us. So much has happened *to* me, not just recently, but over the whole course of my life. I've never really felt like I was in control of my own canoe, but maybe it's finally time for me to embrace my power to steer. Time for me to grow up and accept responsibility for my own destiny.

"Any of it. It just… it would never have happened, not really. I think we both know that deep down. You would never have settled, and I… well, I knew it. I just didn't want to admit it. I was young, thought I could change you." I smile ruefully at my own naivety. "If I'm being honest, we were already doomed long before you left me at the altar."

He sits bolt upright, his brows drawing sharply together.

"What is *that* supposed to mean? We were fantastic together. You said so yourself."

"No, *you* said so," I correct him gently. The words are flowing freely now, as though a long-stoppered dam has finally burst. It feels good to say this, I realise with a jolt of relief. "*I* said we had some good times. But that was all they were. We were children, Ed. We didn't know anything about what made a good relationship. We didn't understand what made something forever. It was for the moment." I sigh. "Maybe if you'd just let it stay that way, it would have been better for everyone."

"So this is my fault too, is it?" He leaps to his feet, glaring at me. "You're saying that you had nothing to do with any of it? That you didn't stand there in front of everyone and agree to marry me? That you didn't tell the story to everyone you met. That—"

"I don't deny any of that." I stare up at his furious face, feeling faintly out of my depth. Why does he always take everything I say and stretch it to its most dreadful-sounding extreme? "And I never said it was your fault. I think it was both of us. We got swept up in an idea. It was intoxicating; it went to our heads. We couldn't see that that's all it ever was, just a vision, nothing substantial. Nothing that could ever have lasted." I take a breath, then say what I really mean. "It wouldn't have worked out between us, even if we had got married that day. I think it's time we both accepted that."

He doesn't look ready to do anything of the kind. Instead, he folds his arms and fixes me with an icy stare.

"What are you trying to do, Belle? Ruin everything we ever had? How do you think that's going to help?"

"I'm trying to get some closure," I fire back hotly. "For both of us. I'm trying to be *honest*. Why can't you do the same?" Frustrated tears prick at my eyes, and I ball my hands into fists at my sides. "Why can't you just let me go, Ed?"

My desperate words fall into the twilit silence. Even the

birds seem to have stopped singing. Ed and I stare at each other for what feels like an endless moment. Then he speaks, his voice disbelieving.

"You think it's me, don't you? You think I'm here because of me, not you. Because *I'm* the one who hasn't moved on."

I open my mouth to interject, but he cuts across me, anger blossoming beneath the surface of his level tone.

"Don't say anything else. I understand totally. I'll get out of your way, shall I?"

"Ed, come on…" I reach for his arm, but he snatches it away. "Look, you're here now. Why don't you come tomorrow?" I sound almost pleading. How has this about-face happened? "We can talk some more."

"No, I'll keep my distance. I know when I'm not wanted. Or at least, I thought I did." He begins to fade, the trees becoming visible through his watery form. "Enjoy the walk back, by the way. Try not to get lost."

And then he's gone, disappeared into nothing. Into the dark.

It's only then that I notice the sun has long since set and the shadows between the trees have deepened into black. Brilliant. That's all I need.

Wrapping my arms around myself with a sigh, I begin the long trudge back.

## Chapter Twenty-Seven

"Are you *sure* he's not here somewhere?"

Tess has appeared in the doorway, chewing her lip as usual.

I tug at my dress, an ethereal column of sea-green chiffon that seems to have made it its life mission to trip me up. A glance in the mirror tells me I don't look too bad, all things considered. Diamond studs sparkle at my ears, and the makeup artist has done this incredible, subtle smoky eye, the kind of which I could never have achieved by myself if I'd spent weeks practising. It makes my eyes look luminous in my face.

The only thing that vehemently refused to conform is my hair. Even after three quarters of an hour, thirty-five pins, Tess's help, my grandmother's help (she wasn't all that helpful) and, eventually, the help of both of them combined, together with the makeup artist and hairdresser who were supposed to be tending to the mother of the bride at the time, still it refused to conform to any sort of updo, let alone the one I'd planned. In the end, I gave up and just let it tumble down my back as usual. To console us all the hairdresser spritzed it with something shimmery, so that it sparkles subtly under the lights.

I am, in effect, wedding ready. Well, almost.

"How should I know?" I reply vaguely. I'm casting around for my shoes, which have somehow worked their way under the bed. How did *that* happen? I swear I left them over by the wardrobe earlier. "I'm not his keeper. He said he'd stay away and I hope he does. I've no time for his ghostly antics today."

I told Tess about what happened last night. Usually, it's something I would have kept to myself, but if I'm going to make an effort to be more open with those around me, then I have to start somewhere.

Tess doesn't look comforted by my disinterest. She's gazing out of the window nervously, as though hoping she'll suddenly spot him down in the rose garden.

"I don't know, it's just… I've got a bad feeling. This day *needs* to go perfectly. And he's always at his most dangerous when he goes quiet."

"Stop fiddling with your hair," I scold her gently. Rosie will have a fit if her updo falls down as well. It's bad enough that I've spoiled her vision of perfect synchronicity. "It's all going to be fine. In just under an hour, we're going to be walking down the aisle." I sit down on a blush-pink upholstered bedroom chair to put my shoes on. "Nothing can possibly go wrong now. You and I are almost ready.

When Ro's finished in there with the makeup artist, all that's left is to get her into the dress, and—"

"In *there*?" Tess points through to the dressing room. "No, she's not in there. They've only just let me go. They're waiting for her now." Then her eyes widen. "I thought she was with you."

"Well, clearly she's not." I grit my teeth, grappling with the dainty silver ankle strap on my left shoe. The buckle is unbelievably fiddly. There's no way I'm taking these off until the end of the night; I'll never get them back on again. "She must still be having her hair done, then."

Tess shakes her head.

"No, they finished with her half an hour ago."

A familiar feeling of disquiet begins to stir within me. I look up at Tess and by the expression on her face, she's thinking the same.

"Okay." I strive to sound calm, like this sort of thing happens all the time. Someone's got to keep their head, and with all the love in the world, it isn't going to be Tess. She already looks half hysterical, and Rosie's only been missing for a few minutes. "I'm sure she's just lost track of time. I'll go and knock on her door."

This place is a maze, corridor after corridor of duck-egg-blue-striped wallpaper and near identical-looking portraits of early Georgian aristocracy. I'm sure many an art historian might swoon in horror at such an assertion, but alas, I'm no expert, and to me, once you've seen one woman in a powdered wig against a romanticised landscape, you've seen them all.

I remember that Rosie's room is directly opposite a niche, which houses a life-sized marble statue of a particularly scantily-clad Grecian goddess emerging from a shell. This should make it easy to find; nonetheless, I still seem to do what feels like three circuits of the entire floor before I locate it.

I knock on the cream painted panel, praying she'll answer. Praying that this weird, uneasy feeling will prove to be nothing more than big-day nerves.

"Ro? Are you in there?"

The door swings open of its own accord, which is never a good sign. In fact, if the American crime shows Rosie loves so much prove correct, it usually means that there's a body in there.

I peer around the doorframe. No body sprawled on the floor. I sigh in relief, then realise in horror that I'd been holding my breath. Was I *really* entertaining that possibility? This whole thing with Ed has certainly heightened my sense of drama.

"Ro?" I call again, picking my way into the room. Even though she's only been inhabiting it for a little over twenty-four hours, the place is like a bomb site. It looks just like her room at home, with clothes strewn across the floor, the bed rumpled. Either housekeeping hasn't made it in yet, or they took one look and resigned on the spot.

The dress is still hanging in its bag on the front of the wardrobe, the white beaded shoes on the dove-grey carpet beneath it. I poke my head into the cavernous marble bathroom, even though I already know she's not here. The room feels still, unoccupied. I get the sense that she hasn't been here for a while. I walk to the window, more out of habit than for any particular reason. Outside, I can see people hurrying across the lawn, straining under the weight of enormous floral centrepieces. It's a comical sight, and I watch them for a moment, unable to help smiling to myself.

Remembering my mission, I turn around, scanning the room once more for any kind of clue. Everything looks normal, except… her phone is still on the bedside table, along with her engagement ring. That doesn't seem right. Rosie *always* wears her ring, even when she's just at home doing nothing. And I can't imagine her being without her phone in the final moments of setup on the morning of her wedding. She was glued to it for most of yesterday, checking up on progress, barking instructions to the various unfortunates who were scattered across the estate performing tasks on her behalf.

The sense of unease is beginning to intensify, becoming harder to ignore. Where *is* she?

A search of the hotel proves fruitless. I check everywhere: the morning room, the library, the kitchens – even the billiard room, although God knows why she'd be in there. I don't think she's ever picked up a cue in her life. There are plenty of other people around, an almost impossible-seeming number, in fact – can all these people *really* be involved in the wedding? – but no sign of my sister's familiar chestnut-coloured head anywhere amongst them.

"Any joy?" Tess pants, as we reconvene by the side door that leads to the great hall.

"Nothing." A feeling of despair begins to creep up the back of my neck and I force it away. It's far too early to lose hope. She's probably just taking a moment to herself somewhere, that's all. Or at least, that's what I'm telling myself. "I'm certain she's not anywhere inside."

"And I looked all over the gardens." Tess's shoulders drop. "I even ran around the bloody *maze*, that's how desperate I got."

I blink. It's almost unheard of for Tess to swear, even mildly.

"There's still plenty of time for her to turn up," I say, with a forced kind of heartiness which sounds empty even to my own ears. "You know what she's like. She'll walk around that corner any moment, wondering what all the fuss is about."

As if on cue, there's a crunch of gravel, and both of our heads whip around to look at the corner of the house. A plump mallard waddles into view, stopping short with an uncertain quack when it sees us both standing there staring.

Tess sidles me a resigned glance out of the corner of her eye.

"I'll keep looking, then. I haven't checked the parkland yet." She lifts up her foot to examine her silver heels dubiously. "This outfit was not made for tramping across a boggy moor. If I'm streaked with mud in all of the photographs, it'll be her own fault."

"I'll start checking the less obvious places," I sigh,

looking up at the looming shape of the house above me. It's enormous. God only knows how many nooks and crannies it has, how many out-of-the-way corridors and forgotten stairwells? Searching them could take all day. And we don't have the luxury of time; the clock on the stable yard tower reads twenty-five past twelve. I bite my lip against a lurch of alarm. That's even tighter than I thought. Thirty-five minutes to go. Over at the chapel, the guests will be starting to arrive, blissfully ignorant of the fact that anything's amiss. Leo will probably be there too. Knowing him, he'll have wanted to be ready early. I imagine his face, as impassive as ever, hiding the nerves which I know will be churning beneath the surface, and my heart contracts.

I sit down on the stone step, dropping my head into my hands. Okay Belle, think. Think harder than you ever have before. You're her sister; you should *know* this. Where would she go?

I sit there, locked in the same position, waiting for an answer. I'm not sure how many minutes tick by. I will the solution to come, then, when it doesn't, decide that I'm trying too hard and let my mind go blank instead. Still nothing.

I lift my head up with a groan of frustration. The truth is, I haven't the faintest idea where she'd go. The truth is that the sister I've always known would never disappear like this in the first place. She'd already be in her dress, ready to go, watching the clock, itching it to reach the hour so she could marry the man she loves.

A quack makes me look down at my feet. The duck has waddled up to me, regarding me with beady, curious eyes.

"If all else fails, maybe we can put *you* in the veil and hope no one notices," I sigh, propping my chin on my hand.

It blinks at me, which draws me up short. I didn't know ducks could blink.

"I can't speak for everyone in there, but I hope the groom at least might."

Both the duck and I look up, startled, as a shadow falls across the steps.

"Nate!" I scramble to my feet, not an easy ask when your legs are tangled up in layers of chiffon. "What are you… why are you here?"

"I was invited," he says, his tone growing defensive. "I know it's not ideal, but Leo is my friend too. I thought I owed it to him to be here. I thought we could be grown-ups, for one day at least. But clearly—"

"No, I mean what are you doing *here*?" My face is turning hot as I realise how abrupt I must have sounded. Of course, he has every right to be at the wedding. It's just, with everything that's happened this morning, I'd forgotten that we might bump into each other. I'd forgotten to be prepared, to steel my heart against the sight of him. As it is, I'm defenceless, and the organ in question is thundering against my ribs. "Aren't you supposed to be in the chapel?"

"Oh, I see." Now it's his turn to look embarrassed. "The best man isn't feeling too fantastic so I volunteered to run back for some painkillers," he explains, holding up the box as proof. "I suspect he was nervous about his speech and overdid it last night. Between you and me, I think I'm going to have to step in. He looked terrible when I left." His expression becomes searching as he takes in me standing out here on my own. "Isn't the more pertinent question what *you're* doing here? Shouldn't you be inside with your sister?"

"I was just… getting some air," I lie glibly. "You know, before I have to deal with all those crowds, endless relatives asking me how my life's going, and such like." Actually, this is going pretty well, I think in amazement. I actually sound credible for once. I carry on, my voice growing faster as I warm to my theme. "And you know what they say about nature, don't you? How it slows down your heart rate? All those negative ions…" Wait, isn't that the sea? Never mind. Carry on. "Nothing better for the soul, they say." Okay, now I sense that I'm beginning to ramble. *Wrap it up, Belle, before you overdo it.* "The birds and the bees and the… er," I swallow. I've lost it. I know I have. He's looking at me like I'm a total idiot. "Ducks," I finish lamely.

Even the duck, still sitting at my feet, looks hopelessly unimpressed.

Nate narrows his eyes at me, folding his arms across his chest. He's wearing a crisp white shirt with the aqua-coloured tie which all the ushers have been given to wear. I know, because I was part of the painstaking process of choosing it. An hour and a half deliberating over thirteen variants of the same hue… the very sight of it should be enough to bring me out in recollective hives, but instead, all I can think is how wonderful the colour looks against his tanned throat. I swallow convulsively, willing myself to keep it together.

"You're a terrible liar, Belle," he says mildly. "You wouldn't last long as an investigative reporter."

"No, probably not," I mumble, not meeting his eye. God, why does he have to be here? This is the last thing I need right now. How am I supposed to focus on the latest crisis when he's standing there looking all infuriatingly handsome like that? "Look, I need to go."

I turn, but he's already caught my arm. The feel of his hand upon the delicate skin of my inner elbow is enough to send a jolt of electricity rocketing through my body.

"Belle, wait. I'm not a complete fool. I can tell something's going on." He looks at me intently. "If there's anything I can do to help, say so."

My eyes travel back to the clock, and I try not to gasp. How has so much time passed? I suck in a breath, knowing that I have little choice now.

"Actually, there is something." I carry on, before I can back out. "I might need you to… stall things at the church. If we're a little late, I mean."

There's no *if* about it. She's not even in the dress yet. If she were to appear this very second, I'm still not sure we could make it on time. But I don't say that to Nate; I don't want to alarm him.

My attempt to downplay the situation clearly hasn't worked, because his face tenses.

"How late are we talking?"

"I… I don't know," I admit. "I wish I could tell you.

Just… make sure Leo doesn't worry, okay? Say it's all in hand. If he asks, tell him it's something to do with her makeup, or her dress. But whatever you do, *don't* let him leave the chapel."

He looks very much like he might be about to either ask more or protest. Wearily, I hold up a hand to silence him.

"Please, Nate. Just… I need you to trust me. All right?"

He looks at me for a long moment, his dark eyes raking my face. I have no idea what he's thinking, and I'm glad. It's probably not wholly complementary, given our history. I haven't exactly given him a lot of reason to trust me recently.

To my immense relief, though, eventually he sighs, his shoulders dropping in resignation.

"I suppose I'll have to, won't I?"

It's not the most ringing endorsement, but it'll do. On impulse, I reach for his hand. As our fingers brush, a jolt of electricity rockets through me, and I snatch my arm back as though I've been burned.

"Thank you," I stutter. "I'll see you at the church, then."

He nods, already turning away.

"I'll hold you to that."

I watch him walk away, darkly inscrutable against the bright summer sunshine. My emotions are raging, trying to break the surface, but I don't have time to examine them now. If there's still a chance to save this wedding, then I'm going to find it.

Before I can take another step, though, there's a commotion, a sound of scattering gravel from around the corner of the house. I look down at the duck, and he looks back at me in mutual bemusement.

Tess comes flying around the corner, holding up the hem of her dress in one hand.

"Tess!" I catch her as she tries and fails to come to a stop on her own, almost knocking us both over. "What the hell—?"

"You're never going to believe this," she gasps. Her updo is beginning to unravel, but somehow, it only manages to look even better than before.

"Believe what?" She doesn't make a lot of sense at the best of times. Now, out of breath and agitated, she might as well be speaking in gibberish. "What are you—?"

"He's found her." Her eyes are wide, luminous with excitement. "Ed's found Rosie!"

## Chapter Twenty-Eight

"So?" I prompt, in an undertone. "Where was she, then?" Ed shifts awkwardly.

"I don't really know if I should—"

"In my car parked down at the bottom of the drive by the gates," Rosie supplies from the opposite side of the room, where she's sitting at the dressing table while Tess dusts highlighter across her cheekbones, having been promoted to unofficial bridal makeup artist. The real one was long gone by the time we returned to the house, which I can't say I blame her for. Even so, I thought Rosie might blow her top, but she didn't. To everyone's amazement, she simply smiled serenely and reached for her emergency cosmetics bag. She raises an eyebrow at my shocked expression. "Well, you shouldn't talk so loudly, should you? I *am* right here."

"Stop moving, will you?" Tess grabs her shoulders and twists her back around to face the mirror. "This is difficult enough to do in a rush without you wriggling all over the place. I'm not qualified for this, remember."

"Sure you are." Rosie waves a dismissive hand. "You did that semester at art college. I remember you telling me about it."

"That was technical makeup. If you want me to turn you into a zombie or give you a prosthetic nose, then fine. That, I can do."

"Well, it'd certainly be different," Rosie says cheerfully.

We all stare at her.

"Are you… feeling all right?" I venture tentatively.

"Fine, why?" She lifts the lid on a cut-glass bonbon dish in front of her and peers inside. "Oh look, sugared almonds!"

I open my mouth to say something, then simply shake my head. This is all too surreal. And that's coming from someone whose phantom ex-fiancé has been following her around for the past ten days. I pull Ed further into the corner, trying to get a little privacy.

"What's the matter with her?" I hiss. "Has she been lobotomised or something?"

He gives me an unimpressed look.

"Don't be ridiculous. She's just… had a change of perspective, that's all."

"A change of…?" That's a phrase to strike fear into any sensible heart. "What *happened* out there?" Then it hits me. I can feel the blood draining from my face. "She was going to leave, wasn't she?"

I feel like the world's turned on its head. My sister, my

solid-as-a-rock, dependable sister, who's always had it so together… she and Leo, they're *perfect*. They're what I've always aspired to. How could she even *think* about walking away from that?

It doesn't make any sense. None of this does.

Then I look up at Ed, who's standing there quietly, and suddenly, everything becomes clear.

"You persuaded her to stay," I whisper in disbelief.

He looks awkward.

"It wasn't hard. Her heart wasn't in it, not really. She was just… overwhelmed by it all. She panicked." He gives a dazzling smile but I sense that it's just a distraction, hiding something beneath. "My specialist subject, as it turns out."

I look at my feet, swallowed by shame and confusion, not knowing what to say. It's like a rerun of six years ago, except, this time, the roles are all reversed. This time, it's Ed who's saved the day, when no one else could. And after everything I said to him yesterday, too. He'd have been well within his rights to let us all go to hell in a handcart.

But he didn't. And after last night, I think I know why.

I gaze up into his eyes, trying desperately to read him. But it's as impossible as ever.

"Did you do this for me?"

It's a loaded question if ever there was one. Even though it falls from my lips in little more than a breath, it sits in the air between us like a heavy weight. I wish I hadn't asked it; I wish I hadn't needed to. But at the same time, it feels like everything's been nudging us towards this gentle confrontation.

Until last night, I'd never really allowed myself to consider whether he might still be in love with me. Jealous about my moving on with someone new, yes, but… well, I suppose I'd sort of assumed that running away from our wedding signalled the end of those feelings on his part, maybe even a sign that they had never really existed in the first place. And besides, anything else was just too complicated, too confusing, too heart-breakingly exhausting to even contemplate.

But now I have no choice. We both have to be honest if we're ever going to move on. Me with my life, him with… wherever he's meant to be going next. We have to close the door on this once and for all. I did my part last night; now it's his turn.

"Not entirely." Then he smiles at me, a persuasive, boyish grin which I remember all too well. It means that he's about to change the subject. "If I said it was though, would that make you forgive me?"

I give a resigned sigh as I realise I'm not going to get a straight answer out of him, for the time being at least. There's a determined levity about his tone that warns me not to pursue it.

"For what?" I say stonily. "There's quite a list."

It keeps growing, too, although I don't add that part aloud.

He shrugs, scuffing his foot along the edge of the skirting board.

"We could start with our wedding. I think it's time, don't you?"

My mouth drops open. The audacity of the man!

"Oh, just forgive him, Belle!" Rosie yells from the other side of the room, making me jump. She looks sheepish. "Um, yes, I could still hear you."

Tess tuts as she brushes clear mascara across Rosie's eyebrows.

"*Some* of us were trying not to listen."

I frown.

"You really think I should let him off the hook? *You*?" I add, for emphasis.

She has the grace to blush a little.

"All right, so I know I haven't always been the most forgiving of people myself…"

"Some might say inexorable," Tess supplies sagely, swirling a blusher brush around the pot.

"Unyielding," I suggest helpfully.

"Pig-headed…"

"Yes, yes, all right!" Rosie says hastily. Tess and I share a private smile over the top of her head. "But the point is, it's my *wedding* day." She turns to me beseechingly. "And he's right, it's held you back for long enough. Can't you find some way to forgive him? What will it take?"

I open my mouth to make some scathing retort, but she cuts across me.

"For me? As a wedding present?"

My mouth slams shut. Damn the woman; she's played an ace. How can I argue with that? Apart from pointing out that I've already bought her a coffee machine, but somehow, I don't think that'll cut it.

Ed's standing there, trying not to look insufferably smug and failing dismally.

"Ed," I say thoughtfully. "Just remind me… you *can* feel pain, can't you?"

He looks wary.

"In this form yes, but why—"

Before he can finish, I've drawn back my hand and dealt him a stinging slap across the face.

"Jesus Christ!" He reels backwards, clasping a hand to his cheek. "What is *wrong* with you, woman?"

"That," I say neutrally, running a hand over my hair to right my appearance. "Was for leaving me at the altar. *Now* we're even."

"I should hope so," he winces. "That bloody *hurt*."

"See?" Rosie beams upon us both like a proud matriarch, having not so much as flinched throughout the entire altercation. "Everyone's happy. I'm thrilled. Now, out with you, Ed. I need to put my dress on."

"Fine," Ed sulks, still clutching his face. "I'll be at the church if you need me." He begins to fade out, then hesitates. "I take it I *am* allowed to come to the wedding now?"

Rosie and Tess both swivel to look pointedly at me.

"Of course," I grind out. I can't exactly refuse now, can I?

"She might even save a dance for you!" Rosie trills, as he disappears.

I scowl at the back of her head as she sheds her green silk kimono. I seem to recall that her dress has a corset back; I make a mental note to give the laces an extra vengeful tug.

"I'm glad you two have made up," she continues, as she steps into the pool of ivory satin. "You know, I can't believe I'm saying this, but I honestly don't think anyone else could have talked me around in that moment. I was convinced I couldn't go through with it, that I couldn't face this circus I'd created. He reminded me that the only thing that matters is Leo and me, that this is only one day, and ultimately, it doesn't mean a lot in the scheme of things." She gives me a look which can only be described as grudging approval. "I never knew he could be so mature. Why didn't you ever *tell* me he had that side to him? I mightn't have been so hard on him all these years."

I fluff her skirt out, letting my hair fall around my face so she can't see my expression. I daren't tell her I'm as stunned as she is. *I've* certainly never seen a mature side to Ed.

Even as I think it, though, I know that it's not strictly true. Since he's been back, I get the sense that he *has* been trying, if not always wholly successfully. Perhaps I haven't been giving him enough credit for that.

"And you're… absolutely sure now?" I venture haltingly. "About the wedding, I mean." God, talk about awkward. There's no question in the whole world I'd rather have to ask less. But even I know when my familial duty calls. It's not like Mum's going to do it. She's probably cavorting with Carlos in a pew as we speak. "Because it's not too late. If you have any doubts at *all*…"

"I don't." Rosie's grey gaze holds mine steadily. "But thank you for asking."

A flash of understanding passes silently between us. Because she asked the same of me, once upon a time, on a blazing hot hillside in Cyprus.

"Anytime." I aim for a jocular tone, but my voice cracks treacherously. "I love you."

For a good half a second, she tries to keep it together, but then her face collapses.

"I love you too," she sobs, throwing her arms around me. "I'm sorry about everything I said." This more quietly into my ear. "I was just in such a state. I never meant..."

"I know." I pat her back soothingly. How strange that for once, *I* feel like the grown-up. The roles have reversed, albeit probably only for a moment. "Don't worry about it."

"Makeup!" Tess chides, pulling Rosie backwards. "You can cry all you like later."

"I never cry," Rosie says haughtily, dabbing at her eyes with her little finger. "This was a one-off. It's just the emotion of the day, that's all. It won't happen again."

She looks so cross with herself that I have to cover a burst of laughter with a cough.

"Yes, you've let us all down," I say solemnly.

She glares at me suspiciously and relief spreads through my chest. At least one thing's back to normal.

Tess peers uncertainly at the back of Rosie's dress.

"I've done it up as fast as I can. It's a bit wonky at the top; do you want me to re-do it?"

"No, leave it. I don't care." Rosie's practically hopping

on the spot with pent-up energy. "I just want to get there now. I want to get *married*." Her eyes widen and a smile breaks across her face. "Oh my God, I'm getting married today!"

"Well, yes," I say simply. "What did you think all this palaver was about?"

"I just never thought about it like that before. I was so busy worrying about organising everything, about the wedding… I never really stopped to think about what it all means." She claps a hand to her forehead. "God, I sound like a total idiot. I've *been* a total idiot. I'm amazed Leo still wants to marry me."

"But he does," I point out, tweaking her veil back into position. "And he's waiting for you."

Tess claps her hands together excitedly.

"Are we going to a wedding, then?"

"Yes." Rosie laughs, running towards the door, dress gathered haphazardly in her arms. "Yes, we are!"

# Chapter Twenty-Nine

The ceremony goes as well as can reasonably be expected when my family are heavily featured. Mum sits at the front, blocking the view of everyone behind in a monstrous hat which I'm certain is larger by surface area than the dress she's wearing, but at least it casts her cleavage into shadow. Even worse, Carlos, for some unfathomable reason, has decided that skin tight leather trousers are the ideal attire for a traditional country wedding. Every time he moves, they make an excruciating squeaking sound against the pew, punctuating the vows at random intervals. I try not to wince, but it's not easy. I'm acutely aware that I'm on show, standing at the front; if I can't keep it together, then we're really in trouble. I daren't look at Nate, who's lurking silently on the other side of Leo. I met his eye briefly as we walked up the aisle and he nodded infinitesimally in that way he has; barely perceptible unless you're looking for it. Whatever he'd told Leo obviously worked; I've never seen my new brother-in-law so relaxed.

And he *is* my new brother-in-law by now. At least, I think so. I'm never quite sure where exactly in the ceremony the marriage becomes official. I'm sure the vicar said something about them becoming husband and wife ages ago, almost at the start, but there are still all of the vows to go. Surely you can't be married until you've said the vows? I wouldn't know myself, of course; I never got that far.

Once, that thought would have caused me a twinge of pain and regret, but now I find I can ruminate on it quite calmly, almost with a sense of relief. For the first time, I can allow that maybe Ed did me something of a favour, running out the way he did. Obviously, I wish it had ended differently for him. No matter how cavalier he might be about death, I know it's not easy for him, watching everyone moving on with their lives while he can't.

After the first hymn we sidle off to sit in the front row. Luckily, Nate has a seat on the groom's side of the church, and with Mum's hat in the way, I can't even see him. Just as well; the extra distance between us makes me feel more able to breathe. I'm still so aware of him, his presence; it makes it difficult to concentrate on anything else.

"Dearly beloved," bellows the vicar, then hiccups audibly. I stare at him. He seems merry enough, round as a snowball in his white cassock, twinkling away behind his horn-rimmed glasses. Perhaps a little *too* merry, I think warily, as he appears to list to the side, only righting himself at the last moment.

"We are gathered…" he begins, then trails off, blinking in confusion. "Where was I?"

"The vows," Leo prompts, with a nervous side glance at Rosie. But she just smiles beatifically.

"Ah yes," the vicar closes his eyes, and there's a pause. Which stretches. And then stretches some more.

"Has he fallen asleep?" Tess murmurs next to me.

As if in response, the vicar emits a faint snore.

With a dawning sense of horror, I swivel around to the other side, where my grandmother is sitting in a shroud of lilac.

"What did you *do*?" I hiss.

She shrugs, looking unrepentant.

"He was nervous. I offered him a bit of Scotch courage, that's all."

She takes a covert swig from her hip flask, which she's decorated with a white ribbon to mark the occasion. I glare at her; I don't even want to ask if she did the same for the now absent best man. I have a feeling I won't like the answer.

"Do you want some?" She waves it under my nose.

"No, I bloody do not!" This come out louder than I'd intended, and several heads turn in our direction in the otherwise deathly silent chapel. I shrink back in my seat.

Without warning, the prayer book jolts in the vicar's hands, whacking him under the chin. He wakes up with a start, blinking in confusion.

"Dearly beloved!" He blurts out.

"We've had that part," Leo deadpans. Rosie smothers a grin and a look passes between them.

I'm smiling too, despite everything. Because I can see what no one else can: a shimmering shape slipping away into the shadows.

"Thank you," I mouth at Ed, who salutes in response.

Out of the corner of my eye, I can see Nate watching me, a faint frown on his face. Hastily, I lean backwards, beyond his view.

After what seems like an eternity, although mercifully one which the vicar manages to remain awake for, Rosie and Leo are pronounced husband and wife (for what I'm absolutely *certain* is the second time. And after the ceremony we've just witnessed, there's a high probability that I'm right). The congregation caterwauls its way through 'Jerusalem', and then, to my immense relief, the organist clangs out the opening bars of 'The Arrival of the Queen of Sheba', signalling an end to the whole saga.

We begin to file out down the aisle, me pondering, for what must be about the four hundredth time, why this song has become such an iconic recessional tune. She's supposed to be *arriving*; it's in the title! One day, perhaps I'll look it up. Or more likely I won't, and I'll be churning through exactly the same thought pattern again in two months' time at the next wedding I go to.

A low voice next to my ear remarks drily, "So you got her back then?"

My heart leaps in my chest, and it takes all my force of will not to turn my head.

"It's a long story," I respond, in an undertone, trying to keep my tone light despite my skyrocketing blood pressure. I'm telling myself it's down to how unintentionally close to the truth his joke was, but I know it's not really that. It's *him;* every time he's near me, I just can't help it. My whole being reacts to his presence. "You wouldn't believe me if I told you."

He replies easily enough but there's a sadness beneath his voice when he next speaks.

"You say that a lot. I just wish that you'd given me the chance to try."

And I know we're not talking about the wedding anymore. But what we are talking about is too raw, too bitterly unfair. Because I never can be honest with him, not really. There'll always be that large, Ed-shaped elephant in the room, looming over everything.

Or more likely, crashing into everything.

Even if Nate were to stay, things would never be the same again. I have to face that, learn to live with it.

And then we're out in the bright midday sunshine, the bells rising and falling in a joyful, deafening melody all around us. Tess is pulling me over to one side, pushing a confetti cone into my hands. I blink away the prickling feeling which threatens behind my eyes, willing myself to smile. Reminding myself that there's another layer to this, one in which my sister is married, in which I'm happier than I ever could have been for my own sake. How is it possible to feel two such contrasting emotions at once? How can they exist like this, side by side, crashing over one another like waves, melding together in a bittersweet mixture which can't be separated? I wish I could put my feelings about Nate into a box, something to be opened later, once he's gone, once all of this is over. I wish it were that simple.

I realise I'm clutching the confetti cone so tightly that it's beginning to crumple. I loosen my grip with an effort, forcing myself to breathe. The falling sound of the bells reverberates through my skull, the light dazzling my eyes. A single dried rose petal falls from the edge of the cone, floating down towards the gravel. It seems to happen in slow motion.

I look at the roll of paper in my hand. It feels like a lifetime ago that we were sitting on the floor in the living room of our flat assembling these. There's a good chance I might have made this one myself; the edge doesn't quite line up. Looking back on that person feels like someone I barely recognise. I could never have imagined what was coming over the next ten days, how much I'd change.

Rosie and Leo burst out of the church in a flurry of light and laughter. I fling my arm out in synchronicity with everyone else, filling the sky with petals.

---

"You need to talk to him."

I take a sip of my peppermint martini. Green, of course,

like everything else. Even the frosted sugar crystals on the rim match the colour scheme.

"I really don't."

I'm trying to sound nonchalant, but in reality, my insides are in knots. It's hard enough as it is to get through the day pretending that my heart isn't breaking. It's hard enough to smile, and make small talk, all the while knowing that the one person I really want to speak to is standing just across the room, yet at the same time hopelessly out of reach. Rosie's nagging is *not* helpful.

"Of course you do!" Apparently she's not picking up on the atmosphere, or else she's wilfully ignoring it. Probably the latter. Frustration colours her voice as she presses, "You're miserable, Belle. I know you are. You have to at least *try* and sort this out." She makes to move forward purposefully, towards the group of ushers. "If you won't do it, then I will."

"God, no!" I grab her arm and haul her back. "I have tried. He doesn't want to know." Realising that I'm snapping, I continue in a softer tone, "I do have some pride, you know."

I've realised that the only way to navigate this evening with any remaining dignity is to avoid Nate all together. Easier said than done when I'm aware of where he is all the time. Wherever I stand, he somehow happens to be in my eyeline. It's deeply vexing.

"Screw your pride! This is more important. Sometimes, Belle, you have to take a leap. You have to be prepared to get it wrong if you want a chance at happiness. You have to allow yourself to be vulnerable. To admit that you're not perfect." She sighs. "Look, I've never told you this, but a few months into our first year at uni, Leo and I had a wobble. He wanted to take a break, and I let him, even though it was the last thing I wanted. I was too proud to try and hold him."

I stare at her, dumbfounded.

"I had no idea."

She shrugs.

"In the end, I realised what a mistake I'd made, how unhappy I was without him, and I went to ask for him back. It was hard, but it changed our relationship for the better. I learned to let a few things go, to compromise." She has the self-awareness to flush a little at my stare. "I'm aware it might not always seem it, but believe me, I'm better than I was. We became a proper partnership that day." She gives me a piercing look. "It's not true that love means never having to say you're sorry. Believe me, it does. I don't want to watch you make that mistake. Not again. Not when it could be real this time."

"Darlings!" Mum clatters over with her usual impeccable timing for ruining a moment. It's like she has a sixth sense. "What a *glorious* party this is. Carlos is just *loving* it."

I glance over at the dancefloor, where Carlos is currently gyrating against one of Leo's cousins.

"So I see."

Rosie clears her throat awkwardly, averting her eyes.

"Where's Gran? We're about to do the cutting of the cake."

"Oh, she'll turn up," Mum waves her cocktail glass airily. "Old people always do. I haven't seen Ed since the church; is he still here?"

"Somewhere," I say noncommittally. Call that an homage to our newfound truce; saving him from a dance with Mum.

"He is *such* a darling," Mum sighs. "Last time he saw me, he said I'd make the most beautiful bride. All in white, like an angel. That's what he said."

"Isn't white supposed to denote purity?" I mutter beneath my breath. Murky grey would be more fitting.

Rosie stomps on my foot and I swallow a yelp.

She needn't have bothered; as usual, Mum is completely oblivious.

"*Such* a handsome boy, too. *Such* fun. If I were a few years younger…"

And maybe if she weren't *engaged*, perhaps? And if he hadn't once been about to marry her *daughter*? I could go on.

"Mum, stop—" I realise I was about to say, "Stop lusting after my dead ex-fiancé" and draw myself up short. "Just… stop, okay?"

"She's got a point, you know," Rosie murmurs in my ear.

I look at her in open-mouthed horror.

"Not about *that*!" She says hastily. "I mean, I haven't

seen him since the church either. Do you think you should go and find him?"

I scowl. Not this again.

"Why is he my responsibility?"

"Because he's haunting you, that's why! And because you were the one who slept with him in the back of his car after the May Ball."

"You know I don't like bringing that up," I hiss. It wasn't my classiest move. Also, not the most divulgeable of 'how did you meet' stories. I always used to skim over that part and pretend we met earlier in the evening.

Even so, I take her point, if grudgingly. I was the one who brought him into our lives, ergo, he *is* my responsibility. And the way things are going, he's probably going to be my responsibility forever, so I might as well get used to it.

Oh, lord. What a depressing thought.

I drain my glass, needing the fortification. I'm feeling distinctly uneasy about this. If there's one thing my grandmother and Ed have in common – apart from making louche statements in public – it's the fact that they're both at their safest when loud and visible.

And now they're both missing.

I pluck Rosie's glass from her hand and drain that too.

## Chapter Thirty

For the second time today, I find myself undertaking a search of the entire hotel and grounds. And with similar success; Ed is nowhere to be found. Eventually, I stalk back towards the barn, silently fuming at being sent on another wild goose chase. Honestly, with each passing day I feel more relieved that I never got around to actually marrying the man. He always did do a consummate disappearing act, even when he was alive. Now he's a ghost, it's even more impossible. I mean, he literally *could* be anywhere. He's not limited by time and space like us mere temporal beings.

I slip into the barn, hoping to stay unnoticed. If Rosie collars me, she'll probably send me back out there to look all over again, which is the last thing I'm up for. The evening has begun to chill, my feet are killing, and I can see that the cake has been dismantled in my absence, neat slices arranged on plates across the long table.

No *way* am I going to miss out on cake. Not for the sake of one errant ex, at any rate.

I'm just reaching for the last piece of chocolate cake – the middle layer, Leo's one and only input into the whole wedding, from what I can make out – when a hand clasps my shoulder.

I freeze.

"I *did* look, Ro, honestly. Don't make me—oh."

Nate's face is tense, although that's not unusual at the moment. Not when he's with me, at any rate.

"Can we talk?"

I watch in mute dismay as a hand reaches across and swipes the piece of cake I'd targeted. Great, now I'm stuck with either fruit cake or that weird green top layer which Rosie insisted upon because she said it would look good in the photographs. Sprout-flavoured, or something equally repulsive.

All right, so it's probably not *really* sprout-flavoured. I think it's matcha. In any event, it's *green*. Need I say any more?

"Belle?" Nate prompts, scanning my face.

For some reason, that sets my teeth on edge. My head whips around.

"Why?" I shoot back. "What's the point? You're leaving anyway."

Something shifts behind his eyes, and I can tell I've hit my mark. Somehow, though, it doesn't feel as good as I'd hoped. I don't feel relieved, or vindicated. I just feel wretched. Because damn it, I *don't* want to hurt him, not really. Not at all. Quite the opposite. I want to fling my arms around him and apologise, but the words get stuck in my throat. That same pride again, holding me back.

He looks away, frustration evident on his face.

"Why are you trying so hard to push me away? Christ, Belle, I don't want to leave it like this. Not with you."

"Because it's easier like this, all right?" I snap desperately. "And because…" I ball my hands into fists at my sides, nails digging into my palms. "Because… you lost me my cake!"

"Your cake?" He looks disbelieving, which I can't blame him for. "You're making this about *cake*?"

I just look at him hopelessly. Of course, it sounds mad to him. It sounds mad to me. But the truth is, it *is* about cake. And stationery cupboards, and flicking rubber bands at Darren, and stolen kisses in the corridor. It's not about the big stuff. It's about the small moments that made up everything we had, everything I'm about to lose, and I just can't—

Behind us, the band strikes up, filling the room with the sound.

"That's our cue," Nate says evenly. "I hope you can waltz."

I try not to look absolutely appalled. I fear that I fail.

"What?" I splutter. "You and me?"

"You're the maid of honour. I'm now the best man. It's expected of us." He shrugs. "It's actually what I came over to talk to you about."

Oh, God. Immediately, I'm engulfed in burning flames

of mortification. Here I am, making out that it's all about us, all about me, when he only came over out of duty. He probably didn't want to have to speak to me at all if he could help it.

Rosie and Leo are already swirling around the dancefloor. Nate holds out an arm to me. With a sense of doom, I take it. I have no choice, even if I want nothing more than to run as far away as possible and nurse my wounds in solitude. I too have a duty to this wedding, to my sister. I'll just have to get through it somehow.

"Don't tread on my feet," he murmurs. "Those shoes look lethal."

"They are," I mutter under my breath, but there's little conviction behind the jibe. I'm still feeling shaken, something which isn't improved by him pulling me closer and placing a hand upon the small of my back. The contact sends shivers up and down my spine and I curse my body for reacting so shamelessly. Especially as he's probably gritting his teeth, just wanting to get it over with, to say that he's done his duty to Leo. He'll let go of me at the end of this dance, and that'll be it. He'll walk away, into his perfectly unruffled life, filled with perfectly explicable goings on. And I'll be left behind, surrounded by regrets and longing and a particularly exasperating ghost. I have to enjoy these last few moments in his arms, to treasure them.

"Can *you* waltz?" I manage, as we begin to move in time to the music.

"Well enough." He sidles me a glance. "My mother

made me take lessons when I was thirteen. She thought it was *rounding*."

He utters the last word with such a barely repressed shudder that the tightness in my chest just fades away. It's impossible to feel awkward when we're talking like this; like we're still friends, like nothing has happened. Somehow, no matter how bad things have got, we can't seem to help falling back into our old conversational patterns. It's like a magnet, pulling us back in.

"Don't even think about laughing," he adds sternly, seeing my face. "It was pretty scarring for a teenage boy, I have to tell you. I was absolutely paralysed with fear that someone at school would find out and I'd become a laughing stock. I used to hide my coat tails at the back of my locker and wait until everyone else had left before I changed."

Okay, now I can't help it. I *do* laugh, rather loudly.

"You're a cruel woman," he mutters, but the corners of his lips are twitching. "I knew I shouldn't have told you."

"I wish this didn't have to end." The words are ripped from me, impulsive and raw. They come from a part of myself beyond my conscious mind, beyond the barriers I've placed to protect myself. I flush, realising what I've just said. "I mean, this *day*. I wish this day didn't have to end."

He hesitates and I watch him, wondering what he's thinking.

"Me neither," he admits at last.

And just like that, everything else falls away. Finally, I understand what people mean when they say that. I know that we're surrounded by people, I know that if I don't keep half an eye on what my feet are doing then we'll probably crash into another couple and cause a pile-up on the dancefloor. But I don't care. I can't see anyone else. I can't see any*thing* else, except Nate's face, the pain and longing that flicker across it as he speaks those words. It changes everything. It makes me want to stop being such a coward, to just say what I really mean.

"It was always real, Nate. You and me." I hold his gaze, trapping him there. Willing him to listen. There are so many things I can't ask of him. I can't ask him to stay, for one. I already did that, and it was wrong of me. I knew it almost immediately. I can't ask him to forgive me either. But I can ask him this one thing, just to hear me out. Just to let me tell him the truth about how I feel, as much as I understand of it myself. When he goes, I want him to take it with him. "I wish you could believe that."

For a moment, he doesn't say anything, just presses gently into my back to manoeuvre us around another couple. How he's managing to stay focused on what's going on around us is a mystery. For my part, I don't understand how people in books hold intense conversations whilst dancing.

"I won't pretend that my feelings haven't been complicated," I continue softly. "And I won't pretend that it wasn't a surprise, to find that I could feel like this again. I didn't think I ever would. But I'm glad it was you. And I'm glad that you know now." I take my hand off his shoulder, beginning to pull away. That's enough of a show for everyone. I've said what I needed to. It's time to go, before I lose my composure. "Good luck in London. I wish you every happiness."

I've only half turned when his fingers suddenly tighten around the hand he's still holding, spinning me back. I'm so surprised that I miss my footing, but he catches me against him, stopping us still in the middle of the dancefloor.

I stare up at him in dizzy confusion. From this close, I can see the olive-green flecks in his eyes. People are whirling around us in a kaleidoscope of colour. It's making my head swim.

"What are you doing?" I manage, in a gasping voice.

"You know," he says slowly, somehow looking both perplexed and resolute at the same time. "I have absolutely no idea."

Then his lips meet mine, and the world spins off its axis…

… For about half a second, that is. Suddenly, the air all around us vibrates with the most tremendous crash. I jolt away from Nate, looking around wildly.

What fresh hell?

A commotion of that magnitude could only be the work of one person. Or one *un*-person, as the case may be.

Tess appears in my sightline from behind a wooden pillar at the edge of the dance floor, chewing her lip and beckoning to me manically. A feeling of abject doom settles upon me. Seriously, can I not just have *one* moment? One tiny moment, where I'm not running around dealing with disasters?

"I have to go for a second." I disengage myself from Nate reluctantly. "Hold that thought, okay?"

He looks nonplussed.

"Really? Right now?"

"I'm sorry. It's just… well, it's about Ed, and…"

In front of my eyes, his face changes. It's as if the precious, dreamlike bubble of the last few minutes simply bursts, and all that's left is resigned recollection.

"I understand." He says quietly. Then he releases my hand.

I open my mouth to speak, but before I can say anything, Tess's signalling morphs into a frantic windmill motion. I grit my teeth. It must be urgent, whatever it is. But after what just happened between Nate and I…

"Look, just… don't go anywhere," I say pleadingly, already turning on my silvered heel. "I'll be back, I promise."

---

"What the hell is going *on* back there?" I demand. Or at least, begin to. But Tess shushes me, grabbing my arm and pulling me through the swing door towards the bar.

I stop short. There are few sights as strange as seeing your sister in full wedding dress crouching over a body.

"What the—?" I begin again, but this time it's Rosie who cuts across me.

"Get down, will you? We don't want to be seen."

Feeling faintly ridiculous, and more than a little

apprehensive, I drop to my knees and shuffle across the floor towards the scene. Tess follows suit. God only knows what we must look like, although to be fair, I have bigger concerns on my mind right now. Namely, the lifeless figure sprawled on the ground. It appears to be covered in a white sheet.

"Oh my God!" I clap a hand to my mouth. Now I'm closer, I can see that it's not a sheet at all. "You've killed the vicar!"

"What?" Rosie stares at me incredulously. "Don't be absurd, Belle. He's just fainted, that's all."

"Oh." Now that my hysteria has faded slightly, I can see that his chest is rising and falling beneath his vestments. "How did you get here so fast, anyway? You were on the dancefloor with me a minute ago."

"Unlike some of us, I came as soon as I heard the crash," Rosie says drily. "But then, I wasn't otherwise occupied with kissing someone."

I flush. Doesn't she miss *anything*? Besides, I was *not* trying to—

"*Kissing* someone?" Ed's indignant voice sounds from somewhere behind me. "Who've you been kissing now?"

I cringe. As if this couldn't get any more embarrassing. He makes it sound like there's a long queue.

"Can we just deal with the matter at hand please?" I hiss, to the room at large. Why does my private life seem to be open for discussion at all times, no matter what else is going on? "What happened here?"

Rosie points at Ed.

"Ask your friendly ghoul. It's his doing."

"It was an *accident*!" Ed whines. "How was I supposed to know he'd be there?"

"He materialised out of thin air," Tess supplies further clarification.

"Seriously?" I whip around to glare at Ed. "How could you be so careless? There are over a hundred people here!"

"I know. I just... got a bit complacent, that's all. I thought it'd be all right behind here."

I groan. I suppose in a way I'm not that surprised. It was only a matter of time before it happened. But now? In front of a man of God, no less?

As if on cue, the vicar snaps awake, sitting bolt upright, his face contorted in fear. He points a shaking finger straight at Ed.

"Demon!" He screams.

Rosie and I meet each other's resigned look.

"Just as well I'd given up on the idea of a perfect wedding, isn't it?" she sighs.

## Chapter Thirty-One

It takes almost half an hour to sort the whole thing out. Leo steps in and manages to smooth everything over in his diplomatic way. Somehow, he contrives to make the sight of the vicar hiding behind the cake table flinging slices of matcha-flavoured Génoise at Ed seem like a perfectly unremarkable occurrence. Mercifully there was no mention of my grandmother – still ominously absent – or her moonshine; Leo's far too kind for that. Besides, I suppose we're officially his family now; protecting our not-so-good name is part of his job.

Eventually, after a bit of undignified chasing and a subtly-executed rugby tackle, the vicar is installed in one of the hotel bedrooms with a cold compress on his forehead and a holy Bible on his chest, the band kicks off again, and order is restored to the party. Finally, it feels more like a wedding again rather than a free-for-all at a Wild West saloon. Rosie is glowing with happiness, Leo is looking palpably relieved, and even his parents look less sour about the whole concept. They're drinking peppermint martinis like they're going out of fashion, which might have something to do with it, but still. All's well that ends well, as they say.

There's just one tiny problem: I can't find Nate.

I mean, I *really* can't find him. Obviously with all the commotion that went on, I don't expect him to have stayed exactly where I left him. But I thought he'd be... well, *around*. I've circled the room four times. With his height, he should be easy to spot, but I can't see his familiar dark head anywhere. I'm genuinely beginning to get anxious.

"Mum," I grab at her arm as she floats past. "Have you seen Nate?"

I'm half expecting her to say "Nate who?" But to my amazement, she says, "He left, darling."

I blink. The way she's looking at me is strange, unfamiliar, it's almost... concerned, and even slightly motherly, and... dear Lord, surely not a bit *pitying*?

My stomach swoops. Things really must be bad.

"But... he can't have left!" My voice is rising in volume. I'm starting to panic. No. This can't be... he wouldn't just have... *gone,* without so much as giving me a chance to explain myself.

*Except, he* has *given you a chance,* a small, unhelpful voice pipes up in my mind. *He's given you no end of chances, hasn't he? He's done everything you asked him to. And all you ever did was lie, and deflect, and expect him to simply accept it. No wonder he's had enough.*

"Belle, darling," Mum shakes my arm. "You look rather peaky. Is everything all right?"

"Actually, no." I'm too shaken to pretend any more. "Not really. I just… I think I might have…"

"That boy." Mum swishes her pashmina around herself with a knowing look. "I knew it. For a while, I thought it was Ed, but then I saw you together at the party, the…" she frowns. "What was it? The hen, stag… whatever?"

"Sten do," I say faintly.

"That's it!" She looks triumphant. "Yes, I saw the way you looked at him then, and I knew."

I blink in astonishment. She did? *I* didn't, not then at least. Besides, this is Mum we're talking about; she never notices anything unless it concerns herself.

She obviously catches my expression, because her face quivers.

"Don't look so surprised, Belle. I know I'm not always an exemplary mother." She looks at the floor, then up, her eyes bright with emotion, and for once, she doesn't appear to be over-acting. "But I do love you girls very much, you know. There's nothing more in my life I want than to see you both happy. I wish you could see that."

"I know, Mum," I say softly. Because I suppose I do, deep down, beneath everything. She does love us, in her own chaotic, self-absorbed way. She does her best. And she's stayed around, for all these years. I can't count the number of boyfriends who've wanted to whisk her away abroad, but she's always said no. Even when we both became adults, she's wanted to be near us. Her way of showing it might not be the same as many other parents, but that doesn't mean it's not real. I pull her into a hug. "And so does Ro. But it might be nice if you told her anyway, especially on a day like today."

She pulls away, cupping my face in her hands briefly. "You'll be all right?"

"Fine," I lie. "It's for the best, really. It couldn't have gone anywhere, I know that." But I'm no actress and my voice is losing its breeziness. "I'll just go out to get some air, I think."

Outside it's cool at least, the heat of the early summer's day having dipped to a still, soft evening. I lean back against the side of the barn, the rough texture of the wood scraping against the thin fabric of my dress.

It would be nice to cry, I think. It would release some pent-up emotion. But despite the rasping in my throat, the pressure building up in my temples, the tears refuse to come.

"What's up with you?" Ed materialises at my side. "You're missing the party. I thought you might like a dance."

He's wearing a blue suit, just like the one he had for our wedding. His blond hair falls across his forehead, burnished amber by the setting sun. He looks more like the man I fell in love with all those years ago than ever. I wait for my heart to flip, but it doesn't. Instead, I just feel empty.

"Nate's gone." My words are flat, dispassionate. They couldn't be more at odds with the tsunami of emotions within. "Although why should you care about that? You're probably glad. It's what you wanted, isn't it?"

He stares at me in bafflement.

"But it doesn't matter how I feel." I continue bitterly. "It never did. I can't escape my past. I'll never be free. *That's* what this is all about, isn't it?" I gesture between us. "That's what they sent you for. To show me that I might as well not bother to try. I'll always be that girl standing outside a hilltop church, waiting for something that's never going to come."

"I don't know," he says simply. "But for my part, I certainly hope not."

That knocks me off my stride. I stare at him numbly.

"I've been thinking about what you said all night," he admits awkwardly, scuffing his shoe along the side of the barn. When he looks up at me, his clear blue eyes are filled with unprecedented sincerity. "Look, I made Rosie swear not to tell anyone what I said to her earlier, but actually, I think you should know."

"You don't have to—" I begin to blurt out, but he holds up a hand to silence me.

"I told her that she isn't like me. That she's a better person, a worthier one. She deserves a lifetime of happiness. I didn't." He looks away, picking at an exposed nail sticking out of the side of the barn, and for the first time, I see something else new; a kind of vulnerability. "I wasn't much of a human, really, I can see that now. I didn't do much good in the world. I hurt the one person who believed in me, who was ready to take a chance on me." He shakes his head, meeting my gaze steadily. "Regrettably, I can't turn back time; that's way above my pay grade. But I can still change what happens next. I can still stop you from making the biggest mistake of your life. Belle, I don't want you to let what happened between us stop you from living anymore."

I've been standing here all the way through this, frozen to the spot. Almost dreading the moment when he finished, and I'd have to say something. Because what can I say? These are the words I've longed to hear, the closure I ought to be desperate for. And yet now, it doesn't seem to mean as much as it should.

Perhaps because I know better now.

"Ed, it's not your fault." I sigh, leaning into the building for support. Suddenly, I feel utterly drained, like everything that was propping me up has left me. "I mean, admittedly, you haven't been the *most* helpful at times…" The pants immediately spring into my mind, in all of their garish, lacy glory, and I suppress a shudder. "But I can't keep on pretending that you're to blame for everything. It's made it all too easy for me." I drop my voice to a softer tone. "I think we both knew our wedding was a mistake before the day even dawned. And you leaving… it just gave me an excuse not to take any responsibility for my own misjudgements. To be honest, I've been using it ever since."

He narrows his eyes at me. The nail's come free from the wood and he curls his palm around it.

"Wait… you've given up, haven't you? I can hear it in your voice. You're not even going to try and get him back." He looks indignant, and a little bit betrayed, as if he's just found out that the tooth fairy isn't real for the first time. "I don't *believe* you! This isn't the Belle I remember. She had spirit; she never gave up."

"She was also hopelessly immature, hence why she got left at the altar," I point out crossly. Is he seriously going to lecture me right now? "This Belle is more grown-up, worldlier. She knows when something isn't going to happen. And this…" I almost choke on an unexpected surge of emotion. "This isn't going to happen, Ed. Nate doesn't want me. Not anymore. I know by now what it means when a man walks away."

"No, you don't," Ed says impatiently. "Look, Belle, if death has taught me anything, it's…" he falters, looking sheepish. "Well, all right, so perhaps it hasn't taught me as much as it might have. But it *has* left me in no doubt whatsoever that we're put upon this earth for one reason only: to be happy. It's the only goal worth fighting for. Love's all that really matters, in the end. I learned that too late; you don't have to." He sighs regretfully. "Look, if the man has even an inch more sense than I had, he'll come running back to you. I only wish I'd done the same. Leaving you was the biggest mistake of my entire life, Belle. My heart stopped beating the day I left you at the altar."

I look back at him, hot tears prickling at the back of my eyes. Oh, God. He *would* have to go and say something like that, wouldn't he? Something so perfect, and beautiful, and heartfelt, that I'm lost for words.

"Ed, I…"

"Not *because* I left you at the altar, obviously," he continues breezily. "Because I crashed into a ravine."

I blink. Oh. Yes, right.

He grins wickedly.

"Sorry, couldn't resist. Come here."

He wraps his arms around me and I settle against his chest, the way we used to when we were together all those years ago. And yet, I know it wouldn't feel the same as it did back then, even if he were alive. So much as changed in the meantime. I've fallen for somebody else, for one thing.

"I know that I have to let you go," he says, so lightly that it's almost a whisper. Then he squeezes me more tightly, just for a moment, before pushing me away. "Find him. Please. Before it's too late. I'll do what I can at my end."

He's weighing the nail in his hand, looking thoughtful. I open my mouth to ask what he's planning, then decide I don't have the time. Gathering up my skirt in one hand, I run towards the house without looking back. In the distance, I can see the gravelled driveway sweeping off into the line of trees. Just one more chance, I pray silently. That's all I need. I won't waste it this time.

My shoes sink into the soft grass of the lawn, slowing my progress, and I'm out of breath by the time I reach the front porch. There's no one in sight, not even the duck, and my heart plummets. I'm too late. He must have pre-packed his suitcase earlier, ready to fling it into the back of the taxi. Clearly, he always planned to make a quick getaway.

The knowledge hits me like a sharp pain to the chest. Obviously he didn't come here today cherishing any hope for a last-minute reconciliation. Whatever I might have said, it wouldn't have made the slightest bit of difference.

I sink down onto the front steps, watching the sun sink low behind the trees, bathing everything pink. Tonight, however, I feel anything but rosy. I feel brittle, like a perished dried petal, the slightest touch enough to make me fall apart.

I try to tell myself that it's not the first time this has happened. That I've been left before, and I survived. Except, it's not working. Because this time, it feels different. It's not Ed who's walked away – cavalier, unreliable Ed, who I always knew, deep down at least, that I could never hold for long. This is Nate, who waited three years just to ask me out. Who's seen me at my worst. Who's forgiven my missteps and my half-truths. Who I thought would always be there.

Yes, I've been left before. But it never hurt this much.

I stand, my dress brushing against the gravel with a slithering sound. Some practical, mechanical part of my brain is directing me now, telling me I can't sit here forever. That it's over. Survival instinct kicking in, sending me back towards the party, to the life that still waits for me. A life filled with family and friends, with a job I like if don't love, with a flat that overlooks the beautiful city I get to call home. A happy life, filled with things to be grateful for.

If only my heart could believe it.

And all of a sudden, he's there, standing in front of me. His silver-grey jacket is draped over his arm, and he's loosened his tie. He looks so indescribably, dazzlingly wonderful that for a moment I can only stare at him, devoid of any opening gambit. To be honest, it's hard to convince myself that what I'm seeing is real, that he truly is still here. The moment feels fragile, suspended in a glass which could shatter under the pressure of one wrong word, the slightest false movement, leaving me here all alone in the watercolour wash of evening.

"I thought you'd left."

Isn't it strange how there can be so much emotion, so much clamouring to be said, and yet all we can manage in the moment is something utterly banal and obvious? It seems like such a waste of a moment, but truly, it's all I can conjure up. My voice sounds faint, as though it's travelled down a very long tunnel.

He shakes his head.

"I had. I did. I got halfway down the drive before I just… stopped. I realised I couldn't do it to you. Not again." His eyes meet mine. "I think you've had enough of people running out on you. This time, I want it to be different. I want…" He scrubs a hand through his hair, looking agitated. "Christ, Belle, I'm getting this all wrong. I feel like I've got everything wrong, ever since we met. I don't know what to do around you. Nothing makes sense. I just know that I don't want to fight with you anymore. I want to stand here and talk it out, for as long as it takes. All night if we have to. Because even after everything, I still think it's worth it. And maybe I'm crazy, maybe I should already be in the taxi getting as far away from all of this as possible, but something is telling me to stay. Something is telling me to fight for this."

I open my mouth, then close it again.

"Please, Belle, give me a reason to think I'm not crazy." His gaze is steady, but his voice reveals the emotion beneath. "Just one will do."

"I'm not in love with Ed," I blurt out desperately. "In fact, I'm not sure I ever really was."

There's a heavy silence. I'm acutely aware of my own breathing. It seems to thunder in my ears. In a way, I'm horrified to hear the words aloud, but at the same time, there's an intense, almost dizzying rush of relief. Because it's out now. Finally. The truth. I didn't even know it myself until recently.

Nate closes his eyes as though in pain.

"Belle, you don't have to say that. I don't need you to protect my feelings."

"I loved him," I say softly. "In a way, I think I always will. But I wasn't in love. I couldn't have been." I give a hopeless shrug. "Being in love means knowing someone inside out, everything they are. I never knew Ed, not really. I only saw the fantasy." Just saying it out loud makes me want to wince, but I persevere. "I think something in me realised that pretty soon afterwards. And that's why I convinced myself I had to keep loving him. To keep me safe from making another mistake like that. I couldn't trust myself to let anyone else in, in case I got it wrong again."

"Wait… that's why you kept me at arm's length?" His face clears. "Why didn't you just *tell* me?"

"And admit what a screw-up I am?" I give a strangled laugh. "Not exactly the image you want to give the guy you're falling in love with. You'd have run for the hills."

Nate's gone very still, I notice.

"You're... falling in love with me?" He says at last, in a strained voice.

It takes a good couple of seconds for my brain to catch up. Oh God, did I *really* say that out loud? I did, didn't I? Horror and mortification burn through me and I turn away, covering my eyes with my hands.

He's close behind me. He puts a hand on each of my shoulders and spins me gently around.

"I don't think those were my words *exactly*," I hedge weakly. "It was more like..."

He shakes his head, a smile playing around his lips. "You can't lie to an investigative reporter, you know. We always get to the truth."

I look up into his warm golden eyes, and suddenly, I realise that I never want to lie to him again.

"The truth is that I'm scared." I gesture between us. "*This* scares me." At least when I still insisted I was in love with Ed, I had some sort of control. Now, it's all spiralling wildly away from me. "I don't know when things started to change, but I never expected you to get through my defences. I never thought anyone could. I had no idea how to deal with it." I breathe out a sigh. "Believe me, I wish more than anything that I'd been brave enough to admit it sooner." Maybe things might have turned out differently. Maybe I wouldn't finally understand what it feels like when your heart's breaking. I stand up straighter, will myself to be strong, just for another few moments. Finally, I understand what people mean when they say that loving someone means letting them go. Who would have thought it would be Ed who'd teach me that? "But look, I meant what I said earlier. I don't expect anything from you. You don't even need to say anything. You can walk away right now, get into your taxi without looking back. I'll understand. I just… don't want there to be any more secrets between us."

There's a pause. I close my eyes, waiting for the crunch of his shoes on the gravel as he turns away. But nothing happens. Instead, he speaks again, quietly.

"I'm afraid I can't do that."

My head snaps up. He's watching me intently.

"Why…" My throat is parched. I swallow, try again. "Why not?"

"Well, for one thing, my taxi's stuck at the bottom of the drive with a flat tyre. Ran over a nail, apparently. They called me a minute ago." He raises an eyebrow. "If I believed in providence, I'd say that someone was trying to keep me here."

"Hmm." I look away, biting my lip. I should have known Ed couldn't resist meddling.

"Also, there's another problem, of rather more magnitude." Nate sounds serious, and my heart swoops. What fresh hell? Please tell me Ed hasn't done anything else, like thrown all of Nate's underwear into the lake or released a plague of rats into the offices of his new paper in

London? I wouldn't put it past him. I wouldn't put *anything* past him.

"You see, I can tell you the exact moment it happened for me." Nate takes a step closer, holding my gaze. "Because Belle, I've adored you since the moment we met."

My heart seems to stop beating. There's a strange crackling sound in my ears as what feels like a wall of energy surges upwards into my head, making it spin. For a brief moment, I wonder if I'm about to faint again and I take a fluttering breath, searching for my voice, which seems to have chosen this moment to go into hiding.

"Really?" I stutter, at last. "The *very* moment? I find that somewhat hard to believe."

He gives a self-deprecating smile.

"All right. So maybe it was more like five minutes in."

"I'll take that." This time, the words rush from my lips as I pull him against me. I don't wait, I don't think. I promised the universe that if I got that extra chance, I would take it.

I intend to keep my promise.

# Chapter Thirty-Two

"We're not late, are we?" I scuttle out onto the porch, tugging Nate behind me. Overhead, the morning sunshine is dazzlingly bright. It promises to be another glorious day. "We sort of… lost track of time."

"I'm sure you did," Mum smirks. I'm about to flush, when I observe that she looks decidedly tousled herself and Carlos is patting a yawn. Talk about the pot calling the kettle; I doubt that she got any more sleep than I did.

Besides, nothing is going to spoil my mood today, I think, as Leo finishes loading their suitcases into the boot of the powder-blue convertible they've hired to drive away on their honeymoon. Rosie flits around in a matching blue dress – old habits die hard – and an oversized sunhat, seeming to issue a lot of instructions without doing much in particular herself. But I suppose that, as she's still technically the bride, she can be excused this time.

"Your gran turned up, by the way," Tess murmurs next

to me. "They found her asleep in the hotel manager's bathtub, covered in glitter and wearing a tuxedo jacket."

She utters all of this so matter-of-factly, as if there's nothing even remotely untoward about that sentence. I stare at her, to which she replies with a cheerful shrug.

"It's all a bit of a mystery, really."

Beside me, Nate's struggling to withhold a smile.

"You might laugh now," I mutter darkly. "You wait till she's ninety. She'll be even worse. We'll be called out in the middle of the night because she's running around Edinburgh with a traffic cone on her head."

"At least we won't be bored," he leans down and brushes a kiss across my lips.

I roll my eyes. I'm still not entirely sure he knows what he's letting himself in for. It's easy to be cavalier now, in the golden glow of new-found love, but my family have a way of wearing you down and draining your soul. Will he still be feeling so benevolent in years to come? Then again, maybe he's not all that sane himself. I mean, the man fell in love with *me*. Hardly the most prudent choice, out of all the female population.

He wraps an arm around my waist and pulls me close. I snuggle into his warmth, his steadiness. I have to keep reminding myself that not everyone is like Ed. For most people, love is stronger than adversity and recalcitrant in-laws. If Leo can manage it, then so can Nate. Lord knows, he's put up with enough from us all already.

"We're about there." Leo strides over. "Thanks for seeing us off, everyone."

He shakes hands with Nate, while Rosie bounds towards Tess and me, pulling us into a group hug.

"I'm going to miss you both so much," she sniffs.

"You're only going away for a week," I tease, but I know what she really means. We all do. Something has fundamentally changed within our group. Two things now, I amend, with a sideways glance at Nate, who's good-naturedly trying to decipher Carlos's wildly gesticulating form of conversation. But for once, I'm not afraid of the future. I know I'll be all right.

"Belle." Leo embraces me. "Thanks for all of your help." Then, in an undertone, so that only I can hear, he murmurs, "Just make sure that ghost of yours behaves himself while we're gone."

I freeze, but he's already pulling away. Our eyes meet for a moment, he raises an eyebrow slightly, and then he's moved away to hug Tess.

I just stand there, feeling floored. How did he…?

"By the way, where's Ed?" Rosie asks, seemingly echoing my thoughts. "I feel he ought to be here, after everything…" she trails off, looking embarrassed.

"I haven't a clue." That's a good point, actually. Normally he'd never miss an opportunity to create havoc.

"I saw him in the rose garden a few minutes ago," Tess offers. "He was standing by the fountain. I asked him if he was coming and he sort of…" She frowns. "Well, actually, it was a bit strange. He said he would be along in a minute."

"There's nothing odd about that," Rosie points out.

"He's unfailingly late to everything. He's probably lost track of time, that's all."

"No, it wasn't that." Tess looks thoughtful, as though trying to find the words. "It was the look on his face. He was smiling, but there was something sad about it. It didn't reach his eyes."

Rosie and I share a familiar look. Tess is probably imagining things again, but still…

"I'll go and look for him," I say with a sigh. If I'm quick, no one will even notice I've gone.

As Tess described, there's a small fountain gurgling away in the centre of the rose garden, sunlight sparkling off it in ripples. A breeze flutters through the otherwise still air, lifting the skirt of my lightweight summer dress. I push my hands into my pockets to weight it down, and as I do so, my fingers brush something cold and metallic. With a puzzled frown to myself, I pull out the mystery object, wondering if I've left an old hairpin in there from several summers ago. I hold it up to the light, and for the second time today, I go completely and utterly still.

It's a ring. But not just any ring. It's *my* ring. My wedding ring. I never knew he even still had it.

"Belle."

I spin around, my heart flying into my throat at the sound of my name. But it's not Ed standing there, it's Nate. Wearing an endearingly concerned, if slightly exasperated expression.

"What on earth is going on? You just… ran off."

"He left this for me." I say, staring at the ring, unable to take my eyes off it. "He's gone, Nate."

*I know that I have to let you go.*

Ed whispered those words in my ear last night. And suddenly, I understand.

He knew. For once, he was telling the truth.

To my amazement, I find that my eyes are burning with tears. I slip the ring back into my pocket, but not before the sun catches it one last time, making the stone sparkle, just quickly. Almost like a wink.

"Are you all right?" Nate's watching me carefully. "Do you want me to leave you for a minute?"

In answer, I step towards him, laying my head against his chest. Immediately, his arms move around me, cocooning me in his embrace.

"You're not going to tell me what's been going on, are you?" He murmurs next to my ear. He doesn't sound irritated, though, I notice. More resigned.

"Nate," I manage, with a watery smile. "Something strange is *always* going on when I'm around."

At least I can say it's the truth. And that's as much as I can manage in this instance. Because this is one secret I really do have to keep; it was never mine in the first place.

He pulls back to look at me, and his eyes are warm.

"I can't deny that."

In the distance, a car horn toots insistently.

"I think that's our summons," Nate says, with a rueful tilt of the lips. "Are you ready?"

I nod.

"And then..." I let the sentence hang, wanting him to finish it. Needing to hear him say it.

"Home," he says simply, and my heart blooms at the word. "Although, who knows if we'll still have jobs waiting for us when we get back. Wasn't the health inspector going around yesterday?

I blink. I'd forgotten about that.

"We'll have to set up our own agency." I slip my hand into his, revelling in how natural it feels. "Delphine and D'Angelo, Investigative Reporters. It has a nice, alliterative ring, don't you think? Maybe we can even adopt Frou Frou as our office dog."

The car horn beeps again, with increasing ire. I can envisage Rosie leaning on it furiously. We share an amused look.

"Come on." He squeezes my hand. "Let's see this wedding out."

"And then no more," I say firmly. "Weddings, I mean. I've had enough of them to last a lifetime."

He looks at me.

"Really?"

I flush as I realise what I've said. And then again as it dawns on me how untrue it is. Because something in my mind's eye begins to take shape; someone with dark hair and a grey suit waiting patiently for me at the altar. And for the first time, it doesn't feel terrifying. It feels...

"Well, maybe not a *whole* lifetime," I hedge quickly. "I mean, that's not to say I couldn't be persuaded, if the right person happened to... you know..."

He leans in and kisses me. And whatever I was about to say flies straight out of my head. As he pulls away, though, something catches my eye. A movement in the trees, a subtle shimmering. Someone standing there, watching us. And even though I can't see from here, I know that there's a smile on his face.

"What is it?" Nate turns to look over his shoulder with a frown. "What are you looking at?"

"Nothing." I pull myself up short with a shake of my head. "Just thought I saw something, that's all."

He raises an eyebrow.

"One of Scotland's famous ghosts, perhaps?"

I shrug lightly.

"Maybe. Who knows?"

And then interlacing our fingers, we begin the walk back together.

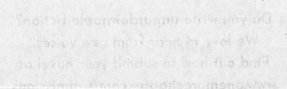